The Mariners

Harbor Messiah

Todd Daley

LitPrime Solutions
21250 Hawthorne Blvd
Suite 500, Torrance, CA 90503
www.litprime.com
Phone: 1 (800) 980-3309

Published by LitPrime Solutions   09/15/2020

ISBN: 978-1-953397-02-7 (sc)
ISBN: 978-1-953397-03-4 (e)

Library of Congress Control Number: 2020915860

Table of Contents

"Whoever walks with the wise becomes wise,

but the companion of fools suffers harm."

Proverbs 13:20

CHAPTER 1

A Hot Lesson

Tom drove his old gray 1964 Pontiac along the meandering Richmond Terrace from Mariners Harbor to Port Richmond to West Brighton to St. George. The oldest road on Staten Island, Richmond Terrace was originally an Indian footpath that was widened into a dirt road by British soldiers during the American Revolution. The preternatural warmth of the November morning surprised Tom, forcing him to lower the front windows to get a welcome sea breeze.

Approaching St. George, he glanced at the New York City skyline, marked by the recently erected twin towers that dominated Lower Manhattan. Tom recalled the first time his mother took him and his sister to Manhattan to see the vaunted skyscrapers—symbols of America's enterprising spirit. Parking on Hamilton Avenue, the skinny young science teacher trudged up the steep hill, looking anxiously at the formidable gargoyles of Curtis High School's limestone facade—symbols of the meticulous workmanship of yesteryear.

On Tom's desk were two glass jars half-filled with black dirt, through which thermometers were stuck. Both jars had been placed in a sunny window for two hours, prior to the lesson. One jar was open at the top, while the other jar was covered with clear plastic wrap. It was the skinny science teacher's practice to start off each lesson with an attention-grabbing experiment to motivate his lackadaisical students. The aim of the lesson was written clearly on the blackboard: "What is the greenhouse effect?"

1

Tom had Wendy, a sensuous long-haired teenager, come up and read each thermometer.

"The open jar has a temperature of seventy-five degrees Fahrenheit, and the covered jar has a temperature of eighty-eight degrees Fahrenheit," she announced in a shrill voice.

"That's awesome girl!" exclaimed Barry, a streetwise black youngster. "You should work in a hospital and stick thermometers up people's asses."

"Ah, stick it up your bony ass!" Manny yelled from the back of the room.

"Why don't you come up here and try it?" Barry replied angrily.

"Now cut it out, both of you," Tom interjected quickly, anxious to avoid a physical confrontation. He knew from past experience that classroom hassles escalate rapidly from verbal to physical, especially on Fridays.

Moving on, the skinny science teacher asked the class, "What can we conclude from this experiment?"

"That today was your lucky day, because your practical experiments seldom work," replied the quick-witted Barry.

Ignoring the wisecrack, Tom called on Riner, a serious student wearing thick glasses.

"The plastic cover prevented the heat from escaping the jar," he replied.

"What if you put a jar with gasoline in a sunny window?" someone asked from the back of the class.

"Why don't you try it in your house and tell us what happened?" Barry said.

Ronnie, a naive black girl, asserted, "That's why you shouldn't leave a dog in your car during the summer."

"Especially with the windows closed," Tom added. "An animal or child left in a car in the heat of summer would suffer heat prostration within a matter of minutes."

Barry raised his hand, and Tom waited for the inevitable negative remark. "So what does all this have to do with the greenhouse effect?"

"I'm really glad you asked that question," Tom said, relieved that the troublesome youngster didn't go off on a tangent.

"I know," said Riner. "The earth's temperature is rising because the gases polluting the atmosphere trap the heat. Just like the plastic wrap did with the glass jar."

"Way to go, Coke-bottle glasses!" interjected the irrepressible Barry.

Ignoring the latter's impudent remarks, Tom explained that such atmospheric gases as carbon dioxide, carbon monoxide, sulfur dioxide, and nitrous oxide act like the glass of a greenhouse to trap the earth's heat. Elaborating, the young science teacher lectured, "The earth's atmosphere allows the sun's shortwaves such as light, ultraviolet rays, and infrared rays to pass through, but it blocks the earth's long waves (low-energy infrared rays). Over time this heats up the earth, causing global temperatures to rise."

"That's fine with me. I wouldn't mind warmer winters," Manny replied.

"Okay, but if the earth's average temperature rises by more than a few degrees, the polar ice caps will melt and ocean levels will rise by several feet, flooding coastal areas—including Staten Island and Manhattan," Tom responded.

"And the burning of fossil fuels sends millions of tons of toxic pollutants into the atmosphere every year, which are harmful to plants and animals," Riner added.

"We should use alternate energy sources like wind and solar energy," Wendy suggested.

"Put a windmill in your own backyard, while I'll let Con Ed run my TV," Manny yelled from the back of the room.

"To each his own," Tom said ruefully as the bell rang and his students dashed for the door, unconcerned about air pollution, global warming, and other environmental issues. The optimism of young people cuts like a two-way sword, simultaneously creating and negating needed innovations.

CHAPTER 2

Harbor Resident

As Tom walked down Morningstar Road, he felt so warm that he removed his jacket. He recalled chilly November days when a coat and a hat were needed for such a walk. Global warming was not an invention of a few eccentric scientists. On the plus side, the skinny science teacher hoped the upcoming winter would be mild enough to make snow shoveling unnecessary. He heard some church bells tolling as he ambled along the gently sloping Morningstar Road.

He wondered about the origin of its quaint name. The Island's earliest settlers were Dutch. Did a colonial Dutchman observe Venus trekking down this very road, from whence its quaint name was given? Was there an Eveningstar Road somewhere else on Staten Island? Turning west on Richmond Terrace, Tom headed for the Mariners Harbor waterfront, which faced the gray choppy waters of the Kill Van Kull. After a while, the abandoned Bethlehem Steel shipyard was before him, in its ramshackle splendor.

He always enjoyed looking at the defunct shipyard—a hodgepodge of rickety warehouses, rotting docks, flaking hulks, and corroded ships with their rusty anchors. From the time of his boyhood, Tom found this maritime scene soothing to his frayed nerves and disquieting thoughts. Although it had its rewards, teaching adolescents wore a person down like few other jobs, with the possible exception of assembly-line worker. None of his friends understood Tom's attachment to the run-down Mariners Harbor waterfront. His high school sweetheart, Joanie Gardello, had observed that "the harbor has seen better days. It's not what you would call picturesque."

Strolling along the sidewalk, the young science teacher noticed a person living in one of the abandoned ships—a ramshackle tugboat. He was a sturdy young man in a T-shirt and dungarees. He was bent over a fishing pole. Then, he pulled up and cast out the line one hundred feet over the murky water. Tom noticed a wire running from a utility pole on the roadside to the tugboat, apparently drawing electricity for the squatter's use. "You can't beat American ingenuity," Tom said to himself with a chuckle. "And Con Ed won't miss the few kilowatts stolen from its coal-powered grid."

Intrigued by the spectacle, Tom walked carefully on the rotting wharf, which led to the tugboat. The stranger waved to Tom and signaled him to come aboard his tugboat. Again Tom heard the pealing of church bells deep in the Harbor.

"Is this your home?" Tom asked as he cautiously stepped onto the tugboat, which was clean despite being in a state of disrepair.

"Indeed it is. As they say, there's no place like home. Ain't fancy but it has all the amenities. And it's bigger than it looks—there are two cabins below," said the stranger, who identified himself as Amon.

"I've seen worse in my day," Tom replied diplomatically.

"I'm sure you have," Amon responded, which gave Tom pause.

"I walk down here all the time. But this is the first time I've seen somebody living in one of those boats. Where are you from? You don't sound like a New Yorker."

"I've been all around this country—north, south, east, west. It's all good," Amon replied.

"America's a great place, but I like Staten Island. I'm a native New Yorker," Tom declared proudly.

"I don't know. I detect South Jersey or Philly in your past."

"As a matter of fact, I lived in Bloomington, New Jersey, as a kid. It was a farming area. So I'm city and country — a hybrid of sorts," the young teacher said, amazed at the stranger's acuity.

The stranger was deeply tanned, like someone who had spent much time outdoors. His age was indeterminate. He might have been in his twenties or thirties. And his dark complexion, jet-black hair, and piercing dark-brown eyes rendered his ethnic identity indeterminate, as well. Amon could have been Italian, Spanish, Middle Eastern, Asian, or possibly Native American.

For no particular reason other than curiosity, Tom asked Amon what his plans were for the future.

"My plans? I haven't figured it out yet. Let's just say I want to do some good in the world," he replied solemnly.

"Well, as a teacher, I start with an objective, formulate a plan, and then implement the plan," Tom said in an offhand way.

"Nonetheless, it's good to be in the heart of New York City, the origin of so many worthwhile endeavors," Amon asserted.

"I wouldn't call Mariners Harbor the heart of New York City or even the heart of Staten Island."

"I like harbors. All the world's great cities are built on harbors — New York, San Francisco, London, Paris, Amsterdam, and Rio de Janeiro," Amon stated, looking toward the brackish water of the Kill Van Kull. Then staring at Tom intensely, Amon said, "So you're a schoolteacher … of what subject?"

"I teach science, chemistry, and physics at Curtis High School. I deal with facts — that is, facts linked by scientific laws."

"Facts about the world as it is or as it should be? Teaching is a noble profession. You do God's work," the stranger observed.

Pausing momentarily, Tom asked Amon if he was some kind of a preacher. He remembered the soapbox preacher in the city who had scared Joanie with his strange talk of impending doom. Stemming from his childhood experiences with scary nuns, Tom had ambivalent feelings about organized religion. He also had problems with the doctrine of trinity, especially the Holy Ghost.

"I'm not a man of the cloth. I'm just a person trying to find his way. The world needs more love and understanding and less violence and greed," he replied.

"I can't argue with that. But unless you're John D. Rockefeller, you have to spend a good part of each day earning your bread. The law of supply and demand forces us to be realistic, rather than idealistic," Tom asserted.

Changing the subject, Amon mentioned Curtis High School. "Isn't that the impressive building with those devilish gargoyles in the front?"

"One and the same. Those damned stone gargoyles used to scare the hell out of me. They're a solemn warning to both students and teachers that education is a serious business," Tom said grimly.

"Teachers are special people. Jesus was a teacher of sorts. His disciples called him Rabboni, meaning 'teacher,'" Amon asserted.

"Some of my students do want to crucify me. Seems like everybody in America is either a teacher or a student. Unlike the apostles who talked about the hereafter, we deal in the here and the now."

"You have an ironic sense of humor. What is your name?" the stranger asked.

"Tom Haley from Elm Park, at your service."

Lyndon Johnson

Lyndon Johnson assumed the presidency in 1963 after the assassination of President Kennedy in Dallas, Texas. He ran on his own in 1964 and was elected by a huge margin. LBJ never forgot his humble origins in southwest Texas, where he began adult life as a teacher of Mexican American children. His favorite biblical verse was "Come now, and let us reason together." As a legislator, LBJ was able to push many laws through Congress because of his ability to compromise. In 1937, Lyndon Johnson was elected to Congress as a Democrat, promoting Franklin Roosevelt's New Deal and working for rural electrification. With regard to foreign policy, President Johnson was rigid, escalating the Vietnam War from 16,000 to 550,000 combat troops in the late 1960s. Widespread opposition to the war forced Johnson to abandon his plans for another term in 1968.

In addition to increasing American troop strength in Vietnam, LBJ started an extensive bombing campaign against North Vietnam. The unintended consequence of this heavy bombing was to bring regular North Vietnamese troops into the war. American army bases were attacked by these troops, allied with the Viet Cong, throughout South Vietnam. The war bogged down to a bloody stalemate with mounting casualties on both sides—and no way out for Johnson.

On the domestic side, Lyndon Johnson passed a comprehensive program of economic reforms designed to alleviate poverty and advance civil rights for black people. LBJ's war on poverty decreased poverty rates in America from 23 percent to 12 percent. President Johnson started government programs like Head Start, food stamps, and model cities, which improved the plight of millions of working-class people in America. LBJ also achieved major reforms in the area of medical care: Medicaid for poor people and Medicare for the elderly. He also provided funds for hospitals and funds to advance medical research. In the area of education, LBJ's Elementary and Secondary Education Act dramatically increased funding for public schools, private schools, and higher education.

In the area of civil rights, Lyndon Johnson advanced the economic and political status of black people. His landmark Civil Rights Bill of 1964, which ended discrimination in public accommodations and housing, and advanced black voting rights, was probably LBJ's greatest achievement. His economic agenda changed America for the better in virtually every segment of our society. Johnson's sympathy for poor people likely originated from his own struggles as a young man. He supported himself though college by picking crops—cotton, corn, and grapes. Along with Abraham Lincoln, LBJ was the only US president to work as a laborer in his adult years. Were it not for the Vietnam War, LBJ would have gone down as one of America's greatest presidents.

CHAPTER 3

Superstition

On Tom's desk were the following items: a broken mirror, a rabbit's foot, a horseshoe, and a card with the number thirteen on it. The aim of the lesson was written on the board: "What is superstition?"

Barry entered the room and began singing Stevie Wonder's popular song "Superstition."

"Very superstitious, writing on the wall. Very superstitious, ladder's 'bout to fall. Very superstitious, nothing more to say. Very superstitious, the devil's on his way."

"Now we'll learn something useful—how to cast an evil spell on someone," exclaimed Manny, who was as rowdy as Barry.

Tom asked the class for some examples of superstition.

"The rabbit's foot and the horseshoe represent good luck," a student called out from the back of the room.

"That broken mirror," said Wendy. "If a person breaks a mirror, it means seven years of bad luck."

"Girl, you break a mirror every time you look into it," Barry snapped.

"Now that's enough from you. Give it a rest already," Tom responded.

"That's right. Saying mean things can bring bad luck. What goes around comes around," Ronnie chimed in.

"And if you can't say anything nice, don't say anything at all," Barry commented in a high voice.

Someone from the back of the class asked why the number thirteen was connected to bad luck.

"Judas sat in the thirteenth place during the Last Supper. He was the person who betrayed Jesus to the Romans," said Riner.

"Wow, Riner! You're an expert on the Bible too, as well as that boring science stuff," exclaimed Barry.

"He's just a learned guy," quipped Manny.

"Also, there are thirteen steps from the prisoner's holding cell to the gallows on death row," Tom indicated.

"How did you know that, Mr. Haley? Have you spent time in jail?" the irrepressible Barry asked.

"It's amazing what a person can learn by reading," Tom said irritably.

"Now that sarcastic remark is immature. I should report you to the principal, Mr. Stout," Barry retorted.

Ignoring the pesky student, the skinny science teacher asked the class about the difference between black magic and white magic.

"Black magic is associated with bad doings, and white magic is associated with good deeds," Riner answered.

"Now that's racist!" Barry called out.

Determined to press on with the lesson, Tom ignored the youngster's remarks.

"All this leads to the pivotal questions: What is superstition, and how did it originate?"

"It's folklore that grew out of coincidences in everyday life. Two things that occur together are often mistakenly connected as cause and effect," said Riner.

"So what's the opposite of coincidence?" Tom inquired.

"It's scientific knowledge based on observations and conclusions. The scientific method is the way we learn about the world," Wendy answered.

"Excellent, Wendy. In the Middle Ages there was a Dutch philosopher, named Spinoza, who said everything in nature operates according to cause and effect," Tom lectured.

"He was a determinist," said Riner. "He didn't believe in random events. Nor did he believe in established religion."

"Sounds like a Communist to me," said Manny.

"Actually, he was a free thinker. And for his troubles Spinoza was excommunicated by both the Catholic Church and the Jewish authorities of Holland," Tom indicated.

"I'll bet you he told those Holy Rollers to go blank themselves," said Barry.

"No, Barry. Spinoza was a stoic who lived a simple life and didn't make trouble."

"If you don't believe in God, you're looking for trouble," retorted Ronnie, who was naive and mild mannered.

"Truly, Spinoza did believe in God. He said God and the universe were one and the same. He also said that when we harm others, we actually harm ourselves," the skinny science teacher continued.

"That's true, Mr. Haley. When I punch somebody, I often get punched back by that somebody," said Barry.

"So why don't you just punch yourself and save others the trouble of punching you back?" commented the winsome Wendy.

"Shut up, bitch!" yelled Barry. But observing his teacher's angry stare, the impulsive teenager changed his tone. "I mean 'Hush, my little hussy.'"

With that unexpected conciliatory remark, the bell ended the lesson on superstation, and the students rushed out of the classroom, as if to avoid bad luck.

The Hermit

On a windy Saturday morning in late November, Tom walked down Morningstar Road amidst the fluttering yellow and red leaves borne by the shifting wind currents. Clad in a light jacket, the skinny young science teacher could feel the chilly autumn air, which was a sign of the approaching winter. Drawn to the rotting docks and abandoned ships of the old Bethlehem Steel shipyard, Tom headed west on Richmond Terrace. As soon as the ramshackle tugboat came into view, Tom saw Amon wave at him. Amon jumped off the boat and approached him on the rotting wharf.

"Let's go for a walk," he shouted to the young teacher. Tom nodded, and the two men walked briskly eastward on Richmond Terrace, passing under the arched Bayonne Bridge. This magnificent steel bridge was matched only by a bridge of similar design in the land down under, Australia.

As the two young men walked beyond the bridge, they came to an overgrown, weed-filled field with a dirt road that was familiar to Tom. They soon reached a dilapidated wooden shack where a red-bearded hermit had once lived. Stopping abruptly outside the shack, Amon said he felt a strange aura, the spirit of dead person.

"He was a recluse who died alone and in despair. May his tormented soul rest in peace," Amon uttered in a low tone.

Tom was amazed that the stranger's perception defied rational explanation. "That's right! In fact, I was the one who discovered his body a few years ago. He was a red-bearded hermit—kind of scary-looking. As a teenager I once delivered a newspaper to him. But when I came back to collect my money, the sight of his face frightened me, and I ran away."

Running his finger along the dust-laden windowsill, Tom asked, "How did you know about the hermit?"

"It's something I've always had. I am able to pick up vibrations that most people miss. It's metaphysics—the realm of reality beyond the five senses," Amon answered in a matter-of-fact manner.

"I'm a science teacher. Scientists deal with real phenomena—matter and energy—susceptible to the five senses and measurable in terms of numbers. It's weird. I gave a lesson on superstition the other day," Tom said.

"There's a good deal of truth in superstition, which is based on folklore passed down through the ages. And there are no coincidences in life. Everything happens for a reason," Amon continued.

"What about random events like flipping a coin or tossing dice?" Tom asked.

"You've heard of gamblers who constantly win at cards and games of chance. It's a gift that some people have—myself not included," Amon replied.

"You seem to be a determinist like the Dutch philosopher Spinoza. We talked about him also. Now that's a coincidence for sure!" the young teacher said.

"I've always had this hypersensitivity to things, similar to animals before an earthquake. We all have a purpose in life. The trick is to find out what it is and try to fulfill that purpose," Amon asserted.

"So what's your purpose?" Tom inquired.

"That's a good question!" Amon replied, shaking his head.

CHAPTER 5

Saturday Morning

It was Saturday morning, Tom's favorite time of the week, when he read the *New York Post* and chitchatted with his mother. Weekday mornings Claire Haley gobbled some toast and slurped instant coffee before dashing around the corner to catch the #3 Castleton Avenue bus to St. George. After crossing New York Bay on a packed ferryboat, his mom walked to the Canadian Bank of Commerce in Lower Manhattan, where she handled stocks, bonds, and securities, and hobnobbed with middle-aged carriers of those aforementioned financial instruments. Unlike her son, who had a love–hate relationship with teaching, Claire Haley loved her job with a passion that mystified Tom.

"I met this guy who lives in an abandoned tugboat in Mariners Harbor," Tom said as he ate his usual breakfast of Wheaties topped with a sliced banana.

"Lives in an old tugboat. What is he, some kind of a nut?" she replied archly.

"No. He's an interesting person. Very resourceful. He seems to have ESP."

"Oh, sure. He reads tea leaves and wind currents from the air. Reminds me of your father. He was always bringing some old drunk around. I'd come home from work to find him sitting on the front stoop, drinking beer with one of his cronies. He'd tell me the old bum had a gift—a gift for taking up space!" his mom complained.

"Mom, you're always comparing my situation with Dad's. You should have an open mind about such things."

"Listen, McGee. You have to live life on a basis of reality. Why doesn't he get a job?" she retorted heatedly.

"I know, Mom—one of your famous old adages. You either go to school or you go to work. A car is a luxury. Use your head for more than a hat rack. And of course, you have to die of something. Such pearls of wisdom that pour forth from thy mouth!"

"Well, don't invite him here. I'm tired of those downtrodden bums sponging off me!" she said with blazing eyes.

"Spoken like a true Marxist. Keep the downtrodden proletariat off my steps. We all make mistakes. To paraphrase Shakespeare … the fault, dear Mom, is not in ourselves, but in the stars."

"Talking about the stars, isn't it about time you trimmed the hedge? It's so high you can't see the stars, or the moon, or the sun," she said stridently.

"Oh, yes. I mustn't forget the hedge from hell. How about another of your infamous tautologies—hedges cannot trim themselves," said Tom, finishing his coffee and leaving the kitchen in a huff.

Richard Nixon

Richard Nixon grew up in poverty in Northern California, attending Whittier College and then Duke Law School, where he graduated in 1937. He served in the navy during World War II and was first elected to Congress in 1946 and to the Senate in 1950. Nixon rose to prominence in 1948 when he investigated Alger Hiss, who was identified as a member of the Communist Party. He attracted the attention of Dwight Eisenhower, who chose Nixon as his running mate in 1952.

In 1960, Richard Nixon ran for president against John Kennedy, losing in a very close election. The highlight was the televised Kennedy–Nixon debate, which Kennedy appeared to win due to his appearance, confidence, and motto to "get America moving again." John Kennedy also talked about economic growth, civil rights, the missile gap, and medical care for the elderly. Nixon's message of eight years of peace and economic progress under President Eisenhower did not resonate with the American people, and Kennedy was victorious.

In 1968, Richard Nixon ran for president a second time. This time, he defeated Hubert Humphrey by a close margin. The Nixon administration recognized Red China, and Mr. Nixon himself visited China and shook hands with its leaders, Mao Zedong and Zhou Enlai. Nevertheless, the Vietnam War continued to rage, with Nixon intensifying the bombing of North Vietnam, Laos, and Cambodia. He began a program of Vietnamization, in which the South Vietnamese Army would take over the fighting. However, the latter was unable and unwilling to fight the Viet Cong and its North Vietnamese Army. A humiliating defeat appeared inevitable as America lost its enthusiasm for the war.

On the domestic front, President Nixon took measures to reduce inflation through wage and price controls. The Nixon administration formed the EPA to protect the environment, passed the Clean Air and Clean Water Acts, and OSHA for the workplace in the early 1970s. However, federal funds for these environmental initiatives were limited. With regard to racial desegregation, Nixon worked quietly behind the scenes to accomplish that objective. Richard Nixon also supported equal rights for women and appointed more women to his administration than Lyndon Johnson had done in the 1960s.

Richard Nixon's downfall was the Watergate scandal, in which he tried to cover up a burglary at the Democratic Party headquarters. There were White House tapes indicating Nixon's involvement in the cover-up. At one point in 1973, Nixon asserted that he was "not a crook. I've earned everything I got." With the tide of public opinion turning against him, Nixon found it impossible to govern. With the threat of impeachment looming, Richard Nixon resigned the presidency in the summer of 1974. His vice president, Gerald Ford, became president for the remaining two years of his term. In his final speech, Richard Nixon talked about his own great effort and devotion in fighting for worthy causes — "knowing both his triumphs and his failures while daring greatly."

CHAPTER 6

Forms of Energy

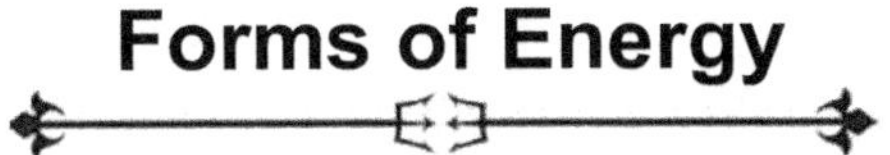

On Tom's desk was a hand-cranked generator connected to a light bulb, plus six-inch lengths of metal, glass, and plastic. The aim of the lesson was written on the board: "How is electricity produced and transmitted?" As his sophomore students filed into the room, a few of them played with the hand generator, turning it to get the light bulb to glow.

"Come over here, Wendy. Put your hand here while I turn the generator," said Barry, pointing to the light socket.

The pretty, long-haired teenager ignored him as she chatted with a heavyset girl who sat across from her. Tom shooed the mischievous student away and began the lesson. Turning the generator handle, which caused the light bulb to glow faintly, the young science teacher asked the class to explain what was happening.

Riner raised his hound. "You're changing mechanical energy to electricity and then to light energy."

"Very good, Riner. So it's clear that energy can be changed from one form to another. By the way, what is energy?" Tom asked.

"I know. Energy is the ability to do work. Now give me ten points extra credit," said Barry.

"If I stopped to give extra points to each person that answered a question correctly, I wouldn't have time to cover all the material I'm supposed to."

"That's exactly the point, Mr. Haley," replied the mischievous youngster with a sly grin.

Moving to the front of the class, the skinny science teacher held an eraser high above his head and then let it fall to the floor. When it struck the floor, the eraser released a cloud of chalk dust.

"You're polluting the air. That's against the law!" Manny called out from the back of the room.

"What's the energy transformation shown here?" Tom inquired.

"Gravitational energy to kinetic energy," Ronnie, a mild-mannered black girl, responded.

"Define those two kinds of energy."

The same youngster answered, "Gravitational energy is due to the height of an object above the ground. And kinetic energy is due to an object's motion."

"That's absolutely right, Ronnie!" Tom exclaimed energetically. He had learned that showing enthusiasm was important when teaching adolescents, whose passion for science was limited.

Tom had Barry come up and turn the generator. He asked what happened when the light bulb was connected and then disconnected from the generator.

"It was harder to turn the generator when the light bulb was connected to it. This is truly amazing, Mr. Haley!" Barry said with feigned excitement.

Tom also bridged the generator circuit with the metal, the plastic, and the glass wires. He demonstrated that only the metal wire could conduct electricity, while the glass and plastic lengths acted like insulators, stopping the flow of electric current.

Turning to the board, Tom told the students to get out their science notebooks. This caused the usual collective sighs and groans, which Tom had learned to ignore. Teaching was akin to marching uphill with one hundred pounds on your back. Talking and writing simultaneously, Tom summarized the outcomes of the day's lesson.

"Energy is the ability to do work and move objects. Potential energy is energy of an object due to its position above the ground. Kinetic energy is energy of an object due to its motion. Electricity is energy of moving electric charges through a wire. Other forms of energy include light, heat, chemical energy, and nuclear energy."

Turning back to the class, Tom asked, "Does anyone know the law of conservation of energy?"

"Energy can neither be created nor destroyed. But it can be converted to different forms," Wendy answered.

"Wow! That girl has smarts," Barry said sarcastically.

"It's called homework. Try it and you'll be surprised at how much you can learn," Tom chided the loquacious teenager.

"Book smarts is all right. But street smarts is better," the youngster replied.

"How about common sense? That trumps everything," someone called out from the back of the room.

"I can't argue with that," the skinny young science teacher responded as the bell rang, ending the hard wrought lesson on energy.

CHAPTER 7

Fallen Angel

Tom went for a walk down Morningstar Road on an unusually mild day in early December. Turning west on Richmond Terrace, the skinny science teacher ambled toward the abandoned Bethlehem Steel shipyard, with its rotting docks, corroded hulks, and derelict ships. Approaching the ramshackle tugboat, Tom noticed Amon perched near the top of a utility pole, working on some wires. Stopping in midstride, he realized that those wires carried high voltage.

Suddenly there was a bright spark accompanied by a crackling noise, and Amon was catapulted off the pole. He fell down hard, crashing on the rotting wharf. Tom ran over to him. Amon was stunned but conscious.

"Are you okay? Don't move! You might have cracked some vertebrae."

"I'm fine," Amon replied, grimacing. "This wharf is soft from dry rot. And I have backup." He showed the young science teacher a greenish metallic cross hanging from his neck on a chain of the same hue.

"That cross is made of copper, actually corroded copper—called verdigris. The Statue of Liberty, as well as the roof of Curtis High School, are made of the same metal. The cross must be very old," said Tom, looking at it closely.

"I found it on that ship over there." Amon pointed to an old freighter some distance away.

After emerging from his tugboat with a pair of rubber gloves, Amon remounted the pole and finished connecting the utility lines to a second wire running to his boat.

"So you believe in good luck charms," Tom said, concealing a smirk.

"I believe in electricity. But divine grace is essential also. The latter is a blessing, as well as an obligation, which I intend to fulfill," he stated bluntly.

"Aha! You are a man of God after all," Tom replied, scrutinizing Amon.

"Sure. This is my congregation. I preach to the fishes, the clams, the oysters, and the squid. And this guy over there," he replied, pointing to a small pig.

"Well, St. Francis of Assisi preached to animals, as well as people. The godly are always looking to expand their flock. We had pigs when I was a kid. Sometimes they'd get out of their pigpen. It was a good excuse for being late to school," Tom reminisced.

"It's tough trying to get people to mend their ways—let the ambitious expand their flock,"' Amon replied.

"Contrary to America's drive for supremacy, bigger is not always better. Remember the huge dinosaurs of days gone by?"

They're not around anymore," Amon responded.

"Scientists believe they were wiped by the Ice Age. And mankind may undergo a similar fate because of environmental pollution," the science teacher replied.

"So you once raised pigs? You're an interesting guy … though a bit weird," Amon remarked with a rare smile.

"That aspect we have in common," the skinny science teacher replied.

George Wallace

George Wallace was known for his segregationist policies in the South during the 1960s and 1970s. Wallace's position opposing racial integration was epitomized by his infamous statement, "I draw a line in the dust and toss the gauntlet before the face of tyranny. And I say segregation now, segregation tomorrow, and segregation forever."

George Wallace was born in rural southeastern Alabama in 1919. Though his parents were dirt-poor farmers, Wallace was interested in politics from an early age. Wallace tried boxing as a teenager and became adept at the sport. In 1937, Wallace went directly to law school from high school. After receiving his law degree in 1942, George Wallace joined the Army Air Corps, flying B-29 combat missions against Japan during World War II.

In 1946, George Wallace was elected to the Alabama legislature as a racial moderate. In 1948, Wallace supported Harry Truman for president, despite his opposition to the latter's civil rights program. Wallace held the Southern point of view that racial segregation was a matter of states' rights. In 1952, Wallace was elected circuit judge of the Third Judicial Circuit Court of Alabama. He gained a reputation for fairness and integrity, treating white and black lawyers with equal respect. Nonetheless, George Wallace opposed the removal of "whites only" signs in railroad stations and blocked federal efforts to review local voting lists, where discrimination was evident.

In 1962, George Wallace was elected governor of Alabama as a segregationist, winning 96 percent of the vote. He was sworn in on the same spot where Jefferson Davis became president of the Confederacy in 1861. This was the occasion of Wallace's statement vowing to maintain segregation in Alabama forever. In 1963, President Kennedy sent federal troops to Tuscaloosa to enforce integration of the University of Alabama. George Wallace stood in the college's front door in a vain attempt to stop the federal order. Later on, Wallace tried to prevent the integration of elementary schools in Huntsville and was overruled by the federal courts.

In 1964, George Wallace ran for president on a platform of opposition to racial integration, plus a tough approach toward street crime. His stump speech included rabble-rousing remarks about pinkos protesting the Vietnam War and outside agitators forcing racial mixing. In 1968, Wallace ran a second time for president on a different platform of ending the Vietnam War within ninety days. With regard to domestic issues, George Wallace favored increasing Social Security and Medicare benefits. However, his racial policies continued to oppose what he referred to as "forced integration."

In 1972, George Wallace ran for president a third time — advocating a moderate approach to racial matters, although he opposed busing to integrate public schools. In the midst of the campaign, Wallace was shot five times, with one bullet penetrating his spinal column. For the remainder of his life, George Wallace was paralyzed from the waist down. In his final term as Alabama governor, Wallace made a record number of black appointments to state jobs, including two black members of his cabinet. Unapologetic about his race baiting in the 1960s and 1970s, George Wallace asserted that he had evolved politically in the area of civil rights. Wallace's record of four gubernatorial terms across three decades was a national record. For better or worse, George Wallace had an enormous impact on America's racial politics during the twentieth century.

CHAPTER 8

Big Boned Girl

Tom sat down on a stool in the dimly lit, sour-sweet–smelling Kaffman's bar, drinking a locally brewed Ballantine beer. As usual, the first one was on the house. Rudy Kaffman's generosity was in memory of his father, Thomas Haley, who had regularly spent a good chunk of his house painter's salary in this neighborhood bar—one of many dotting Staten Island's North Shore. The hazy old saloon was jammed with customers celebrating the upcoming Christmas holiday, which was scarcely a month away. Journeymen alcoholics use any excuse to imbibe, and Christmas was as good as any.

Tom was anticipating the arrival of his girlfriend, Martha, to Kaffman's. On Friday nights, they met for a few drinks at Kaffman's or K. C.'s before doing some bowling in Port Richmond. The place was a shabby bowling alley, called Gooley's, on Richmond Terrace, a few doors from the seedy cockroach-infested Empire Theater, which regularly showed X-rated foreign films. Unable to convince Martha to see these movies, Tom occasionally saw these avant-garde films himself on a weekday night, clad in a soiled old raincoat.

The skinny young science teacher mused over the ups and downs of his teaching week at Curtis High School. There had been no fights or flare-ups, and his lessons on household chemicals, electricity, and energy went over reasonably well for this time of the year—the lead-up to the Christmas break. Tom put a lot of effort into his planning, especially the initial classroom experiment, as well as the following material. He had learned through bitter experience to fill up every moment of the lesson with information, concepts, and principles.

His students may not have appreciated it, but they regularly left his class with something concrete to take away — the vital material required for everyday life. It could be said that, as a teacher, Tom was a putter-inner and not a taker-outer. However, these post–Aquarian Age kids were tough customers. They had little intrinsic interest in learning for its own sake. Their focus appeared to reside in the realm of money and material things.

Fortunately the torturous American–North Vietnamese negotiations, orchestrated by Henry Kissinger, were bringing the seventeen-year-long Vietnam War to an end. For many young men of Tom's generation, it was a light at the end of a long winding tunnel. Even ex–Cold War warrior Richard Nixon was ready to accept a stalemate after his brutal bombing campaign against North Vietnam and the Ho Chi Minh trail — running though Laos and Cambodia — had not driven the Viet Cong into submission. Reportedly, Nixon had admitted to Mr. Kissinger that his bombing had accomplished "zilch."

Unlike many of his peers who went into teaching only to avoid the draft, Tom opted to continue teaching science for the foreseeable future. He was basically a creature of habit. Resisting his mom's prodding, Tom decided to forsake the business world, with its promise of big bucks and golden parachutes. A young man of modest needs and dogged endurance, Tom accepted the bumps and bruises, the mediocre salary, and the lack of future advancement, for the elusive joys of the classroom. Of course, teaching had its consolations — Christmas and Easter breaks, plus the cherished ten-week summer vacation.

Tom's rambling thoughts were interrupted by the breezy entrance of his girlfriend, Martha, into the dingy bar. Tall, big-boned, bouncy, and upbeat, Martha had a way of stirring things up wherever she went in life. Tom ordered his girlfriend some white wine and himself another Ballantine beer.

"Don't look so glum, Tom. It's Friday, thank God!" she exclaimed, plopping her voluminous but shapely derriere on the stool and grabbing Tom in a tight bear hug with kisses that left him breathless. Years ago his mother, aka Little Mommy, would grasp him and his sister, Cara, in a similar vice-like hug that rendered the two of them dizzy and out of breath.

Kissing the tall, pretty brunette on the forehead, nose, and lips, Tom said, "I just realized I'm a veteran teacher with two and a half years' experience under my belt. You could say that I'm locked into teaching for life. I'll be doing this for the next fifty years!"

"God willing. And what's so terrible about teaching? At least you earn a decent salary. Try working for the Staten Island Diocese," she responded.

"No, thanks. I'm not into vows of poverty and chastity. As St. Augustine said, Lord give me chastity but not yet," he remarked.

"You're just a spoiled naughty boy who needs a good spanking," she exclaimed.

"I'll settle for that — as long as I can reciprocate," he replied, smirking.

She shoved the skinny science teacher playfully, and Tom would have lost his balance had Martha not grabbed him with her strong arms. Dating Martha — a veritable Amazon who often whipped him at bowling, ping-pong, and basketball — was physically demanding. Upon consummating their union, she would denote her satisfaction by slapping him smartly in the face.

"But my favorite saint was Saint Teresa, who used to beat herself with a wooden stick so she could have visions of Jesus Christ," he said.

"For someone who never enters a church, you know a lot about the saints. That's what you need — a good beating with a stick," she asserted angrily, downing her wine in a few gulps.

"With regard to chastity, Tom, a girl like me does not relinquish that particular vow lightly. And the time is fast approaching when you will be obliged to make me an honorable woman. Beneath all that 1960s idealism, you're a selfish, immature boy," she retorted angrily.

"Stop fretting. You do remind me of Saint Teresa, who said, 'Let me suffer or let me die.' I am not selfish. I'm generous with my affection," he said, turning to Rudy, and ordered another round of drinks.

There ensued an awkward silence between the two lovers as each stared bleakly into their respective glasses, allowing the din of the crowded bar to mask their isolation. Looking up momentarily, Tom did a double take as he saw a familiar face approaching. It was a face from the past—Jake Gardello, his old girlfriend's cousin.

"Tom, can I talk to you for a few seconds?" Jake inquired in an undertone.

Turning red, the skinny science teacher nodded, got up, and followed the husky young man out of Kaffman's bar onto the chilly sidewalk.

"Joanie's back on Staten Island. She's in St. Vincent's Hospital. There's a tumor in her brain, and it's affecting her sight," Jake stated hurriedly.

"What? A brain tumor? Oh my God!" Tom replied breathlessly.

"I need to tell you she's married now. But she wants to see you, Tom. So don't say anything stupid, and don't upset her!"

"Of course not. I'll respect the sensibilities of everyone," Tom replied quietly.

"Good. You were always a classy guy. Visiting hours are from 4:00 to 8:00 p.m. Here's the room number," Jake said, handing the young teacher a small piece of paper, which Tom folded carefully and put in his wallet.

Returning to his stool at Kaffman's, Tom could see that Martha was furious.

"I know who that guy is. He's Joanie's cousin. If you start seeing her, we're finished," she asserted, getting up from her stool.

"Martha, the girl has a brain tumor. Have a heart!" he replied, near tears.

CHAPTER 9

Pretty Invalid

Except for the lost weight, pale skin, and close-cropped hair, Joanie looked pretty good to Tom. Her big brown eyes, full red lips, and warm smile tugged at the skinny teacher's heart, as always. Happy to see Joanie after more than two years, Tom struggled to keep his emotions in check.

"Oh, Tom! It's actually you. It's so nice of you to visit me ... a twenty-two-year-old invalid."

"Joanie, you're not an invalid. Before you know it, you'll be up and out of here," he replied optimistically.

"Come over here, Mr. Teacher Man, and give me a hug and a kiss," she demanded.

Tom did so readily, observing with apprehension that his old girlfriend appeared frail and fatigued.

"It's wonderful to see you, Joanie, after so many years. You look good. Just do whatever the doctors tell you," he remarked, trying to mask his concern.

"Of course I cooperate, but it's kind of annoying. They're always examining me every day—X-rays, brain scans, electrodes on my scalp, poking and prodding me every which way," she said stoically.

"What happened to you? How did it all start?" he questioned in a faltering voice.

"I began getting severe headaches. Then my vision was affected — fuzzy and double images," she revealed.

"I'm sure the doctors will get to the bottom of it. They can do so much nowadays. Medical science has advanced significantly in the past few years," Tom commented.

"Thanks to science teachers like you. How is your teaching going?"

"It's not bad. It took a while, but I've learned how to keep my students under control … for the most part. The secret is to keep them busy. Work their little their butts off," he asserted.

"Remember that cute girl, Mimi? She had a big crush on you," Joanie said, smiling, especially when the young teacher began to blush.

"Nah. She felt sorry for me because the kids gave me a hard time. Once, she popped me in the nose, giving me a nosebleed, when I pulled her off a classmate," Tom mentioned.

"You were always getting nosebleeds. You're just a softy. Which is why I liked you from the start. Do you still have that old red bike?" she said.

Nodding and shrugging his shoulder, Tom asked Joanie how she liked Indiana.

"It's nice. But I miss Staten Island. I have a good life in Indiana. My husband, Joe, is a lawyer. He is very ambitious. He works long hours, trying to get ahead," she said, as if reading from a script.

At this point, a nurse entered the room and began examining the pretty, young patient. The nurse, a stern middle-aged woman, told Tom that he had to leave because Joanie was being brought to another floor for further tests. Tom gave his ex-girlfriend a kiss on the cheek and left the room hastily, trying to hold his feelings in check. He understood that the major events in life — illness, birth, death, and love — are inextricably linked on an emotional level.

CHAPTER 10

A Stray Cat

Tom walked westward along Richmond Terrace on another mild Saturday in December. He noticed a red sedan parked near the old Bethlehem Steel shipyard, where Amon had made his home. Hurrying over to the site, Tom saw Amon bent over a black cat on the sidewalk with a chubby, middle-aged woman watching the proceedings with concern.

"What happened?" the skinny science teacher asked the woman, who was clearly upset by the accident.

"My car struck the cat. It darted out into the road, and I couldn't stop in time," she replied tearfully.

"It's okay, lady. I hit a squirrel the other day on Walker Street. Never had time to stop. It could have been worse. Some parts of the Island have deer crossing the road," Tom said, noticing a frown on Amon's face.

The cat was howling and writhing in pain as Amon stroked its belly and murmured some soothing words to the distressed animal. It appeared to have an internal injury to the head, which was bleeding.

"Maybe we can bring it to the vet," Tom suggested to the woman, who was visibly shaken.

Turning back to the injured cat and Amon, Tom was surprised to observe the cat, which was pure black, purring and licking Amon's hand with affection.

"My God! It looks like he's feeling better," Tom exclaimed.

"Of course he's better. It's a gift I've always had. My hands can heal," Amon stated calmly, stroking the cat under its chin.

Ecstatic, the chubby woman clapped her hands joyfully. "What can I give you?"

"Nothing." Then Amon paused a for a moment and said, "The next time you pass by, perhaps a few cans of soup, a loaf of bread, and some cat food. I'm going to keep this little guy," he said, stroking the cat.

"For sure. Anything you need," she replied joyfully.

"So you're not only a soothsayer, but also a healer. You're an amazing guy," Tom said, scrutinizing Amon with renewed interest.

"To paraphrase Henry James, I work in the dark, do what I can, and I give what I have," Amon recited with a half smile.

Shirley Chisholm

Shirley Chisholm was the first African American woman elected to Congress, representing Bedford-Stuyvesant from 1968 to 1983. In 1972, she was nominated for president at the Democratic convention, becoming the first African American candidate for the nation's highest office. Born in Brooklyn, Shirley Chisholm was sent to Barbados to live with her maternal grandmother until the age of ten. Because of her early years in the Caribbean, she spoke with a strong West Indian accent. Returning to Brooklyn, Shirley Chisholm attended New York City public schools, including Girls High School, which at the time had an excellent academic reputation, attracting girls from all over Brooklyn.

In 1946, Shirley Chisholm graduated from Brooklyn College with a bachelor's degree in education. While working in a nursery school in the late 1940s and early 1950s, she attended graduate school and earned a master's degree in education from Columbia

University in 1952. At this time she met and married Conrad Chisholm, a private investigator specializing in negligence lawsuits. Running a day care center, Shirley Chisholm became known as an authority on early-education issues. She first became involved in politics by working as a volunteer for political clubs, as well as the League of Women Voters in the 1950s.

In 1965, Shirley Chisholm was elected to the New York State Assembly, where she served for three years. In the State Assembly, she obtained unemployment benefits for domestic workers. In addition, Mrs. Chisholm sponsored and helped to pass the SEEK program, which helped disadvantaged students attending college through extensive remedial services in New York City high schools. In August 1968, she was elected as the Democratic National Committee woman from New York State.

Later in 1968, Shirley Chisholm was elected to Congress from the newly redistricted Bedford-Stuyvesant area of Brooklyn. Her campaign slogan was "Unbought and unbossed." With her victory, she became the first black woman elected to Congress. One of her early successes in Congress was to expand the food stamp program. In particular, she started the WIC program, which provided milk and food to poor children. Her congressional staff consisted of only women, of which half were black. From her own experience in the New York legislature, Mrs. Chisholm always believed that she had been discriminated against because of her sex, rather than her race.

In the 1972 presidential election, Shirley Chisholm made a bid for the Democratic nomination for president. Calling for a "bloodless revolution," she formally announced her candidacy at a Brooklyn Baptist church. However, her campaign was hampered by poor organization and a lack of funds. Many party regulars did not consider Shirley Chisholm a serious candidate for president. She received little support from her black brothers, complaining that "men are men." Culturally, many black men were hung up by the "black matriarch" thing. Her husband, Conrad Chisholm, supported his wife: "I have no hang-ups about a woman running for president." Shirley Chisholm's base of support was ethnically diverse, including prominent women like Betty Friedan and Gloria Steinem.

Shirley Chisholm often reached out to people of opposing political views. She visited George Wallace in the hospital after he was shot in 1972. Later on, Wallace supported Mrs. Chisholm in her effort to give domestic workers the minimum wage. The former Alabama governor lobbied Southern congressmen to get the bill through Congress. In her congressional career, Shirley Chisholm worked hard to improve the living conditions of inner-city residents. With regard to foreign policy, she opposed the military draft, the Vietnam War, and the expansion of nuclear weapons. After leaving Congress, Mrs. Chisholm resumed her teaching career at Mount Holyoke College. In the 1980s, she campaigned for Jesse Jackson in his bids for the presidency. Shirley Chisholm was a pioneer for the rights of black people and women, blazing a path to be followed by a new political generation in subsequent years.

More Wonders

A few weeks later, Tom was sitting with his mom in the kitchen, reading the *Advocate*, the local Staten Island newspaper. "Wow! Remember that guy living in the Bethlehem Steel shipyard I told you about?" he asked, pointing to the community news section of the paper.

"Yes. He sounded like a crackpot, living on an old tugboat. In this day and age, some people will do anything rather than work for a living. There are no free lunches in this country," she said cynically.

"Well, it says here Amon—that's his name, by the way—assisted a little boy who fell from a tree. According to eyewitnesses, the boy appeared to have a broken leg. But after the stranger stroked his leg, while chanting a prayer, the child's leg was completely healed. The kid got up and walked away, as if nothing had happened. The boy's parents visited Amon in his tugboat residence, offering him money, which he refused. Later, they returned with a donation of food, which he accepted gratefully."

"That *Staten Island Advocate* is a scandal sheet—a rag that I wouldn't use to wipe my behind. I'll never forget the front-page story they did about your father's nephew, Rusty. Remember when he turned up at the house with a bag of money from robbing a liquor store?"

"How could I forget, Mom? You used to remind Cara and me about that story twice a month, as a sort of weird object lesson. I was afraid to go within fifty feet of, much less enter, any liquor store on the North Shore!" Tom replied.

"Sure. You of all people, who frequents the saloons of Elm Park more often than you go to the public library. Anyway, this kook has everybody fooled. I wonder what his real game is," she continued.

"So what are you saying, Mom? That he's up to some kind of scam or racket?"

"If the shoe fits, wear it, my naive son."

"From my own observations, Amon is a charismatic person with amazing gifts that elude rational explanation. And unlike so many of our fellow citizens, Amon is not concerned with pecuniary matters."

"Just keep an eye on your wallet. For a science teacher, you're pretty gullible. And don't talk about that man to your students or the teachers at Curtis High School. They'll think you flipped your lid!" she warned her son.

"Mom, not everything in life can be explained in terms of cause-and-effect laws of science. There is a spiritual side of life too," Tom retorted.

"Here's a spiritual thought—cleanliness is next to godliness. So go clean up your sloppy room, and take out the garbage," Claire Haley commanded her son.

"And don't forget that old standby—life must be lived on the basis of reality," Tom recited as he left the kitchen.

Yet he couldn't blame his mother for her cynical attitude toward mavericks as a result of past experiences with shady characters, like his father. As a middle-aged person who had experienced the ups and downs of life, her unhappy yesterdays greatly exceeded her sunny tomorrows.

CHAPTER 12

Visit to the Hospital

So you want me to see this woman friend of yours at the hospital?" Amon asked, fixing the skinny science teacher with an intense stare.

"Joanie's only twenty-two years old. She's too young to be so afflicted. I'll drive you there. Just look at her. Please," Tom implored.

"Well, there's no harm in that. But remember, I'm no miracle worker. Despite what the local papers say."

Joanie squealed with joy when Tom and Amon entered her room. After an exchange of pleasantries, Tom nodded to his friend. Joanie looked at Amon with grateful eyes, sensing he was there to help her.

"How are you feeling, sweetie?" Amon asked in a low voice, looking at the pretty, young woman reverently.

"Not too good. I woke up with a fever and a bad headache," she said agitatedly.

The three young people began chatting amiably. Joanie talked about her whirlwind dating with Tom back in high school.

"Tom is a very nice person. I used to see him delivering papers early in the morning on his old red bicycle, years before we started dating," she related.

"Absolutely, my friend Tom is the best. He's one of those people you feel you've always known—even before you actually meet him," said Amon.

"There was this softball game, and I kept yelling at him to get his attention. Then, he collided with another player and I ran out on the field to help him."

"It was fate. You and Tom were supposed to meet. That incident on the field was truly an act of God," Amon stated bluntly.

Going over to Joanie, the stranger said, "Just close your eyes for a minute, sweetheart, while I keep my hand on your forehead."

Joanie did as she was instructed and soon fell into a deep sleep. Amon signaled Tom, and the two young men left the room.

"You're still in love with her, my friend. There's definitely something between you," Amon asserted.

"Oh, no. We're just friends. Joanie's married, you know. Just old friends, that's all," Tom replied in a determined manner.

CHAPTER 13

Martha and Mary

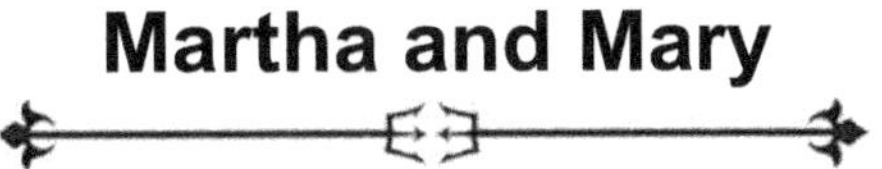

Tom stopped his old gray Pontiac on Richmond Terrace, adjacent to the abandoned Bethlehem Steel shipyard, where Amon lived on his refurbished tugboat. Out of the beat-up sedan emerged Tom, his girlfriend Martha, and her friend Mary. Like Martha, Mary taught at St. Mary's school in Port Richmond, farther down on Richmond Terrace. Carefully, the threesome walked on the rotted old wharf that led to Amon's tugboat. Tom carried a shopping bag of some clothes and a pair of shoes for Amon, who greeted them warmly and accepted the donations with his customary gratitude.

"Thank you so much. As you can see, my clothes are threadbare, and my boots have seen better days," he said with no hint of embarrassment.

"I want to introduce you to Mary. Of course, you've already met Martha," the skinny young science teacher said hesitantly. It was clear that Martha was not fond of Amon, which only made Tom more determined to maintain his friendship with the gifted young man. Smiling, Amon gave both young women a hug and welcomed them to his home. Mary immediately asserted herself, telling the young stranger to sit down on a chair while she removed his old boots and frayed socks.

"Your feet are filthy. Martha, look for a basin. I'm going to wash those God-awful feet," Mary declared forcefully.

"Now this is ridiculous! He's a grown man, capable of washing his own feet," Martha replied, annoyed by the entire situation.

"Martha, don't fret over such matters. If this lovely woman wants to be kind to me, let it be," Amon lectured the impetuous schoolteacher.

Within a few minutes, Mary was washing the stranger's feet. In addition, she scrubbed his face, neck, hands, arms, and upper body, to the amusement of Tom and the chagrin of his girlfriend. Then Mary, who clearly liked Amon, told him to "wash your lower half, and put on the new clothes, because we're all going out for a bite to eat."

While the stranger busied himself with washing and dressing in his new wardrobe, Tom looked around Amon's living quarters, noticing two big stacks of old newspapers going back to the 1950s — the *Staten Island Advocate*. Tom wondered if Amon's knowledge of the red-bearded hermit's death may have been due to the latter's perusal of that local newspaper.

Upon Amon's insistence, it was agreed that they would walk to the restaurant. Amon decided on a small, dingy diner going west on Richmond Terrace, a few blocks after Union Avenue. Just as Tom was a fan of Elm Park, Amon was a confirmed enthusiast of Mariners Harbor in all its offerings.

Strolling along Richmond Terrace, Tom noticed the run-down Victorian apartment house, where his parents lived when he and Cara stayed with their foster parents in South Jersey. So much had happened in the ensuing fifteen years. Thomas Haley had died of a heart attack, Cara was now a married woman, and Tom was a veteran science teacher at Curtis High School. He recalled looking at the tugboat and ship traffic from their second-floor window as a boy, amazed and dismayed at the busy North Shore neighborhood, which faced the gray choppy waters of the Kill Van Kull.

"You lived there at one time, Tom?" Amon inquired, pointing at the dilapidated apartment house.

"How did you know that?" Tom replied, amazed at the stranger's uncanny perception.

"It's obvious the way you scrutinized the place that it had been your home," Amon replied in a matter-of-fact manner.

"What a guy! I always wanted to go out with a person with ESP," Mary exclaimed as Martha shook her head petulantly.

"They opened up a new pizza place on Forest Avenue, which claims to serve the biggest pizza in New York," Martha said, attempting to change the subject.

"Martha, there's a place in Brooklyn where the pizza is a tabletop, supported by four cardboard legs. So you would just eat the table — a meal fit for a big-boned girl like you," Tom wisecracked to his girlfriend.

Martha responded with a hard punch to the skinny science teacher's gut, which left him breathless momentarily.

Arriving at the gloomy diner, the four young people took seats in a booth. There were a few middle-aged patrons eating at the counter and in the booths. A gaunt gray-haired waitress took their order: hamburgers and french fries for the gentlemen, and BLT sandwiches with coleslaw for the ladies.

"It's my treat, folks. I just got a promotional pay raise for my master's degree," Tom announced proudly as his companions congratulated him.

"Hard work pays off in many ways, especially the intrinsic satisfaction of work itself. Who said, 'Do not squander time, for that's the stuff life is made of'?" Amon inquired.

"That was Ben Franklin, who also said, 'Lost time is never found again,'" Tom declared, proud of his recall of that founding father's assertions.

"Ben Franklin, of course. Early to bed and early to rise, makes a man healthy, wealthy, and wise," Mary chimed in with a smile.

"Franklin also said the sleeping fox catches no chickens and the used key is always shiny," Tom proclaimed happily.

"Will you stop already with those stupid Ben Franklin sayings!" Martha said stridently.

"Okay, we'll quote Richard Nixon, with his false promises of ending the Vietnam War through Vietnamization. Or when he talks about his wife's Republican cloth coat. Or when he says, 'Let me make one thing perfectly clear,' before bullshitting the American people," Tom replied.

"You seem to be very knowledgeable about American history," Amon observed.

"Next to science, it's my favorite subject. Occasionally I fill in for absent history faculty at Curtis," the skinny teacher replied.

"Tom is a jack-of-all-trades: teacher, scholar, athlete, drinker, and rabble-rouser. In the Middle Ages, they would have hung him," Martha commented sourly.

"Thank God we're living in a secular world, where reason holds sway over fanaticism," Tom replied.

Suddenly, there was a crash as a customer seated at the lunch counter fell to the floor. Amon instantly sprang into action, quickly joined by his companions. Assessing the elderly man closely, Amon declared that he must have had a heart attack. The diner's owner said he'd call an ambulance. Mary put her ear onto the victim's chest, trying to ascertain if his heart had stopped beating.

"It's hopeless. I don't hear a heartbeat, and he's not breathing," Mary said tearfully. The waitress said the man, whose name was Danny, often complained about chest pains.

"Where there's faith, there's hope." Amon stroked the old man's forehead and placed his hands on his chest, pushing rhythmically and whispering some words, which none of the spectators could hear.

Suddenly, the stricken man gasped for breath and opened his eyes. "Just rest awhile, my friend. And then go forth and live your life," Amon proclaimed solemnly, aware that he had an audience.

"You're amazing! A soothsayer and a faith healer. You're my hero, Amon," Mary said, hugging the young man ardently.

Even Martha was impressed. "Now I've seen everything."

Gloria Steinem

Gloria Steinem is a leader of the American feminist movement, as well as a journalist and political activist. She has written numerous articles for *New York Magazine* and founded *Ms. Magazine* in 1971. A native of Toledo, Ohio, Ms. Steinem was of mixed Scottish and Jewish background. Her paternal grandmother was prominent in the women's suffrage movement of the early twentieth century.

Gloria Steinem's mother suffered a nervous breakdown—experiencing delusions and outbursts—resulting in hospitalization for mental illness. Her father was a traveling antiques dealer. Consequently, the Steinems spent many years traveling the country in a trailer. As a youngster, Ms. Steinem was struck by the indifference of doctors toward her mother. She also noted the difficulty her mother had in obtaining work, as evidence of the general anti-woman attitudes of the country at that time.

Gloria Steinem graduated from Western High School in Washington, DC, and then moved on to Smith College, where she graduated Phi Beta Kappa in 1956. While working as a journalist for *Show Magazine*, Ms. Steinem wrote an exposé about Hugh Hefner's Playboy Club, where she worked as an undercover waitress. The article, "A Bunny's Tale," featured a photo of the author in a Bunny uniform and explained the humiliations a waitress had to endure at the club. Her work as a Playboy Bunny resulted in a negative label on Ms. Steinem's reporting ability, preventing her from working in the field for some time. In the meantime, she began writing for a TV show: *That Was the Week That Was*.

In the late 1960s, Gloria Steinem became involved in the abortion issue. She, herself, had obtained an abortion in London in 1959. This was the beginning of Ms. Steinem's career as an active feminist. It angered her that women, who were forced by circumstances to have an abortion, were labeled as evil. Ms. Steinem asserted that "if men could get pregnant, abortion would be a sacrament." She believed women have the fundamental right to "take responsibility for their own life and not just let things happen to them." Gloria Steinem invented the phrase "reproductive freedom" — the freedom to have children or not to have children.

In the realm of political activism, Gloria Steinem signed the "War Tax Protest" pledge in 1968, refusing to pay income tax as a protest against LBJ's Vietnam War. The following year, she spoke before Congress in favor of the Equal Rights Amendment. She also wrote articles on a utopian world in which men and women were truly equal. In 1972, Ms. Steinem ran as a Democratic Party delegate for Shirley Chisholm but lost. She also worked on women's equality issues in the workplace for such occupations as waitressing, airline stewardesses, and medical workers. Active in the civil rights movement, Ms. Steinem was arrested for protesting South African apartheid in the late 1970s.

Gloria Steinem has criticized pornography, which she said humiliates, degrades, and exploits women. She also has been critical of obscure deconstructionist discourse, which produces arcane knowledge that is neither accessible nor helpful to people. Ms. Steinem grew up reading Wonder Woman comics. She restored this female superhero visually on the cover of the first issue of *Ms. Magazine*. Ms. Steinem firmly believed that sex and race were easy and visible differences used by the system to separate people into superior and inferior groups, especially in regard to cheap labor upon which capitalism depends. Gloria Steinem's solution: "A society in which there will be no other roles other than those chosen or earned. We are really talking about humanism."

CHAPTER 14

What Is Life?

Displayed on Tom's desk were a tomato plant, a toy car, a fish bowl with two goldfish, a petri dish with green molds, and a rock. On the blackboard was a chart depicting the amoeba, a one-celled organism. The aim of the lesson was written on the board: "What is life?" A few of Tom's sophomore science students lingered by his desk, examining the tomato plant that bore green tomatoes and tapping the fish bowl, causing the two goldfish to dart around their small home.

"How do we know something is alive?" Tom asked as he picked up the rock.

"The rock is only alive when you throw it," someone called out from the back of the class.

"Anything that moves is alive. Like those goldfish, which I'd like to fry for lunch," Barry replied, getting up from his seat.

"Sit down, please. What about this particular thing?" Tom inquired, letting go the windup car, which zoomed across his desk.

"Very tricky, Teacher Man. But once the spring unwinds, the car will move no more," Manny yelled from the back of the room.

"Some living things don't move. Like that green mold, plus bacteria and viruses, and the amoeba in that chart moves very slowly, when you look at it under a microscope," Wendy pointed out.

"That's true, Wendy. What other life forms move rather slowly?" the skinny young science teacher asked.

Riner raised his hand. "Plants move slowly. If you put a potted plant on its side, it will slowly bend and grow toward the sun."

"What about the Venus flytrap? It moves pretty fast. They say there are giant man-eating plants in the Amazon jungle," Barry asserted.

"It's clear that with the exception of microorganisms, all living things move: animals walk, fish swim, birds fly, insects crawl, and green plants grow toward the sun," Tom responded.

"You're talking about photosynthesis, which is necessary for green plants to make their own food," Ronnie said.

Turning to the board, Tom wrote the equation for photosynthesis:

Carbon Dioxide + Water $\rightarrow$ Carbohydrates + Oxygen.

"In addition, why are plants important to us?"

"Because we eat them. Though I prefer meat to vegetables any day of the week," said Barry.

"Well, meat does provide protein—necessary for growth and energy. But fruit and vegetables are also needed for a well-balanced diet," Tom lectured.

"Also, plants take in carbon dioxide and give off oxygen. So plants are really more important to our survival than animals," Wendy added.

"You go, girl!" Barry exclaimed, causing the long-haired youngster to offer the rambunctious teenager a rare smile.

"Another property of living organisms is the ability to respond to stimuli," Tom stated.

"That's right," said Manny. "When you touch a hot stove, you respond by moving your finger away quick."

"Unless you're a masochist who enjoys feeling pain," said Barry.

"Speak for yourself, man," Manny retorted.

"Listen to him, Mr. Haley. He's being disrespectful to honest scientific inquiry," Barry said half-seriously.

Ignoring the two teenage boys who liked to butt heads, Tom acknowledged Ronnie.

"Can a person return from the dead?"

Barry squealed, "You never heard of zombies, girl?"

Tom asserted that there have been cases of "people brought back to life, who had been clinically dead — no breathing or heartbeat — for a minute or two."

The next day, Tom continued the lesson on what is life. He reviewed the basic concept that, excepting bacteria and viruses, all living things — plants and animals — move through growth and by responding to stimuli. He also went over photosynthesis, though which green plants produce food in the presence of sunlight.

"What are the five necessary conditions for life?" he asked the class.

Riner, a high-strung bespectacled youngster, answered, "Oxygen, water, food, moderate temperature, and normal atmospheric pressure."

"Awesome, Riner! You are my hero," Barry called out in a high voice.

"The real heroes of the world are green plants, without which we wouldn't be around," Tom replied.

"So you're suggesting we worship green plants, Teacher Man?" Manny called out from the back of the classroom.

Ignoring the latter's remarks, Tom told his students to get out their science notebooks as he began writing the conclusions of the last two days' work.

Photosynthesis: the process by which green plants manufacture food in the presence of sunlight.

The Five Conditions for Life
1. Oxygen: needed to oxidize food to obtain energy.
2. Water: all plants and animals need water; man is 80% water by weight.
3. Food: provides chemical energy for animals.
4. Moderate Temperature: temperatures ranging from 30 °F to 100 °F.
5. Normal Atmospheric Pressure: 14.7 lbs/sq in.

Near the end of the lesson, Tom brought up the concept of food chain, which he said is the transfer of food energy from one form of life to another. However, there is a loss of energy as it proceeds up the food chain. The ratio of output energy to input energy is called efficiency:

Efficiency = Output Energy / Input Energy."

The skinny science teacher mentioned that usually humans are at the top of the food chain. Ronnie drew exception, saying that sometimes bears eat people, and alligators also have been known to eat people.

"Suppose a hunter kills a grizzly bear, which has eaten a person. And then the hunter eats the grizzly bear. So is the hunter a cannibal?" Manny asked from the back of the room.

"That's an interesting philosophical question. My answer is to stay out of wooded areas where there are grizzly bears," Tom replied.

"Like everything in life, it's all a matter of luck," Ronnie offered.

"Yeah. Sometimes you eat the grizzly bear, but other times the grizzly bear eats you," Manny called out from the back of the room.

"Talk about having a bad day at the office. That would be your last day at the office!" Barry shrieked.

Smiling, Tom withheld comment. Just then the bell rang, ending the lesson with those gloomy remarks from the irrepressible black teenager. With a three-day weekend approaching, the young teacher happily anticipated a respite from the classroom wars.

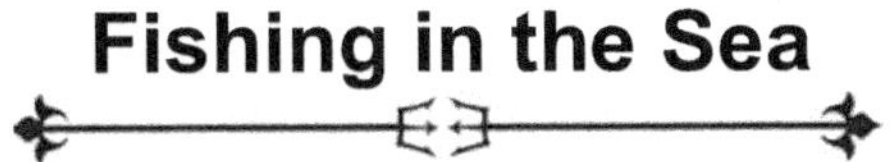

CHAPTER 15

Fishing in the Sea

On a mild February morning, Tom celebrated Lincoln's birthday by going for a walk along Morningstar Road and turning west on Richmond Terrace toward the defunct Bethlehem Steel shipyard. Tom thought about America's sixteenth president, whose Emancipation Proclamation freeing the slaves was probably the most significant presidential statement in history. He also recalled Lincoln's stirring words that "government of the people, by the people, and for the people shall not perish from the earth" in his Gettysburg Address. Sadly, the current crop of American politicians seemed like petty pip-squeaks when compared to giants like Lincoln, Washington, Jefferson, and Hamilton.

As Amon's repainted tugboat came into view, Tom noticed that he had set up six fishing poles that dangled off the side of the boat at intervals. He kept an eye on the fishing poles from a rickety rocking chair.

"What are you doing? Planning a grand feast for half of Mariners Harbor?" Tom called out.

"You got it. I'm starting a project to help people in the community who are down on their luck," Amon replied as he watched the poles.

"That's commendable. By the way, the poles are starting to vibrate," the skinny science teacher observed.

Immediately, Amon sprang into action, grabbing a pole and reeling in the line, which had a sizable fish hooked onto it. Tom ran onto the tugboat and helped Amon reel in the fish, which were numerous and hefty. Each time Amon put a new line into the gray choppy waters of the Kill Van Kull, the pole shook with a squirming, churning fish at the end of it. The fish were thrown into a large, ice-filled tub, which was soon filled to the brim.

"Not a bad day for a novice fisherman. I guess we have enough to feed half of Mariners Harbor on Sunday," Amon asserted with a wry smile.

"Beginner's luck, I would say," Tom commented, hiding his astonishment at the spectacle before him.

Looking at the murky water of the Kill Van Kull, Tom wondered about the mercury contamination in the fish flopping about in the icy tub.

"Ah. Ecologists have found high levels of mercury in certain fish—sharks, swordfish, tuna, mackerel, and sea bass," he asserted.

"Just about everything you eat has some kind of toxic elements in it. What are you gonna do, stop eating?" the young man replied.

"So what are your plans?"

"We're planning to fix up an old house on Simonson Avenue, right off the Terrace. It will be a place for the homeless—you know, vagabonds, hobos, alcoholics, drug addicts, the lost souls of Mariners Harbor."

"Sounds good to me. How can I help?" Tom asked.

"As a matter of fact, we need some carpenter tools like hammers, saws, chisels, screwdrivers, planes, sandpaper, paintbrushes, and the like. As well as some helping hands to pitch in. What we used to call elbow grease," Amon said.

"Come with me to my house. I have some tools in my cellar. They were my dad's. I can give you a hand on weekends," Tom suggested.

The two young men walked up the long sloping hill on Morningstar Road. They went past the abandoned railroad tracks that once transported commuters from Mariners Harbor, Elm Park, Port Richmond, and West Brighton to the St. George ferry. Approaching Innis Street, they ambled past an auto repair shop, where Benny, the amiable, grease-covered mechanic, was bent over the open hood of a 1950s Chevy.

As they trudged up the Morningstar hill, Tom saw an old man shambling toward them. It was one of his father's drinking buddies, a grizzled alcoholic who had lived with Thomas Haley in a little house at the end of Pulaski Avenue.

"How are you, sir? Are you still living in the neighborhood?" Tom inquired.

"I can't complain. I got a room across the street. Tom, you're the spitting image of your father—minus the blue eyes and his big thirst for the bottle," the old man replied in a scratchy voice.

Turning to his newfound pal, Tom said, "This is my friend Amon, who helps folks down on their luck."

Amon asked the old man his name and invited him to his upcoming dinner at the old Bethlehem Steel shipyard. "You can't miss it. We're going to have signs posted all over the area," he asserted.

The old man did not appear to be interested in Amon's invitation and shuffled away.

Continuing on Morningstar Road, the two young men turned right on Booker Place, where they ran into Harry the Horse, wearing paint-spattered overalls. Years ago, Harry the Horse would march down Pulaski Avenue, carrying a Spalding and broomstick bat—the basics for a street game of stickball. Everybody, boys and girls included, participated in a boisterous running-bases stickball game that occasionally ended in a broken window. Often the shattered glass was the result of a screaming line drive off the bat of one of the street urchins.

Always the good sport, Harry paid for the broken window and bore the verbal attacks of neighbors, like Mrs. Egger, whose hostility toward Harry and his gang was virulent and strident.

"There he is. The stickball champ of Pulaski Avenue," Harry exclaimed loudly.

"How are you doing, Harry? Better known as the Pied Piper of Elm Park," Tom replied.

Introducing Harry the Horse to Amon, Tom said that Harry always had time for a game of stickball — unlike the other dads of Elm Park.

"That's awesome. Grown-ups should always make time for kids. You know the biblical saying: Suffer the little children," Amon responded.

Harry looked at the young stranger suspiciously. "I like to play ball, but when it comes to church stuff, count me out."

"I totally understand. Good work trumps holy words any day of the week," Amon replied diplomatically as Harry went on his way.

Reaching Pulaski Avenue, the two friends encountered Granny Schmidt, making her daily pilgrimage to the neighborhood liquor store on Morningstar Road.

"Look what the cat is dragging along! The wise guy of Elm Park. Where's your low-life buddies carrying on in the street?" the frumpy dowager growled.

"Hello, Granny. Why the hostility? Remember the day I helped you when you passed out on the street?" Tom replied calmly.

"That's supposed to make up for all those wisecracks from you and your buddy Harry the Horse," the old woman squawked.

"Listen, Granny, I'm hosting a dinner in Mariners Harbor to raise money for the homeless and ..."

Cutting the young stranger off, the irascible old alcoholic yelled, "It sounds like bullshit to me. Get a job, and leave everybody alone!" Muttering curses under her breath, she walked away in a huff. Tom did his best to stifle a laugh.

"Whew! Talk about hard sell. The folks in Elm Park don't want to hear anything about helping their fellow human beings," Amon said, shaking his head.

"We're hard-nosed, hard-drinking, hardworking, down-to-earth SOBs. That's for sure!" Tom replied with a smirk.

As they strolled along the sidewalk of Pulaski Avenue, Amon stopped abruptly. Pointing to a cracked, jutting part of the sidewalk, he said in a somber tone, "This is where your father died of a heart attack. It occurred suddenly. He gasped for breath, clapped his right hand on his chest, grimaced in pain, and fell hard onto the concrete. I'm so sorry, Tom."

Incredulous, Tom asked, "How do you know all that?"

"It's something I see in my mind's eye. Just like the red-bearded hermit dying alone in that wooden shack off Richmond Terrace," Amon replied in a matter-of-fact manner.

Tom was amazed at his friend's uncanny ability. However, he wondered about the stacks of old newspapers, the *Staten Island Advocate*, which Amon had in his tugboat. When they first became acquainted, Amon told Tom he liked reading those old newspapers to learn about the Island.

Gerald Ford

Gerald Ford grew up in Grand Rapids, Michigan, where he was a star athlete and captain of his high school football team. At the University of Michigan, Ford was a center and linebacker for the nationally ranked Wolverines in 1932 and 1933. At Michigan, he befriended a black teammate, Willie Ward, with whom he roomed on the road. After graduation, Ford applied to Yale Law School, where he earned his law degree in 1941.

During World War II, Gerald Ford served on an aircraft carrier in the Pacific Ocean, participating in air strikes against the Philippines. For his naval service, Ford received a medal and nine engagement stars. After the war, he married Elizabeth Bloomer Warren, a fashion model and dancer in the Martha Graham Dance Company, in 1948.

The same year, Gerald Ford was elected to Congress, where he represented Grand Rapids, Michigan, for twenty-five years. In 1963, Ford served on the Warren Commission, investigating the assassination of John Kennedy. As part of his work for the commission, Ford prepared a biography of Lee Harvey Oswald, the alleged assassin.

As Republican minority leader of Congress, Gerald Ford began criticizing Lyndon Johnson's handling of the Vietnam War. He asserted that the White House did not have a plan to bring the war to a successful conclusion. His speech angered President Johnson, who accused Ford of playing "too much football without a helmet." Johnson also said that Gerald Ford was so dumb that he "couldn't walk and chew gum at the same time."

Under Richard Nixon, Gerald Ford helped Congress pass several of his initiatives, including environmental protection, tax reform, and revenue sharing. As testimony to his ability and integrity, Ford was selected by Congress to replace the disgraced vice president, Spiro Agnew, in 1973. Following Richard Nixon's resignation from the presidency, Gerald Ford became president, serving until January 1977. One of his first actions as president, Ford pardoned Richard Nixon for any crimes committed while in office. This may have led to his defeat by Jimmy Carter in the 1976 presidential election.

The Ford administration tried to combat inflation with "WIN" buttons. In addition to 12 percent inflation, the country was beset with high unemployment and the swine flu. To deal with the latter problem, President Ford launched a massive program of vaccinations, inoculating 25 percent of the population against the flu. Gerald Ford was an early supporter of the Equal Rights Amendment for women. Ford's wife, Betty, spoke in support of the Supreme Court's Roe v. Wade decision to permit abortions in the United States.

In the area of foreign policy, President Ford signed the SALT treaty to limit nuclear arms with Russia, and entered into the Helsinki Accords, which established basic human rights for all the world's people. Ford's greatest contribution was the termination of America's military role in Vietnam, ending that bloody nineteen-year war. The Paris Peace Accords, signed by Henry Kissinger and Le Duc Tho in 1973, brought that unhappy chapter in American history to a close. During President Jimmy Carter's inaugural address, he praised Gerald Ford and thanked him for returning integrity to the office and "for all he had done to heal our land."

Visit to Elm Park

Arriving at the flat-roofed, white stucco, two-family house with the number 269 emblazoned between the double front doors, the two young men paused for a moment.

Looking at the concrete porch steps, Amon said, "I can almost see your dad sitting here with that old man we just spoke to, drinking beer and waiting for your mom to arrive from work."

"Wow! Now you're starting to scare me, Amon," Tom said, getting spooked.

Tom showed his friend the alleyway, which led to the backyard. To his surprise, Cara was sitting on a stool, painting the view going toward the Caprinos' backyard, which was a veritable oasis of rose bushes, flowers, shrubs, plus an ancient olive tree. Awkwardly, Tom introduced the young stranger to his sister, who carefully explained her painting technique to the curious young man.

"My God! Your work is awesome. You've inherited your dad's talent—and then some," Amon exclaimed.

"How did you know our dad was a painter?" Tom asked incredulously.

"A gift like that doesn't fall from the sky, like a tiny sparrow falling from the branch of a tree."

"Thank you. It's something I've always enjoyed," Cara said, looking southward toward the Caprinos' backyard, which was two yards away. "Painting has kept me sane in a world gone crazy. I have a stressful job in the city and a mad-dog husband," she continued grimly.

Examining Cara's work, the young stranger observed, "Your depiction of your neighbor's backyard is dramatic and compelling."

"Well, thank you, Amon. You just made my day," Cara replied, setting her brush down.

"The artist holds a mirror to the world, providing a truer picture of reality than any photographer could provide," Amon commented.

"Did anybody ever tell you that you talk funny?" Cara inquired as the three young people laughed in collusion.

"Unlike the other dads of Elm Park who spent their free time boozing in the neighborhood gin mills, Mr. Caprino enjoyed working in his garden," Tom mentioned.

"Would that there were more devotees of the French philosopher Voltaire," Amon commented.

"Wasn't he the guy who told people to cultivate their garden?" Cara inquired.

"Excellent, Cara! Voltaire was known for that particular piece of advice," her brother exclaimed.

"You're astonished that I've read a book or two," she replied, looking at Tom. "You can't believe how shitty it was being this guy's sister. The damn teachers were always getting on my case about my low grades compared to Mr. Honor Roll," she continued irritably.

"Each one of us has something special to contribute. It's just a matter of time finding exactly what it is that we should offer to the world," Amon replied.

Putting down her brush momentarily, she asked, "So what do you offer to the world?"

At that moment, Tom's old buddy Joey Caprino came out of his house and waved to the threesome. Anxious to change the topic, Tom urged the young stranger to come with him to meet the ex–stoop ballplayer.

After awkward introductions, in which Joey repeatedly inquired about Amon's occupation, the conversation shifted to sports. Joey talked about his job as a Wall Street stockbroker and his baseball-playing exploits in the local semipro Staten Island baseball league.

"My pitching arm is shot, so I'm now playing the outfield for the Elm Park Aces. Mike Palermo and Gene Munski are on the team and some of the younger guys from the neighborhood," Joey said.

"How is Mike doing? I haven't seen him in ages," Tom said.

"He's the same dumb Guinea. Still thinks he should be pitching in the big leagues," Joey replied disdainfully.

"What does that expression 'dumb Guinea' mean?" Amon asked.

"Where are you from, Squeedunk?" the burly stockbroker replied. Before Amon could answer, Joey ran inside his house and emerged with a couple baseball gloves and a baseball. Tom said he would dig up a glove from his house so they could play a game of catch on Pulaski Avenue, as in the old days.

Before they left the yard, a bee flew off the olive tree and stung the young stranger. Jerking his arm in pain, Amon cursed the buzzing insect and the old tree in uncharacteristic anger. The swirling bee stopped flying and fell abruptly to the ground dead, and the leaves of the olive tree appeared to shrivel before the young men's very eyes.

"How the hell did you do that?" Joey inquired.

"It's just a little black magic or white magic … depending on your perspective," Tom asserted as Amon examined the well-worn baseball gloves like they were fossils from a bygone era.

The three young men began a game of catch on Pulaski Avenue. It was evident that Amon had never played baseball, which he openly admitted.

"Are you some kind of an immigrant?" Joey asked the awkward young man.

"I never had much time for games as a kid. We were always working on the farms in the area. Picking tomatoes, beans, corn, and the like," Amon replied.

"I did my share of corn picking and pig feeding as a kid, but there was always time for playing baseball and stuff like that," Tom mentioned.

Joey showed Amon how to hold his glove when catching a ball to his left or right. He also showed him how to throw the ball with his arm extended, plus the correct shoulder movement. A quick study, Amon was soon catching and throwing like somebody who had been doing it all his life.

"Not bad. Not bad at all. Want to play for the Elm Park Aces? We could use a spare outfielder," Joey said.

"He's a natural athlete and the best fisherman I've ever seen," Tom exclaimed.

Loosening up, the three men began tossing the baseball with more force. As luck would have it, one of Amon's strong throws sailed over Tom's head and crashed through Mrs. Egger's first-floor windows. It was a déjà vu moment from the past when one of Harry the Horse's errant throws broke the very same window. Immediately, the irritable middle-aged woman stuck her head out of the window directly above the broken window.

"Goddamn you, Tom. You broke my window again. Why can't you take your stupid ball games to the school yard?" she yelled.

"Sorry, madam. It was my fault entirely. I'll fix it immediately," Amon called out as he headed for Perry's junkyard, which was next door.

"Fix it immediately, you say? I'll believe it when I see it."

Within minutes, Amon had removed the broken pain and replaced it with a glass of exactly the same size. Borrowing tools from Tom and some putty from Joey, Amon had completed the repair on the window within twenty minutes, to the amazement of the three spectators.

Mrs. Egger was so pleased with Amon's work that she asked him if he could repair a leaky faucet in her upstairs bathroom. Agreeing, Amon entered the cantankerous woman's house while Tom and Joey waited outside in total astonishment at the peculiar turn of events. Emerging from the two-family house a half hour later, Amon carried a shopping bag full of canned goods.

"You're sort of weird, but you're some kind of miracle worker. With some practice, you'd probably be the best player on my team!" Joey said, looking at him closely, as if he had discovered a new baseball prospect.

"Indeed. He's a soothsayer, a faith healer, a handyman, and an awesome fisherman—all rolled up into one amazing person," Tom concurred.

"When you have good intentions, anything is possible," Amon asserted calmly.

CHAPTER 17

Laws of Motion

On Tom's desk was his windup car, a baseball, a rock of the same size, and a few balloons. Written on the blackboard was the aim of the day's lesson: "What are the three laws of motion?" In groups of twos and threes, his sophomore science students sauntered into the room, tossing their books onto the desks, and chatting aimlessly with their friends. As was their custom, Barry and Manny examined the items on their teacher's desk in a desultory manner. By the afternoon, high school students often exhibit academic fatigue through impatience, boredom, inattention, and irritability. Tom knew he had to act fast to maintain their interest.

Accordingly, the skinny young science teacher started the lesson with a jolt by releasing an inflated balloon toward the open door. The whooshing balloon darted into the hall, to the amusement of his students, who reacted vociferously.
Before Tom could stop him, Barry grabbed a balloon, blew it up, and sent it out of the room on a similar trajectory.

"Who can explain what happened here?" Tom asked the class.

Riner raised his hand. "Action and reaction. The air is forced out of the balloon backward, and the balloon moves forward in the opposite direction."

"Very good. It's called Newton's third law of motion: For every action, there is an equal and opposite reaction," Tom stated.

"I know Fig Newton. He's the guy that dropped the two rocks from the Leaning Tower of Pizza," Barry replied.

"Actually, it was Galileo who did that experiment from the Leaning Tower of Pisa, which proved that all objects fall at the same rate of speed due to gravity."

"Whatever. Show us the windup truck already," the irrepressible teenager responded.

Tom sent the windup car across his desk, which did not impress his students, who had seen that notorious car earlier in the semester. Then, as the science teacher sent the car on its way across his desk, he dropped the rock on it.

"So what happened here?"

"The car slowed down because of the added weight of the rock," Wendy quickly responded.

Next, Tom sent the baseball rolling across the desk with a slight push. Then he sent it rolling faster with a harder push.

"Who can summarize the first experiment with the car and the second experiment with the baseball in a law of motion?"

"The acceleration of an object varies inversely with its mass and varies directly with the applied force," Wendy answered.

"That's absolutely correct, Wendy," Tom replied. "One more thing, folks. I'm going to roll the baseball across my desk. What property of matter is shown here?"

"That round objects tend to roll forever?" Manny responded.

"Well, yes. But let's make it more general."

"That an object in motion stays in motion. And an object at rest stays at rest," Ronnie answered.

"That's absolutely correct, Ronnie," Tom replied.

"How come whenever a girl answers a question right, you say it's absolutely correct. But when a boy says something right, you barely acknowledge it," Barry complained.

"That's because I like girls better than boys."

"That's discrimination. I'm going to report you to the principal, Mr. Stout."

Ignoring the pesky student's complaint, Tom turned to the board. He instructed his reluctant pupils to take out their science notebooks. The following conclusions of the day's lesson were written on the blackboard.

Isaac Newton's Three Laws of Motion

First Law: An object at rest tends to stay at rest, and an object in motion tends to remain in motion.

Second Law: An object's acceleration varies directly with the applied force, and varies inversely with its mass.

Third Law: For every action or force, there is an equal and opposite reaction or force.

As the class drew to a close, Tom took out a match-head–filled, tin-can rocket. As expected, the rocket immediately grabbed everyone's attention. Years ago, Tom had set off a similar rocket, aiming it toward the hallway. Unfortunately, the rocket slammed into Mr. Stout's ample backside, to the joy of his students and the consternation of the grumpy school administrator.

Experience being the wisest teacher, Tom aimed the rocket toward the ceiling. Lighting the fuse with a match, the rocket seemed to tremble momentarily before it whizzed upward, smashing into the classroom's high ceiling. The class roared in delight as the room filled with sulfur fumes. Amazingly, the tin can rocket stuck onto the ceiling tile, where it remained for many weeks, as a reminder of their teacher's fun lesson on Newton's laws of motion.

"Now that was a truly awesome practical experiment! You should do more stuff like that, Mr. Haley," Barry yelled.

"If I did something like that every day, I'd lose my job," Tom replied as the class exited the room joyfully. Besides the jammed rocket, the room had filled with sulfurous fumes that wafted along the hallways.

CHAPTER 18

Home Repairs

As Tom walked along Richmond Terrace, he thought about Amon's plan to fix up an abandoned old house on Simonson Avenue, right off the Terrace.

Tom had worked at a defunct appliance factory as a security guard near the run-down house years ago. The young science teacher was impressed by Amon's philanthropic impulses. Tom occasionally donated money to charity, but he understood that giving one's time and energy for a worthy cause was a much greater commitment.

As he approached the ramshackle Bethlehem Steel shipyard, Tom saw Amon grappling with some lumber and supplies to transport to the construction site on Simonson Avenue. He hurried over to help his friend. Stepping from a moored rowboat to Amon's tugboat, Tom tumbled into the water as the rowboat broke free. The skinny young teacher panicked and thrashed about, desperately trying to grab the skittering rowboat.

Instantly, Amon ran over to the edge of his tugboat and dived into swirling gray water. With a strong arm, he grabbed the floundering science teacher and pulled him over to the rotting wharf. Dripping wet and shivering from the cold salty water of the Kill Van Kull, the skinny teacher climbed up to the rotting boards of the ancient wharf.

"You saved my life! I'm not a very good swimmer." Tom gasped, realizing how tenuous the boundary between life and death is.

"That's apparent. A person living on an island should be able to swim," Amon commented.

"It was the one course at CCNY I was failing. Then I got an excuse note from Dr. Atlas to get me out of it. He wrote something about recurrent sinus infections."

"Dr. Atlas, you say? I went to him recently for a checkup and a flu shot. He charged me five dollars—quite a bargain by today's standards," Amon said.

"Dr. Atlas is a rarity among doctors. He still makes house calls," Tom added.

"By the way. When you stepped from the rowboat to my ship and it went backward, doesn't that have something to do with action and reaction? I still remember that fact from my high school days."

"You're right about that also. You can't move forward without pushing something back. It's Newton's third law of motion: For every action there is an equal and opposite reaction. I was teaching Newton's three laws of motion the other day but forgot to apply it to everyday life," Tom said ruefully.

"It's clear that you are a theoretician and not a pragmatist. But I'm guilty of the same flaw myself," Amon remarked.

"Yeah, common sense has never been my strong point. I once painted a chair red and then sat on it before it dried. They called me Red Ass for months."

Clearly, the house on Simonson Avenue needed a lot of work. The clapboards were bare in places where the paint had flaked off. The leaky roof was marked with missing shingles and a crumbling red brick chimney. The backyard was overgrown with weeds and crabgrass, and the unruly front hedge hadn't been trimmed in years. Inside, the torn linoleum needed replacement, and the faded walls needed a paint job. The bathroom and kitchen sinks leaked, and the toilet dripped continually. Many of the windows were broken or cracked, and the locks on the front and back doors were broken.

Amon had roughly a dozen volunteers helping him. Mostly amateurs with regard to home repairs, they were a motley group of grizzled alcoholics, scruffy drug addicts, and down-and-out drifters. The charismatic young man called them "my posse of misfits." Amon had them cleaning the interior of the house — picking up accumulated debris, sweeping and mopping the floors, sanding the walls, and washing the windows.

Tom offered to trim the formidable front hedge. It was a task for which he had ample experience, as a result of his years-long battle with the eight-foot-long, six-foot-high hedge fronting his white stucco house on Pulaski Avenue. Martha's friend Mary was at the Simonson Avenue house on weekends and some weekday nights, cleaning and scrubbing with the fervor of a fanatic. Her loyalty and devotion to Amon was remarkable. Martha was annoyed by her fellow teacher's compliance with the young stranger's pronouncements and endeavors. She also resented the time Tom was spending on Amon's reclamation project.

"Martha's on my case because of my helping you here," Tom said to Amon as they sat on the front porch of the Simonson Avenue house.

"I'm not the person you should be talking to about such matters. I don't have extensive experience in those types of relationships. Do you love her, Tom?"

"I guess so, but things have been rocky lately. She's temperamental and dogmatic. The word 'compromise' is not part of her vocabulary."

"As with most things in life, let your heart be your guide," Amon said as he examined the rotting front steps of the old house, which needed repair.

"That sounds like something Ann Landers would say," Tom replied, thinking about some of the girls he had dated before Martha.

There was a woman named Madeline, with politically conservative views, who lived in Manhattan. Despite their political differences, Tom would have continued to date her were it not for the burden of running back and forth to the city. In those halcyon days, women like Madeline were classified as "GU" — geographically undesirable. On the other hand, Martha could be classified as "TU" — temperamentally undesirable. Of course, the worse classification for a women was "PU" — physically undesirable.

The Camp David Accords

On September 17, 1978, the Camp David Accords were signed by Egyptian President Anwar el-Sadat and Israeli Prime Minister Menachem Begin, after twelve days of secret negotiations mediated by President Jimmy Carter. The Accords were the culmination of intense talks taking place at the Camp David presidential retreat in Maryland. The negotiations were spurred on by Carter's relentless drive to achieve peace in the Middle East.

The peace initiative began when President el-Sadat announced his intention to go to Jerusalem and speak before the Israeli Knesset. Sadat's speech led the Israelis to invite the Egyptian president for a three-day visit. Egypt's goal was to regain the Sinai Peninsula, which was lost by Egypt during the 1973 Yom Kippur War.

With regard to Israel, Menachem Begin was willing to cede the Sinai for a relaxation of tensions along the Sinai–Israeli border and the establishment of diplomatic relations between Israel and Egypt. As the dominant Arab country in the Middle East, Egypt exerted great influence in the region. Thus, Menachem Begin preferred negotiations with Anwar el-Sadat to dealing with Arab countries like Syria, Jordan, and Iraq, who adamantly refused to recognize Israel's very existence.

It had been a long-term goal of Jimmy Carter to rejuvenate the Middle East peace process. The Yom Kippur War actually made negotiations possible on the basis of Israel ceding land in exchange for diplomatic recognition and permanent peace. President Carter was also interested in resolving the Palestinian issue in terms of granting those displaced people the right to govern their territory in the West Bank and in Gaza.

Because of Sadat's and Begin's expressed interest in resolving these issues, secret talks began in the American embassy in Cairo in 1977. When progress was made in these talks, both leaders were invited to Camp David for more negotiations. There were times when the talks reached an impasse, but Jimmy Carter got both men back together with compelling personal appeals. Nevertheless, the mutual antipathy between Begin and Sadat was such that they seldom had direct contact. Each man resided in a separate cabin, with Carter and his national security aide, Zbigniew Brzezinski, shuttling back and forth with proposals and counterproposals.

Near the end of the negotiations, Jimmy Carter took both men to Gettysburg, Pennsylvania, the site of the big Civil War battle, which resulted in the deaths of 15,700 men plus 46,000 casualties on both sides. This object lesson on the horrors of war was not lost on the two leaders. Both men invested enormous political capital, and in the end, a historic agreement was achieved.

The fundamental outcomes of the Camp David Accords were the withdrawal of Israel from the Sinai Peninsula, the establishment of diplomatic relations between Egypt and Israel, and the provision for autonomy by the Palestinians over the West Bank and Gaza. Another consequence of the Egyptian–Israeli peace treaty was America giving billions of dollars in foreign aid to both countries. In the enduring years since the Camp David Accords, there have been no outbreaks of war between Israel and its neighbors.

CHAPTER 19

Brouhaha in a Bar

Entering Kaffman's bar and sitting on a stool, Tom ordered a Ballantine beer, locally brewed on Staten Island. Looking around, Tom saw that the place was sparsely filled with customers, particularly for a Friday night.

"Mackie's back in town. Where have you been?" said the red-faced bartender, sliding a sudsy glass of beer toward Tom.

"I've been helping this guy fix up a house for the homeless in Mariners Harbor," the young science teacher said after taking a sip of the beer.

"One of them do-gooders? Hold onto your wallet," Rudy warned.

"Nah. It's nothing like that. He doesn't give a shit about money."

"Sounds like your dad. He liked to buy drinks all around when he was flush."

"Which wasn't very often," Tom replied cynically.

"Then your mom would come around and curse me out for serving him. She was one tough lady," Rudy observed.

Just then Martha burst into the hazy saloon and plopped hard on the bar stool next to Tom, giving him a sloppy kiss and a tight squeeze that left the skinny teacher breathless.

"What a day I had today. You know that redheaded kid Jimmy? He kept on jumping out of his seat. I was this close to belting him!" she complained.

"Do the nuns still hit kids when they're out of line?" Tom asked.

"Of course not. This isn't the 1950s. The only one who needs a good spanking is yours truly," she replied angrily.

"You can spank me anytime. As long as I get to return the favor … with your britches off."

"Let's go bowling first. And then we'll see about who's gonna spank who in your run-down old Pontiac," she replied with a wry smile.

"Well, I had other plans. I thought you might like helping Amon with that house on Simonson Avenue. Mary will be there lending a hand also."

"Mary's in love with a zealot. Some life she'll have with him, living on that old, rat-infested tugboat," Martha exclaimed.

"He's not a zealot. He's a person who tries to do the right thing in life. He has some amazing powers. I'm beginning to believe that he is an avatar."

"Sure, Tom. He's the messiah—the Messiah of Mariners Harbor," she yelled as some of the patrons stared at the angry young woman.

"I told him I'd stop over tonight. We'll go bowling tomorrow night, I promise. No reason to get all bent out of shape," he called out to his feisty, big-boned girlfriend as she stormed out of Kaffman's, nearly knocking an elderly man who had just entered the dingy bar.

CHAPTER 20

Nobody's Perfect

The next morning, Tom was sipping his second cup of coffee while his mom perused the *Staten Island Advocate*, with which she had a love-hate relationship. It was customary for mother and son to linger over breakfast and chat on Saturday mornings. Weekday mornings both members of the Haley family ate hastily and were out of the house before 8:00 a.m.

"I stopped in Kaffman's bar the other night, and he's still talking about you. Back in the old days when you cursed him for serving Dad."

"Selling liquor to alcoholics is blood money. There's a special place in hell for such bloodthirsty buzzards! Furthermore, stay out of those places," she exclaimed.

"I think Martha and I might be breaking up. She doesn't like my spending so much time with Amon, whom she calls the Messiah of Mariners Harbor."

"You're still messing around with that Amon fellow? I thought he was just a passing fad with you," she replied, leafing through the *Advocate*.

"Mom! I said I could be breaking up with my girlfriend, and you're so matter-of-fact about it," Tom replied, annoyed with her indifference.

"Well, nothing lasts forever. Except your father's love for the bottle."

"Gee, thanks, Mom."

"Speaking of the devil, there's something in the paper about Amon. It seems some of his Mariners Harbor neighbors don't appreciate the residence he's fixing up for the homeless. Which I have to admit is a worthwhile undertaking. If we lived in a Marxist society, homelessness wouldn't exist," she replied in a singsong voice.

"How would you like to contribute to the cause? I'll match—no, I'll double—your contribution," Tom offered.

Surprising her son, she reached into her pocketbook and took out a five-dollar bill. "There you go. Now go cut that front hedge."

"I'm amazed, Mom. And I didn't see one moth fly out of your handbag!"

"Very funny, McGee. As far as that Martha woman is concerned, she was not my favorite. Reminded me of a nun, the kind that tied her gown with a rope belt. Maybe you should get back with Joanie, who was likable."

"Mom, Joanie is married and lives in Indiana!"

"Nobody's perfect."

CHAPTER 21

Work in Progress

Considerable progress had been made on the Simonson Avenue house during the past few months. The twelve-room Victorian house's exterior had been repainted a light blue, torn roof shingles had been repainted, and the cracked sidewalk had been patched up. Tom himself had done much of the outside painting, working carefully on a stepladder. He told Amon that his father had been a skilled housepainter, in between periodic drinking binges and stints in the local jail to dry off.

"Why wasn't he placed in a hospital instead? Alcoholism is a disease, not a crime," Amon replied.

"Those were the dark ages. Alcoholism was considered a character defect. He did attend AA meetings with my mom, to little avail," Tom replied.

Tom recalled reading about Bill Wilson, the founder of AA, who was an inveterate alcoholic. He had discovered that the chronic drinker could not break the habit by himself in a moment of remorse. More effective was the group concept of AA, in which alcoholics discussed their drinking habit with fellow sufferers.

"In the end, the individual has to see the light of God to extricate himself from the bonds of alcohol or drugs—whatever has entrapped him," Amon said.

"My dad never saw any light, except for the lights of the neighborhood bars."

At this moment, a statuesque blonde approached the two young men with a smile on her pretty face. "Hello, Tom. What are you doing here?"

"We're fixing up this house for the homeless. It's my friend Amon's project," he replied, jestering toward the young stranger.

"Don't you remember me?" she asked.

Pausing for a moment, Tom said, "I never forget a pretty face. You're Jennifer. I took you to a movie—the Ritz, or was it the Paramount?—some years ago."

"And what was the movie?" the blonde woman inquired.

"It must have been a lousy movie, because I never saw you again."

"It wasn't the movie. I told you that I was seeing a soldier, who had been sent to Vietnam. I'm married now to the same guy. But you were the perfect gentleman," she replied with the same dazzling smile.

"Well, you caught me at a good time. When I was behaving myself," the skinny science teacher said with a sly grin.

She turned to Amon. "Anyway, we have some stuff we're throwing out—lamps, end tables, chairs, sofas, a bed, and some blankets. Would you like them?"

"Thank you, by all means. I'll round up some help, and we'll get it out of your way," Amon said happily.

At this point, Martha pulled up in her shiny new Dodge. Emerging from the car in a huff and giving Jennifer a dirty look, she asked Tom what was going on.

Flushing bright red, Tom mumbled awkward introductions and indicated that the blonde woman was donating some stuff for Amon's house.

"It's very kind of you, Jennifer. We do what we can, and we give what we have," Amon said hurriedly.

"We're all here for the greater good," Tom intoned blandly.

"Don't bullshit me, Tom. I see through your phony idealism," she yelled, giving the blonde woman a dirty look. Martha jumped back into her glossy turquoise sedan and slammed the door.

"Your friend has a hot temper," Jennifer said as his girlfriend gunned the sleek car.

"We all have our moments. Martha's good people," he said, watching the shiny Dodge barrel down Simonson Avenue.

"She does have a nice set of wheels," Jennifer remarked.

"Yeah. She's well equipped," Tom said dryly.

CHAPTER 22

Lovers' Lane

Gooley's was an ancient dimly lit six-lane bowling alley situated on Richmond Terrace, near the junction with Richmond Avenue, roughly 150 feet from the murky Kill Van Kull. It had smoke-filled air, poor lighting, no air-conditioning, and few amenities—except for a bargain-priced bar. The latter feature was a big attraction for Tom and his cohorts when the notion of bowling struck them. There were newer bowling alleys on the South Shore and in mid-Island, but Tom preferred shoddy to fancy, when given the choice. Despite his recently attained professional status as a Curtis High School science teacher, Tom was fundamentally working class.

The skinny science teacher had arranged to meet Martha at Gooley's for their customary Saturday night date of bowling, followed by a bite to eat at the diner on the corner of Morningstar Road and Forest Avenue. A creature of habit, this unpretentious eatery was the place where his old girlfriend Joanie had given him the terrible news of her family's move to Indiana seven years ago. Next to the move of Cara and himself from his foster parents in South Jersey to his real parents on Staten Island, the unexpected breakup with Joanie was the most traumatic event of his life. These traumatic events represented two gaping holes in his heart that he felt could never be repaired.

Bursting into Gooley's, Martha was all smiles until she realized Tom was wearing the paint-spattered clothes that he had worn earlier in the day.

"Go home and change! It's Saturday night, and I won't have you looking like a pig," she harangued loudly so that a few of the bowlers stopped their games to stare at the vociferous young woman.

"Pigs are meticulous animals. I used to take care of them as a kid," Tom replied, trying to make light of the situation.

"I don't give a shit about your farm-boy stories. Either you change into something decent, or I'm going home," she retorted.

At this point, Martha noticed Amon and Mary, who were similarly attired in paint-spattered overalls. Growing even more livid, Martha exclaimed, "I can't deal with this shit anymore. Good-bye." With those remarks, the tall brunette picked up her pocketbook and proceeded to exit the bowling alley.

"Lord, she's one angry young woman," Amon said as Tom smiled sheepishly.

"She's just the girl-next-door type who uses the carrot-and-stick approach. Except lately, I've gotten the stick much more than the carrot," Tom said ruefully, eyeing the undulations in Martha's ample backside as she walked away.

"She'll be all right. Martha wears her heart on her sleeve. You know beneath it all, she loves you, Tom," Mary replied, defending her friend and coworker.

"She sure has a funny way of showing it," Tom said, shaking his head.

The threesome decided to do some bowling anyway. Tom got beers for himself and Mary, and a soda for Amon. The latter had never bowled before, so Tom took some time showing him how to hold and throw the ball. After throwing a couple gutter balls, Amon soon got the knack. By the end of the night, he was bowling in the low two hundreds—besting Tom and Mary, to their amazement. Just as with the game of catch with Joey Caprino on Pulaski Avenue, Amon was a fast learner in the realm of athletics.

"You're a good fisherman, a soothsayer, a faith healer, a great athlete, a superb bowler, an expert carpenter and painter—the list goes on and on!" Tom exclaimed.

"Amon has ESP. He's intuitive, kind, and generous," Mary chimed in.

"It's a God-given gift that we all have. It's just a matter of channeling it to do something good for the world," he replied, looking around the hazy bowling alley. Tom noticed wherever the charismatic young man went, he was the cynosure of the crowd — much like his ex-girlfriend Joanie.

As a young man with physical and emotional needs, Tom feared a breakup with his impetuous girlfriend, whom he had been dating for more than two years. He recalled a particular night in June when they played midnight basketball after a long bout of drinking. Martha grabbed him under the backboard and kissed him passionately. The skinny young teacher suggested they drive to a secluded road in Mariners Harbor. It was a well-known lovers' lane, surrounded by dense foliage and thick fir trees.

Once there, the athletic Catholic school teacher ripped off Tom's shirt and unzipped his pants while Tom clumsily tried to return the favor. Not nearly so adept as his girlfriend, he managed to jam her sweater zipper, which annoyed the impetuous young woman. The skinny science teacher also banged his elbow on the steering wheel. A few moments later, overcome by passion, Martha slammed his head against the dashboard. It seemed their amorous encounters were often wrought with pain for the young man. Fortunately, forbearance was an integral part of the skinny teacher's character. Thus, both young people persevered in their weekend lovemaking, fulfilling mankind's urge to merge.

Panting, sweating, groping, and kissing on that sultry night in June marked the first time that the novice teachers were able to consummate their budding romance within the confines of Tom's old gray Pontiac. It was the start of a fervent love affair. The assignation brought to mind his mom's characterizing the automobile as a hotel on wheels. It could truly be said that Henry Ford's epoch-making invention was the engine of the sexual revolution.

Plagued by lover's remorse the next day, Tom questioned the St. Mary's elementary school teacher about contraception.

"Not to worry," she responded. "I practice the rhythm method of birth control, like any good Catholic."

"I scored at the right time," he said to himself, with a sigh of profound relief. But from that point forward, Tom opted to carry prophylactics whenever he dated the sensual parochial school teacher. There was one place Tom never took Martha in their romantic assignations. This was the old wooden bench in the cemetery on Walker Street opposite PS 21, where he sat with Joanie after a pizza at DeNinno's on Richmond Avenue. He remembered the last night they were together before receiving the dreadful news of her family's impending move to Indiana. They had engaged in intense kissing and petting, and talked lightly about Peter Stuyvesant purchasing the island of Manhattan from the Lenape Indians for the outrageous sum of twenty-four dollars.

At Curtis High School, Tom often sought fatherly advice from Dick Grimsby, who always had a keen eye for his female colleagues, despite being married with with children. Tom told his colleague about the unsatisfactory state of his relationship with his longtime girlfriend. Dick pondered things momentarily and then recommended sending flowers and chocolates to the difficult young woman. To Tom's surprise, the peace offerings worked like magic, and Tom reaped the rewards that his sagacious fellow teacher envisioned.

In another effort to mend fences, the skinny science teacher opted to spend more time with Martha. After all, charity begins at home, he rationalized.

In the full bloom of youth, Tom enjoyed giving, as well as receiving, physical affection. And nothing in the world relieved the bruising stress of teaching unruly adolescents like the palliative of sex. Even his saintly friend, Amon, appeared to enjoy spending time with his soul mate, Mary, sequestered away in his refurbished tugboat on the rolling waters of the Kill Van Kull.

The Fair Housing Act

The Fair Housing Act was passed in 1968 during the administration of Lyndon Johnson, as part of his landmark civil rights legislation. America had a long history of housing discrimination going back to the Civil War. In the South, Jim Crow laws were in effect, prohibiting the right of Afro-Americans to purchase homes and rent apartments in white neighborhoods. In the North, de facto segregation existed, limiting the same rights to housing in middle-class neighborhoods. Since 1917, various federal courts had ruled that such housing discrimination was illegal. Nevertheless, many states and municipalities ignored these court mandates, permitting real estate brokers and landlords to continue their discriminatory practices against racial and ethnic minorities over the years.

The primary purpose of the Fair Housing Act was to protect a buyer or renter of dwellings from discrimination by sellers and landlords. This federal law makes it illegal for sellers and landlords to refuse to sell or rent a housing unit to an individual because of his race, religion, ethnic background, or economic class. The goal of this landmark law was to open up the housing market to all people regardless of their color or ethnic background. The advertisement of sale or rental housing cannot include references to a prospective buyer's or renter's race, class, or ethnic background. In addition, coercing, threatening, intimidating, or interfering with an individual's enjoyment or exercise of his housing rights—based on discrimination—is expressly prohibited.

The Fair Housing Act also created the Department of Housing and Urban Development (HUD), charged with the authority to administer and enforce the Fair Housing Act. HUD's Office of Fair Housing and Equal Opportunity has a staff of 600 people in 54 offices around the country who enforce the Fair Housing Act. It is one of the largest federal civil rights agencies. Anyone who believes that he has been discriminated against with regard to fair housing can file a complaint with HUD's fair housing office. Most states have equivalent fair housing laws, enabling such individuals to refer complaints to the local fair housing office. There is also a network of private nonprofit agencies, which operate with private donations, that help victims of housing discrimination. Rooming houses with three or more tenants would be under the jurisdiction of this law. However, landlords renting rooms or apartments to fewer than three tenants, in their primary residence, are exempt from the Fair Housing Law of 1968.

With regard to the ultimate success of the Fair Housing Law, the results are inconclusive at best. Millions of dollars have been recovered in housing discrimination cases over the years. Yet these discriminatory court cases only scratch the surface of unfair housing practices occurring across the country. Poor implementation of the law results in only 1 percent of all instances of housing discrimination being addressed. From 1970 to 1990, the extent of racial and ethnic minorities living in impoverished areas has increased. The percentage of blacks and Hispanics living in central urban areas has increased, while the percentage of white people living in such low-income areas has decreased significantly. This demographic phenomenon has significance for blacks and Hispanics because of the inferior quality of inner-city schools, hospitals, and services. Thus, the racial geography of housing patterns in America tends to perpetuate the limited access such ethnic groups have to attaining the American dream of a white-picket-fence house in the suburbs.

CHAPTER 23

Visit to the Tugboat

One windy afternoon in March, Tom took two of his colleagues, Tony Tumali and Dick Grimsby, to meet Amon on his refurbished tugboat in Mariners Harbor. The two teachers stepped carefully from the rotted wharf to the tugboat, admiring the improvements undertaken by the clever young stranger.

Both men, more practical than Tom, recommended improvements that Amon said he would implement. Tony noticed a corroded freighter anchored in the Kill Van Kull a few hundred yards from Amon's ship. Amon offered to row him in his rebuilt rowboat, while Tom and Dick poked around the tugboat, noticing the stockpiles of canned goods, brooms and mops, fishing rods, and stacks of the local newspaper — the *Staten island Advocate*.

On makeshift shelves, there was a Bible, a dictionary, assorted encyclopedia volumes, and some soft-cover books, all presumably donated by friends and members of the local North Shore community. In one corner were assorted paintbrushes and rollers, half-full containers of paint, turpentine, and paint rags.

Propped against a wall were a dozen or so fishing rods, along with fishing hooks and tackle. Tom mentioned Amon's uncanny ability as a fisherman, telling Dick about the day when numerous fish were biting simultaneously at the cast rods while Amon struggled to reel them in.

Shortly, Amon and Tony returned, with the latter carrying an old TV set he had found on the derelict freighter. With mock solemnity, Tony donated the television, which was a twelve-inch black-and-white Motorola model, similar to the set Tom's foster family had back in the 1950s. Amon plugged it in, and to everyone's surprise, the set seemed to work. More surprising, there was a show about local neighborhoods of New York, of which the region showcased was none other than Mariners Harbor.

"It's yours to do what you want with. Except no X-rated shows, since you're supposed to be a man of God," Tony said with a tight-lipped smile.

"I don't watch TV, but I'll bring it over to the house on Simonson Avenue we've been working on. Thank you very much," Amon said, ignoring the young biology teacher's barb.

Then turning to Dick, Amon asked about his atrophied leg, which was in a steel brace. "It's polio—contracted after World War II. You learn to live with such things, but it does limit me so much," he replied grimly.

"May I look at it?" he inquired. Dick obliged by lifting up his trousers to reveal a starkly thin leg, totally devoid of muscle. The young stranger rubbed the leg lightly while murmuring a prayer, which Tom did not comprehend.

"Holy shit! I just felt a tingling sensation. That leg has been totally numb for twenty-five years. How did you do that?" Dick exclaimed.

"It's a God-given gift. How I acquired it is beyond me. As soon as you get home, remove the brace, because your leg muscles will begin to expand. You will be walking normally within a week or so as your leg strengthens."

Laughing and whooping with excitement, Dick took out a hundred dollars from his wallet. "Here's a donation for the house on Simonson Avenue."

"Oh, no. I don't accept money. Food donations and a helping hand would be more than welcome, Dick," Amon replied.

"Count me in also. I'll come around Saturday and pitch in," Tony added.

"Super, we can always use extra hands."

"But watch this guy. He's a menace with a hammer and saw," Tony added, pointing to Tom.

"And his classroom experiments endanger the entire school," Dick added.

"Remember that sulfur smoke bomb he set off last year?" Tony chimed in.

"It triggered the fire alarm, so everybody got a fifteen-minute break from teaching. What's wrong with that?" Tom replied.

"Tom's relegated to our painting crew, where he can do the least harm," Amon said, smiling at the skinny young science teacher.

Household Chemicals

Displayed on Tom's desk were bottles of Clorox, ammonia, vinegar, orange juice, seltzer, kitchen cleanser, sugar, salt, photographic film, lawn fertilizer, and limestone. The aim of the lesson was written on the board: "What are some common household chemicals?" In groups of twos and threes, his sophomore science students trudged into the room, enervated by the oppressive June heat. Immediately, Barry walked up to Tom's desk, grabbed the Clorox, and put the bottle to his lips. As Tom quickly reached for the bottle, the black teenager put it down, grinning.

"Ha-ha! You thought I was gonna drink that nasty stuff."

"Some people will try anything for a laugh," Wendy commented.

"Shut up, bitch! I mean refrain from negative talk," Barry replied, restraining himself as he noticed Dick Grimsby passing by in the hall.

Tom paused momentarily as he observed his colleague walking unemcumbered by the steel leg brace. Excited, he waved to Dick and continued with his lesson.

The skinny science teacher showed his students the materials on his desk, eliciting their uses in the home. Holding up the piece of limestone, Tom asked for its use. Someone from the back of the room mentioned plaster and wallboard. Tom said it was also found on the Curtis building. "Those scary gargoyles that decorate our school's facade. They're made out of limestone."

"Like a rhinestone cowboy. Riding on a horse in a star-spangled rodeo," Barry sang nasally, sounding more like Johnny Carson than Glen Campbell.

"Oh God! Heaven help us," Wendy, the buxom teenager, exclaimed.

Tom couldn't help laughing at Barry's off-key singing, breaking one of the cardinal rules of teaching—never laugh at a student's effort to sidetrack a lesson. But such humorous asides were often welcomed by the skinny young teacher himself, as a break in the humdrum routine of teaching science.

Holding up the bottles of Clorox and ammonia, Tom stated, "Let me make one thing perfectly clear. Never mix Clorox and ammonia. It will produce a poisonous gas, greenish in color, which is very dangerous."

"You sound like our dumb president, Tricky Dicky," said Manny, another unruly youngster who often clashed with Barry.

Holding up samples of salt and sugar, which were similar in appearance, Tom asked what kind of substances they were.

"Salt is a compound sodium chloride, and sugar is an organic compound composed of carbon, hydrogen, and oxygen," Riner, a serious student, answered.

"Wow! You're so intelligent, Riner. Someday you'll invent a bomb big enough to destroy the world," Barry intoned.

"Mr. Haley, are you gonna set off any rockets today?" Ronnie asked.

"No. There will be no pyrotechnics today. And now it's notebook time. Folks, get out your science notebooks and copy the following information down."

Household Chemical: Its Use
Ammonia: Cleaner
Clorox: Bleach

Acetic Acid: Vinegar
Citric Acid: Orange Juice
Salicylic Acid: Aspirin
Sulfuric Acid: Battery Acid
Milk of Magnesia: Antacid
Limestone: Plaster
Lye: Drano
Sodium Chloride: Salt
Carbohydrate: Sugar
Silver Bromide: Film
Potassium Nitrate: Fertilizer
Tincture of Iodine: Antiseptic

Tom had good timing, because the bell rang just as he finished the long list of useful household chemicals. He knew how to fill up a forty-minute period with little time left over for teenage tomfoolery. Gathering his materials and erasing the board, Tom headed down the hallway, looking for his rehabilitated colleague, Dick Grimsby.

Catching up with the easygoing biology teacher, Tom queried him about his leg.

"As you can see, the brace is gone and my leg is getting stronger day by day. Pretty soon I'll be able to challenge you in one-on-one basketball. That friend of yours performs miracles like he's a magician making a rabbit disappear in his hat," the congenial middle-aged teacher exclaimed.

At that moment, the two science teachers were joined by Curtis principal Lou Stout, who hadn't even noticed the change in Dick Grimsby. "What's up, Dick? Why are you so happy? You look like you just got laid."

"Give me some time and I'll be pumping away before the day is over … now that I've got my legs back," Dick replied, jumping up and down before the astounded school administrator.

"Did you have surgery on that bad leg of yours over the weekend?" the principal asked, examining Dick closely.

Dick started to relate his experience with Amon, but a signal from Tom caused him to change his story, so he mentioned a new medical procedure performed over the weekend at St. Vincent's Hospital on Castleton Avenue.

CHAPTER 25

Impromptu Fisticuffs

A few weeks later, Tom was helping Amon with the house on Simonson Avenue, along with some of the new residents—a motley crew of former drug addicts, alcoholics, and vagrants of different backgrounds and hues. Renovations had progressed to the point where the house was in mint, live-in condition. Amon's project had been publicized in a lengthy article appearing in the *Staten Island Advocate*, which included pictures of the young stranger, Tom himself, and the residents of the refurbished Victorian house.

Tom was painting a second-floor window frame, when he noticed three sullen men emerge from a black sedan and approach Amon, who had been sweeping the sidewalk. From their hostile looks, it was clear the men were not part of a welcome wagon.

After identifying themselves as part of a "community watch group," the men told Amon that they didn't appreciate his "housing undesirables in Mariners Harbor" because of the threat of crime to a decent neighborhood.

"You and your do-gooder friends are bringing criminals, drug addicts, drunks, and prostitutes into this area. And we're not gonna put up with it," said a burly middle-aged man who looked anything but law-abiding.

Annoyed by the group's aggressive intrusion, Tom climbed down the ladder and talked to the heavyset man in a didactic manner.

"Listen, sir. We have obtained permits from city hall for the building. Everything Is legit," he replied.

"Anyone who comes to our door is welcomed, regardless of circumstances, color, or creed. Everybody pitches in, and no one is questioned about their past," Amon added.

"That's great! Take any lowlife that walks off the street," one of the men said.

"There's a need for housing for the poor. Who could object to such a worthwhile endeavor?" Tom answered, as if he was lecturing one of his students.

"I heard about you. You're a teacher at Curtis High School. I'm a personal friend of Lou Stout. So keep your mouth shut, sonny boy!"

"Are you threatening me?" said Tom, growing angrier by the minute.

"That's right." With that, the heavyset man punched Tom in the jaw, instantly knocking him to the ground."

Then he turned toward Amon, while his cohort attempted to grab Amon from behind. With a sudden powerful movement, the young stranger flipped the wiry thug behind him and blocked an attempted punch by Tom's attacker, twisting the latter's arm so severely that a loud snap of a broken wrist was heard, accompanied by a squeal of pain from the middle-aged bully. The third member of the group raised his hands in surrender, asking Amon if he could call for an ambulance.

"Gladly. The sooner your friends are removed from the premises, the better," Amon said, stooping down to look at Tom's bloody nose.

Looking up at his friend, the skinny teacher said, "It's not the first time I've been decked."

"Whenever there's a disagreement, why does it always come to this?" Amon asked rhetorically. He bent down and started rubbing his assailant's broken wrist. Immediately his attacker stopped moaning and looked up at the stranger with a look of total surprise.

"My arm feels better. How the hell did you do that?" he exclaimed.

"It's mind over matter. You'll be fine. All I ask is that you tell your friends in the neighborhood to leave us alone," Amon replied.

The man nodded and left with his stunned cohorts, with Tom watching in amazement, as if he had just witnessed a supernatural event.

"I'll say one thing, Amon. You definitely know how to handle yourself."

"It's something I picked up along the way. But violence is not the answer."

"When words fail, blows succeed … unfortunately," the skinny science teacher observed.

"Might does not make right. Kindness and virtue make right," Amon said somberly, dabbing Tom's bloody nose with a handkerchief.

"Violence is as American as apple pie. It goes back to our frontier days," Tom replied, examining the bloody handkerchief.

Muhammad Ali

Muhammad Ali was one of the most electric characters of the late 1960s and early 1970s. Unlike most boxers, who are from the underclass, Muhammad Ali had a middle-class background. Actually, his origins were black Southern middle class, which, according to writer Toni Morrison, "is not white middleclass at all." Ali was born in 1942 in Louisville, Kentucky, with the birth name of Cassius Clay. After winning the heavyweight title from Sonny Liston in 1964, he took on the name of Muhammad Ali — becoming a Muslim. As a toddler, Ali was a fast taker and the center of attention at all family gatherings. His father was a sign painter and part-time artist. The Clay family was troubled by his father's drinking, bad temper, and infidelity. Years later, the famous boxer occasionally mentioned his dad's roving eyes for women. Joking, Ali would talk about it: "My daddy is a playboy." Nevertheless, it was apparent that his son had psychological scars, as a result of his father's behavior.

Ali took up boxing when someone stole his bicycle — a new $60 red-and-white Schwinn. He began at the age of twelve in Martin's gym on the south side of Louisville. Well-coordinated, quick on his feet, and fast with his hands, Muhammad Ali soon developed his well-known style of boxing, which entailed lightning jabs, circling the ring continually, and leaning back to avoid his opponent's knockout punches. Ali had not only hand quickness and punching power, but the ability to see everything happening in the ring, as well as the capacity to think clearly when he was in trouble in a bout. Never panicking when caught by a hard punch, Ali had an iron chin and a powerful will to win, enabling him to win all but five of sixty-one professional fights. His boxing career stretched over twenty-one years — from 1960 to 1981. Muhammad Ali often taunted his opponents with insults and comments before and during his bouts, aimed at disrupting their concentration in the ring.

In 1964, challenger Muhammad Ali fought heavyweight champion Sonny Liston, a bruising puncher who was a seven-to-one favorite. Liston had soundly defeated the former champion, Floyd Patterson, in two first-round knockouts. Ali appeared to be very confident before the fight, as he repeatedly teased Liston with barbs like "Ugly bear"—in contrast to his unmarred good looks. The fight was a stunning upset, as Ali evaded Liston's wild punches and repeatedly peppered him with sharp jabs and lightning combinations. Except for one round when the young challenger appeared to be blinded with a chemical in his eyes, Muhammad Ali completely dominated the hulking Sonny Liston. After taking a pounding in the sixth round, the bruised and battered Liston threw in the towel, citing a torn shoulder muscle.

After becoming heavyweight champion at age twenty-two, Muhammad Ali defended his belt eight times in the next four years. He easily defeated an array of challengers, including Sonny Liston, Floyd Patterson, George Chuvalo, Henry Cooper, Brian London, Cleveland Williams, Ernie Terrell, and Zora Foley. In March 1967, Ali refused to be inducted into the armed forces, stating that he had no argument with North Vietnam and stating bluntly that "no Viet Cong ever called me nigger." Consequently, Muhammad Ali lost his boxing license in every state and was stripped of his heavyweight title. Ali did not fight for three and a half years—covering the prime years of his boxing career from the age of twenty-five to nearly twenty-nine.

In 1970, a federal court decision forced the New York State Boxing Commission to grant Ali a license to box. Public opinion had changed toward the former heavyweight champion, as opposition to the Vietnam War increased and Ali's status as a spokesman for Afro-Americans grew. In his comeback, Muhammad Ali fought Jerry Quarry and Oscar Bonavena in tune-up bouts. Then he met the undefeated Joe Frazier in the "Fight of the Century." The match was an action-filled contest, with Ali absorbing many hard shots from the hard-hitting Frazier. The fight was close until the fifteenth round, when Frazier knocked Ali down with a vicious left hook. Ali's iron chin withstood the punch, and he was back on his feet within a few seconds. Nevertheless, Ali lost the fight by a unanimous decision—his first defeat ever. Muhammad Ali and Joe Frazier fought twice more in brutal, hard-fought contests, with Ali winning by close margins.

In 1975, Muhammad Ali fought a new champion, George Foreman, in Zaire, where Ali was favored by the Africans. The local people cheered Ali wherever he traveled, yelling "Ali *bomaye*" (Ali kill him). Sensing that Foreman tended to run out of gas in his matches, Ali employed the "rope-a-dope" strategy, in which he leaned against the ropes, allowing Foreman to pummel him. In the eighth round, Ali turned on Foreman with a flurry of punches that sent the latter to the canvas for the count. It was a monumental upset that rivaled Ali's victory over Sonny Liston eleven years earlier.

Muhammad Ali continued to box well into the 1970s, fighting an assortment of journeyman boxers to earn paychecks. His opponents included Chuck Wepner, Joe Bugner, Jimmy Young, and even a Japanese martial artist—Antonio Inoki. Fighting the powerful Ken Norton in 1973, Ali lost a split decision and suffered a broken jaw. As time progressed, Ali's boxing skills declined, and he absorbed more blows to the head from younger opponents than he had ever experienced in his career. In 1980, Ali was soundly defeated by Larry Holmes, getting struck in the head repeatedly. Medical experts assert that the one-sided Holmes fight probably contributed to Ali's Parkinson's syndrome—common to long-term boxers.

In retirement, Muhammad Ali was a well-known celebrity, adored by millions of fans all over the globe. He portrayed himself as the "people's champion" and as a symbol of oppressed minorities in America and in the developing world. Ali sought a psychological edge over his opponents, using trash talk to disrupt their concentration. The King of Trash Talk employed this tactic against Sonny Liston back in 1964 by describing him as a "big ugly bear who even smells like a bear" and vowing to "donate Liston to the zoo after I beat him." Ali's unique swift-footed, rapid punching style was epitomized by his famous quote: "I float like a butterfly and sting like a bee." But Muhammad Ali's most revealing quote was "I am an ordinary man who worked hard to develop the talent I was given. I believed in myself and I believe in the goodness of others."

CHAPTER 26

A Time to Build

Cara sat on a chair before an easel, painting the old Bethlehem Steel shipyard, with its rotting wooden docks, corroded ships, abandoned hulks, and defunct vessels trailing rusty anchors. Amidst this ship graveyard was Amon's repainted tugboat, standing out among its ramshackle companions. From time to time, Amon and his girlfriend, Mary, came over to commend Cara's work, which depicted the stark, somber beauty of the once-bustling Mariners Harbor waterfront and the gray, choppy water of the Kill Van Kull.

Tom and fellow teacher, Tony Tumali worked on the rotting wharf that led to Amon's tugboat, replacing the rotting boards and some of the supporting two-by-fours. Tom always felt contentment when he could spend his spare time on productive physical labor. It allowed him to rest his frayed nerves after a week of handling his restive science students at Curtis High School. In addition, working to improve the lives of the poor tended to raise his spirits—something that teaching rarely did for him. In some ways, Amon reminded the young teacher of American evangelist Billy Graham.

Reverend Billy Graham—spiritual adviser to Presidents Truman, Eisenhower, Johnson, Nixon, Ford, Carter, and Reagan—had made a big impact on the country during the 1950s and 1960s. He had moved away from anti-Semitic statements and indifference toward the civil rights movement to embrace a more inclusive brand of Christian fundamentalism. Yet his opposition to Communism and homosexuality was explicit and unyielding.

Tom admired Reverend Graham's admitting his mistakes and even altering his narrow-minded views—something that people in the public arena rarely did.

"We have been proud and thought we were better than any other race … but we are going to stumble to hell because of our pride," Billy Graham had warned white Southern segregationists.

Working on the ramshackle Mariners Harbor docks, the young science teacher recalled the philosophical reflections in Ecclesiastes. The world-weary preacher talked about the seasons of one's life—"a time to plant and a time to harvest, a time to build and a time to destroy, a time to weep and a time to laugh, a time to keep and a time to cast away, a time for war and a time for peace, a time for love and a time for hate. Is there anything new under the sun?"

Tom asked Amon if he had ever read Ecclesiastes.

"As a matter of fact, I was looking at that part of the Old Testament the other day. It's remarkable the way the preacher stipulates times for different activities—building, destroying, planting, harvesting, war and peace, love and hate. His basic message is to allocate our time wisely, because both our energy and our time are limited."

"The preacher also said to enjoy the days of your youth while you have them," Tom replied.

"Absolutely. I'm blessed to have a partner in life—Mary. It's time you found your soul mate, Tom."

"I have one—Martha," the skinny teacher asserted, trying to sound convincing.

CHAPTER 27

History Class

Walking into the front entrance of Curtis High School, Tom ran into Lou Stout, the hefty principal, who greeted him with a slap on the back. Suspicious of the shrewd administrator, Tom took a deep breath.

"So who's got the flu bug?"

"No one. Alan Katz has to attend a big union meeting in Brooklyn."

"And he needs people to cover his classes," Tom said in an annoyed tone.

"You're against the union? They just got you a 12 percent raise, spread over three years," Stout replied.

"Not at all. I love unions. Without unions we wouldn't have a middle class in this country. I just don't like covering classes for people."

"It's his sixth-period class. I'll get you out of your building assignment."

"Good. I hate patrolling the front entrance and staring at those horrible limestone gargoyles in front."

"Limestone, you say? I thought those devils were made out of plaster."

"Plaster would never hold up after seventy-five years of wind and rain," Tom replied.

"Anyway. You'll find the material for Alan's lesson in his mailbox. He's in room 325, sixth period."

"Sure. Don't forget to put me on your I-owe-you list," Tom said as he reached into Alan's mailbox.

"That damn list is so long, I'll never get to you," the administrator replied as he headed back to his office.

Walking into Alan Katz's history class later in the day, Tom saw some familiar faces — Barry, Manny, Riner, Wendy, and Ronnie — who were in his sophomore science class. Ignoring the boos, catcalls, and cheers, Tom wrote the aim of the lesson on the board: "What are the consequences of war?" Next he unrolled a chart listing the nine major wars in American history: the American Revolution, the War of 1812, the Mexican War, the Civil War, the Spanish–American War, World War I, World War II, the Korean War, and the current Vietnam War.

War / Duration of War / Battle Deaths
American Revolution / 1775–1781 / 25,000
War of 1812 / 1812–1814 / 15,000
Mexican War / 1846–1848 / 13,280
Civil War / 1861–1865 / 750,000
Spanish–American War / 1898 / 2,450
World War I / 1917–1918 / 116,500
World War II / 1941–1945 / 405,400
Korean War / 1950–1953 / 36,500
Vietnam War / 1956–1973 / 58,282

"What about the Cold War?" Manny called out from the back of the room.

"That is just a stalemate. Had it broke out into a fighting war, we wouldn't be here today," Tom replied.

"Why don't you do one of your practical experiments, like setting off one of those match-head rockets?" Barry complained.

Ignoring the pesky youngster's question, Tom asked, "Why do we have wars?"

"Because of greed. Countries are just like people — they want more land, more power, and more stuff," Wendy, a nubile teenager, answered.

"That's correct. There are land grabs, stolen resources, shortages of food and water, as well as ethnic and religious reasons for war," Tom replied, glancing at Alan's notes.

"War is evil. It breaks one of God's commandments: Thou shall not kill," said Ronnie, a naive black youngster.

"Stop talking church stuff, girl. You're so holier-than-thou!" Barry reprimanded his classmate.

"That brings us to an interesting question. Suppose two countries go to war. And the people of both countries pray to God for victory. Whose side should God take?" Tom inquired.

"Not the country that started it. But the country that was defending itself," Riner responded.

"Are there any just wars?" Tom asked.

"Yeah. The Civil War, which was fought over slavery," Manny said.

"How about World War II? We wanted to stop Hitler and his Nazi storm troopers. He was putting the Jews into concentration camps," Riner said.

"Was the American Revolution a just war?"

"Nah. George Washington and his friend were slaveholders. I would have preferred living under the British king, myself," Barry said half-seriously.

"Doesn't it say somewhere that if you live by the sword, you will die by the sword?" said Lora, a new student at Curtis, who reminded Tom of Mimi from his first year of teaching.

"Wait a minute. If someone jumps me in the street, I have to fight back. Otherwise I won't be able to ever walk the streets again," Manny yelled from the back of the room.

"Has there ever been a nuclear war?" Tom asked the class.

"Americans dropped atomic bombs on Hiroshima and Nagasaki during World War II," Riner replied.

"Man! That's cold. I thought we were supposed to be the good guys," Barry shouted.

Referring to his notes, Tom read: "During the Second World War, Franklin Roosevelt stated the four freedoms: freedom of speech, freedom of religion, freedom from want, and freedom from fear."

"That just about says it all," Wendy commented.

"What about the Vietnam War? America was not attacked by North Vietnam. So why are we fighting there with so many people dying on both sides?" Tom asked, speaking more for himself than for the sake of the lesson.

"That's a good question, Mr. Haley. I ain't got no arguments with them Viet Congs. They're not messing around in my neighborhood. So leave them the hell alone!" Barry intoned angrily.

"Live and let live. That's my motto," Lora chimed in with a cute smile. Barry got out of his seat, ran over to her, and bowed before her in mock submission.

Everyone cheered and applauded her message of harmony and peace, ending Tom's hastily fabricated lesson on war.

As the young science teacher walked down the hall, Riner caught up with him.

"Mr. Haley, you forgot to mention the Philippine–American War in your list of American wars."

Glancing at Alan Katz's notes, Tom responded, "You're right. The Philippine–American War. Somehow I omitted it."

"I'll bring it up tomorrow so we can add it to our notes," the earnest young man declared.

"Very good. The next time I cover his American history class, I'll have you copy the notes on the board."

At that moment, Tom bumped into Dick Grimsby, walking briskly down the hall with no sign of a limp. "Hey, Tom. I got somebody I want to bring to your friend Amon. She has a bad case of psoriasis."

"Dick, you promised not to talk about that stuff. Soon, the whole island will be knocking on his door."

"It's Miss Atkins from the English department. You've seen her skin. It's a hopeless case."

"All right. I'll ask Amon to look at her. But that's it. This guy is catching flak from his neighbors. Things are getting out of hand," Tom asserted.

The skinny young science teacher wondered if there were limits to Amon's amazing powers. *At some point, the well must run dry — even for an avatar. The admiration Americans have for celebrities is short-lived. After a meteoric rise, a meteoric fall is almost inevitable in our culture. The tide of public opinion will turn against him,* Tom thought with a shudder.

Basketball Game

Tom pulled up at Amon's rebuilt wharf one Saturday morning in early April. Amon was tinkering with some electric wires that ran from a utility pole on Richmond Terrace to his tugboat.

Walking from the docks to his tugboat, Tom yelled up to his friend, "Come with me. You need a break. We'll play some basketball."

Amon, wiping the sweat from his face, readily agreed. "I haven't played hoops in years. You'll have to show me how native New Yorkers play the game."

"Yeah, sure. You picked up baseball pretty quickly, as I recall," Tom responded.

He remembered the impromptu game of catch on Pulaski Avenue with Joey Caprino in February. One of Amon's hard throws whistled through Mrs. Egger's window, which the able young man quickly repaired.

The two young men arrived at the PS 21 school yard in Tom's 1964 gray Pontiac. They headed for the nine-foot baskets where Tom had spent countless hours as an adolescent, perfecting his sweeping hook shot, line-drive jump shot, and awkward banked layups. As they warmed up, it was clear that Amon was more than rusty. It appeared that he had never played the game and knew little about its rules and techniques.

As with science, Tom was a patient teacher of basketball. He showed Amon how to dribble and how to shoot a two-handed set shot and a one-handed jump shot—allegedly invented by Bud Palmer. As in the case of tossing and catching a baseball, the young stranger was a quick study at mastering the techniques of schoolyard hoops like a native New Yorker. Initially, Tom didn't guard Amon too closely, allowing him to shoot and dribble without interference. At first, the young man was off target as his shots slammed off the metal backboard and clanged off the iron hoop. Tom was rusty, as well, as his line-drive jump shots and his sweeping hook shots were errant.

Then, a transition began to occur. Amon began hitting his shots. His main offensive weapons were a high-arching two-handed set shot and a soft looping jump shot. Tom was surprised by the high trajectory of Amon's shots. Usually a good defender, Tom could do little to hinder Amon's shooting. In terms of physical stature, he was about the same as Tom's six-feet two-inch height but appeared to be twenty pounds heavier. Amon's jumping ability was exceptional, along with his uncanny ability to accelerate after an initial step or two.

At a certain point, Amon began to play defense, swatting away Tom's layups and forcing him to take his jump shots from beyond the foul line. He even tipped a few of Tom's sweeping hook shots, which surprised the latter. Little by little, Amon closed the gap between himself and the skinny teacher. Time seemed to slow down as both young men huffed and puffed from the exertion of the hotly contested game. Amon was repeatedly leaping so high that his wrists reached above the nine-foot rim. With the game tied at twenty apiece, Amon throw up a high set shot that seemed to hover over the basket for a second, before falling cleanly through the hoop.

"Wow! For a beginning hoopster, you're not bad at all," Tom exclaimed.

"You're not too shabby yourself. I'm totally winded, but it was exhilarating."

"That it truly was. Man, you could have played high school basketball and been a star!" Tom said, gasping for breath.

"It's just focus. Once you're in the groove, your body does what you want it to," Amon replied, catching his breath faster than Tom.

The two young men decided to sit on the bench of the old cemetery that faced the school yard across Walker Street. Tom had brought along two cans of soda, which they sipped slowly, cooling off in the gentle April breeze.

Looking around and running his finger on the old wooden bench, Amon said, "I can just picture you years ago, sitting with Joanie and talking about waxing and waning moons, and Peter Stuyvesant purchasing the island of Manhattan from the Indians for twenty-four dollars."

"Holy shit! I'm beyond amazed. I'm absolutely astounded. How the hell did you know that?" Tom replied, incredulous at Amon's remarks.

"It's something I can perceive — a feeling, an aura, a scene — which gradually comes into focus."

"I wish I could see stuff like that. What a gift that must be!" Tom declared.

"It's not so great to see such things. It can be a burden," Amon said gloomily.

CHAPTER 29

The Elements

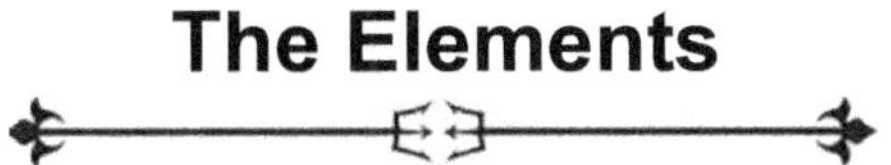

Displayed on Tom's desk were samples of various elements: copper, iron, aluminum, sodium, magnesium, potassium, Clorox, tincture of iodine, a lead pipe, an old nickel, a lead pencil, charcoal, a horseshoe magnet, and Tums. As customary, Barry and Manny hung around the front desk, picking up the magnet and testing which metals were magnetic. The aim of the lesson was written on the blackboard: "What are the elements?" Barry opened the Clorox and sniffed it, making a face. Tom sent both youngsters to their seats and began the lesson.

Picking up the horseshoe magnet, Tom asked, "What elements are magnetic?"

Someone from the back of the room called out, "Iron, steel, and lead."

Riner disagreed, stating that the three magnetic elements were iron, nickel, and cobalt.

"That's absolutely right," replied the young science teacher as he picked up the iron nail and the old nickel with the magnet, while the lead pipe, copper, and aluminum were not attracted to the magnet.

"Wait a minute," Barry called out. "Try this nickel here."

Tom went over to the spunky teenager and held the nickel to the magnet. It definitely was not magnetic.

"Can anyone explain why this nickel is not magnetic?"

Wendy raised her hand. "Because nickels today are not pure nickel. They are made mostly of copper and tin."

"Then it should be called a tinkle, not a nickel!" Barry snapped.

"By the way, lead is not an innocuous element. When it is found in water or paint, it can be very harmful to children if ingested," Tom stated.

"I'll remember that the next time I want to nibble on some paint chips," Manny called out from the back of the room.

"Isn't that why they're forcing the oil companies to take lead out of gasoline?" Wendy inquired, to which Tom assented.

"Why do compasses point north?" Ronnie asked.

"That's because compasses are tiny magnets, and they point to the earth's magnetic north pole. Actually, the earth's magnetic and geographic north poles do not coincide. So there's a slight deviation between magnetic north and true north," Tom lectured.

"So when somebody has a magnetic personality, it's because they always point north?" Barry asked.

Ignoring the obstreperous teenager, Tom moved on. He showed the class a number-two pencil and asked what it contained.

Someone from the back of the class yelled out that it was made out of lead.

"No, that's a misnomer. Lead pencils contain carbon or graphite. Another form of carbon is charcoal," he commented, showing the class the piece of charcoal.

"I've heard that diamond is mostly carbon that has been transformed through heat and pressure over millions of years," Wendy asserted.

"That's right, missy. Remember, diamonds are a girl's best friend," Barry said in a singsong voice.

"I prefer copper myself," said Lora, a new student who jingled her copper bracelets and anklets.

Lighting a match, Tom asked what was the key element in matches. No one knew the answer, so Tom indicated it was sulfur.

"Are you gonna set off one of your match-head rockets today?" Manny asked.

"Not today. But I will show you two unusual metals — sodium and potassium," he responded, holding up samples of these metals, which were stored in special containers.

"Unlike most metals, which are hard, glossy, strong, and ductile, sodium and potassium have the consistency of clay." Tom cut small, pea-sized pieces of each metal. Then he threw them into a beaker of water. There was a loud pop, and each metal burst into flame.

"Do it again, Mr. Haley. But use bigger pieces this time," Manny urged.

Throwing caution to the wind, Tom cut larger pieces of the two metals. First, he threw the sodium into the beaker of water. It made a louder pop, bursting into a bigger flame. Then, he threw the potassium, which was more active than sodium, into the water. It exploded like a gun going off with a bigger flame. The burning piece of potassium landed on the skinny science teacher's jacket, burning a hole in his suit jacket.

The students cheered and applauded loudly, just as Mr. Stout, Curtis's principal, walked by the class. He stuck his head into the room. "Another one of your practical experiments backfired?"

"Yeah. He's a menace to the school, but mostly himself," Barry called out.

"Here. I'll reimburse you for the cost of the jacket," said the chunky administrator, handing the young teacher a five-dollar bill.

The class applauded, showing its appreciation for the principal's unusual generosity. Tom said he'd donate the money to Curtis High School's scholarship fund, which he did at the end of the day. As the bell rung, Lora, who had just enrolled in Tom's general science class, smiled at the young teacher.

"I hope you don't have any more accidents, Mr. Haley. You're a cool teacher, but you're a klutz!"

"Well, I'll take that as a compliment," he replied, examining his damaged suit jacket and gathering his materials.

CHAPTER 30

A Vulgar Experiment

The next day, Tom continued his lesson on the elements. On his desk were a small beaker of concentrated sulfuric acid and a large beaker containing some table sugar. The previous day's aim was written on the blackboard: "What are elements?" Since they had not gotten to that pivotal question, Tom asked it again.

The new student, Lora, raised her hand. "An element is a pure substance that cannot be broken down chemically."

"Excellent, Lora. All matter is composed of elements, which are the building blocks of nature. What are compounds?"

Riner raised his hand. "A substance composed of two or more elements, chemically combined."

"Very good, Riner. Who can give me some examples of compounds?"

"Water, which is H_2O, and salt, which is sodium chloride," said Riner.

"Isn't sugar a compound also?" asked Wendy.

"Absolutely, sugar is an organic compound, composed of carbon, hydrogen, and oxygen. You guys are on your game today!"

"That's because you're a great teacher," Barry said with a smirk.

"I wouldn't go that far. Moving on, there was a guy named Berzelius, who devised a system of symbols for the elements, using the first letter or first two letters of its name. For example, the chemical symbol of oxygen is O, and the symbol for hydrogen is H, while the symbol for carbon is C."

"And the chemical symbol for lead is L," Barry interjected.

"No, the symbol for lead is Pb, from its Latin name, *plumbum*."

"Now that's messed up. Latin is a dead language," Barry replied.

"Excuse me. I took four years of Latin in high school," Tom declared.

"What? Were you studying to be a priest?" Manny asked from the back of the classroom.

"I don't think so," Barry cracked.

Ignoring the two impertinent teenagers, Tom pressed on. "Before we get to the elements, I'm going to show you an example of a chemical reaction."

Holding up the small beaker of concentrated sulfuric acid, which he identified, Tom poured it into the wide beaker of table sugar. A large amount of heat was released, along with clouds of vapor. A column of black carbon rose from the sugar as it combined with the acid.

"My, my, Mr. Haley. That thing looks obscene. If you catch my drift," Barry proclaimed, to the amusement of his classmates.

The class roared in laughter as the black column continued to grow in size. Tom, himself, had trouble keeping a straight face.

"What's the fancy word for that, Mr. Haley? I know — phallic symbol!" said Lora loudly.

"You mean prick? Or dick? Or cock? Or wang? The scientific term for that part of the male anatomy is penis," Barry chimed in.

Tom shook his head. He had done that particular experiment before, with hardly a peep from his students. But this motley group of youngsters was an entirely different species. And Lora was beginning to remind him more and more of Mini, whom he had once pulled off a classmate that she was pummeling. He had received a bloody nose from one of her wild punches in the process.

"Okay, folks. It's science notebook time." The class booed as he moved to the blackboard, summarizing the material covered in the last two lessons.

Element: pure substance that cannot
be broken down chemically.
Compound: two or more elements chemically
combined in definite proportions.

Symbols of Key Elements

Carbon: C
Hydrogen: H
Oxygen: O
Nitrogen: N
Sulfur: S
Phosphorus: P
Fluorine: F
Iodine: I
Uranium: U
Helium: He
Aluminum: Al
Chlorine: Cl
Calcium: Ca
Magnesium: Mg
Zinc: Zn
Nickel: Ni
Lithium: Li
Radium: Ra
Iron: Fe
Lead: Pb
Gold: Au
Silver: Ag

Copper: Cu
Sodium: Na
Potassium: K
Tungsten: W

Just as his students were finishing their notes, Lora raised her hand, and Tom braced himself for an off-color remark.

"I have an old penny here. How come it's turning green?"

"Copper turns a greenish compound, called verdigris, when it corrodes. The roof of Curtis and the Statue of Liberty are made of copper. Years of exposure to the atmosphere—especially moisture—turns copper into that sickly greenish color," Tom explained patiently.

"Copper bracelets are supposed to cure arthritis," Ronnie asserted.

"Better than that. Copper can make a person more amorous. That's why I have copper bracelets on my arms and legs," Lora said, proudly displaying the metal trinkets on her appendices.

"Send her to the dean. That girl's definitely out of line," Barry screeched in mock terror.

Before Tom could react, he was saved by the bell. The class dispersed out of the room with Lora following them, her copper bracelets jingling in the hallway.

Kareem Abdul-Jabbar

Kareem Abdul-Jabbar was an all-star center for the Milwaukee Bucks and the Los Angeles Lakers from 1969 to 1989. During his twenty-one–year professional career, Jabbar scored a total of 38,387 points—an NBA record. This total exceeded Wilt Chamberlain's career record of 31,419 points. Chamberlain, also an all-star center, holds the single-game record of 100 points—occurring in 1962 against the New York Knicks. The first time Kareem played against him, Wilt knocked the slender seven-footer out of bounds. On the next play, Jabbar faked Chamberlain, came across the middle, and dunked on the legendary center. In addition to total points, Kareem holds the NBA record for total minutes played—an astounding 57,446 minutes. Standing seven feet two inches, Jabbar was best known for his patented "sky hook," which he had developed in college, playing for the UCLA Bruins. While playing at UCLA, Jabbar was scratched in the cornea, requiring that he play with goggles to protect his damaged left eye from that point onward.

Upon graduating from UCLA, Kareem Jabbar was offered a million-dollar contract to play with the Harlem Globetrotters. Instead, he played for the Bucks for five seasons, and then in 1975, Jabbar was traded to the Los Angeles Lakers, where he played for the next sixteen years. With his unstoppable sky hook, good passing, strong rebounding, and tough defense, Kareem led the Lakers to five NBA championships. Kareem's stamina and longevity could be attributed to his physical fitness regimen, which included yoga and kung fu to enhance his flexibility and strength. Always a team player, Jabbar said that he tried to do the right thing at the right moment in the game to achieve victory. "You can't win if you don't play as a unit."

While in college, Jabbar converted to Islam, changing his name from Lewis Alcindor to Kareem Jabbar. He had studied the Koran under a Turkish imam of the Hanafi School, refuting any connections with the Nation of Islam. Kareem asserted that he saw

Islam "as the correct way to live and I have chosen to try to live that way." The former NBA all-star absolutely refutes the violent extremist version of Islam, which would perpetrate horrific violence upon nonbelievers in the ensuing years. Since retiring from the NBA, Kareem Jabbar has coached the Los Angeles Clippers and written articles, newspaper columns, and books.

Kareem Jabbar sees himself as an advocate for all black people. "When I was a kid, no one would believe anything positive about black people. That's a terrible burden." Consequently, Jabbar has spoken out on black–white relations in America. People tend to discredit his statements about race and religion, labeling him as just a high-paid athlete. Jabbar defies that stereotype: "I can do something else besides stuff a ball through a hoop. My biggest resource is my mind." In addition, Kareem Jabbar has a recommendation for youth of all colors and stripes: "Start spending as much time in the library as you do on the basketball court."

CHAPTER 31

Legal Advice

One weekday night, Tom was mulling over his general science notes, trying to plan his lessons for the next few days. In his first few years of teaching, he spent countless hours preparing lesson plans for his recalcitrant students. From his own standpoint, Tom couldn't quite grasp the notion that most adolescents had little curiosity about the natural world. This apparent lack of intrinsic interest in science forced him to devote time and energy planning the initial practical experiment, designed to grab the attention of his reluctant scholars. Of course, once you got their attention, how did you keep it? *Aye, there's the rub!* A forty-minute lesson often seemed to go on forever, especially the last five minutes when the typical teenager's reservoir of patience was depleted.

Suddenly the young science teacher's ponderings were interrupted by the harsh ringing of his old-fashioned, rotary dial phone. It was Mary, Amon's girlfriend, who sounded nervous and scared.

"Amon's been arrested on trumped-up charges," she exclaimed in a shaky voice.

Through Mary's halting words, the story emerged. Following a neighbor's complaint, police arrived at the Victorian house on Simonson Avenue, where they found marijuana. Amon, plus some residents of the house, had been taken into custody. Immediately, Tom left the house with his checkbook, ignoring his mom's strident words to stay out of the situation.

"That man is a fool! Taking people off the street and putting them in his house. Your father was the same way. Always helping his alcoholic friends with nothing to spare for his family," she yelled from the front door as Tom hopped into his old gray Pontiac.

A few days later, Tom and Amon parked on Morningstar Road, adjacent to Mislicki's bakery, which along with Karisi's grocery story had been a neighborhood mainstay since Tom and Cara first came to Elm Park a dozen years ago.

Stan Mislicki worked in the family business through high school, college, and law school. When he hung his attorney's license in a second-floor office above the bakery, Doris Schmidt's husband, Eddie Pelchanski, worked in his place, as his flour-covered face and clothes clearly indicated.

Before walking into the tiny law office, Amon looked at the square on the opposite side of the street, which also served as the entrance to the Bayonne Bridge and the Staten Island Expressway.

"You and Cara had an emotional encounter with your foster parents that first summer you moved to Staten Island. They had rye bread steak sandwiches for you, which you couldn't even eat," he related in a matter-of-fact manner.

"You're absolutely right. Too bad you can't market that gift of yours. You'd be a millionaire—living on Todt Hill with all of Staten Island's rich folks."

"But if I sold out, what would happen to the people on Simonson Avenue who depend on me?" Amon inquired.

Stan Mislicki welcomed the two young men into his small book-filled office, which had a picture of John Kennedy displayed behind the congenial young attorney. "I remember when you, Joey Caprino, and Mike Palermo played stickball on Pulaski Avenue, along with Harry the Horse."

"I saw Harry recently. He doesn't have as much time for street games as he used to," Tom replied.

"Back in the day I used to follow the exploits of the Elm Park boys in the little league. Joey and Mike played for Tony's Tigers at that time, but didn't you play for a different team — the Salvation Army Red Shields?" Stan asked.

"Yeah. The Red Shields took players who couldn't make the better teams," Tom mentioned sheepishly.

"But unlike the other kids, you became a teacher, doing something worthwhile with your life," Stan observed.

"It has its ups and downs. But the reason I'm here is because of my friend Amon."

Tom introduced Amon to the attorney, and the former related the reason for the their visit to his office. The perspicacious lawyer grasped the situation quickly and offered his services pro bono. An avid reader of the *Staten Island Advocate*, Stan knew about Amon's good deeds in Mariners Harbor and realized his financial resources were limited. Writing on a yellow legal pad, Stan asked Amon his surname, which Tom didn't even know.

"It's Takoda — Amon Takoda. I'm American Indian on my mom's side."

"What does it mean?" Tom asked, recalling that the names of Native Americans had specific connotations.

"Literally, *takoda* means 'friendly to everyone,'" the young man replied.

"I'll get you off those charges readily. But from this point onward, you have to scrutinize any new tenants to your Simonson Avenue house. Secondly, you have to inspect all the rooms of your boardinghouse on a regular basis," he said.

"I've been remiss. But I assure you, sir, I'll be more careful in that regard from this point onward," Amon asserted.

"No offense intended. Have you ever been arrested before?" the young attorney inquired, looking at Amon intently.

"As a matter of fact, I was arrested in the Midwest for stealing a loaf of bread from a grocery store. Hunger can drive you to desperate actions."

"What was the outcome?"

"I was given a suspended sentence for petit larceny. The police labeled me as a vagrant and told me to leave town pronto."

"So basically, you have a clean record. And you've had great publicity from the local papers for your good work with the poor. It should to be an open-and-shut case, depending on the judge we get." Turning to the young science teacher, he continued, "Tom, make sure you show up with us in court. Most judges tolerate attorneys, but they genuinely like teachers."

"Yeah. Teachers, nuns, social workers, and moms are favorites nowadays."

"Do you know any movie stars, Amon? That could help," Stan said half-seriously.

"Only those celebrities who are down on their luck. There was a man who said he acted in movies back in the 1940s. His name was Adolphe Menjou," Amon mentioned.

"I remember that guy. I recognized his face right away. He talked about Joseph McCarthy, who was a hero to him," Tom observed.

"He didn't stay very long. He left abruptly one day when his agent told him he had a part on a TV show," Amon said.

"Too bad you don't know Richard Chamberlain."

"Who, Dr. Kildare? How about a real doctor, like Dr. Atlas?" Tom suggested.

"Dr. Atlas is a great doctor. He helps everyone who walks in his office, whether or not the person has the money to pay him," Amon declared.

"Not everybody is driven by pecuniary concerns," Stan asserted.

CHAPTER 32

Civil War Lesson

Walking down the dark first-floor hall of Curtis High School, Tom thought about his friend Amon. Newspaper articles about the man were no longer glowing, due to reports of drug use by residents of his Simonson Avenue rooming house. A nonsmoker, non–drug user, and teetotaler, the benevolent young man reminded Tom of Phillies pitching great Robin Roberts, who had refrained from such bad habits during a nineteen-year career. The Philadelphia workhorse had won twenty games six years in a row for a weak-hitting second-division ball club.

However, Roberts' status as a perennial pitching ace was diminished by his reduced effectiveness in the latter part of his career. There was something contrary about American culture that builds up a person like Roberts or Amon as a folk hero, and then tears him down as a charlatan. The skinny teacher's ruminations were interrupted by a tap on the shoulder. It was his favorite administrator wearing a sheepish smile and holding some handwritten lecture notes.

"Just tell me where and when, and I'll be on my merry way."

"You're Curtis's super-sub and clutch hitter," Lou Stout asserted with a straight face.

"I know. If the game was on the line, you'd pick me," Tom replied sourly.

"Well, I wouldn't go that far. Especially if your old friend Mike Palermo was pitching."

"I once hit a triple against him. I swung late and hit a line drive over first base," Tom related.

"Mike probably knocked you down on the next at bat," the principal replied.

"No. He struck me out on three pitches," Tom said grimly.

The boos and catcalls began the moment Tom crossed the threshold of the room. He wrote the aim on the board: "The Civil War: Its causes and effects."

"What? No practical experiment today? How boring!" Barry exclaimed.

"Maybe you could set off a cannon to get things rolling," Manny yelled from the back of the room.

"Sorry, folks. No pyrotechnics or histrionics today. Just the plain facts of America's bloodiest war," Tom said.

He realized that teachers of history, English, and mathematics could not avail themselves of the initial experiment, which grabbed the students' attention. Yet most youngsters needed something concrete to move from the material world of everyday objects to Plato's world of ideas, where scientific theories existed. In that regard, Tom considered science teachers lucky to have this pedagogical weapon at their disposal.

"But I do have a picture of these two guys, who played pivotal roles in the Civil War. Does anyone know who they were?" he asked, showing the class pictures of Robert E. Lee and Ulysses S. Grant.

Riner raised his hand. "The first one is General Lee, who commanded the South. And the second man is General Grant, who led the North."

"Very good, Riner. And who were the political leaders of the two opposing sides?" Tom asked.

"Abraham Lincoln was president of the North, and Jefferson Davis was the president of the South," Wendy answered.

"Excellent, Wendy. Abraham Lincoln was our sixteenth president and arguably our greatest president. Where was the capital of the Confederacy?"

No one answered. Looking over Alan Katz's notes, Tom said it was Richmond, Virginia. He told the class about Lincoln's visit to the abandoned Confederate capital near the end of the war, during which Lincoln walked around the city and sat in Benjamin Davis's chair. At one point Lincoln was confronted by some freed slaves who bowed down before him. The sixteenth president told them never to bow to any person in the future, but to go forth and live their lives as free men in America.

"But the freed slaves weren't treated so well in the South or in the North," Barry said bluntly.

"You're absolutely right. The oppression of black people led to the civil rights movement, spurred by Dr. Martin Luther King and others," Tom replied.

"Whatever happened to the Confederate leaders — guys like Jefferson Davis and Robert E. Lee?" Ronnie inquired.

"They were sent to prison as traitors. But during Reconstruction, most of them were released after a few years," Tom said after perusing Alan's notes.

"They should have been hung. Thousands of people died in the Civil War," Manny called out from the back of the room.

"Well, the federal government did seize Robert E. Lee's plantation in Northern Virginia and used it for a burial ground for Union soldiers," Tom stated.

Lora, the feisty new student, raised her hand. "I know what you're talking about. It's called Arlington Cemetery. I saw it last summer with my family."

"Very good, Lora. There was another famous Union general besides Grant. His name was William Sherman. He waged all-out war through Georgia, cutting a 100-mile swath of destruction through that state—still recalled to this very day as Sherman's March to the Sea."

"War is hell," Barry proclaimed.

"You can say that again," Tom concurred.

"War is hell," Barry repeated as the class laughed, and Tom shook his head.

"Anyway, the Civil War resulted in a total of six hundred thousand deaths—more casualties than all other American wars combined. In the Battle of Gettysburg, which took place over three days, there were forty-six thousand casualties, including 7,860 battle deaths. The Northern army repulsed Pickett's Charge with the heaviest cannon barrage in the Civil War, causing Robert E. Lee to retreat for the first time in the war. After that battle, the Southern armies never ventured into the North again. It was their high-water mark. The rest of the war was fought in the South, as the North's bigger numbers and greater resources began to prevail."

"That must have been a hell-raising street fight," Manny commented.

"It was said that the roar of cannons was heard fifty miles away in the city of Philadelphia, during the Battle of Gettysburg," Tom declared.

Riner raised his hand. "Was that the point in time when Lincoln gave his Gettysburg Address?"

Tom nodded as he looked over Alan Katz's notes. "Lincoln said how the nation was conceived in liberty and dedicated to the proposition that all men are created equal. He resolved that the soldiers who died at Gettysburg should not have died in vain. Lincoln called for a new birth of freedom and that—"

"Government of the people, by the people, and for the people shall not perish from the earth!" Barry intoned.

"Wow. You ought to run for president someday," Lora exclaimed — a notion for which the entire class seemed to concur.

On that rare note of unanimous acclaim, the bell sounded, ending Tom's lesson on the Civil War. Tom wondered if he should have been a history teacher. But his practical classroom experiments would have never become part of Curtis High School's folklore — just as Harry the Horse's street stickball games and Thomas Haley's notorious drinking binges would not have become part of Elm Park's colorful folklore. And Amon's exploits and his waterfront tugboat would not have become part of Mariners Harbor's picturesque history. Remembering his early days with Cara on their foster parents' farm in South Jersey, Tom believed that there was a residue of those experiences in that remote country town.

Perhaps the emotional aura remaining in an area was what Amon detected with his keen superhuman sensibility. Would that his rare gift was more widespread in the population, along with Amon's genuine concern for his fellow human beings. But there was a groundswell of bad feelings surging in the country — what President Nixon referred to as the "silent majority," in which the man in the street rejected programs for the poor as wasteful and misguided.

CHAPTER 33

Complaints and Regrets

Things had become somewhat shaky between Tom and Martha lately. The latter was definitely not a fan of the Mariners Harbor phenom. She was suspicious of Amon's motives and efforts on behalf of the poor. And she doubted his alleged psychic abilities — labeling him a quack.

"I can't believe an educated person like you, a science teacher, could be so damn gullible," she commented.

"Martha, I've seen him in action many times. His hands are capable of healing, and he knows things about events that occurred in the past that elude rational explanation."

"He's a charlatan who uses cues to get information about people. Nobody can read a person's mind, know the past, or predict the future from tea leaves or whatever object they conjure up," she retorted.

"You were there at that diner in Mariners Harbor when he brought back that elderly man from the dead. How do you explain that situation?"

"He had a heart attack that wasn't fatal. It happens all the time. Hopefully, he's been to a real doctor since that incident. Rubbing a person's chest and saying some mumbo jumbo is not established medical procedure."

"That's what you need. Someone to rub your chest and mumble sweet nothings in your ear," Tom replied with a smile.

"You can rub me anywhere … after we go shopping for a ring."

"Martha, Martha. You shouldn't dwell on such bourgeois concerns. Look at the big picture," he chided.

"With you in it, it's a bleak picture—with a future I cannot contemplate."

"It sounds like you need a drink. Let's stop into Kaffman's for a couple of beers."

"Yeah, a few beers. That's your answer to everything. Just like your poor old dad, drinking his whole life away."

"Hey! Bringing up my father is hitting below the belt."

"If the shoe fits, wear it," Martha replied irritably.

It was another Saturday morning as Tom mused about the ups and downs of his relationship with Martha and the pitfalls of his teaching job. He recalled a line he had read somewhere that we measure our lives with spoons dipped in coffee cups. As usual, his breakfast mate was his mom, who was poring over the *Staten Island Advocate* and sipping her coffee with her usual slurping sound.

"It says here that there was a fire in that Mariners Harbor house run by your friend Amon. It purportedly started in the basement, where there were some old newspapers and debris of various types. Fire officials suspect arson. But your friend was praised for going into the burning building repeatedly to rescue some residents living in his Victorian twelve-room house."

"I'm willing to bet someone from the neighborhood started it. There was some flak from the local yokels. Angry words escalated into fisticuffs, but Amon handled himself very well, as I recall," Tom related.

"He ought to give you lessons. Maybe you wouldn't have gotten so many bloody noses as a kid," she said sourly.

"That was my secret weapon. I'd repeatedly smash my nose and my jaw against their fists until my opponent quit because his knuckles were sore."

"Right. You're a hard-nosed competitor. They should have called you Rocky."

"Not everyone goes around picking fights with the entire neighborhood. Every store owner and bartender in Elm Park was subject to your virulent outbursts," Tom replied, remembering his mother's arguments with the local merchants.

"You're damned right I fought with those SOBs! Selling booze to a hopeless drunk like your father. That's what I call blood money—the vital juice of corrupt capitalism. Selling liquor to alcoholics should be against the law."

"Mom, they tried prohibition in this country years ago. It didn't work."

"Lucky for you. If it wasn't for those damn gin mills, what would you do with your weekends?"

"I'd make my own bootleg whiskey, like they did during the 1920s," Tom asserted.

"It must run in your blood. Your dad said he had made moonshine liquor with his brothers back in the day."

"Now I know where I got the idea for my famous practical home experiments," Tom declared.

"Yeah, I heard about those experiments. Someday you're gonna blow yourself up!"

"Teachers are performers. There's no business like show business," he replied, leaving the kitchen to look at the formidable front hedge, which needed a trimming.

CHAPTER 34

Celibacy versus Debauchery

Pulling up in his old gray Pontiac at the corner of Richmond Terrace and Simonson Avenue, Tom saw a flurry of activity by the residents of the big Victorian house. Amon was replacing the basement windows shattered during the recent fire. Fortunately, the damage was limited to the basement and part of the first floor directly above the fire. The young man blamed himself for not removing stacks of old newspapers and piles of discarded clothes from the dungeon-like cellar.

When Tom questioned him about the origin of the fire, Amon was noncommittal. "Stuff happens. God only knows who started the fire. Some of my folks are careless with their cigarettes."

"Yeah, but we all know there are people in the neighborhood who are troublemakers. I wouldn't put it past them to pull a stunt like that," Tom said.

"Arson is a serious crime. I'm not going to make accusations. The fire department is investigating, and the police promise to step up their patrols."

"At least your tugboat has not been violated. That's something to be thankful for," Tom commented.

"Actually the wires supplying electricity to my tugboat were cut," Amon said quietly, almost as an afterthought.

"Shit! How is Mary handling all this?"

"She's truly a saint—the joy of my life," Amon declared fervently. "And how is Martha doing? I haven't seen her lately."

"She's her usual vociferous self. Lets you know when she's unhappy," Tom replied ruefully.

"Well, we have to keep our women happy. That's the eleventh commandment."

"I don't know. There's something to be said for celibacy," Tom said grimly.

"Wasn't it St. Augustine who spoke on behalf of celibacy?" Amon asked.

"That was after he had spent his early years messing around with peasant girls. It's good to know that saints have human failings like everyone else. But St. Augustine did renounce physical pleasures after finding religion."

"Nothing worse than a reformed drunk or a reformed womanizer," Amon commented wryly.

"The road to salvation is marked with detours and setbacks," Tom concurred.

"Which means there's hope for all of us," Amon replied happily.

George Harrison

Born in Liverpool, England, to a working-class family, George Harrison was a member of the Beatles, along with Paul McCartney, John Lennon, and Ringo Starr. His mother, a self-styled singer with an interest in exotic music, encouraged George to play the guitar. As a youth, Harrison was influenced by Cab Calloway, Carl Perkins, and Slim Whitman. When he was thirteen, George's father bought him an acoustic guitar. A friend of his dad's taught him how to play that guitar. A few years later, he met Paul McCartney, who would eventually bring George Harrison and John Lennon into his band: the Quarrymen.

In 1960, at the age of sixteen, George Harrison joined the singing group, which had changed its name to the Beatles. In addition to McCartney, Lennon, and Harrison, there was the group's drummer: Ringo Starr. Known as "the quiet Beatle," Harrison was a gifted guitar player, singer, and songwriter. In addition to rock and roll, Harrison explored non-Western music, playing the Indian harp in "Strawberry Fields Forever." He also played the *warmandal* (small Indian harp) and the tabula (Indian wooden drum). Harrison was influenced by the socially relevant protest songs of Bob Dylan and the British rock group the Birds.

George Harrison's modest demeanor belied his immense songwriting ability, putting him on par with the celestial level of McCartney and Lennon. More spiritual than either of his famous bandmates, such Harrison songs as "Here Comes the Sun," "Something," "My Sweet Lord," "Taxman," and "Bangla Desh" all have eternal themes of love, justice, and godliness, which reached a wider audience than typical pop songs. In 1968, Harrison met Bob Dylan, establishing a friendship and the creative latitude that did not exist within the Beatles band. Despite the internal strife and competitive impulses, the Beatles recorded their final album, *Abbey Road*, which featured Harrison's megahits "Here Comes the Sun" and "Something."

Of all the songs written by George Harrison, "Something" has the most universal appeal. Frank Sinatra recorded it for an older audience and asserted it was the greatest love song of the past fifty years. After the Beatles breakup in 1970, Harrison wrote and recorded "My Sweet Lord," which expresses his devotion to God—a profoundly spiritual message that resonated over the years. In the early 1970s, Harrison organized a concert for Bangladesh, in response to a request from Ravi Shankar. This small Asian country was beleaguered by warfare, floods, hunger, and poverty. Harrison's goal of raising millions for Bangladesh was hampered by poor planning and fiscal mismanagement. Nevertheless, Harrison's concert raised awareness about the plight of the Bengali peasants. In the end, the George Harrison Humanitarian Fund for UNICEF did donate $450,000 for the cyclone victims of Bangladesh.

Of all the Beatles, George Harrison was the one who was most focused on spiritual themes, ethical issues, and third-world poverty. The so-called "quiet Beatle" never suffered from the egomania that seemed to consume McCartney and Lennon, and that led to the ultimate breakup of that legendary British rock group. When the Beatles made their first trip to America in 1964, Harrison expressed doubts about the venture: "America has everything. Why should they want us?" Low-key about fame and fortune, Harrison asserted that "the nicest thing is to open the newspaper and not find yourself in it." Always modest about his status as a rock-and-roll icon, George Harrison once said, "Life goes on within you and without you."

CHAPTER 35

Coupling Interrupted

It was a busy Saturday night at Gooley's, which was located at the corner of Richmond Terrace and Richmond Avenue in Port Richmond. Patrons mingled in the hazy, dimly lit bowling alley, moving from the tiny bar to the well-worn alleys in a desultory fashion. Tom understood that most people went there to socialize and drink, rather than to engage in some serious bowling. Nevertheless, Tom and Martha played three intense games of bowling, in which the parochial school teacher topped the skinny science teacher by narrow margins. The two young people bantered and joked, forgetting at least for the night their differences about Amon and his doings in Mariners Harbor. Martha wore a snug sweater and tight jeans, which showed off her ample physical assets.

Upon the completion of their bowling games, Tom suggested a drive to their secluded haunt on South Avenue on the western end of the Island. Martha readily agreed, with a mysterious grin on her face. Arriving at the tree-lined clearing, which was a hundred feet off the main road, Tom removed Martha's pink sweater, revealing her bulging lacy brassiere. The St. Mary's teacher did the same thing for her longtime boyfriend. As their blood pressure surged, their breathing quickened, and their bodies heated up — despite the chilly forty-degree temperature outside.

Just before consummating their love, as was their Saturday night custom, Martha signaled Tom to hold his fire.

Panting and aching with desire, Tom pulled back. "What? Is there something wrong?"

"I'm not using any contraceptives," she said abruptly.

"Well, I'll put something on," he replied, reaching for the glove compartment.

"No. I don't want to take that chance anymore. Especially when there's no commitment on your part. I'm just an easy lay to you."

"Hey! I've never thought about you in that way," Tom replied, becoming aggravated at the unusual turn in events.

"Sex without a real commitment is wrong," she said.

"Sex without love is wrong. I love you, Martha. You know that."

"I don't know what to think about you or our relationship. We're at a crossroads right now, and where we go from this point on is up to you," she said, putting her sweater on and smoothing over her hair.

Tom backed up his old gray Pontiac and drove toward Martha's house, off Morningstar Road. To make matters worse, the heater in his car had stopped working, and the radio emitted more static than music. There was a stony silence as both of them dwelled on bleak thoughts about a relationship that appeared to be heading nowhere.

A few days later, Tom called Martha to try to patch things up. The prospect of a breakup frightened him, and he was desperate to avoid what he viewed as a calamity. When Joanie moved to Indiana, he spent his college years and his first two years of teaching alone, accept for the occasional date that left him emotionally and physically unfulfilled.

After initial awkward preliminaries, Tom asked Martha out for the upcoming Saturday night. After a long pause, Martha said that both of them needed a "break in the relationship … a sabbatical of sorts."

"Sabbaticals are given to teachers after seven years, not to boyfriends who have been true and loyal," Tom replied.

"You had a different upbringing than I had, Tom. All that stuff with your foster parents and your dad's heavy drinking. What's more, your real parents weren't even married," Martha commented.

"I'm not against marriage. It's just that I'm not quite ready for it. After all, I'm only twenty-four years old, working on my master's degree and helping my mom with her household expenses. Not to mention my helping Amon with his rooming house on Simonson Avenue."

"Of course. You have plenty of time for everybody except for me. I feel lucky that you can spare a Saturday night for me," she complained.

"So when am I going to see you?" Tom asked, growing nervous.

"I'll be around. Unfortunately, we're from the same neck of the woods," she said coolly.

Hanging up the phone, Tom remembered a prayer he had heard years ago in the Methodist Church in Port Richmond: "Lord forgive me for not doing what I should have done, and for doing what I shouldn't have done."

CHAPTER 36

The Atom

Tom recalled his years in elementary school when air-raid drills were regularly held and certain public buildings were designated as fallout shelters in the event of nuclear war. The late 1950s and early 1960s was the height of the Cold War. He remembered waking up from scary nightmares of Russian jet bombers dropping bombs from the sky as a youngster. During times of crises between America and Russia, both countries had giant bombers continually flying in the air, carrying atomic bombs equivalent to millions of tons of TNT. There were even tales of America launching its nuclear bomb–laden B-52s, triggered by a "V" formation of geese flying over Northern Canada. Fortunately, the deadly bomber fleet was called back before nuclear Armageddon.

In order for his students to understand nuclear energy, Tom realized that they first had to grasp the basics of the atom's structure. Written on the blackboard was the aim of the lesson: "What is the structure of the atom?" There was a planetary model of the helium atom on his desk and Mendeleev's periodic table of the elements hanging from the board.

Barry walked into the room with his usual rolling gait, stopping at the front desk, where he began fiddling with the helium atom model, until he plopped into his chair. Tom asked the class why it was called the planetary model of the atom.

Wendy raised her hand. "Because it works like the solar system. The electrons orbit around the nucleus just as the planets orbit around the sun."

"Excellent, Wendy. And just like the solar system, the atom is mostly empty space. Many years ago, a scientist named Ernest Rutherford bombarded a thin sheet of gold with alpha particles. Most of these high-speed particles went straight through, as if there was nothing there," Tom lectured.

"So that steam pipe holding boiling hot steam over there is mostly empty space?" Manny asked skeptically.

"The molecular bonds holding iron atoms together are very strong. Now there are two important concepts I want to discuss," Tom said, turning to the board.

"Oh, goody. It's notebook time. But mines is filled to the brim," Barry said, showing the class a notebook in which every page had notes from all his classes on it.

"Somebody give Barry a piece of paper to copy his science notes on."

Lora gave the boisterous student some paper, which he sniffed loudly.

"My oh my. This paper smells like perfume," he exclaimed.

"If you're nice, I'll let you smell my feet," she replied coyly.

Barry started to leave his seat when Tom told him to sit still and copy the science notes.

The Bohr Model of the Atom
The three subatomic particles are protons, electrons, and neutrons. The protons and neutrons are packed tightly together in the nucleus, while the electrons revolve around the nucleus in orbits or shells. Electrons have a negative charge, protons have a positive charge, and neutrons are electrically neutral.

Atomic Number = Number of Protons
Number of Electrons = Number of Protons
Atomic Weight = Protons + Neutrons

Lora raised her hand. "This stuff about the atom is okay, but what use is it in my daily life? I don't need to know about atoms to iron my clothes, wash the dishes, or dust the furniture."

"Well, dust adheres to furniture because of molecular forces, which are electrical in nature," Tom commented.

"I'll keep that in mind the next time I dust the furniture," she replied dryly.

"More importantly, I might give you some questions like this on your next science test."

The young science teacher wrote out the following:

#1. Carbon has atomic number of 6 and atomic weight of 12.
#2. Beryllium has atomic number of 4 and atomic weight of 9.
#3. Fluorine has atomic number of 9 and atomic weight of 19.

Find the number of protons, electrons, and neutrons for each element.

Riner raised his hand. "Carbon has six electrons, six protons, and six neutrons."

Ronnie raised her hand. "Beryllium has four electrons, four protons, and five neutrons."

Barry raised his hand. "Fluorine has nine electrons, nine protons, and ten neutrons."

"Very good. You guys are on your game today. That's for sure."

On that positive note, the bell rang, ending a good lesson for Tom, despite the fact that there was no practical experiment to start off the lesson—and despite Lora's lack of conviction about the utility of atomic theory. The clanging sound of her copper trinkets had a mournful note as she strolled down the dimly lit Curtis hallway.

CHAPTER 37

Nuclear Energy

On the following day, Tom reviewed the Bohr model of the atom, in which electrons orbit a central nucleus composed of protons and neutrons packed tightly together. Tom also reviewed the electrical charges of the three subatomic particles: electrons were negative, protons were positive, and neutrons were uncharged. On his desk was a series of inverted matches set in clay, arranged in a row that led to a strip of magnesium. The aim of the lesson was written on the blackboard: "What is nuclear energy?" Before starting the lesson, the young science teacher shooed Barry and Manny away before they could tamper with the carefully arranged match heads.

Tom asked someone to define nuclear fission, and no one responded. Then he asked someone to define nuclear fusion, with no answer forthcoming. Shaking his head, the skinny science teacher said, "Well, I guess nobody did their reading last night."

"Some of us have other things to do besides homework, like hanging out with our friends and playing hoops," Barry commented.

"Yeah, Mr. Haley. We have other things on our minds besides schoolwork," Lora chimed in.

"Going to school is your job. It's preparation for life," Tom replied.

"Then we should get paid like any job. How long would you teach kids like us if you weren't paid?" Manny yelled out from the back of the room.

Ignoring the latter remark, Tom turned to the board and wrote the following definitions for his students to copy into their science notebooks:

Nuclear Fission: the splitting of the nucleus into smaller nuclei with the release of energy.
Nuclear Fusion: the combining of smaller nuclei into a larger nucleus with the release of energy.

Tom went on to explain that only very heavy elements are fissionable, like uranium and plutonium. Slow-moving neutrons are used to split uranium. In the reaction, neutrons are released, which in turn causes more and more uranium atoms to split. The process is called a chain reaction. Huge amounts of energy are released in both fission and fusion, which originate from nuclear binding energy holding the nucleus together.

"Why is the term 'atomic energy' a misnomer?" Tom inquired.

Riner raised his hand. "Because the energy comes from the nucleus and not the entire atom."

Turning to the blackboard, Tom wrote down Einstein's famous equation: $E = mc^2$ where E = energy, m = matter, and c = speed of light.

Tom explained that a small amount of matter can be converted into a huge amount of energy because c^2 is a very big number. He also stated that, according to Einstein, matter and energy were really the same thing.

Somebody from the back of the class asked about fusion.

"Thermonuclear fusion is the source of energy in hydrogen bombs. This process occurs in the sun, where hydrogen is fused into helium under great heat and pressure with the release of energy in the form of heat, light, ultraviolet light, and gamma rays."

"So you're saying that atomic and hydrogen bombs are the most powerful weapons in the history of the world," Barry said.

"Absolutely. A few hundred pounds of uranium could blow up Staten Island," Tom replied.

"Wow! Where can I get my hands on some uranium?" Manny asked.

"Near the end of World War II, in 1945, atomic bombs were dropped on the Japanese cities of Hiroshima and Nagasaki, virtually destroying both cities," Tom declared, turning to the blackboard.

City / Population / Number Killed
Hiroshima / 350,000 / 140,000
Nagasaki / 260,000 / 80,000

"In addition to the above numbers killed instantly, thousands more died from radiation sickness. Nuclear bombs emit deadly alpha rays, beta rays, and gamma rays, which cause radiation sickness, cancer, and harmful mutations," Tom stated grimly. He was aware of the scars on his mom's face after exposure to radium as a teenager. In the early twentieth century, doctors were ignorant of the terrible effects of that radioactive element.

Riner, an intense young man, raised his hand. "Aren't hydrogen bombs much more powerful than uranium bombs?"

"That's true. And both America and Russia have stockpiles of thousands of these nuclear bombs — capable of totally destroying each country. An all-out nuclear war would bring the civilized world back to the Stone Age," Tom asserted grimly.

"The caveman didn't have it so bad. Hunting the saber-toothed tiger and the woolly mammoth with clubs and spears might be fun," Manny called out from the back of the room.

"Hydrogen bombs use fissionable uranium as a trigger. They can be made very large or very small. Nuclear warheads in intercontinental ballistic missiles are hydrogen bombs. A fifty-megaton hydrogen bomb dropped on Manhattan could wipe out all of New York City, including Staten Island," Tom recited from his extensive notes on nuclear energy.

"I think I'm going to move in with my granny. She lives in the backwoods of old Mississippi," Barry replied.

"The radioactivity from a nuclear war would kill you anyway," Riner responded.

"In a thermonuclear bomb, two isotopes of hydrogen are utilized, called deuterium and tritium, which are found in trace amounts in ocean water," the skinny teacher stated.

"When are you gonna do your practical experiment?" Lora asked, bored with the discussion about nuclear weapons. She was aware of her teacher's reputation for botched classroom demonstrations.

"Oops, I almost forgot my match-head version of a chain reaction."

He struck a match and held it to one end of the closely arranged match heads.

Sweeping through the matches, the flame darted along the row of match heads until it reached the magnesium strip, which burst into a bright white flame. Then the unexpected happened. Tom had left the class's homework papers, which he had intended to return to the students, next to the magnesium strip. The burning, white-hot magnesium set the papers on fire, causing the class to roar its approbation for this unexpected event.

"Mr. Haley, you're the best. You can have this copper bracelet as a token of my esteem," Lora said gleefully.

Tom shook his head, suggesting that she bring him an apple the next day. The bell rang, and the students left the class joyfully, laughing and chattering about the spectacle they had just witnessed. Cleaning up his desk and gathering his materials, Tom chuckled over the dramatic ending to his lesson on nuclear energy.

He realized that these unforeseen mishaps made up for the boredom inherent in day-to-day classroom teaching. Yet he wondered if his message about the awesome destructive power of nuclear weapons had gotten through. Scanning his notes, he noticed a fact that he had overlooked: the United States and Russia had conducted over twenty thousand tests of atomic and hydrogen bombs since the 1940s. Children all over the world were breathing air contaminated by radioactive isotopes, which have permeated the soil, the water, and the atmosphere of this fragile planet earth that we call home.

CHAPTER 38

Hamilton and Burr

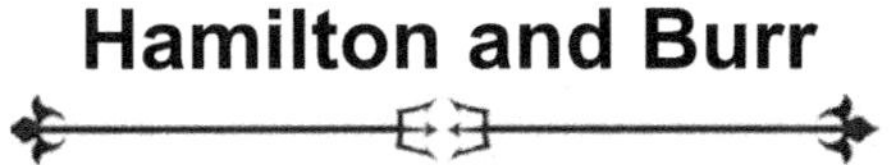

One Saturday afternoon, Amon asked Tom to drive him to Port Richmond, where he could have his old work boots resoled. There was a tiny shoemaker's shop located near the Ritz Theater, where Tom had seen many movies going back to his high school days. A block from Richmond Avenue was PS 20, his elementary school alma mater. He recalled the older school building, erected in 1891, which had an impressive clock tower. Like his neighborhood of Elm Park, Port Richmond was the locus of so many fond memories for the skinny science teacher. As a teenager, he had a *Herald Tribune* newspaper route covering a three-square-mile area, ranging from Port Richmond to Elm Park to Mariners Harbor. He used to get up before school each day to deliver this comprehensive newspaper, which never caught on with North Shore readers.

After Amon's boots were done, the two young men walked down Richmond Avenue toward the Terrace. Reaching the end of Richmond Avenue, they noticed a plaque on an ancient brick building, stating that Aaron Burr died there in 1836. In the nineteenth century, the building was known as the St. James Hotel, the last home of Burr. Tom said that Aaron Burr was the notorious killer of Alexander Hamilton, America's first treasury secretary, under George Washington.
The infamous Hamilton–Burr duel occurred in 1804 at Weehhawken, New Jersey.

"Dueling was common in the early days of the republic. The two men were bitter enemies, especially after Hamilton supported Jefferson over Burr in the presidential election of 1800," Tom related.

"I guess you could say that duels and shootings are part of our heritage in this country," Amon said.

"Guns have played a big role in our history. It might have been due to our frontier past. You know, driving the Indians off their land to settle the West."

"Don't remind me. So was Burr arrested after killing Hamilton?" Amon asked.

"There was a warrant issued for him. Jefferson, who was no angel himself, had declared that Aaron Burr was a traitor on trumped-up charges. Supposedly, Burr had a scheme to start a new nation in Florida and Louisiana territory and appoint himself king," Tom stated.

"So, how did Aaron Burr wind up in Port Richmond? Did he want to create a new fiefdom on Staten Island?" Amon inquired.

"No. By then he had become a practical man, marrying a wealthy widow and starting a lucrative law practice. Like many people, Burr was a complicated man. He could be kind and generous to poor people, especially children. Burr died in 1836 after suffering a stroke at this site, the infamous St. James Hotel," Tom related.

"Except for idealists like you and me, most of us have our price," Amon replied.

"My motto is: When you come to a fork in the road, choose the path which is less profitable," Tom said with a wry smile.

"I hear you. Money isn't everything, though it's a necessary evil," Amon responded. "How do you know so much about Aaron Burr?"

"I had to cover a history class for a colleague, Alan Katz. He has excellent notes. All I have to do is follow them, and I look like an expert to my students."

"The folks in my residential house on Simonson Avenue feel the same thing about me. They think I have all the answers," Amon said gloomily.

"It's called charisma. Get used to it because it's a label that doesn't wear off easily," Tom replied.

Roe v. Wade (1973)

Roe v. Wade was a landmark US Supreme Court decision overturning a Texas law prohibiting abortion, making abortion legal in the United States. The court ruled seven to two that the right to privacy under the due process clause of the Fourteenth Amendment extended to a woman's decision to have an abortion. Basically, the Supreme Court stated that a person has a right to abortion until viability. And viability was defined as the ability to live outside the mother's womb without artificial aid.

The court said that restrictive abortion laws in effect in most states were of relatively recent vintage. With regard to history, abortions were done in ancient Greece and Rome, and in Europe. In the United States, abortion was sometimes considered a common-law crime. However, the criminalization of abortion did not have roots in English common law. This historical analysis of abortion laws was provided by Justice Harry Blackmun, who said that nearly every state had laws banning abortion since the 1900s.

In 1970, a US district court in Texas ruled in favor of defendant Norma McCorvey (alias Jane Roe), who falsely asserted that she had been raped in order to obtain an abortion. Texas law permitted abortion in cases of rape and incest. Though ruling in McCorvey's favor, the district court declined to grant an injunction against the enforcement of Texas laws barring abortion. Eventually, Norma McCorvey gave birth before the case was decided.

In December 1971, Justices Stewart and Blackmun agreed that the Roe v. Wade case ought to be heard. The seven-to-two decision in favor of legalizing abortion was based on the assertion that abortion was a fundamental right under the "right to privacy" clause of the Fourteenth Amendment of the US Constitution. Justice Henry Blackmun stated that this amendment guaranteed a woman the right to terminate her pregnancy within the constitutional guarantee of personal privacy. In addition, the court explicitly rejected the fetal "right to life" argument. This fundamental right to privacy could not be abrogated without a "compelling state interest."

Nevertheless, the Supreme Court created a trimester framework to balance the fundamental right to abortion with the government's two legitimate interests: protecting the mother's health and protecting the "potentiality of human life." At the point of viability in the third trimester, the state's interest in "potential life" would become compelling and the state could regulate and even proscribe abortion to preserve the life and health of mother and fetus. In addition, the court preserved the right of the physician to practice medicine freely in this area, absenting compelling state interest.

Support for Roe v. Wade has ebbed and flowed over the years, depending on the nation's political climate. The majority of voters in the United States favored the legalization of abortion, particularly among younger Americans. With respect to presidential opinions toward legalizing abortions, Richard Nixon never commented about it, Gerald Ford opposed it, while Jimmy Carter consistently supported a woman's right to abortion.

CHAPTER 39

Hospital Revisited

Later that week, Tom was awakened in the middle of the night by a phone call from Mary, who was beside herself with fear. "Amon's been shot! He's been sent to St. Vincent's Hospital."

Tom rushed down to the North Shore hospital in his old gray Pontiac. St. Vincent's was located off Castleton Avenue on a large shrub- and tree-filled lot. The densely populated area, known as West Brighton, was home to many of Tom's students at Curtis High School.

Arriving at the young stranger's room, Tom was relieved to learn that it was a superficial wound in his left shoulder. Looking like he just woke up from a pleasant siesta, Amon smiled as soon as he saw his friend. Mary sat next to her lover, holding his hand and looking at him with concern and adulation.

"Sorry to stir you from your beauty rest, but Mary desperately wanted you to be here," Amon said in a steady voice.

"Some people will do anything for publicity," Tom replied, feigning annoyance.

"I'm sure it will be on the front page of the *Advocate*."

"How did it happen?"

Amon explained that he had been puttering around in his refurbished tugboat, when he heard a sound like a firecracker going off and felt a sharp pain in his shoulder. Fortunately, Mary was on the vessel with him and called an ambulance. In addition, his girlfriend had insisted that Amon install a phone there in case of emergencies.

"Everybody working with Amon felt that things were getting out of hand with the local Mariners Harbor people," Mary replied.

"I cannot accept the idea that some of my neighbors are capable of such things. I believe most people are good and well-meaning," Amon stated unconvincingly.

"Jesus said a prophet is without honor in his own country," Tom asserted.

"Well, I'm no prophet. I'm just trying to put a roof over people's heads."

"You'd get more acclaim if you were burning villages in Vietnam," Tom commented, thinking about the horrors occurring in Southeast Asia.

"Enough idle talk. Let him rest, Tom. We need you back in the Harbor. And don't get out of bed without the nurse's permission," Mary warned Amon, fixing his blanket and beckoning Tom to leave the room.

She had mentioned that Amon had gotten out of bed to help his roommate. After administering his own type of healing, the middle-aged man was soon released from St. Vincent's with a clean bill of health. Doctors could find no trace of the liver tumor that had showed up in X-rays a few days earlier.

On the drive back from the hospital, Tom was keyed up. He decided to stop and have a drink at K. C.'s on Morningstar Road, which was still open despite the late hour. He ran into Harry the Horse, the perennial stickball player who was never too busy or tired to join the Elm Park kids in a game of stickball on Pulaski Avenue.

"What are you doing here on a Wednesday night? Don't you have to teach tomorrow?" he asked the young science teacher.

"I just came from St. Vincent's Hospital. Remember that guy Amon I introduced you to back in the fall? He was shot by some nut in Mariners Harbor."

"Shit! The North Shore is going downhill. It's all those people from Brooklyn."

"I like this area. The people here are down-to-earth. They tell it like it is. You're beginning to sound high-class, Harry. Soon you'll be ordering tea and biscuits at the Staaten, instead of a beer at K. C.'s or Kaffman's," Tom responded.

"I'm just a working stiff. But the neighborhood is changing."

"Where are you gonna move, Tottenville? You can't play stickball on dirt roads or cow pastures. You'll be stepping in cow manure."

"Have you seen the streets around here lately? They're full of dog shit!" Harry complained.

"You're right about that. It seems I'm always stepping in it," Tom related.

"Sure, I'm right, Tom. But you always had a knack for stepping or sitting in it."

"Tell me about it. The other day I almost started a fire doing one of my practical classroom experiments."

"So the menace of Elm Park is now the menace of Curtis High School. Remember the time you were playing stickball and hit a pop-up that landed in your neighbor's tub of concrete?" Harry related with a wry grin.

"Don't remind me. Have you ever noticed that people don't really change? A ten-year-old is pretty much the same person when he's an adult," Tom observed.

"For better or worse, we're stuck with ourselves forever. How's Granny Schmidt? Does she still get her booze every day from that liquor store on Morningstar Road?"

"Yup, some things never change. Consistency throughout life is good in a world that's constantly changing. I'll drink to that," Tom said, downing his Ballantine beer, bidding Harry good-bye, and getting up from his bar stool.

Walking out to the street, Tom wondered whatever happened to that concrete-covered Spalding, which had been on his bookshelf for so many years.

Such relics, along with old photos, were more enduring than a person's recollections, which grew fainter with each passing year. He realized that his mom's old shoebox of canceled checks from his foster family held good memories, as well as representing a long-standing debt owed her by her children.

CHAPTER 40

Martha, Martha

Desperate to save his relationship with Martha, Tom had an idea. For the first time in years, he skipped a Saturday night elbow-bending session at Kaffman's.

After playing some late-night basketball at PS 21, the skinny science teacher treated himself to an ice cream cone at Ralph's in Port Richmond. Reading the *New York Post* briefly, he was ensconced in his sun-porch bedroom and asleep by 11:30 p.m. Why to bed so early? Tom had plans for Sunday morning. Visions of the tall, voluptuous brunette filled his head, along with the din of Saturday night traffic on Pulaski Avenue.

Neatly dressed in one of his old teaching suits, a light-blue polyester garment purchased at J. C. Penny, Tom hoped that Martha was in attendance at St. Mary's church on Richmond Terrace. The small chapel was lightly attended for a pleasant Sunday in early May, Tom imagined. He assumed that church attendance fell during the bitter days of winter and rose with the balmy days of spring. Then he saw her, clothed in a formfitting pink dress, with a matching pink bonnet.

Trying to focus on the priest's sermon, Tom did his best to disregard her blooming presence. The subject of the priest's sermon was the role of marriage in providing stability for children and society as a whole. When it came time to receive communion, Martha went up to the front of the church to receive communion.

She must have gone to confession and told the stern, middle-aged priest about her sexual transgressions. Somehow, that thought did not bode well for a reconciliation between the two teachers.

As Tom emerged from the church, he waited for his old girlfriend. Approaching her with trepidation, the young science teacher said hello.

"Tom! This is the last place I'd expect to see you. Did you have a scary dream about a burning bush?" Martha said, adjusting her pink bonnet.

"Maybe I had a revelation, and I'm turning over a new leaf in life," he replied.

"Tom has found religion. You of all people? Why don't you sell me the Brooklyn Bridge?" she commented with a wry smile.

"Martha, Martha. You are worried about so many things. I never knew you to be so cynical."

"Stop with that 'Martha, Martha' crap from the Bible. It's a joke worn thinner than your bony ass."

"Ouch! You really know how to hurt a guy."

"You haven't seen anything yet, Mr. Newspaper Boy," she exclaimed in a loud voice, attracting some of the bystanders' attention.

Walking away, Tom stumbled and fell on the sidewalk, tearing a hole in his light-blue trousers. The trousers were part of a suit he had purchased during his first year of teaching. He was sentimental about clothes, refusing to discard them no matter how wrinkled, frayed, or faded with chalk the garment was.

Now she thinks I'm back to early-morning drinking, a habit he had long ago given up. *I keep digging myself into a deeper and deeper hole with Martha.* As with so many things in life, luck plays a big role. And he was out of luck with the tall buxom brunette. At least he wasn't wearing one of his newer bell-bottom trousers — the rage of the 1970s. A few weeks earlier, the skinny teacher had tripped on his wide cuffs walking up Hamilton Hill, drawing giggles from his students. Yet he had to laugh at his own clumsiness. It reminded him of a heavyset softball player from Elm Park who had stumbled and fell hard on the pavement while running out a ground ball on the PS 21 playground years ago. Everybody turned away, struggling to keep from laughing at the funny spectacle of all that abundant soft flesh bouncing on hard concrete.

CHAPTER 41

Angry Cleric

On a sunny Easter morning, Amon decided to go to church with his girlfriend, Mary, and his steadfast ally and friend, Tom. Both young men were neatly attired for the occasion. Tom wore the light-blue suit that had been patched up by an old tailor situated at the bottom of Morningstar Road, right before the junction with Richmond Terrace. Somehow, Tom felt an affiliation with this elderly man, because he worked in the same profession as his maternal grandfather. From occasional tidbits given by his mom, Tom gathered the impression that his progenitor was a hardworking and gentle soul.

Amon was resplendent in an off-white summer suit, which fit the strapping Mariners Harbor resident perfectly. The suit had been purchased by his girlfriend, Mary, especially for the occasion. The generous young woman was instinctively in tune with Amon, appearing to know his preferences, as well as his exact suit size.

"That's a great outfit, Amon. You look like one of those Southern plantation owners from days gone by," Tom declared, admiring his longtime friend.

"I'm sorry I can't return the compliment. Your suit has definitely seen better days. Who's your tailor?" Amon responded with a smile.

"When it comes to sartorial matters, you know I'm a Scotchman. Actually, the guy who patches up my clothes has a shop near this area," Tom replied.

"If it wasn't for the likes of you, the man would have to go out of business."

"That reminds me of a big heavy guy from Elm Park, called John Kish. He was slow-moving and clumsy, but he could hit a softball a country mile. One day Kish hit a monstrous home run that cleared the left-field fence, plus the brick wall across the street. The poor guy got so excited that he stumbled and fell hard, ripping his extra-large pants. Well, everyone did their best not to laugh, but it was so damned funny we couldn't help ourselves."

"So what's your point, Tom?" Mary inquired,

"Nothing at all. But if I suddenly start laughing in church, you'll know why. Kish fell so hard. I swear the ground shook," Tom replied with a giggle.

"I don't know. We can't take this guy anywhere," Amon said ruefully.

As the threesome entered St. Mary's church on Richmond Terrace, Tom scrutinized the congregants, searching for his old girlfriend. His heart skipped a beat when he observed her, dressed in a white dress, adorned with yellow flowers. As with all of Martha's outfits, the dress displayed her ample assets.

The theme of the priest's sermon was concerned with the alleged conflict between an individual's material wants and his spiritual needs. The requirement to support one's family does not have to threaten one's religious values at all. The preacher seemed to indicate that family responsibilities and socioeconomic pressures do not necessarily endanger one's faith, particularly in America, where individual freedom and material greed are engrained.

"Yes, Jesus told us to render unto Caesar that which is Caesar's and render unto God that which is God's. And never forget that we live in a beneficent country where anyone who works hard can achieve a level of affluence unparalleled in human history. There is no fundamental conflict between materialism and spiritualism. Indeed, America, a shining city on a hill blessed by God, has blazed the path of prosperity and freedom for all the world to follow," the middle-aged cleric intoned righteously.

Tom turned and glanced at Amon. It was clear that the Mariners Harbor resident did not agree with the priest's views about America's beneficence and the harmony between materialism and faith. Sensing Amon's discomfort, Mary grasped his hand, whispering her dismay over the direction of the priest's doctrinaire discourse.

Then it struck Tom that the priest's sermon was directed at Amon himself. Somehow he had been notified of Amon's presence in the congregation. He wondered if that stunning voluptuary in white, decked with yellow flowers, had tipped off the stern-looking priest about Amon's activities in Mariners Harbor.

After the service, people milled about the entrance of the church as the cleric shook hands and chatted with the congregants. Tom, Amon, and Mary stood in a little group, with Martha a few feet away, engaged in deep conversation with some elderly churchgoers. Tom noticed Martha nodding at the priest, who had a pink complexion, bloodshot blue eyes, and a porcine face. Tom dismissed him as the stereotypical Irish cleric—hard-drinking, well-fed, and cynical. The red-faced priest accosted Amon, cognizant of his unofficial title: the Mariners Harbor Messiah.

"I've heard a lot about you, young man. It seems that the *Advocate* does a feature story about you regularly. Your efforts on behalf of the homeless are exemplary," the cleric said, looking at Amon intensely.

Tom was struck by the difference between the content of his words and the tone of his message. It reminded him of the Native American saying that a person spoke with a forked tongue.

To everyone's surprise, Amon spoke bluntly to the priest, saying he disagreed with the latter's message. "Materialism and spiritualism are diametric opposites. The church ought to speak out about American greed and the awful plight of the homeless in our country."

"Young man, there is no fundamental conflict between supporting one's family and following the teachings of the Catholic Church. They go hand in hand in America. Our free-enterprise system has created unparalleled abundance for the American people. It is the Communists who extol materialism to the exclusion of the teachings of the Gospel. When man loses his fear of God, then we become fearful of each other. That's what happened in Nazi Germany and what is occurring today in Russia and in China," the priest lectured sternly.

"Actually, I've given out Bibles to all our residents on Simonson Avenue, and we have Bible readings for all those who are so inclined," Amon responded.

Surprising himself, Tom spoke up. "Didn't Jesus say that a camel has a better chance of passing though the eye of a needle than a rich man has of going to heaven?"

Ignoring Tom and turning abruptly to Mary, the middle-aged cleric said, "I haven't noticed you in church lately. Where are you Sunday mornings?"

Mary blushed and stammered an answer that was inaudible.

"I understand you teach third grade at St. Mary's. We expect our faculty to attend church regularly. After all, you are a role model for our youngsters."

Without further comment, the unsmiling cleric left the three young people. Tom also noticed that his old girlfriend had also retreated from the front entrance of the church.

Trying to make light of the situation, Mary said, "I think we've been excommunicated by Father McGuire."

"That's his name? It's no surprise. There's nothing worse than a pious Irishman!" Tom replied sardonically.

"I like the Irish better when they're drunk," Amon commented.

"Is it possible to be excommunicated by your girlfriend?" Tom asked, trying to get a final look at his sensual ex-girlfriend.

"I'll have to look that up," Mary replied as the threesome walked along Richmond Terrace.

CHAPTER 42

Magnetic Lesson

Displayed on Tom's desk was a compass, a bar magnet, a horseshoe magnet, a hand-cranked generator connected to a tiny light bulb, a wire coil connected to a galvanometer, and a flashlight. The aim of the lesson was written on the board: "How is electricity generated?" As usual, Barry and Manny played with the magnets and the generator. And as customary, the young science teacher sent the two hyperactive teenagers back to their seats so he could begin the lesson.

Tom began turning the crank generator, which caused the light bulb to glow weakly. "What is the energy conversion shown here?"

Ronnie raised her hand. "You're converting mechanical energy to electricity and then to light."

"Very good, Ronnie."

Next, Tom called Manny up to the front desk to turn the crank generator.

"What happens when the light bulb is screwed on and off?"

Manny said it was much harder to turn the generator when the light bulb was turned on.

"That's such an astounding practical experiment, Mr. Haley!" Barry exclaimed sarcastically.

"But why is it harder to turn with the light on than off?" Tom persisted.

Riner, an intense student, responded, "With the light bulb on, the electricity turns into light energy. With the light bulb off, there is no energy output, so it's easy to turn the generator."

"Excellent, Riner."

"How come when anyone else answers a question, you say 'good,' but when four-eyes answers a question, you say 'excellent'?" Barry complained.

"That's an excellent point, Barry. I'll keep that in mind."

Next, Tom took the wire coil connected to the galvanometer and moved the bar magnet through the coil, causing a current to flow through the coil, as indicated by the movement of the needle on the galvanometer. The same thing occurred when the horseshoe magnet was moved through the coil. He asked the class to explain what had just occurred.

Barry raised his hand, and Tom braced himself for a wisecrack. "A moving magnetic field near a wire can generate electricity. Which is what happens when you turn a generator."

"Excellent! That is absolutely right, Barry."

"Give me extra credit for that answer, Mr. Haley."

Ignoring the pesky youngster, Tom moved on with the lesson. He turned on the flashlight while holding it near the compass. "What's going on here, class?"

Wendy answered, "It demonstrates that an electric current has a magnetic field around it."

"That's correct, Wendy. There is a symmetrical relationship between magnetism and electricity. This was first discovered by Michael Faraday and is called Faraday's law. Everybody, get out your science notebooks and copy this down: 'Faraday's Law: A moving magnetic field can generate an electric current, and surrounding an electric current is a magnetic field.'"

"So what you're saying is that all generators have some kind of magnet with a coil of wire that rotates," Manny called out from the back of the class.

"That's correct, Manny. And a motor operates in the opposite sense from a generator. An electric current applied to a motor causes its coil to turn or rotate under the influence of a magnetic field," Tom stated.

"Isn't the rotating coil of a motor called the armature?" Riner inquired.

"That's correct, Riner. You guys are doing well today," Tom said happily.

"Since we're doing good today, we deserve a day off from homework," Barry commented.

"I wouldn't go that far. Homework is the vital fuel that feeds our minds," the skinny teacher replied.

There was some time left before the period ended, so Tom decided to press on.

"There is another law that's important in electricity called Ohm's law. Does anybody know Ohm's law?" Nobody answered, so Tom wrote it on the board for the students to copy on their notebooks: "Ohm's Law: The electric current flowing through a wire varies directly with the voltage and inversely with the resistance."

"Why do people in science have such weird names? Newton, Faraday, Ohm, Einstein, Bohr, Planck, Ampere, Volta—I could go on and on," remarked Lora.

"It's almost as strange as wearing copper bracelets on your arms and legs," Barry snapped.

"If you really want to know why, I'll tell you," she replied, going over to her classmate and whispering something in his ear. The obstreperous youngster smiled and clapped his hands.

"The world needs more young ladies like you. That's why I'm easy. Easy like Sunday morning, as the song goes." Barry sang off-key.

On that harmonious note, the bell rang, ending the magnetic lesson on Faraday's and Ohm's laws. As the class disbursed and Tom gathered up his materials, Lora went up to the skinny young teacher and offered him a small copper cross, tied to a string.

"I want you to wear it, Mr. Haley. It will ward off evil spirits," she asserted.

"Really? Then I'll wear it. Thank you. Even though teachers are not supposed to accept gifts from students," Tom said, putting the cross around his neck.

Smiling, the perky teenager happily left the class with the clanging sounds of her copper arm and leg bracelets echoing down the hall.

Marvin Gaye

Marvin Gaye was born in Washington, DC, to a Pentecostal pastor and a maid in 1939. He began singing in church at the age of four, accompanied by his father on the piano. The Pentecostal church adhered to strict conduct, following both the Old and New Testament. Marvin Gaye loved to sing as a youngster, but he was whipped brutally by his father, whom he described as peculiar, cruel, and all-powerful. His mother was kind to him, consoling the boy and encouraging him to pursue singing. Gaye had a brief stint in the air force but was soon discharged because he refused to obey orders.

Early in his career, Marvin Gaye was a backup singer for Chuck Berry in the hit "Back in the USA." In 1960, Gaye moved to Detroit, where he was a backup singer and drummer. In 1962, he wrote "Beachwood 4-5789," sung by the Marvelettes, and "Together," which he sung with Mary Wells. He also wrote his solo hit "How Sweet It Is" that year.

In the middle 1960s, Marvin Gaye recorded a series of duets with Tammi Terrell, including "Ain't No Mountain High Enough" and "Ain't Nothing Like the Real Thing." Terrell collapsed during a performance with Gaye, and it was discovered that she had a malignant brain tumor. The latter's poor treatment by the record company disillusioned Gaye about the record business. In the late 1960s, Marvin Gaye recorded "I Heard It Through the Grapevine," which reached number one on the charts. There were several more hits in the late 1960s, but upon the death of Tammi Terrell, Gaye experienced bouts of depression.

In the summer of 1970, Marvin Gaye wrote and recorded his greatest song, "What's Going On." The song was motivated by acts of police brutality against blacks that Gaye had personally witnessed. Initially, the record company refused to release the record, but strong protests from Gaye resulted in its release. The haunting record was a smash hit, reaching the top of the charts and selling over two million copies. This was followed by two more top hits: "Mercy Mercy Me" and "Inner City Blues." These records had a profound message that resonated throughout the country and enhanced Marvin Gaye's reputation beyond the world of pop music. As a result, Gaye received the Grammy Award, plus recognition from the NAACP.

In the late 1970s, Marvin Gaye developed a serious addiction to cocaine. He moved to Europe to cope with his addiction and to escape his financial woes, including alimony payments and owed back taxes to the IRS. His career went into decline, hampered by drug dependency problems. Tragically, in 1984, Gaye was visiting his parents in California, when an argument ensued with his father. Becoming enraged for reasons unclear, Gaye's father shot him at point-blank range. Marvin Gaye died in a California hospital at the relatively young age of forty-five.

Marvin Gaye had a wide vocal range. He actually had three distinct voices: a smooth tenor, a growling rasp, and an unreal falsetto. Critics said it was one of the sweetest voices ever heard. In addition to his versatile voice, Gaye was a maverick in the new genre of social and racial commentary. During the 1960s, Motown artists were told not to delve into political or social criticism of America. But the racial injustices of that era moved Marvin Gaye to express these themes in his songs, especially in "What's Going On," which has endured beyond the 1960s and 1970s.

CHAPTER 43

Vietnam Remembered

One pleasant Friday evening in early May, Tom pulled up at the Mariners Harbor waterfront in his gray Pontiac, looking for Amon. Stepping from the old wharf to Amon's repainted tugboat, he found his friend sitting in his rickety rocking chair reading the *Advocate*.

"Where's Mary tonight? You guys are usually inseparable," Tom remarked.

"She's helping out at St. Mary's. They're having a spaghetti dinner to raise money for the school."

"It seems like everybody's got their hand out nowadays."

"Well, it's for a good cause … I suppose," Amon replied.

"You look exhausted. Is everything okay?"

"Had to break up a fight between two winos at the boardinghouse. And the neighbors are always snooping around, especially when there's trouble."

"Well, the press has given you rave reviews on your work in the Harbor," Tom said, trying to boost Amon's morale.

"Those people at the *Advocate* would love to dig up some dirt about me. It sells papers," Amon replied sullenly.

"Come on with me. You need a break. I'll buy you a beer at Kaffman's," Tom said, jiggling his keys restlessly.

"I don't drink, nor do my boarders. You know my rules," Amon asserted.

"It's May Day—when people celebrate fertility and the rebirth of nature. We'll make an exception for May Day."

The two young men entered Kaffman's, where the skinny science teacher was welcomed by Rudy Kaffman with his usual comment about the prodigal son returning. Thomas Haley had been a longtime customer, spending a big chunk of his paycheck on himself and his cronies. Tom ordered locally brewed Ballantine beers for himself and Amon, who sipped his beer tentatively.

Looking around the crowded, sour-sweet–smelling saloon, Amon observed that the place seemed friendly enough.

"Kaffman's is like one big family. Most of the patrons are from the neighborhood. Wow, there's Granny Schmidt downing some whiskey at a table. That's a first," Tom said, thinking she must have come into some money.

"So this is where the heavy drinkers of Elm Park congregate?" Amon asked.

"The younger crowd hangs out here, while the veteran drinkers patronize K. C.'s, which is down the block."

"I can feel your dad's presence here. He usually sat at that stool in the corner near the window. He'd drink his beer, followed by a whiskey chaser."

"You're right! How the hell do you know that stuff?"

"Because I can see him as clearly as I see you right now. Heavyset man, curly hair, piercing blue eyes, somewhat bloodshot, and a wry smile—more like a grimace," Amon recited, looking at the corner stool, which was unoccupied.

"Did you always have the ability to see things like that?"

"Pretty much all of my life. But I didn't understand their meaning as a kid. I thought everybody could see such things," Amon replied.

Just then, Tom noticed a face from the past staring at him in the mirror. He shuddered when he realized it was Wayne O' Toole, the old neighborhood bully.

The latter recognized Tom and gave him a too-hearty hello, accompanied by a hard slap on the back.

Turning to Amon, Wayne yelled, "Do you know this guy? Curtis High School teacher and fancy-dressing draft dodger."

"Teaching is an honorable profession. Tom's a good guy. He's helped me to fix up a home for down-and-out folks, many of them Korean and Vietnam War veterans," Amon asserted, eye-balling the bully intently.

"Were you in 'Nam?" Wayne asked, sensing that Amon was no pushover.

"Have you heard of the Ia Drang Valley?"

Wayne's demeanor toward Amon changed as he leaned toward him, rapt with attention.

"I was with a battalion from the First Cavalry Division. We were trying to flush out the Viet Cong who had been taking potshots at us for about a week. They were good at hit-and-run attacks, looking to catch us off guard," Amon said.

"Yeah, those sons of bitches could hide in the underbrush five feet away. Then, they'd jump out and fire at you from point-blank range," Wayne yelled, attracting the attention of the bar patrons nearby.

"As we were moving through the dense underbrush of the Drang River, I told my sergeant to slow down because I felt the enemy's presence around us. But he disregarded my warning, and we marched straight into a Viet Cong ambush. The sergeant and several of my buddies were shot dead within seconds. I got hit in the shoulder," Amon related, showing Wayne and Tom a gaping hole in his right shoulder.

"So how did you survive the ambush?" Tom inquired.

"They called in air strikes and artillery fire, which drove them away. Later on, we found out that regular North Vietnam army troops had been fighting alongside the Viet Cong. They had come down from the north via the Ho Chi Minh trail, which ran through Laos. That was when the war changed from a guerrilla war to a conventional war of pitched battles, along with hit-and-run attacks," Amon related.

"The war must have been like a trip to hell and back," Tom replied.

"I was in the central highlands protecting the air force base at Pleiku, where the VC harassed us with their sneaky attacks, firing at us and then running back into the jungle. So we cleared the entire area surrounding the base with defoliants plus napalm shot from our jets. Have you ever seen a person burned with napalm? It ain't a pretty sight. The smell of human flesh burning is terrible. Since Vietnam, I don't eat barbecue hamburgers or steak," Wayne exclaimed.

"In 1965, the war went from a counter-insurgency to an all-out ground war. The battle of the Ia Drang Valley resulted in roughly 300 Americans killed, plus 600 wounded. Army headquarters claimed that we had killed 3,500 and wounded over 1,200 of the enemy," Amon related grimly.

"I remember the Defense Department talking about kill ratios of ten to one. It was always in the TV reports about the war," Tom said.

"Strange as it may sound, Vietnam was a beautiful country. Thick forests, green mountains, rolling hills, giant hedges, lush rice paddies, thatched huts, a great climate, and really nice people — simple peasants who just wanted to live out their lives in peace," Amon said mildly.

"It didn't matter because the VC recruited people from all over Vietnam—North and South. They were happy to be cannon fodder—those fucking gooks," Wayne chimed in bitterly.

"It was an unnecessary war, hatched by the politicians. A no-win situation," Tom commented.

"If the fuckin' politicians hadn't tied our hands, we could have won that war in six months," Wayne stated matter-of-factly.

"Anyway, I thank both of you for your service to our country. What are you drinking, Wayne?"

He indicated Scotch, which the skinny teacher ordered from Rudy. Wayne quickly downed his drink, and Tom promptly ordered another round for the three young men.

Observing a buxom blonde on the other side of the bar, Wayne nodded to Amon and headed in that direction.

"Wayne's an old friend of yours?" Amon asked with a sly grin.

"More like an acquaintance. He once flipped my bike, bending the front wheel. It wobbled for weeks until I could afford to fix it. Those were my newspaper route days, so my bike was a necessity," Tom said.

"Sounds like a guy with issues."

Just then a short, homely middle-aged man walked into Kaffman's. He was a longtime customer of the saloon who was said to be a lothario of sorts. As soon as the other customers recognized him, they began to clap.

"Why are they clapping?" Amon asked.

"Rumor has it that the dumb bastard caught the clap from his many sexual conquests," Tom replied, eyeballing him with admiration.

"Another guy with issues," Amon commented.

"Just about everyone in this place has issues," Tom replied, ordering another Ballantine beer.

Flinching, the skinny science teacher felt a rap on his back. It was Granny Schmidt, staring at him wall-eyed.

"Hey, wise guy. Buy me a drink. You owe me," the dowdy old lady shrieked.

"How's that? I rescued you when you passed out on the street last year," Tom replied.

"You and Harry the Horse playing ball and making noise right below my window on Pulaski Avenue," she complained, ignoring Amon.

Rather than argue with the drunken dowager, Tom ordered a whiskey from Rudy Kaffman. Seizing the whiskey-filled tumbler, Granny Schmidt downed it in one big gulp, belched loudly, farted explosively, and walked out of the saloon.

"Talk about issues. That lady has a disorder," Amon observed.

"At least Granny could pass Lyndon Johnson's IQ test," Tom remarked.

"What in heaven's name is that?" Amon inquired.

"She can walk and fart at the same time," Tom snapped.

Getting up from his stool, Amon turned to Tom. "I've seen enough. It's time to leave this zoo."

Gulping his Ballantine beer, Tom followed his friend and emerged from the hot hazy bar to the fresh balmy air of the May evening. The young science teacher had to walk fast to keep up with his impetuous friend.

"My time is running out, and there's so much to do," he murmured.

Poetry Lesson

Tom walked into the Curtis High School front entrance, scarcely noticing the limestone gargoyles looming overhead. At one time, those fierce stone creatures frightened the rookie teacher, but the sight of Lou Stout at the front door gave him pause. The burly principal was clutching some papers that looked like lecture notes.

"Don't tell me. I see a class coverage in my future."

"It's a lesson on poetry, courtesy of Mrs. Hannity, who has the flu," the heavyset administrator replied in a businesslike manner.

"What the hell do I know about poetry?"

"About as much as you know about history, but it didn't stop you from doing a good job," Lou replied, handing Tom some notes from the absent teacher.

"You and Mrs. Hannity owe me big-time. Too bad she isn't good-looking," Tom said grimly.

"If Mrs. Hannity was good-looking, I'd cover her classes myself," Lou Stout replied with a Cheshire cat smile.

Huffing and puffing after climbing to the third floor, Tom walked into a chorus of boos and hoorays from the students, many of whom were recognizable from his science classes. The irrepressible Barry was talking to Wendy, the long-haired nubile teenager; the bespectacled Riner was perusing his poetry book; the naive Ronnie was looking over her notes; Lora was playing with her copper bracelets; and Manny was slouching in the back of the classroom. Shuffling through his notes, Tom wrote the aim on the board: "What is the value of poetry?"

"Chuck the poetry, and do one of your famous experiments," Manny called out from the back of the room.

"Yeah. This is faggot stuff. Nobody goes around reciting poetry — unless he's crazy or on drugs," Barry exclaimed.

"Poetry is a waste of time. It's frivolous," Riner concurred.

Tom almost concurred. He had read somewhere that poetry costs money, but he persevered. Glancing at Mrs. Hannity's notes, he read, "Poetry brings down walls. For poetry, people have been jailed, whipped, and even killed."

"Anything can happen when people get bored," Barry retorted.

"Here are some lines from well-known poems," Tom said, proceeding to read from his notes:

"Pride goeth before destruction, and a haughty spirit before a
fall."
"She has a heart too soon made glad."
"How like a serpent's tooth an ungrateful child!"
"They serve who only stand and wait."
"Let us be up and doing with a heart for any fate."
"Shall I compare thee to a summer's day?"

"That line about a girl's heart becoming glad too soon reminds me of someone in this room," Manny called out, pointing to Lora.

"You give off bad vibrations," Lora replied, pointing her finger back at him and shaking her copper bracelets.

"My mom tells me I'm ungrateful, but she never said I was a serpent's tooth. She just says I'm a pain in the ass," Barry complained.

"Here's a poem by William Blake. Tell me what you think: 'He who would do good to another must do it in minute particulars.

General good is the plea of the scoundrel, hypocrite, and flatterer.'"

"I disagree. I would never give any money to a beggar or panhandler," Riner exclaimed. Several others in the class concurred with the mild-mannered boy's scrooge-like sentiment.

Tom thought about all the times he gave money to street people, especially alcoholics, whom he connected to his father. He felt that such spontaneous generosity brought him good luck in life.

Changing the theme, Tom read the following lines from Shakespeare:

> Shall I compare you to a summer's day?
> Thou art more lovely and more temperate:
> Rough winds do shake the darling buds of May.
> But thy eternal summer shall not fade.

"That's very lovely, Mr. Haley. I wish guys were into poetry. All they care about is screwing!" Lora complained.

"Send her to the dean for obscene language," Barry called out, wagging his finger at the provocative teenager.

Ignoring the obstreperous youngster, Tom read another excerpt:

> April is the cruelest month, breeding
> Lilacs out of dead land, mixing
> Memory and desire, stirring
> Dull roots with spring rain."

"It's from The Waste Land by T. S. Eliot," Tom said, reading his notes.

"That's a very exciting poem. Like watching paint dry on a wall. Or my dumb neighbor raking leaves on a windy day," Manny called out.

Tom read another poem, written by E. Y. Harburg during the Great Depression:

> Once I built a railroad, I made it run,
> Made it race against time.
> Once I built a railroad, now it's done.
> Brother, can you spare a dime?"

"I like that poem because it tells a story. Though it's a sad story," Ronnie remarked.

"Here's another poem about iceberg lettuce, by Gerald Locklin: 'At any rate, I really enjoy a salad with plenty of chunky iceberg lettuce, the more the merrier, drenched in an italian or roquefort dressing.'"

"Now, who in their right mind would write a poem about lettuce?" Riner asked.

"Riner! I'm shocked at your negative attitude toward poetry," Barry said with a straight face.

"Riner's right. Poetry is just a bunch of words that sound pretty but doesn't mean anything," Manny called out from the back of the class.

"I disagree. Words are the key to meaning in our lives. Just think about it: love versus hate, friend versus enemy, good versus evil, peace versus war," Wendy replied.

"Excellent, Wendy. I couldn't have said it better myself. Poetry can bring down walls. Poets and writers have gone to jail because of their words," Tom said, reading from Mrs. Hannity's notes.

Next, Tom read the three witches' lines from Shakespeare's Macbeth:

> Where hast thou been, sister?
> Killing swine
> Sister, where thou?

A sailor's wife had chestnuts in her lap,
And munch'd, and munch'd, and munch'd —
But in a sieve I'll thither sail,
And like a rat without a tail,
I'll do, I'll do, and I'll do."

"Man, that stuff makes no sense at all," Barry proclaimed, gathering his books and getting ready to leave the room.

Lora raised her hand, jingling the copper bracelets on her arm. "Here's a poem dedicated to Mr. Haley: Roses are bright red, daffodils are quite yellow. My teacher is boring, but he's a nice fellow."

As the class cheered and applauded Lora's ditty, the bell rang, and the class disbanded. Lora smiled as she left the room, her copper bracelets and anklets jingling poetically in the long, narrow hallway.

CHAPTER 45

Rescue at Sea

Without anything planned for Saturday night, Tom decided to drive Amon and Mary to St. George, where they would walk to the ferry for a pleasant ride to Lower Manhattan. Amon was neatly dressed in a plaid lumberjack shirt and clean dungarees. Under Mary's solicitous tutelage, Amon had been dressing better on their dates. Like Tom, he paid little attention to his wardrobe unless pressured by the fairer sex to look presentable on a date.

Parking on Hamilton Avenue, near Curtis High School, the three young people stopped to admire the school's impressive facade, with its fierce sandstone gargoyles. In his early years at Curtis, Tom would hurry into the school, trying to avoid a look at the grimacing creatures.

"Those stone goblins are interesting. Wouldn't you say so, Mary?" Amon said, pointing toward the school, which was a North Shore landmark.

"Rather garish and probably paganistic, I would assume," Mary said, eyeballing them with strained curiosity.

"You remind me of Martha — always on guard for signs of heathen influences," Tom remarked.

"Not at all. There's something to be said for paganism. Wouldn't you agree?" she replied, turning to Amon.

"I respect all religious persuasions. No one faith is better than any other."

"Speaking of pagans, how is my old flame Martha doing? Still keeping her pupils in line with her fiery temper and her iron fist?" Tom asked, trying to sound matter-of-fact. He missed her large voluptuous presence, especially on Saturday nights.

"Martha quit St. Mary's. She got a job teaching in the public schools—PS 21."

"For real? PS 21 was the first school my sister and I went to on Staten Island," Tom mentioned.

"I can see you there with Cara, hanging out in that school yard with a pretty curly-haired girl, memorizing a poem for some kind of a recital," Amon said.

"There you go again. The Mariners Harbor clairvoyant at work."

"I call him the Mariners Harbor Messiah," Mary cooed, throwing her arm around his waste.

"I'd give my right arm for that kind of insight into the past and even the future," the skinny science teacher replied.

"It's an unwelcome gift, but my vision of the future is clouded at best."

Boarding the large orange-hued ferry, the threesome looked out across the bay toward the distant Manhattan skyline, with its vaunted skyscrapers dominated by the newly erected World Trade Center towers. Under John Lindsay's spirited leadership, "fun city" had experienced a building boom, a business resurgence, and a cultural renaissance. The big rumbling ferry, rocking with the strong currents, barreled out of the ferry slip, bouncing off the weathered docks, which reminded Tom of the old docks of the Mariners Harbor waterfront.

Sitting on the outside of the boat's second level, Tom noticed a face from the past. It was Perry Pantino, an old Port Richmond High School classmate.

Tom took leave of his two friends to accost Perry, whom he hadn't seen in many years. The years had changed Perry's appearance in added weight, long hair, and a scruffy beard. His dark eyes darted back and forth, never focusing on one object for very long.

"How are you doing, Perry? Long time no see," Tom called to his former classmate.

"I'm okay. I haven't seen you since those long friggin' subway rides to City College," Perry replied, looking toward the choppy waters of the bay with bulging eyes.

"Yeah. That Seventh Avenue IRT was the subway from hell," Tom concurred.

"That's why I quit going there, plus those queer professors. I had this goofy English professor with a goatee — looked like that Flash Gordon villain, Ming."

Turning to Amon, Tom introduced Perry to the Mariners Harbor resident.

"I couldn't stand those fuckin' faggots at City College. Can you blame me?"

"Live and let live. That's my motto. We're all God's children after all," Amon replied, studying Perry closely.

"What are you? Some kind of a preacher or some kind of a nut?" Perry asked with undisguised hostility.

"A little of both. We do what we can and give what we have," Amon intoned diplomatically.

"Butt out! I don't want anything from you," Perry yelled with sudden fury. Then he left the two young men abruptly without any good-byes.

"That's not the Perry I used to know," Tom said. "He was always making jokes, followed by a high-pitched cackle. Kind of a happy-go-lucky guy."

"He doesn't look like a happy customer to me," Mary offered, watching the peculiar young man as he walked to the other side of the boat. His gait was rapid, and he seemed to be nodding his head, as if conversing with an invisible sidekick.

"Keep your eyes on him, Mary. He's in trouble — that's for sure," Amon replied in an undertone.

"His parents used to have a deli on Richmond Avenue near DeNinno's Pizzeria. I think he had a younger sister — don't recall her name. They were a close-knit family. Once some wise guy came into the store and harassed Perry's mom when she accused him of stealing something. Perry beat the crap out of him. After that, nobody disrespected his mom — or his dad, for that matter."

"He seems like a person who's had some setbacks in life. Wears his heart on his sleeve," Mary said, looking over to the other side of the ferry.

"The only difference between an average person and a troubled person is the intensity of his feelings," Amon commented.

"You're right," Tom said. "I've gone through rough times when things looked pretty shitty. You look for a way out, and there's isn't any."

"Going through tough times can make you stronger. Sometimes a little misfortune is good," Amon replied, signaling to Mary to follow Perry in his peculiar meandering around the outside aisles of the ferry.

Mary sauntered to the other side of the boat, looking at the Statue of Liberty, which appeared through the windows. She gave the strange young man a cursory glance, pretending indifference to his frenetic wandering. Suddenly, Perry climbed over the outside railing and stood on the ferry's ledge, which overlooked the pounding waves surging by the boat. Screaming, Mary rushed over to him and grabbed his shirt. Shaking loose from the young woman's grip, the desperate young man leaped into the churning water.

Stirred by his girlfriend's scream, Amon sprang into action, tossing off his shoes and his lumberjack shirt and diving off the rail of the ferry into the turbulent greenish-blue water. Tom grabbed a roped flotation doughnut, which was anchored to the boat via a thick iron ring. A powerful swimmer, Amon was within a few feet of Perry, who was thrashing frantically in the rough sea. Within seconds, Amon had collared the unhappy young man and swam back toward the boat, where he grabbed the doughnut. Tom and another male passenger tugged desperately on the rope, slowly pulling it toward the ferry. By this time, deckhands had arrived on the scene, lowering a rowboat to the floundering twosome.

Arriving in New York City, the three friends were interviewed by the police, while the victim was placed in an ambulance and taken to Bellevue Hospital in Lower Manhattan. Perry appeared subdued and remorseful. He had attempted to apologize to Amon before being taken away, but the medics wouldn't allow it.

Amon did manage to go over to Perry, and the two spoke quietly for a few minutes. As with all mishaps and calamities, newspaper reporters appeared suddenly on the scene, plying the modest young man with questions. A grizzled reporter turned to Mary, who was holding Amon's hand, for her reaction to his heroic actions on the Staten Island ferry.

"This was a typical day for my boyfriend. He's always helping people, especially the poor and the downtrodden," Mary related to the reporter.

"He's rescued people from fires, fed the hungry, provided a home for the homeless. You name it, Amon's done it," Tom chimed in.

"On Staten island, he's known as the Mariners Harbor Messiah," Mary added, to Amon's chagrin.

"Mariners Harbor Messiah, you say? That's kind of catchy," the veteran reporter said, writing furiously on his pad.

Pumpkin Pie

Walking to the front entrance of Curtis High School and barely noticing the limestone gargoyles grimacing from the school's distinctive facade, Tom caught sight of the principal, Lou Stout. He held some notes carefully collected from an absent pedagogue.

"Just tell me it's not a poetry lesson from the semi-beautiful Mrs. Hannity.

"No, it's something you're comfortable with—a lesson on decimals, courtesy of Dr. Gootstein," the burly administrator replied.

"Goody Gootstein. He hates the thought of my having a free period to relax and mull over my lesson plans."

"We all know you use the same dog-eared lesson plans that you wrote up as a rookie teacher."

"How can you improve on perfection? All my lessons start off with a bang," Tom retorted.

"Yeah. Half the time the entire science wing is filled with fumes, or you burn your suit jacket from one of your practical experiments."

"Hell, that's the fun of it. I like to break up the humdrum routine of teaching. When the sparks fly from a botched experiment, a teacher blowup, or student fisticuffs, that's when it gets interesting," Tom said.

"No. I don't want the unexpected. Just give me dull, boring, uneventful days. The big shots at the Board of Education don't want surprises either. Remember, there is no learning without discipline," Stout replied before heading back to his large, sofa-chaired, picture-filled office.

Looking over Dr. Gootstein's notes, Tom was happy to learn he would be teaching math basics—decimals and fractions. The prospect of spending his prep period poring over advanced algebra or trigonometry notes would not have made him happy—not that he was lacking in scholarly interest in academic areas outside of science. On the contrary, the skinny science teacher enjoyed studying diverse subjects, from science to mathematics, history, and even literature. He wondered how he would motivate such a basic topic as fraction–decimal conversions. Then, an offbeat notion struck him: the way to a student's mind is through his stomach.

Bursting into the remedial math class, Tom was greeted by a chorus of Bronx cheers. However, when the motley group of teenagers saw that the popular science teacher was carrying a large pumpkin pie, the boos turned to actual cheers.

Tom was also happy to observe familiar faces in the room—all of whom had their eyes focused on the jumbo-size pumpkin pie, which had just emerged from the oven of the teacher's cafeteria. The chief cook of the Curtis High School cafeteria, Maggie, had hurriedly baked the pie—induced by a sizable tip and her connection to Tom as a fellow Elm Park resident.

Waving her hand, which jingled with the pretty teenager's copper bracelets, Lora asked if she could cut the pie for the skinny young teacher. Tom said that he would do the honors. Setting the jumbo-size pie carefully on his desk, he wrote the aim of the lesson on the blackboard: "What are fraction–decimal conversions?"

"We already know about fractions and decimals. How about doing a practical experiment, like setting off one of your match-head rockets?" Riner complained.

Ignoring the student's complaint, Tom asked the class to define fractions.

"Fractions represent parts of a whole. If you cut that pie into four parts, each part is one-fourth of the pie," Wendy replied.

"Very good, Wendy. What are the two kinds of fractions?"

Barry raised his hand. "Polite and vulgar."

"Very funny. The two kinds of fractions are proper and improper," Ronnie responded.

"How do proper and improper fractions differ?" Tom inquired.

"Proper fractions have numerators that are smaller than the denominators. And improper fractions have numerators that are larger than the denominators," Wendy answered.

"Mr. Haley, this is stuff we learned in elementary school. Our regular math teacher was doing signed numbers," Riner declared in an annoyed manner.

"What's the matter? Are fractions beneath you? You wouldn't be able to follow a recipe without knowing about fractions," Barry snapped at the studious boy.

"I still hate fractions," Lora responded.

"Suppose somebody offered you half a million dollars? Would you turn him down because you hate fractions?" Tom asked the winsome youngster.

"You have a point there, Mr. Haley. I'd spend the money quick to get rid of the annoying fraction," she replied dryly.

Turning to the board, Tom wrote out the following problem: "4.5 x 5.25."

The students struggled over the problem before realizing they had to convert the mixed numbers to improper fractions in order to multiply them. And then they had to convert the answer back to a mixed number.

"Why is it necessary to change improper fractions back to mixed numbers?" Lora asked petulantly.

"Would you go to a butcher shop and ask for 5/2 pounds of chop meat? He wouldn't know what you meant. But if you had said 2.5 pounds, there'd be no misunderstanding," Tom offered.

"So you're saying butchers are stupid? My uncle is a butcher," Manny called out from the back of the room.

"I would never insult a person with a cleaver," Tom snapped. "But moving on, let's talk about those important numbers called decimals."

"What's so important about them?" Lora asked, fiddling with her copper ankle bracelets, which caused several of the boys to stare at her shapely ankles and calves.

"Well, if you like money. Our money system is based on decimals. A penny is 1/100 of a dollar, a nickel is 5/100, a dime 10/100, a quarter is 25/100 of a dollar, and a half-dollar is 50/100 of a dollar," Tom replied, going to the blackboard.

Coin / Fraction of Dollar / Decimal Value
Penny / 1/100 / $0.01
Nickel / 5/100 / $0.05
Dime / 10/100 / $0.10
Quarter / 25/100 / $0.25
Half-Dollar / 50/100 / $0.50
Dollar / 100/100 / $1.00

"Come on, Mr. Haley. Let's do something besides money, which is the root of all evil," Ronnie complained.

"But it is a necessary evil. Without it we would be living on the street," Lora replied, fiddling with her copper armbands.

"Yeah. If you had money, you'd be wearing gold bracelets instead of those dumb copper bracelets on your arms and legs," Barry retorted.

Wagging her hands and shaking her legs, Lora started to say something about the sexual benefits of wearing copper, but upon further thought said nothing.

"It's interesting when we look at ancient civilizations and their use of different metals. The metal bronze, which is a mixture of copper and tin, was used in Africa and the Middle East about four thousand years ago. Whereas iron was first used in China, India, and the Middle East about three thousand years ago," Tom explained.

"When man first used bronze, it was called the Bronze Age, and when people started using iron, it was called the Iron Age," Riner observed, having overcome his boredom with the topic of the day.

Tom took advantage of this brief interlude to introduce the English and metric systems of measurement. "In the areas of science, engineering, and construction, we need an accurate system of weights and measures."

Turning to the board, the skinny teacher wrote down the following information.

English System	Metric System
Length	
12 inches = 1 foot	10 millimeters = 1 centimeter
3 feet = 1 yard	100 centimeters = 1 meter
660 feet = 1 furlong	100 meters = 1 hectometer
5,280 feet = 1 mile	1,000 meters = 1 kilometer
Weight	
480 grains = 1 ounce	1,000 milligrams = 1 gram
16 ounces = 1 pound	10 grams = 1 decagram
100 pounds = 1 hundredwt	100 grams = 1 hectogram
1,000 pounds = 1 ton	1,000 grams = 1 kilogram

"Getting back to fractions and decimals, it's often useful to convert fractions into decimals. How is that conversion done?" Tom inquired.

Wendy raised her hand. "You divide the numerator by the denominator."

"Very good. Everybody convert the fraction 5/8 into a decimal."

The class performed the indicated division, coming up with the answer: 0.625.

Tom went over the decimal equivalents of the basic fractions 1/2, 1/4, and 3/4. He went on to explain that not all fractions convert into exact decimals. Some fractions convert into repeating decimals. He then had the class convert 1/3 and 2/3 into decimals.

Barry raised his hand. "The first one is 0.3333 repeating, and the second one is 0.6666 repeating, which is a sign of the devil. I wouldn't mess with 2/3 if I were you. Especially if you go around with those devilish copper bracelets."

"What are you talking about? Copper is a good luck metal, unlike silver and gold," Lora replied indignantly.

"We're getting off topic. How can you tell if a fraction will convert into an exact decimal or one of those scary repeating decimals?"

Riner raised his hand. "A fraction is exact only if its denominator can be converted into a power of ten."

"Excellent, Riner!" Going to the blackboard, Tom did the following computations:

$$1/2 \times 50/50 = 50/100 = 0.5$$
$$3/4 \times 25/25 = 75/100 = 0.75$$
$$5/8 \times 125/125 = 625/1000 = 0.625$$

"It's clear why these fractions are exact decimals and not repeating decimals."

"My favorite fraction is 23/33 because it converts to the decimal 0.696969," Manny called out from the back of the room.

"You're disgusting!" Lora exclaimed as the bell rang, mercifully ending Tom's lesson on fractions and decimals.

Everyone helped themselves to a small piece of the pumpkin pie that the skinny teacher had brought up from the cafeteria — everybody except Lora, who stormed out of the class with her copper bracelets jingling loudly.

CHAPTER 47

Food Drive

As a two-and-a-half–year veteran of teaching, Tom was aware of the economic status of his students. Nearly half of Curtis's students qualified for the free-lunch program. Working in the student cafeteria, the skinny science teacher knew that much of this free food was dumped into the trash receptacles at the end of lunch period. Whether this was due to the poor quality of the hot lunches or willful teenage wastefulness, it was hard to determine. Nevertheless, there was a connection between cognition and malnutrition. Tom had done a master's thesis on the relationship between a low-protein diet and maze-learning ability in rats. After running the white rats through a maze, he found that rats raised with adequate protein could run the maze with fewer mistakes.

With the Thanksgiving holiday approaching, Tom began soliciting faculty and student contributions toward purchasing food for holiday gift baskets. The holiday food baskets were actually cardboard boxes filled with canned goods, cereal, rice, and canned hams and turkeys. The idea originated with Tom himself, but Curtis principal Lou Stout took credit for the program. And Tom was wise enough not to intrude on the administrator's glory for this worthy program benefiting Curtis's impoverished students.

A few days later, Tom mentioned to his friend Amon the annual food-basket drive that was under way at Curtis High School. The latter said he would get the residents of the Victorian house on Simonson Avenue to donate some canned goods for the drive.

Tom indicated he was hesitant to involve these folks who had little to offer but good intentions.

"It has been said that those who give will be given back generously. Indeed, it is a bountiful world we live in," Amon responded.

"Sounds like someone has been reading the Bible," Tom observed. Yet experience told him that poor people were more generous than the wealthy.

"Enduring the slings and arrows of outrageous fortune, I seek the comfort of Him whose suffering makes my plight seem trivial."

"What's going on? Has there been some more trouble from the local people?" Tom asked, recalling the bullet that had glazed Amon's shoulder the year before. He worried about his friend, as well as Mary, who spent weekends in his refurbished tugboat helping him. Mary's loyalty to this young man, whom she lovingly called her "Messiah," was boundless.

After a few weeks of the food drive, Tom and his peers at Curtis had accumulated two dozen cartons of canned goods, including canned hams and frozen turkeys. Understanding Amon's predicament, Tom hesitated to involve his friend in the endeavor. A phone call from Mary reminded the skinny science teacher never to doubt his charismatic friend's ability to go beyond the expectations of ordinary human beings.

"Tom, you have to help us get this food to your Curtis students. There's barely room for us to move around here," she exclaimed.

"We're starting tomorrow. It would be great if Amon could help deliver the food baskets. I think he'd make a nice impression on the students."

Hanging up the phone, Tom wondered if his friend had performed another one of his quasi miracles. Maybe he multiplied the stockpiled food by a wave of a magic wand he had hidden away somewhere in his boat.

The operation of delivering the food baskets was accomplished by teacher–student teams who worked on the Wednesday afternoon prior to Thanksgiving. Tom was teamed up with Barry, the outspoken teenager who stirred the pedagogical pot in his general science class. Amon was teamed up with Lora, the jangling wearer of copper bracelets and anklets. Barry was unusually quiet as Tom drove through the hilly streets of St. George to the first family on the list provided by Curtis's grade advisers.

Arriving at a ramshackle house on Westervelt Avenue, Barry mounted the rickety front porch steps with the food basket, accompanied by the skinny teacher. After trying the doorbell, the youngster knocked on the front door, which was opened by an elderly black woman who appeared perplexed by the visit. Barry mumbled something about a present from Curtis High School.

The wizened woman was beside herself with gratitude, shaking Tom's hand and kissing Barry on the cheek, to his surprise and consternation. After placing the heavy package into the woman's hand, Barry ran back to the car while Tom exchanged pleasantries with the grateful lady. Back in the car, Tom drove a few blocks toward Jersey Street, where he pulled up at an old brick apartment house. Growing up in the working-class neighborhood of Elm Park, Tom was accustomed to dreary streets, but this New Brighton area was totally run-down.

The two of them walked along the cracked sidewalk, bordered by crabgrass and weeds, and trod up the creaking stairs, huffing and puffing as they reached the front door and knocked loudly.

A disheveled Spanish woman opened the door, accompanied by a frisky toddler who wrested the food basket from Barry. He began searching the basket for something to eat — obviously a candy bar. Fortunately, Tom anticipated this scenario and produced a Hershey bar, which the rude child grabbed and gobbled in a few big bites.

"Somebody's got a sweet tooth," Barry exclaimed in a friendly tone.

"Sorry, Jacobo loves chocolate more than anything," the young woman said.

"That's quite all right, ma'am. We're all guilty of that affliction," Tom replied.

Walking down the rickety stairs, Barry asked his teacher if he had another Hershey bar. Giving him the treat, Tom suggested they stop at McDonald's for a bite to eat, to which the youngster readily agreed.

Meanwhile, Amon was accompanied by Lora, the copper bracelet lass, on his food basket route in New Brighton. The curly-haired teenager was nervous in the presence of the good-looking charismatic young man. Amon borrowed Mary's car to deliver the items to several needy Curtis families stipulated on the list. As they drove to the first destination off Bay Street, Amon quietly asked Lora to refrain from rattling her copper bracelets and anklets.

"I'm not familiar with this part of the Island. So I'm just as nervous as you are. Just think of the good we're doing in giving food to the needy."

"It's just my way. My moms is always telling me to stop fidgeting," Lora replied, examining some green tarnish on one of her bracelets.

"I'll bet Mr. Haley explained why copper changes into a greenish veneer after exposure to air and moisture."

"Yeah. He said copper forms a compound called verdigris on its surface. He told us the Statue of Liberty and the roof of Curtis High School are made of copper."

"It could be worse. If your bracelet was iron, it would rust. And if it was silver, it would turn black from tarnish," Amon explained.

"That's all I need. Wearing black metal bands on your arms and legs is a sign of the devil," she exclaimed, showing him her arms and legs inadvertently. Keeping his eyes on the road, Amon turned the car onto a narrow rut-filled, tree-lined street with run-down Victorian houses set back on weedy lots.

Checking his neatly typed list, Amon said this was their first house. The two of them got out of the car, with Lora carrying the food basket, jangling her bracelets and anklets all the while.

"There's one thing for sure, Lora. You'll never be able to sneak up on anybody."

"My moms is always telling me the very same thing, Mr. Amon."

"At the risk of sounding pedantic, the word is *mom* — not *moms*."

"You remind me of Mr. Haley. But you're a lot cooler," she offered.

"Your science teacher is a very special person, Lora."

"Yes, he's great. There's only one thing wrong with him."

"What's that?"

"He's a teacher. You know, they're different from normal people," she replied, fiddling with her copper bracelets and anklets.

Climbing the stoop of the front porch, the twosome had to tread lightly due to some loose floorboards. The screen door had gaping holes, and the doorbell hung from the facade by means of exposed wires. The stark squalor of this ancient edifice gave pause to Amon and his youthful companion. Lora began to knock tentatively on the door, as if she was afraid to damage the splintered front door.

Shaking his head, Amon knocked on the door loudly, calling out, "Is anybody home? We're making a food basket delivery here."

After waiting a few minutes, the strapping young man and the curly-haired teenager turned and walked gingerly down the rickety steps. Suddenly, the front door swung open to reveal a straggly-haired blonde woman and her towheaded little girl.

Smiling at the child, Lora announced that they were "delivering food baskets—paid for by Curtis students in honor of Thanksgiving."

"Why, that's such a nice gesture. Tell all the Curtis kids that I thank them from the bottom of my heart." Turning to the little girl, she said, "What do you say, Sally?"

The cute towhead did not speak at first. Noticing Lora's copper bracelets, she reached out and touched a bracelet. "Can I have one?"

Amon whispered to the teenager, "Give and it will be given to you."

The bracelet-wearing Curtis sophomore hesitated momentarily and sighed. A gentle breeze rustled through her curly hair, and a sparrow alighted on the front stoop momentarily.

"Sure, sweetie. My moms makes them for me. They're easily replaced." Handing one of her shiny bracelets to the child, Lora wished her a happy Thanksgiving.

As they descended the rickety stairs, Amon gave the youngster a hug. He murmured how proud he was of the pretty teenager, who managed to walk without jangling her copper bracelets and anklets.

Catching Amon by surprise, Lora asked the charismatic young man if he was afraid of dying. Pausing for a moment, he replied, "We all have that fear. But then I remember a passage from the Bible: 'I am the resurrection and the life, saith the Lord: he that believeth in me shall never die.'"

CHAPTER 48

Herculean Tug

A few weeks later, Tom took Amon shopping for some winter clothes—a coat, a hat, scarves, gloves, and some work boots—at the army-navy surplus store on Richmond Avenue. Tom insisted on paying for the clothes, overcoming the Mariners Harbor resident's objections.

"I haven't been around to help you lately. This is the least I can do."

The two young men emerged from the store carrying several bundles of clothing and walked along Richmond Avenue, which was decorated with red and green lights, holly wreaths, and silver bunting—befitting the upcoming Christmas holiday. Since his early days on Staten Island as a wide-eyed twelve-year-old, Tom always associated Christmas with the bustling Port Richmond shopping area.

These quaint family businesses were the places he spent his meager paperboy income to buy holiday gifts for his congenial sister, Cara, and his hard-to-please mother. The holiday music emanating from loudspeakers enhanced the festive mood of local North Shore residents, who threw themselves wholeheartedly into the upcoming holiday.

Suddenly, the squealing sound of a car coming to an abrupt stop interrupted the two friends' holiday musings. A beat-up 1960s sedan had come to a stop after striking a female pedestrian. The woman was lying precariously under the sizable car, trying to free herself from the front wheel, writhing and moaning in pain. A puddle of blood oozed from beneath the car along the pavement. Instantly, Amon dropped his packages and ran to the car, with Tom following him, discarding his bundles one by one as he arrived at the scene of the accident.

With a herculean tug, Amon lifted the full-size car — which was an old DeSoto — allowing the injured woman to slide her bleeding leg from under the front wheel. Tom gave Amon his handkerchief, with which he wrapped the victim's ankle to staunch her bleeding. The charismatic young man murmured soothing words to the injured woman as he gently stroked her forehead and cheeks. Almost immediately, the woman (whose name was Evette) stopped moaning and rested serenely — apparently free of distress and out of pain.

Fortunately, passersby notified the owner of Kresge's, who promptly called an ambulance. Within a few minutes the ambulance arrived, and the woman was taken to St. Vincent's Hospital, off Castleton Avenue in West Brighton. Later on in the evening, the two young men visited Evette, a black woman in her thirties. Coincidentally, she lived In Mariners Harbor — on the crest of Union Avenue, where it overlooks the defunct North Shore branch of the Staten Island Railroad. Miraculously, she had suffered only lacerations and bruises on her legs. There were no broken bones, concussions, or other trauma.

"The good Lord was looking after me today. When that big old car barreled into me, I thought that my life was over," Evette exclaimed feverishly.

"I don't know how that driver hit you. He must have been distracted," Tom said.

"And I wasn't looking either. You know how it is this time of the year. By the way, how did you lift that car?" she asked.

"That was just adrenaline. Fortunately, the driver wasn't going very fast. And you're one tough lady," Amon observed

"As soon as you stroked my cheek and talked to me, I felt a lot better. Young man, I swear, you have that golden touch," she whispered reverently.

"It just wasn't your time, Evette. God has plans for you," Amon asserted matter-of-factly as the woman looked up at him wide-eyed.

"My friend is a determinist. He believes that everything that occurs in life is for a reason, according to some grand scheme," Tom declared wryly.

"So what's the plan?" the woman asked, looking from Tom to Amon with a mixture of awe and fear.

Alcoholics Anonymous

In 1955, Alcoholics Anonymous was officially turned over by its founders, Bill Wilson and Dr. Robert Smith, to elected representatives from AA groups throughout the United States and Canada. Born in Vermont in 1895, Bill Wilson was raised by his maternal grandparents after his parents were divorced and his mother moved to Boston to study osteopathy. At age eighteen, Wilson suffered a nervous breakdown when his childhood sweetheart died from a botched surgery to remove a tumor. Notwithstanding the Wilson family history of excessive drinking, Bill Wilson took his first drink at age twenty-two, after enlisting in the army as an artillery officer. The magic of those first few drinks led him to an addiction to alcohol, which plagued him for the next seventeen years of his life. Bill Wilson discovered that he loved drinking, especially in social situations.

After the war, Bill Wilson became a successful stockbroker on Wall Street until the stock market crash of 1929. The 1920s was the era of Prohibition, when the sale and use of liquor was illegal in America. A habitual drinker, Wilson found ways to get around the law, fermenting grapes at home to make liquor or going to an after-hours speakeasy where bootleg whiskey was served. During the day on Wall Street, Wilson would abstain from drinking. But once the stock market closed at 3:00 p.m., he would drink himself into a stupor, crawling home with no memory of where he'd been. Repeatedly Bill Wilson wrote pledges (in the family Bible) to his long-suffering wife, Lois, promising to give up drinking. Over the years, he lost many well-paid jobs, and his reputation as a shrewd market analyst was eroded by his drinking problem. The investment company Wheeler and Winans forced Bill Wilson to sign a no-drinking contract before hiring him, which he soon violated.

Alcoholics are adept at hiding their addiction. They can pull themselves together, take long showers, act smarter, and be more alive than most people. Alcoholics have to be one step ahead of their cohorts. There is psychic energy to keeping their addiction secret. Nevertheless, by 1934, Bill Wilson had hit rock bottom. Desperate, he exclaimed, "If there be a God, let him show himself!" Suddenly, the room blazed with an indescribable white light, and he was seized with ecstasy. "You are a free man!" A profound change took place, and Bill Wilson never drank again for the rest of his life.

Actually, Bill Wilson and his friend Dr. Robert Smith made the fundamental discovery that a group of alcoholics talking about their drinking problem was more effective than the lone alcoholic, in a moment of remorse, promising never to drink again. Wilson realized that "he needed the alcoholic as much as he needed me." He also understood that each alcoholic has his own drinking story and his own road to sobriety. Bill Wilson and Dr. Robert Smith founded Alcoholics Anonymous on June 10, 1935 — built on the concepts of group conscience, total honesty, anonymity (first names only), humility (no leaders), restitution (to family and friends), spirituality (seeking God's help), and service to fellow alcoholics. The two founders insisted that AA function as a network of autonomous groups with no leaders and no accumulation of money or power. The only requirement for membership in Alcoholics Anonymous was the desire to stop drinking.

By the late 1960s, after years of smoking, Bill Wilson's lungs were clogged with tar and he was dying of emphysema. He needed an oxygen tank to get through the day. By the fall of 1970, Wilson had gone to bed permanently with round-the-clock nurses, plus his wife, Lois, attending him. A measure of the power of alcohol was illustrated through his deathbed request of three shots of whiskey. When turned down, Wilson became upset and belligerent. Most alcoholics never stop wanting to drink. They love to drink — it works for them. Through all his ups and downs in life, Bill Wilson developed a pragmatic philosophy: "Life is just a day in school. All our experiences are but lessons in some form or other which condition us to a larger destiny. It's a problem world. What matters, and what only matters, is what we do with the problems."

CHAPTER 49

M & M's

In late November, Tom passed under the gruesome limestone gargoyles, noticing Curtis's hefty principal, Lou Stout, shuffling though some notes.

"Don't tell me. Somebody decided to go Christmas shopping, and I have the joy of covering one of his or her classes," Tom said in a sarcastic tone.

"Don't be a Scrooge. 'Tis the season to be jolly. It's a basic arithmetic class, courtesy of Dr. Gootstein," the administrator replied calmly.

"So whose class am I covering?" the skinny science teacher inquired.

"Mrs. Murray's arithmetic class. You know Rosie Murray? The one with the big ass," Stout said with an evil smile.

"Put me on your naughty-and-nice Christmas list, because you owe me, big-time," Tom said, snatching the notes from Lou Stout and heading for the time clock, which was decorated with mistletoe and holly.

What a waste, he thought. If there was one good-looking female teacher at Curtis, it was the unavailable Mrs. Murray. He often fantasized smothering her with holiday kisses and grabbing her nice round butt. At least she'd give him a nice smile the next time he encountered her in the hallways.

Later on, Tom marched into the remedial math class, grimacing resolutely and clutching Dr. Gootstein's notes on ratios and rates.

The skinny teacher recognized that it was the same arithmetic class he had covered a few weeks earlier, with familiar faces from his general science class. Familiarity breeds not contempt but a comforting sense of the routine for the classroom teacher. Aside from the usual pleas for a free period, the class grudgingly got out their math notebooks and settled down.

Tom produced a big jar of M&M's, which immediately grabbed the attention of the youngsters. Truthfully, average teenagers are motivated to learn not from their intrinsic curiosity about the world but from such extrinsic rewards as money, tangible items, and passing grades. Notwithstanding the idealists of the world, like his friend Amon, most people are motivated by self-interest, greed, and material wants.

"Mr. Haley, can I have some of those M&M's? I didn't eat them nasty sloppy joes they make on Mondays," Barry said, staring at the jar.

"First, we're going to have a lesson on ratios and rates. Work before rewards."

"What are we, Pavlov's dogs, learning how to salivate when the bell is rung?" Riner observed petulantly.

"Only a pencil-head like you would know about Pavlov's dogs," Ronnie said.

"Ronnie! I'm surprised by that comment. Usually you're nicer than nice," the skinny teacher replied.

"Sorry, Mr. Haley. It's been a long, hard day. We had to write this boring composition in English about the real meaning of Christmas," the naive youngster complained.

"Anyway, the task before us is to figure out the ratio of red M&M's to blue M&M's. How can we do it?"

"That's easy. Just pour them out on your desk and count 'em," Barry replied.

"That would take too long. Just take out a few handfuls and count them. They look to be evenly distributed in the jar," Wendy responded.

"Excellent, Wendy. We can see that the red and blue M&M's seem to be evenly distributed throughout the jar. I need a volunteer to help me with the counting," Tom said as he poured a sizable quantity of the red and blue candies on a large dinner plate. From a sea of hands and a chorus of "Pick me," Tom chose Lora, who pranced to the front of the room, jingling her copper bracelets and anklets.

The saucy curly-haired sophomore laboriously counted the M&M's, arriving at a total of forty-two red candies and 35 blue cndies. Turning to the board, Tom wrote down the ratio: "42 to 35 = 42/35 = 6/5 = 6 to 5 ratio of red to blue."

"What would be the reverse ratio of blue M&M's to red M&M's?" he asked.

Ronnie raised her hand. "Blue to red would be 5 to 6."

Looking around the room, Tom asked, "What is the ratio of chairs to desks in this room?"

After a pause of half a minute, Manny called out from the back of the room, "There are 34 chairs and 17 desks, so it's 34 to 17 or 2 to 1."

"What 's the ratio of girls to boys in this class?"

"Sixteen girls and 14 boys, 16 to 14, which reduces to 8 to 7," Riner answered.

"Wait a minute. You didn't count Mr. Haley. So the ratio is 16 to 15," Lora said.

"Teachers don't count, because he was talking about girls and boys," Ronnie responded.

"So you're saying Mr. Haley is not a boy. Are you saying he's gay?" Barry replied impudently.

"Teachers are grown-ups, which are their own category," Ronnie chimed in.

"Teachers are like robots. They have no gender," Lora said, waving her copper bracelets back and forth, as if to cancel out their gender.

"Girl, that's flagrantly obtuse. Teachers are normal people who like to party and raise hell … like everybody else," Barry commented with a knowing grin.

Shrugging his shoulders, Tom pressed on with the lesson. "How do rates differ from ratios?"

"Ratios are expressed as fractions, and rates are expressed as decimals," replied Wendy, who was as smart as she was pretty.

"That's right, Wendy. Also, ratios compare quantities of the same units, whereas rates compare quantities of different units." Then the skinny science teacher wrote the following problems on the blackboard:

Ex 1: A compact car drove a total of 275 miles on 12.5 gallons of gasoline. Find the car's mileage rate in miles per gallon.
Ex 2: A train travels for 4.5 hours, covering a distance of 350 miles. Compute the train's average speed in miles per hour.
Ex 3: A 16-ounce can of root beer soda costs 40 cents. Find the unit price of the soda in cents per ounce.
Ex 4: A 12.5-pound bag of grass seed is needed to cover 250 square feet of lawn. Compute the rate of seed coverage in pounds per square feet.
Ex 5: A 26.5-pound turkey costs $11.66. Find the unit price of the turkey in dollars per pound.
Ex 6: A 15-ounce bar of silver costs $87.50. Calculate the unit price of silver in dollars per ounce.

Tom gave his students ten minutes to solve the six rate problems. After they had finished working on them, he had various students work them out on the board.

Ex 1: 22 mi/gal

Ex 3: 2.5 cents/oz

Ex 2: 77.8 mi/hr

Ex 5: $0.44/lb

Ex 4: 0.05 lbs/sq ft

Ex 6: $5.83/oz

As a result of this activity, Tom discovered a useful fact that he would utilize in his science classes: Students love going to the board, sharing their knowledge, and displaying their physical assets to their classmates. In particular, Lora captured the class's attention, jangling her copper bracelets as she slowly computed the high price of silver per ounce. Her short skirt gave everyone a nice view of her shapely legs, offset by the impressive copper anklets.

When the bell rang, Lora came up to the desk, telling Tom a second reason for her affinity for copper. "It's a lot cheaper than silver and gold. And copper does influence a person's romantic impulses. Speaking of romance, does Amon have a girlfriend?"

"Indeed he does. Besides, Amon is an adult. And you should enjoy being a high school student and a teenager. This carefree time of your life will pass very quickly—I can assure you," Tom said with a hint of melancholy.

"Adult or not, Amon is very cool," the cute curly-haired youngster replied, leaving the room jingling her copper bracelets and anklets.

At this moment, there was a loud crash as the big glass of M&M candies spilled over and a river of M&M's spilled over the front desk and onto the floor.

Barry, Manny, Riner, and a few other boys were scooping up the candies from the desktop and floor and eating them. Tom tried to dissuade them from gathering the scattered M&M's and eating them.

"It's okay, Teach. Remember, M&M's melt in your mouth and not in your hands," Barry exclaimed through a mouthful of the popular candy.

Union representative Alan Katz was passing by in the hall and noticed the commotion in Tom's class. "What happened, Tom? Did one of your famous practical experiments backfire?"

"No, I used a jar of M&M's to show ratios. And at the end of the lesson, my students inadvertently tipped the jar over, trying to get at them."

"The guy who invented M&M's—Forrest Mars—got the idea during the Spanish Civil War, where the soldiers ate chocolate beads in hard sugar shells. Mars realized the chocolate encased in a sugar coating wouldn't melt during hot weather," the popular history teacher related.

"Why are they called M&M's?" Tom asked.

"The candies were named after the two owners of the Newark candy company: Forrest Mars and Bruce Murrie."

"And the rest is history," Tom said.

"Offbeat and sugar-coated, which is not often the case in history. That factory in Newark has a big machine, which coats 3,300 pounds of chocolate centers per hour," Alan related.

"I've got to remember that story and tell it to my students."

"You can also tell them that M&M's were the first candy rocketed into space. NASA sent it with the astronauts as a snack in 1981," the union representative replied with a grin.

Alan Katz was not only a stalwart UFT chapter chairman, but also a superb history teacher. He was wont to spin offbeat but true-to-life tales that intrigued his students, making an often-dull subject compelling and tangible to teenagers. Like their peers throughout America, Curtis students appeared to have little interest in events that had occurred prior to their own existence in the world. Tom recalled a quote from philosopher George Santayana: "Those who do not learn from the past are doomed to repeat it."

CHAPTER 50

Notice to Vacate

Exhausted from his week of teaching, which included three class coverages from absent Curtis teachers, Tom planned on stopping at Kaffman's bar at the corner of Morningstar Road and Walker Street for a couple beers. He was not a fan of teachers using their union-mandated personal days to do Christmas shopping. There was plenty of time on the weekend to go Christmas shopping. Besides, Tom didn't have anyone to buy a present for, except his mom and his sister, Cara. Of course, he would have to get Amon something. The man did so much and got little but aggravation in return.

At the last minute, Tom felt a vague sense of anxiety. The idea of sitting in a hazy, sour-sweet–smelling saloon did not appeal to the skinny science teacher. So he went home and had some potato chips and soda—his usual unhealthy early-afternoon snack. Lately, his breakfast was equally unhealthy, consisting of a slice of apple pie, downed with a cup of instant coffee. Sitting on the faded red living room couch, he started to drift into a light sleep, dreaming about his high school sweetheart, Joanie. The skinny teacher's dream was interrupted by the jarring ring of the telephone.

"Tom, we got to talk to that lawyer friend of yours. I got a letter from the city telling me to vacate my tugboat. They're condemning all the boats in the harbor for some kind of project."

Tom said he'd call Stan Mislicki, the amiable lawyer whose office was directly above his family's bakery on Morningstar Road. As luck would have it, Stan said he was hanging around his office, finishing up some paperwork. If Tom could get there with his friend in a half hour, he'd wait for them.

Amon showed Stan the notice that was posted on his tugboat. There were identical notices posted on the rotting docks, crumbling buildings, rusty ships, and corroded hulks, which had remained dormant for years. The studious young attorney read the document carefully while Tom and Amon exchanged worried looks. Amon felt helpless before the weight of municipal government–welding power, which could change the course of his life and the lives of people who depended on him.

The lawyer asked Amon if he lived alone on the tugboat, and the latter replied that his girlfriend, Mary, lived with him.

"No children?" the congenial lawyer asked with a straight face.

Blushing, the charismatic young man said no. Tom was startled to see his usually unflappable friend's face turn red. Doubtlessly, there was a powerful bond between Amon and Mary.

"Are there any children living in the residential house on Simonson Avenue?"

Amon started to shake his head, and then his face brightened. "There's this woman who talked about moving into the Simonson Avenue house, but we have no vacancies." Turning to Tom, he said, "You know who I'm talking about — Evette. She has a little boy who goes to PS 44."

"Is there room for her and the boy on your boat?" Stan inquired.

"We'll make room for her. There's a cabin we use for storage in the bow," Amon replied.

"Well, things might get kind of cramped in your boat," Stan offered.

"Evette is very accommodating. She likes to help out. I came to her aid when she was struck by a car in Port Richmond," Amon commented.

"He saved her life or at least prevented her leg from being amputated," Tom interjected, to Amon's distress and the lawyer's amazement.

"That might work. The city does not want to put families on the street. Of course, the builder won't be happy. But most judges can be convinced to issue an injunction where children are involved."

"Well, that's settled. I knew you could do it, Stan," Tom chimed in.

"These builders have money and influence. So nothing's settled. They'll come back in six months and apply for a building permit again, after they've greased the skids a bit."

Amon shook his head in disgust, and Tom patted him on the back. "We're buying some time, but as Yogi Berra says, 'it ain't over till it's over.'"

Amon asked Stan for a bill. "This is the second time you've helped me, and I want to pay you for your time."

Holding up his hands, the young attorney said he was working pro bono.

As the two young men started to leave the office, Stan said that he had read in the *Advocate* that Joey Caprino was pitching again on the local men's baseball team.

Tom was surprised because he thought his old friend had given up on baseball entirely for "the good life as a Wall Street stockbroker."

"He still works on Wall Street, but on weekends he pitches for the Staten Island Seagulls. There was a story about him in the paper — he's developed a knuckleball that's just about unhittable."

"Good for him. It's nice to hear about an Elm Park kid making good," Tom said.

Joey had been the first kid he made friends with when he and Cara had moved to Staten Island years ago. The stocky youngster used to spend hours playing stoopball, throwing a Spalding against his front porch steps and catching the carom endlessly. Less talented than the hard-throwing Mike Palermo, Joey had had the gift of perseverance and baseball smarts. He also had an uncanny ability to do arithmetic computations in his head, especially the batting averages of his favorite team – the old Brooklyn Dodgers.

CHAPTER 51

Supply and Demand

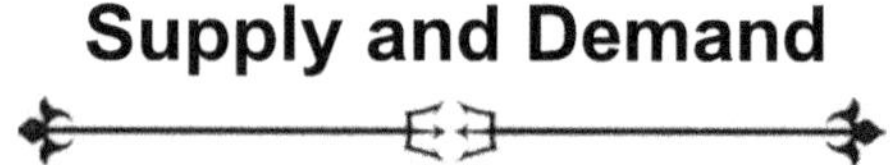

The week following his coverage of Rosie Murray's arithmetic class, Tom was given the honor of covering another one of her classes—economics. Because she was a good-looking woman, Tom accepted the assignment from his steadfast supervisor with hardly a contrary word, though he knew little about the subject. He had heard that economics was referred to as the dismal science.

Handing Tom Mrs. Murray's economic notes, Lou Stout remarked, "I know what you're thinking. Forget about her big ass. What happened to that girlfriend of yours? She had a pretty nice derriere, as I recall."

"Martha? We broke up over political differences. She's a Republican, and I'm a Democrat," Tom replied unconvincingly.

"Yeah, sure. My wife's Catholic, and I'm a Buddhist," the principal replied, heading back to his wood-paneled office, with its pictures of Curtis baseball and basketball teams coached by Stout in his younger days.

Walking into Mrs. Murray's economic class later that day, Tom was astonished to find many of his own students in the class. He and the voluptuous teacher had one thing in common: the same motley crew of Curtis sophomores.

Too bad she didn't live in Elm Park. Unfortunately, Rosie Murray was part of a growing contingent of South Shore people who taught at the North Shore high school.

As Tom got ready to teach the class, he was greeted by a chorus of boos—with the exception of Lora, who clapped and rattled her copper bracelets.

"Don't worry, guys. Mrs. Murray has prepared a lesson on supply and demand for your edification," Tom said as he shuffled through Mrs. Murray's extensive notes on the subject.

Maggie tapped on the door, and Tom beckoned her to enter the room. She was carrying a large platter of M&M's and salted peanuts in separate piles.

Then, Tom had the curly-haired Lora walk around the class, allowing the students to choose either the peanuts or the M&M's. The cute sophomore's rattling copper bracelets and anklets, plus her other charms, distracted the students so much that Tom used the time to write the aim on the board: "What is the law of supply and demand?" He also had time to draw the supply and demand curves on a "price versus quantity" axis on the board, which were similar to the positive and negative sloping lines of coordinate algebra.

After her merry jingling around the room, Lora brought the plate back up to the front desk. It was apparent that the class overwhelmingly favored the M&M's over the peanuts. Tom asked the class, "What can we conclude from the appearance of the plate?"

"That most normal people prefer M&M's to peanuts ... except for weirdos like Riner and Ronnie," Barry said as he munched on the popular candy pieces.

"I have diabetes, so I can't eat sugar," Riner replied defensively. He was a mild-mannered brainy kid, except when his medical condition was involved.

"And I happen to prefer peanuts to those sugary M&M's. Is that a crime?" Ronnie asked petulantly.

"Only your face is a crime," Barry snapped.

"Look who's talking, Mister Skin and Bones," the naive youngster retorted.

Barry got out of his seat and headed for Ronnie, when Lora put herself between the two angry teenagers, who were ready to escalate their quarrel into a physical confrontation.

"Come on, guys, get ahold of yourselves. We've been together since junior high. Love is stronger than hate," Lora said, giving Ronnie one of her copper bracelets.

"So what do I get?" Barry asked with a smirk.

"I'll give you a kiss," she replied, handing the vociferous black teenager a Hershey Kiss. He accepted the token grudgingly, expecting a different kind of kiss from the cute miniskirted youngster.

"Thank you, Lora. Now let us proceed with Mrs. Murray's lesson on the law of supply and demand."

Pausing a few seconds to scrutinize the latter's lesson, Tom asserted that three distinct laws were involved: "The law of supply, the law of demand, and the law of supply and demand—each with their own graphs."

Turning to the blackboard, Tom explained the three graphs he had carefully drawn on the board.

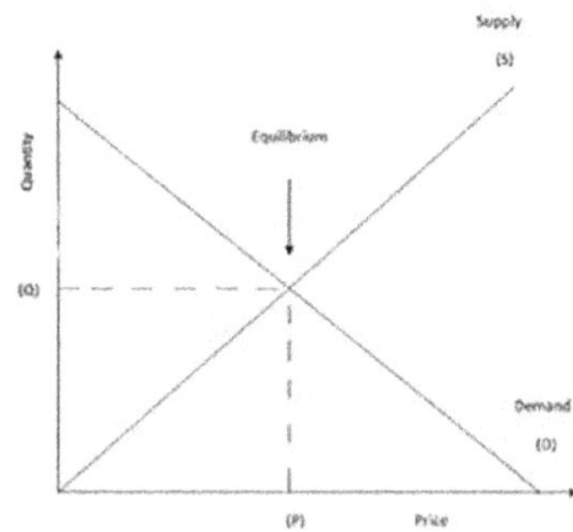

"Notice the supply graph is a positively sloping line, whereas the demand graph is a negatively sloping line. Why is that?"

Riner raised his hand. "Because as the price of a product, like bread, goes up, there will be more bakers making the bread. And as the price of bread goes up, there will be fewer customers buying the bread."

"Excellent, Riner. In other words, there is a direct relationship between price and supply, which is the law of supply. But there is an inverse relationship between price and demand, which is the law of demand," Tom lectured.

Then turning to the third graph showing the positively sloping supply line intersecting the negatively sloping demand line, the skinny science teacher said it represented the law of supply and demand. "Here we have producers and consumers operating together—bakers of bread and buyers of bread."

"I know what's going on. Can I go to the board and explain it?" Barry exclaimed excitedly.

Tom nodded, and the lanky black teenager ambled to the board. Barry pointed to the left side of the graph. "Demand is greater than supply, which pushes the price of bread up." Then pointing to the right side of the graph, he continued, "Supply is greater than demand, which pushes the price of bread down."

"Excellent, Barry. That's absolutely right! So market forces operate to set the price of bread where the supply and demand for bread are equal—no surpluses and no shortages."

"So long as there's a free market with plenty of producers and lots of consumers," Riner interjected.

"Well, that's true. It has to be an ideal free market, with no single company holding a monopoly over any given product," Tom stated, reading from Mrs. Murray's notes.

"That doesn't hold for car companies, 'cause there's only three of them: General Motors, Ford, and Chrysler," Manny called out from the back of the classroom.

"What about Japanese cars?" Wendy asked.

"I hate those tinny little Jap cars. If you get into an accident with one of them, you're dead," Barry exclaimed.

"My dad says buy American and keep factory jobs here," Lora said, shaking her copper bracelets and anklets.

"How about those weird bracelets you wear? Are they made in America?" Manny called out from the back of the room.

"They're not weird. My mother makes them herself, for your information," Lora replied, piqued by the slouching teenager who liked to stir the pot.

"So what did the peanuts and the M&M's have to do with the law of supply and demand?" Barry asked.

"There were fewer M&M's left than peanuts because of the greater demand. If I were selling M&M's in the cafeteria, I'd set them at a higher price than the peanuts," Tom replied.

"All processed foods cost more than natural foods, and they're bad for your health," Riner observed.

"How come folks who eat fruits and veggies look wasted, while guys like me who eat junk food are high-energy phenoms?" Barry asked half-seriously.

"Are you wearing any copper?" Lora asked.

"My underwear is lined with copper. Do you want me to show you, missy?"

"That's the last time I'll give you one of my kisses," the cute sophomore replied.

Fortunately, the bell sounded, ending the class and dispersing the students to the four winds. As Tom gathered up his notes and the big plate filled only with peanuts, Lora approached him.

"Why are boys such assholes?"

Shrugging his shoulders, Tom realized that Martha would say the same thing about himself. Taking a philosophic approach, he said, "They'll catch up, and things will get better."

"I wish I could believe you," she replied, walking slowly out of the room, with hardly a tinkle from her copper bracelets and anklets.

CHAPTER 52

Shoveling Snow

On a snowy Saturday morning in January, Tom lingered over his second cup of coffee as his mom leafed through the *Staten Island Advocate*. As the snow accumulated in the backyard and alley of the white stucco house, Tom became more sullen. He despised winter—its long nights, bitter temperatures, biting winds, as well as heavy, drifting snows that made driving a perilous undertaking. His thoughts turned to his ex-girlfriend Martha and her predilection for cuddling during such frightful weather. However, she was a strong-willed woman—much like his mother—refusing to accept the skinny teacher's procrastination with regard to marriage.

He mused about Rosie Murray, whose arithmetic and economic classes he had covered before the Christmas break. *What an ass on that woman!* In aboriginal cultures, women so endowed were shared among the elders of the tribe. *Now, that's true socialism—sharing material assets and female asses for the common good.*

"I see your friend Amon has done something heroic again. It says here he saved a little boy from drowning when he fell off a tugboat in the Kill Van Kull."

"He pulled me out of the water when I fell off a wharf last year," Tom replied.

"That's no surprise. You're not only a klutz—you're a klutz who can't swim."

"Thanks, Mom. You're always so cheery and encouraging on Saturdays."

"It goes on to say that he's been given notice by the city to vacate the waterfront area because of an impending construction project. However, he's earned a lot of goodwill because of his work with the homeless. This is funny. Do you know what they call him?"

"Tom Haley's best friend?"

"No. He's referred to as the Mariners Harbor Messiah," his mom read loudly.

"Which makes me an apostle — a heavenly being. Since I'm his best friend."

"And if you don't start shoveling that snow, you'll be heading for the hereafter sooner than you expect," she snapped.

Huffing and puffing, Tom shoveled the snow from his front steps and sidewalk. Not content with clearing his own sidewalk, he cleared a part of his neighbor's on each side, plus the area around his car. He was soon joined by other Pulaski Avenue inhabitants — Mr. Eggert across the street, Granny Schmidt next door, and Joey Caprino two houses away. Joey waved at him and threw a fast snow ball at him, which Tom smartly blocked with his shovel.

"If that bastard hits me with a snowball, I'm gonna smack him with my shovel," Granny Schmidt yelled as she shoveled her sidewalk.

"I'll do your sidewalk. Go inside before you have a heart attack," Tom replied, crossing over to his neighbor's side and clearing the snow from her pavement.

"Thanks, wise guy. How about five bucks for a bottle of whiskey," the bad-natured hag demanded.

"What? I'm paying you for the privilege of shoveling your sidewalk."

"You owe me. You and that loudmouth Harry the Horse … always barking up at me from the street," Granny complained.

Handing her the money, Tom watched Granny Schmidt shuffle away toward the liquor store on Morningstar Road, cursing and mumbling to herself in her own unique way.

"Ah, Granny. Parting is such sweet sorrow," Tom uttered as he pushed the snow toward the curb.

Granny had a habit of watching the doings of the neighborhood from her second-floor window. Years ago, Harry the Horse liked to heckle the old woman while playing stickball on the street with the kids. Elm Park probably had more alcoholics per square mile than any other neighborhood on the Island's North Shore. Indeed, drinking appeared to be the most popular pastime of the residents of Pulaski Avenue.

Oddly, once he got into it, the skinny teacher actually enjoyed the snow shoveling. He had recently begun an exercise routine that he had undertaken in high school. It involved calisthenics such as push-ups, sit-ups, and knee bends from a Joe Weider bodybuilding course. He spent extra time on sit-ups, trying to whittle down a growing beer belly (from too many hours of elbow bending at Kaffman's and K. C.'s on Morningstar Road). Teaching itself required a degree of physical fitness, because it entailed standing, writing on the board, and walking around the classroom to check on the students' work. Tom vividly remembered how exhausted he was after his first week of teaching at the St. George school.

Later on in the afternoon, Tom paid a visit to Amon, who was shoveling snow in front of this Victorian rooming house on Simonson Avenue. The skinny teacher grabbed a shovel and joined Amon in removing the snow, which became heavy and wet with the rising afternoon temperatures. He was helped in this endeavor by a few elderly men — reformed alcoholics who lived at the Simonson Avenue house. Tom asked his friend about the rescue incident reported in the local newspaper.

"That was Evette's boy, Willie. He had stopped breathing momentarily, but I revived him. We moved mom and son to the house here. My boat is not fit for children," Amon replied.

At that point, a shiny blue Chrysler with a New York City logo emblazoned on its doors pulled up next to the refurbished Victorian house. A burly curly-haired man emerged from the house, smiling at the two young men. He introduced himself as Sid Davidoff, Mayor Lindsay's community point man.

"Hello, gentlemen. I'm Sid Davidoff from the mayor's office. Is it okay if I take a look at your boardinghouse and the boats on the waterfront?"

"Sure. Come with me. This is Tom Haley, friend and helper. And Curtis High School science teacher and founder of the school's food basket program," Amon replied, nodding toward his friend.

Mr. Davidoff shook hands with both young men and followed them on a tour of the Simonson Avenue house. Satisfied with his inspection, the mayor's troubleshooter trudged in the snow with them to take a look at Amon's tugboat on the Kill Van Kull. He appeared to like the freshly painted boat, but the rotting wharfs, broken docks, corroded ships, rusted hulks, and ramshackle warehouses gave the John Lindsay aide pause.

Amon and Tom anxiously awaited Sid Davidoff's verdict.

"Well, we can save your boat, but the remnants of the old Bethlehem Steel shipyard will have to go. It will be condemned and removed. Then builders will come in and put up pricy condos, new docks for yachts and boats, paving stone walkways, flowers, shrubs, and trees."

"Sounds depressing to me," Tom remarked, which caused Lindsay's troubleshooter to smile.

"It's called gentrification, which is the current rage today," Davidoff remarked.

"When will the construction begin?" Amon inquired sadly.

"There will be competitive bidding, etc. The city moves like a snail on big projects like these. Nothing will happen until the summer," Davidoff replied.

"That's fortunate. Thank God for bureaucracies — they're as slow as molasses," the charismatic Mariners Harbor resident declared bitterly.

"If it was up to me, I'd leave the Harbor as it is. The place has character. The old docks and rusty ships are picturesque," Davidoff said as he surveyed the Kill Van Kull waterfront.

"So the city will allow my boat to remain here in the harbor?"

"I have the mayor's ear, and I'll do my best. Mayor Lindsay is aware of the good work you've done in Mariners Harbor and your reputation as a miracle worker," Davidoff replied, shaking hands with both of them and heading back to his shiny blue Chrysler.

"What do you think? Can we trust this guy, or will the giant cranes and wrecking balls descend on us tomorrow?"

"Sid Davidoff is a good guy. When the students sat in at Columbia University to protest the war, Davidoff negotiated with them and lowered the flag, honoring the four students killed at Kent State," Tom related.

"How about his boss, Mr. Fun City himself?"

"John Lindsay is a decent man. He cares about working people. And he gave teachers the best contract we've ever had, along with transit workers, sanitation workers, cops, and firemen."

"Then why does everybody put him down?" Amon asked.

"They see Lindsay as an aristocrat because he comes from the silk stocking district in upper Manhattan. The blue-collar workers despise him because of his empathy for black people and his opposition to the war," Tom related.

"He seems to be a maverick. We ought to extol such idealists. Instead, we want to tear them down and stone them," Amon replied somberly.

"And take away their homes," Tom said, pointing to Amon's brightly painted tugboat, bobbing up and down in the polluted Kill Van Kull.

The Bee Gees

The Bee Gees were a pop group who wrote and recorded many hit songs in the 1960s and 1970s. Like Brian Wilson's Beach Boys, the group was composed of three brothers: Barry, Robin, and Maurice Gibb. Born on the Isle of Man, the Gibb brothers moved to Manchester, England, with their parents in the 1950s. Later on, the Gibb family moved to Australia, where they began performing to earn pocket money. In 1960, the Gibb brothers were hired to entertain the crowds at Redcliffe Speedway in Queensland, Australia. Initially, they performed under the name BG's, which was later changed to Bee Gees.

In the early 1960s, the Bee Gees were appearing on Australia's TV shows, singing such songs as "Time Is Passing By" and "Wine and Women." In 1962, the Bee Gees appeared with Chubby Checker in a concert at Sydney Stadium. By 1966, their record company, Festival Records, was on the verge of dropping them, because they failed to catch on in the pop music field. However, an engineer/producer, Ossie Byrne, was intrigued by the Gibb brothers and allowed them to record in his St. Clair studio in the latter part of 1966. During this period, the Bee Gees recorded their own songs — including their first big hit, "Spicks and Specks" — plus their own versions of songs by other rock groups like the Beatles.

In 1967, the Bee Gees moved to England, where they caught the attention of Brian Epstein and Robert Stigwood. The latter obtained a recording contract for the group, under which their records would be produced and promoted in England and the United States. The Bee Gees recorded "To Love Somebody," which reached the US Top Twenty level. In the same year, the Bee Gees made their first appearance on British television. The Gibb brothers had attained a popularity that put them on the same level as the Beatles, the Rolling Stones, and the Dave Clark Five. In 1968, the Bee Gees made a promotional tour to the United States and sang their number-one UK single, "Massachusetts." Later that year, the Bee Gees toured Germany and the Scandinavian countries, performing with Procol Harum, who sang "A Whiter Shade of Pale." Robin Gibb remarked that the "Germans were wilder than the fans in England at the height of Beatlemania." In Zurich, the mad rush of fans literally crushed the Bee Gees' car, smashing the windows and forcing the Gibb brothers to huddle on the floor.

Toward the end of 1968, the Bee Gees recorded some more big hits, including "I've Gotta Get a Message to You" and "I Started a Joke." But the strains of extensive touring took its toll on Robin Gibb, who collapsed from nervous exhaustion. There were some more hit singles in the early 1970s, but a period of decline ensued with the Bee Gees. The single "Don't Forget to Remember" was a big hit in the United Kingdom but a flop in the United States. Later on in 1971, the Bee Gees recorded two massive hits: "Lonely Days" and "How Can You Mend a Broken Heart."

In the middle 1970s, the Bee Gees seemed to be in a rut — relegated to playing in small clubs. There was a change in musical tastes in the United States. Rock and roll had been replaced by dance-oriented disco. Spurred by this sea change, the group recorded two disco hits: "Jive Talkin'" and "Nights on Broadway." In these records, Barry Gibb sang an R & B falsetto that would become a trademark of the group. The Bee Gees' new R & B disco sound catapulted them to a level of stardom not previously achieved in the United States. A big break occurred when the Bee Gees agreed to participate in the creation of the soundtrack for the 1970s hit movie *Saturday Night Fever*.

John Travolta asserted that the Bee Gees weren't even involved in the early stages of this movie. Incredibly, the Gibb brothers wrote the songs for *Saturday Night Fever* in a single weekend, and the movie's producer flipped out. Barry Gibb said that they worked with a rough script of the movie, with no exact concept of its storyline. *Saturday Night Fever* kicked off the disco music trend and reinvigorated the Bee Gees as pop music superstars.

Four Bee Gees songs from that popular movie — "Stayin' Alive," "Night Fever," "How Deep Is Your Love," and "More Than a Woman" — reached the pinnacle of American and British charts in 1978. They also wrote "If I Can't Have You" — a song by Yvonne Elliman — which became a number-one hit in the United States. Only the Beatles, way back in 1964, had achieved such record chart dominance as the Bee Gees attained in the year 1978.

The Bee Gees have earned a high place in the rock-and-roll and disco legacy. John Lennon praised them for their groundbreaking songs in the 1970s: "They do a damn good job. There was nothing else going on then." Michael Jackson, who was influenced by the Bee Gees, said, "I cried listening to their music." The consensus of people in pop music was that the Bee Gees were not only brilliant artists but really nice people — minus the big egos that haunt pop stars. Some of the lyrics from their hits are haunting: "You are the reason for my laughter and my sorrow, blow out the candle and I will burn again tomorrow," and "We're living in a world of fools, breaking us down, when they all should let us be."

CHAPTER 53

Marx vs. Keynes

Walking into Curtis High School's main entrance, Tom noticed that the limestone gargoyles appeared more gruesome than ever. Maybe the bitter January weather had gotten to those formidable creatures, changing their homely smiles to horrible grimaces. Punching his card in the time clock, the skinny science teacher noticed that the holiday holly and mistletoe had been removed. Right in front of Tom was the notorious Rosie Murray, dressed in a tight skirt that showed her voluminous ass to maximum advantage.

"Oh, Mr. Haley. I never got the chance to thank you for covering my classes when I came down with a cold before the holidays," she said in a bubbly manner, adjusting her snug-fitting skirt.

"No problem. My name is Tom, by the way."

"And I'm Rosie — short for Rosemary. Actually, I need a coverage today because of some personal business I have to take care of."

"No problem. Our aim at Curtis is to please."

"I have the notes here. We're covering micro- and macroeconomics," she said, dropping the notes and bending down to pick them up. "I don't know how to thank you."

"You did that already," Tom exclaimed, getting an eyeful of her wonderful derriere.

Walking into Mrs. Murray's economics class, Tom had doubts about how he would teach such a dry subject. Stopping off at the social studies department office, he managed to get glossy pictures of Karl Marx and John Maynard Keynes. As with his previous coverage of her classes, Tom was greeted with a chorus of boos. Some of the students demanded a free period, which the skinny teacher rejected. Say what they might about the young science teacher, he always taught something whenever he entered a classroom. Lou Stout's dictum resonated with Tom: "Keep them busy, or they'll fry you for lunch."

Posting the pictures of the two famous economists on the blackboard, Tom asked the students to identify the two men.

"They look like serial killers, especially the old guy with the beard," Manny called out from the back of the room.

"The man on the left is Karl Marx, and the other one is John Maynard Keynes," answered Riner, who was studious and serious.

"That's correct. Can anyone tell the class what the bearded man is known for?"

Again, Riner raised his hand. "He formulated the theory of communism, in which the state owns the natural resources and the factories. There would be no private property and only one class — the proletariat, or workers."

"Excellent, Riner," said Tom, looking at Mrs. Murray's notes. "Marx also said that surplus value is built into the price of goods, which represent the capitalist's profit. And the conflict between the capitalists and workers will result in victory by the latter — known as class warfare."

"If that's so, why do the Russians and Chinese live in mud huts no better than pigpens?" asked Marty, a student whom Tom didn't know.

"That's because Marxism looks good in theory, but in practice it doesn't work," said Wendy.

"Don't get me wrong. But the idea of a classless society isn't so bad. If everybody had the same stuff, there would be no crime," said Barry, an outspoken teenager whose clowning hid a good mind.

"If everyone was exactly the same, it would be kind of boring," commented Lora, jangling her bracelets.

"You can say that again. Imagine if every girl went around with those dumb copper bracelets and anklets. Why don't you wear one of them on your neck, like a dog collar?"

"Go fuck—I mean shut up! Who asked you for your opinion?" she replied angrily, fiddling with her bracelets.

"Did you hear that, Mr. Haley? Send her to the dean," Barry demanded half-seriously.

"What about the other economist, John Maynard Keynes?"

"He said countries should borrow money during recessions to put more money into circulation. This stimulates demand so consumers can buy goods and put workers back to work in factories," Riner replied.

Checking Mrs. Murray's notes, Tom concurred. "Keynes believed that governments must change their taxing and spending policies to modify the boom-and-bust fluctuations of the business cycle."

"The problem with Keynesian economics is that many governments run bigger and bigger deficits that are never paid off. America now has a $10 billion deficit, which grows every year," said Marty, who seemed to be into these arcane subjects.

Perusing Mrs. Murray's notes, Tom stated that the English economist (Keynes) had many supporters in the US government, "which routinely runs deficits during good and bad economic times, and during wars."

"Yeah. LBJ used to talk about not having enough money for guns and butter," commented Marty, who was well-informed about politics.

"John Keynes was opposed to the gold standard. What is the gold standard?"

"That's where money is backed by its equivalent value in gold," Wendy replied.

"America's gold is stored in Fort Knox. That would be a bank heist to die for, busting into that place," Barry replied with a sly grin.

Checking Rosie Murray's notes one more time, Tom asked the class to define "usury," which was unknown to them. "'Usury' is charging of interest for loans. The Jesuits opposed this practice during the Middle Ages, but it's basic to banking throughout the world."

"Why should you pay interest for a loan? That sucks!" Barry retorted.

With time running out, Tom went over key economic concepts listed in Mrs. Murray's notes, which he wrote on the board for the students to copy into their notebooks.

Microeconomics: the pricing of goods and services under the market forces of supply and demand.

Macroeconomics: the behavior of national economies with respect to prices, employment, consumption, savings, and output.

Gross National Product: market value of all goods and services produced by a country in a given year.

Aggregate Demand: the total demand for goods and services by an economy in a given year.

Business Cycle: the boom-and-bust cycle of the economy caused by changes in aggregate demand.

Tom's timing was good, and the students had finished transcribing the economic terms when the bell sounded, ending the lesson. Despite its label as "the dismal science," the economics lesson was not too boring. The skinny teacher realized the antics of his students, far from being an encumbrance, added spark to what would have been a dull lesson.

As Tom took down the posters of Karl Marx and John Maynard Keynes, Lora approached him. "I'm sorry for cursing at Barry, but he is so obnoxious, I can't help it, Mr. Haley."

"It's fine. That's just his way. That's the way boys are. They call attention to themselves by being provocative."

"Sometimes I wish they would just leave me alone," Lora said sadly.

"I hear you. But being left alone can be as vexing as being annoyed by one's classmates," he replied in a consoling manner.

"What about you? Do you have a girlfriend?" she asked abruptly.

Caught off balance, the young science teacher stammered, "Ah … not at the moment."

CHAPTER 54

Dalton Trumbo

One Saturday night with nothing to do, Tom stopped over to see Amon and Mary in their refurbished tugboat. The two were finishing a dinner of fried fish caught in the gray choppy waters of the Kill Van Kull. Tom suggested he treat the two of them to a movie at the Ritz Theater in Port Richmond.

"What's playing? I'm in the mood for something light. The residents in the Simonson Avenue house have been bickering about everything," Amon replied.

"He's too easygoing. There are some troublemakers—alcoholics, drug addicts, and thieves—who should be tossed out," Mary complained.

"Mary, I'm not going to put anyone on the street, especially in the middle of winter. No matter how desperate and lost a person is, there's always hope of redemption."

"Amon believes there's an inner core of goodness in everyone. I'm not convinced of this universal goodness trait," the parochial school teacher remarked.

Responding diplomatically, Tom said he wasn't sure about the universality of goodness in human nature but asserted that most people had positive impulses. The skinny science teacher mentioned a new film with an antiwar message, called *Johnny Got His Gun*, which he wanted to see.

His two friends looked at each other and shrugged. "Why not?"

Amon said, "It will get my mind off all the bullshit that's going on around here."

"I couldn't have said it better myself," Tom replied as the three young people walked in the snow toward his old gray 1964 Pontiac.

The movie, shown at the Ritz Theater, told the story of a young American who is called upon to serve in Europe during the First World War. Severely wounded by an artillery shell, the soldier has lost his arms and legs, as well as his facial features—eyes, ears, teeth, and tongue—in the blast. The young man is unable to commit suicide and must endure a tortured existence. Alternating between consciousness and unconsciousness, reality and fantasy, and thoughts of his early life and his teenage sweetheart, the wounded soldier is trapped in a semicomatose state.

The only comfort the young man receives is from a dedicated nurse who strokes his forehead and is distressed by his suffering. At one point she tries to end his suffering by clamping his breathing tube but is prevented by a superior. The soldier's wish to be placed in a glass coffin as a grim warning of the horrors of war is also denied. Consequently, the young man is confined in an immobile state—paralyzed, helpless, and alone—trapped by his melancholy thoughts.

As the threesome walked down Richmond Avenue in a somber mood, Tom asked Amon if he still was convinced about the fundamental goodness of human nature. "There have been two bloody world wars in the twentieth century, plus numerous limited wars like Korea and Vietnam, causing the deaths of millions of soldiers and civilians alike."

"This movie presents a different picture of war. I often wonder about my own students at St. Mary's. Will one of them be drafted in a future war and have his life cut short?" Mary replied.

"People want to live in peace and do the ordinary things of life. It's greed, fear, prejudice, and crooked politicians that drive men to fight wars. It's the screwed-up world we live in that corrupt us, turning folks away from their good instincts. I was drafted to fight in Vietnam without anyone asking me about my opinions," Amon related.

"The Vietnam War drove me into teaching, which actually turned out to be a good thing. Who knows what I could have become otherwise," Tom said.

"Yeah. You might have become a wealthy businessmen," Amon commented.

"On the contrary, knowing your honest inclinations, you probably would have gone bankrupt," Mary asserted.

"I've been blessed, surviving that war unscathed. I could have wound up like that soldier in that Dalton Trumbo movie. And it's one of the reasons I try to do some good in the world," Amon declared.

"Trumbo never actually fought in World War I, but his grasp of the horrors of war were uncanny. He was blacklisted in the 1950s for refusing to reveal other other members of the Communist Party," Tom said.

"I wasn't aware of that situation. I thought there was freedom of speech and freedom of association in this country," Amon responded.

"Well, there is … except for the Cold War era during the fifties. Trumbo asserted that the artist speaks the truth that no one else can speak. And everyone loses when the artist is suppressed," Tom replied.

"So freedom of speech is not paramount in this country?" Amon inquired.

"In America, we are absolutely free to sink or swim," Tom responded grimly.

CHAPTER 55

Harry the Horse

As the three young people meandered along Richmond Avenue, Tom asserted that science and art are related in that "both represent a search for truth by different means."

"Speaking of art, that yonder house is a work of art," said Amon, pointing to an old colonial-style house, which was situated between a three-story brick apartment building and an abandoned factory.

"It looks like it goes back to the early twentieth century. Kind of reminds me of my mom's stucco house on Pulaski Avenue."

Suddenly, there was a loud snap, followed by an awful sound of wood tearing. Then the sound of a man wailing emanated from within the house. Before Tom and Mary could react to the situation, Amon dashed into the house, heading for the ground floor. Upon arriving at the scene, Tom saw Amon struggling to lift a heavy wooden beam, under which a workman was trapped.

"Tom, help me lift this beam, while you pull him out, Mary," Amon gasped as he hefted the wooden brace.

Together, the two young men hoisted the heavy beam a few inches while Mary grasped the man by his shoulders and pulled him from under the thick wooden beam. The man gasped in relief but was unable to speak. It appeared that his chest had been crushed by the beam that fell on him.

Tom was astonished to recognize the man. It was Harry the Horse, the notorious Pied Piper of Elm Park, who used to lead the neighborhood kids in boisterous games of stickball on the Pulaski Avenue. Unlike the other dads of the neighborhood, who were too busy working or drinking at Kaffman's or K. C.'s, Harry always had the time and the inclination to play street games.

"I think I broke my collarbone," he exclaimed, obviously in pain.

"Just rest a minute," Amon replied as he rubbed his forehead, arms, and chest.

After a few minutes, Harry appeared to revive. "I'm feeling a little better. Are you some kind of faith healer?"

"Not at all. Most people are capable of healing themselves. A working man like you has the strength to bounce back from a minor injury."

"Wait a minute. I've met you before in Elm Park." Looking over toward Tom, he said, "You were with this guy, the worst stickball player in the neighborhood. But at least he made something of himself, teaching those brats at Curtis High School."

"I think you're feeling better already. Back to your usual good-natured self," Tom snapped.

Standing up and dusting himself off, Harry said he bought the ramshackle house for a song. "I'm tired of paying rents in Elm Park. So I'm fixing this place up in my spare time."

Turning to Mary, he exclaimed, "And thanks to you, young lady. Yours was the first face I saw when I came through. I thought I had died and gone to heaven."

Mary blushed sweetly. "It's something anyone would do under the circumstances. I'm so glad you're okay."

Looking around the debris-filled house, Tom declared, "I guess it's what real estate brokers call a fixer-upper."

Shaking Amon's hand, Harry said, "I wish I could repay you in some way. But between this place and my job, I'm busier than a one-armed paper hanger."

"No. Just keep doing what you're doing. That's reward enough for me. But when you finish this place, I'd like to see it," Amon replied.

"I'll have the three of you here for a meal. My wife's a great cook. You like Italian food?"

"Nothing's better. But there is one thing. You'll have to show me how the fast-pitch game of stickball is played. I'm a county boy who's ignorant of that sort of game," Amon said.

"You're on. I can tell right away that you're a natural. Unlike this guy here," Harry replied, rapping Tom on the shoulder.

"What do you mean? I wasn't bad as a stickball player," Tom retorted.

"Yeah, sure. He once broke Mrs. Eggert's window. Another time he hit a pop-up that landed in a concrete tub a man was using to fix his sidewalk," Harry said.

"Tom's a real menace, but he means well," Amon replied.

"Tom's a good guy. Loyal and true blue," Mary concurred, giving the skinny teacher a hug.

Later on, the three young people sat at a luncheonette on Richmond Avenue, sipping coffee and eating some apple pie. Amon was trying to extricate a large splinter from his right hand — the result of his lifting the heavy wooden beam from Harry the Horse's chest.

"Wait a minute," the pretty young woman said as she took out a small sewing kit from her pocketbook. "Hold still, and don't be a baby. I'll get it out pronto."

"Do you always go around equipped with needles and first-aid stuff?" Tom inquired.

"I have no choice. This man's an accident waiting to happen," she exclaimed, giving Amon a resounding thump on the chest.

"We're two of a kind. Partners in crime when it comes to mishaps," Amon said.

Looking down the lunch counter, Tom noticed a former classmate, Perry Pantino, who had been rescued by Amon last year after jumping off the ferry.

Perry greeted the threesome with a too-loud "Hi there, guys!" followed by his customary high-pitched laugh.

The high-strung young man reached over and shook hands with Amon. "The last time we met I was swallowing that pissy seawater in the New York Bay."

"How are you doing, Perry?" Amon asked, eyeing the obstreperous young man closely.

"Not great. But I'm hanging in there, doing some work for the Salvation Army. I drive a truck for them. Remember Tommy Spider? Work with him, talking about the girls we left behind at Port Richmond."

"It's good you're working," Tom said encouragingly.

"If you don't work, you don't eat. Yesterday, I was having bacon and eggs, and a guy came in here barefoot and sat down next to me. He didn't seem to have any money, so I bought him breakfast."

"That was very generous of you," Amon remarked.

"I've been there, done that. So I ask him where he hung out last night. He says to me, 'Do I look like I know where I slept last night?'" Cackling with shrill giggles, Perry left a $5 bill and hopped out of the luncheonette.

Tom sensed a bitterness to his humor as the place echoed with his harsh laughter.

"Shall I follow him to make sure he's okay?" Mary asked.

"No. We're far from water, thank God," Amon replied, shaking his head and shrugging his shoulders somberly.

CHAPTER 56

The Story of Buddha

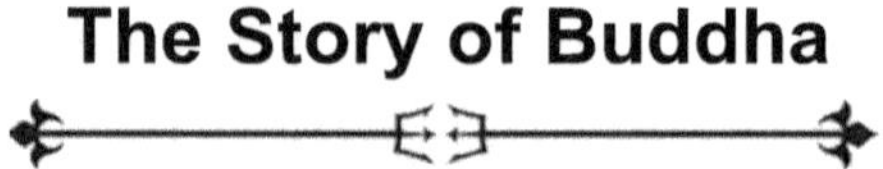

Waking into Curtis High School, Tom was greeted by Lou Stout, the school's steadfast principal, carrying some papers. The skinny science teacher knew it was a bad sign. Sighing loudly, he asked his boss, "Whose class is it this time?"

"Your favorite. Mrs. Murray has the flu. She'll appreciate it greatly."

"I'd like something more substantial from that one—like a piece of her ass," Tom replied, somewhat annoyed.

"Wouldn't we all. I'd give my right arm for a tumble with her. Just the thought of her big ass keeps me awake at night," Stout said, looking at a cute coed who happened to be walking by. It was Lora, one of Tom's students.

"Lora, I don't hear you rattling your copper bracelets. What happened to them?" Tom asked the flaky teenager.

"I'm soaking them in ammonia. Trying to remove the green coating," she replied.

"That green compound is called verdigris. I think acetone, nail polish remover, would work better."

Handing Tom Mrs. Murray's notes, the administrator said, "It's a lesson on … let me see … Eastern religion. Sounds kind of interesting."

"Sounds boring as hell. What do I care about Eastern religion? I've been excommunicated by two major religions: the Catholic Church and the Protestants."

"Doesn't matter. Knock yourself out. Set off one of your match-head rockets to get them in the mood for the apocalypse," Stout replied, leaving Tom and heading for his cozy office.

Later that day, Tom entered Mrs. Murray's room to a raucous chorus of cheers and boos. He placed a picture of Siddhartha Gautama, founder of Buddhism, at the front of the room. Then he wrote the aim on the board: "What is Buddhism?"

"So after years of barhopping, you finally found religion," Barry snapped.

"What are you talking about? I neither barhop nor shun spiritual matters," Tom replied, trying to look sincere.

"I know who that dude is. He's Buddha—the guy who started Buddhism," Manny called out from the back of the room.

"That's correct. His real name was Siddhartha Gautama—a sage who lived in India around the fifth century BC," Tom stated, reading from Rosie Murray's lengthy notes.

"Siddhartha was born in Nepal, to a royal family. And he gave up a life of wealth to become a wandering beggar," said Riner, who was a conscientious student.

"That's right. Siddhartha became a mendicant, walking around India seeking truth about the meaning of life. I guess you could call him an avatar—the embodiment of the ideal in human form."

"Like your friend Amon, the Mariners Harbor Messiah."

"You know that guy? I heard he can bring people back from the dead," Barry said, scrutinizing his teacher for signs of mysticism.

"Don't believe everything you read in the newspapers—it's overstated," Tom replied. "Anyway, Siddhartha renounced the good life for a life of poverty."

"You mean Buddha left his palace and his stuff, plus his good-looking servant girls, to walk around begging for scraps of food? That's messed up," Barry exclaimed.

Perusing Mrs. Murray's notes, Tom replied, "Siddhartha believed that wisdom can only be attained through suffering—hunger, poverty, sickness, deprivation, and death."

"Was Buddha into meditation like those Vietnamese monks?" Wendy asked.

Checking Mrs. Murray's notes, Tom read, "After Siddhartha spent forty-nine days meditating, he became enlightened. Buddha realized that a person must be free of greed, hatred, lust, violence, ignorance, and other afflictions to attain peace of mind."

Lora raised her hand, rattling her copper bracelets, which drew everyone's attention. "I know what perfect peace of mind is called: nirvana."

"Nirvana? Isn't that when a woman has an orgasm?" Manny yelled.

"Why don't you shut your filthy mouth!" Lora shouted, astonishing the entire class, including their young teacher.

Glancing at his notes, Tom stated, "Nirvana is the state of supreme liberation in which all people behave decently, showing kindness and love, practicing mindfulness and meditation."

"Sounds utopian to me. Like Karl Marx's ideal classless society where everybody is equal, everything is shared, and the state withers away," said Marty, a conservative student who was into politics.

"In every religion there are warnings about corruption and greed. The biblical prophet Amos spoke out against rich landowners who exploited the poor. Jesus cast out the money lenders from the temple and blessed the meek, the poor, and the persecuted. In the Koran, Muslims are urged to help the needy and the weak through zakat, a charity tax. And Hindus emphasize the spiritual over the material in the Bhagavad-Gita," Tom recited from his notes.

"There's too much greed and violence in this country. What we need is more love and less hatred," asserted Ronnie.

"It's probably a remnant from the Old West, when everybody — the guys in the white hats and the guys in the black hats—all carried guns," Tom replied.

"The Beatle George Harrison—didn't he record some of that Eastern music with that Indian guy, Ravi Shankar?" inquired Marty, who was a news junkie.

"Yes. Harrison gave a concert to benefit the people of Bangladesh after they went through a catastrophic flood in 1970," Tom mentioned.

Lora raised her hand, minus her copper bracelets. "I saw these Hare Krishna guys chanting in New York City last summer."

On cue, Barry got out of his seat, chanting and dancing. "Hare Krishna Hare Krishna Krishna Krishna Hare Hare Hare Rama Hare Rama Rama Rama Hare Hare."

Transfixed by the mischievous teenager's antics, the class ignored the bell as Barry invoked the Hindu god Krishna. As luck would have it, Lou Stout was passing by in the hall. Stopping, he called out to Tom, "Man! You must have inspired your kids with that lesson on Eastern religion."

"What can I say? I'm an inspirational teacher."

"Yes, he is, Mr. Stout. He's the avatar of the teachers," Lora concurred as she left the class sans her jingling bracelets.

Hank Aaron

Hank Aaron played twenty-three seasons in the major leagues, in a career that began in 1954 with the Milwaukee Braves and ended with the Milwaukee Brewers in 1976. Aaron held the career record in home runs—755—until it was surpassed by Barry Bonds in 2007. Aaron hit at least thirty home runs in fifteen seasons. Over the course of his lengthy career, Hank Aaron attained a lifetime batting average of .305. Aaron's other batting records included total RBIs (2,297), extra base hits (1,477), and total bases (6,856). Hammerin' Hank was also in the top five for career hits (3,771), runs (2,174), and at-bats (12,366).

Born and raised in Mobile, Alabama, Hank Aaron started his professional career with the Negro Baseball Leagues. In 1949, at the age of fifteen, Aaron had tryouts with the Brooklyn Dodgers and the New York Giants. But the Braves offered him a fifty-dollar contract, which he signed. Later on, Hank Aaron declared that fifty dollars was the only thing that kept him from becoming a teammate of Willie Mays. This is particularly noteworthy, since Mays and Aaron have been rated in the top five of the Sporting News list of the "100 Greatest Baseball Players."

A longtime teammate of Hank Aaron was third baseman Eddie Mathews, a notorious home run hitter in his own right. The two Milwaukee Braves sluggers hit a record total of 863 home runs as teammates. Aaron's uniform number—44—was the maximum number of home runs hit by him in a season, attained in four different years. Hank Aaron's best year was 1963, when he hit 44 homeruns, drove in 130 RBIs, batted .319, and stole 31 bases.

In his early years, while a minor league player, Hank Aaron experienced many instances of overt racism. During the 1950s, he was not allowed to eat in the restaurants of southern cities, including Washington, DC. Aaron was also forced to live in separate motels in those times as a minor league player. Years later, in 1973, Aaron received hate mail when he was on the verge of breaking Babe Ruth's career home run record of 714. There were letters containing death threats, as well as threatening phone calls to reporters covering Aaron's home run chase. At the end of 1973, Hank Aaron was given a plaque by the US Postal Service for receiving more mail (930,000 pieces) than any other nonpolitician in history.

In response to this racial bigotry, there was an outpouring of public support for the veteran Braves slugger, who was low-key and modest. Aaron himself expressed the conviction that baseball wasn't about breaking records, but simply playing to the best of one's ability. Early in his career, Hank Aaron was tutored by Mickey Owen, who changed his batting stance, enabling him to hit the ball with power to all fields. In 2001, Aaron received the Presidential Citizens Medal by President Bill Clinton. And in 2002, Hank Aaron was recognized for his professional and humanitarian work by President George W. Bush with the Presidential Medal of Freedom.

CHAPTER 57

Elm Park Revisited

One blustery day in March, Tom went for a walk down Morningstar Road, happily looking for signs of spring in the sprouting crabgrass and the blooming daffodils scattered in the front yards of the one- and two-family houses along the way. A few brave sparrows and striking red robin fluttered about the stark bare-limbed trees, which had not begun to grow leaves. Despite the biting wind, the skinny teacher felt a sense of hope brought on by the incipient vernal season. Turning onto Richmond Terrace, Tom headed west, where he was buffeted by the north wind coming off the frigid choppy water of the Kill Van Kull.

Looking toward Amon's brightly painted tugboat, Tom saw the sturdy young man working on the ropes from which the boat was moored to the old wooden docks. Resourceful and hardworking, Amon was up and about from early morning to late at night. The old black-and-white television set given to him by fellow Curtis teacher Tony Tumali was seldom used by the Mariners Harbor resident. When he had spare time, Amon liked to relax by reading the paperback novels donated by various local people. He also perused the *Staten Island Advocate,* which occasionally featured articles about the man they called "the Mariners Harbor Messiah."

"You need a break, my friend. Let's go for a walk," Tom called out.

"Okay. Let me tie this rope to the dock. With the wind blowing, the boat has been moving around all night. If it breaks free, I'm up a creek without a paddle."

"You have an anchor, don't you?" Tom inquired.

"A very old one connected to the rustiest chain you ever saw. The engine doesn't work—not that I have any fuel. With a vessel like this, you need some backup."

"Just like my '64 Pontiac. The #3 Castleton Avenue bus, which makes a grand tour of the North Shore, is my backup. And the old red bike sitting in my cellar is the backup to the bus … in case of a transit strike," Tom replied.

"Sounds like a plan. Which is what I like about you, Tom. You always have a plan in case of unforeseen circumstances."

"I'm a teacher. We don't do anything without a plan, except when it comes to women, with whom you have to wing it."

Finishing his mariner's chores, Amon soon joined Tom as they headed toward Morningstar Road. Unbeknownst to the charismatic young man, Tom had a plan for that windy Saturday morning. Walking up Morningstar Road with the stinging wind at their backs, the two young men talked about their boyhood. Tom woke up every morning to deliver the *Herald Tribune* before going to school, while Amon picked corn, weeded the truck garden, and took care of cows in his family's farm.

"There's kind of a joy that comes from doing the nitty-gritty things that make up everyday life," Tom asserted.

"Working is a hard-wrought habit that does have its rewards," Amon agreed.

"But trying to convince my students of the value of hard work and learning ain't easy," the skinny teacher replied.

Approaching Booker Place, the two young men noticed the irascible Granny Schmidt tramping toward them. She was making her daily pilgrimage to the liquor store on Morningstar Road.

Amon bade the unkempt dowager a hearty good morning, while Tom tipped his knitted winter hat to the Elm Park matron.

"Hey, wise guy. Give me a coupla bucks for some sneaky Pete."

Tom reached into his wallet and gave the old woman two dollars. Amon wasn't happy but said nothing.

Snatching the money, she started to move on. Then she turned and said the first nice thing that Tom had ever heard from her. "You're not bad for a kid, but who the hell likes kids."

"I'll take that as a compliment," Tom replied with a grin.

Approaching his flat-roofed white stucco house on Pulaski Avenue, Tom invited Amon inside. "It's time you met my mom, the notorious Claire Haley."

Amon sat across the kitchen table from Tom's mom, while Tom sat in the middle of the sturdy wrought iron table, which faced the wall opposite the oven and the refrigerator. The small kitchen was bright and sunny during the morning hours.

"Every time I pick up the *Advocate*, there's a story about you. You're Staten Island's biggest celebrity," she exclaimed.

"I guess I have realized the American dream of ten minutes of fame. It will pass like all things in life," Amon replied in a matter-of-fact manner.

"Everybody and everything has his moment in this crazy world of ours," Claire replied gloomily.

Tom mentioned seeing Granny Schmidt trudging to the liquor store that morning. "I think Elm Park has more alcoholics per square mile than any community, with the possible exception of the Bowery."

"Alcoholism is no joking matter, McGee. When his father was in the midst of his drinking binges, I went to all the local bars and stores and told them not to sell him any liquor," Claire related.

"Did they listen to you?" Amon asked.

"They did, but Mr. Haley just went out of the neighborhood to indulge his habit. You may have noticed that there's a gin mill on every block of the North Shore," she replied angrily.

"Mom, there's money in booze."

"Yeah, blood money. It's a symptom of the capitalist system. Businessmen will sell their soul to the devil to make money."

"My mom is a proud Marxist. Though she doesn't believe in charity," Tom said sarcastically.

"Listen, smart aleck. I typed envelopes at five cents apiece plus worked during the day for low pay to feed, clothe, and keep a roof over you and your sister's head."

"And your son appreciates it. He talks about you all the time. How hard you worked. Doing it all with no help from your husband. He mentioned your walks to the Mariners Harbor waterfront when he was a kid — something he still likes to do."

"Yeah, we lived there years ago. It's very good of you, fixing up that rooming house for the poor on Simonson Avenue," she replied.

"Well, your son has been very helpful in that regard. Not only with his own sweat equity, but getting me legal help when we were threatened with eviction by some big-shot builders."

"Sweat equity, you say? I can barely get him to take out the garbage or cut the hedge in front."

"Trimming the hedge? I love that kind of stuff. Where are the clippers? We'll do it right now, Mrs. Haley."

As Amon waited on the sidewalk, Tom ran into the dungeon-like cellar to get the hedge clippers and rake necessary for trimming the formidable six-foot-high-by-eight-foot-long hedge.

Handing Amon the clippers, Tom declared, "I hereby grant you the honor of trimming that friggin' hedge. Hedge trimming, lawn mowing, and flower planting are noble rites of spring."

Amon started clipping the hedge with energy and alacrity that amazed the skinny science teacher. In contrast, Tom's hedge-clipping methodology was meticulous and deliberate. In less than an hour, the hedge was trimmed, its scattered cuttings raked up and deposited in the rusty garbage can.

As the two young men finished tidying up the front yard, they noticed Joey Caprino sitting on his stoop, watching their grounds maintenance work.

"Hey, Joey, how about a catch?" Tom called out to his neighbor.

Joey nodded, retreated into his house, and returned with two baseball gloves and a yellowish baseball. Tom ran into his sun-porch bedroom to get his worn baseball glove. Without further fanfare, the three young men began a three-way catch in the middle of Pulaski Avenue, keeping as far away from Mrs. Eggert's house as possible. In the past, errant tosses and batted line drives had wound up in the grumpy woman's first-floor front window.

"Stan Mislicki said you've developed a knuckleball. You're pitching for the Seagulls in the men's baseball league?" Tom said.

"Yup. I'm their ace, and Mike Palermo plays third base and relieves me late in the game. It pisses him off to be playing second fiddle to me when he was a star pitcher in high school."

"I heard he threw his arm out in the minor leagues."

"Sure did. The dumb Guinea never developed a curveball or changeup he could control. He's a good hitter. Could have made it on his hitting ability if he had some smarts at the plate," Joey replied with a grim smile.

After warming up, Joey began throwing his knuckleball to Tom, who couldn't handle it. Tom missed a dipping knuckler that "rang his bell," glancing off his glove and striking him in the groin. After that, Joey threw to Amon, who proved to be a very adroit catcher, despite never having played that position as a youngster.

"Want to be my catcher on the Seagulls? You're better than the guy we have right now," Joey told the Mariners Harbor resident.

"Wish I could do it, but my time is kind of limited right now."

"Shit. You play the game like a semipro. And that olive tree you cursed out last year withered away and died."

"Beginner's luck, that's all," Amon said with a shrug.

Face from the Past

In early April, the air was fragrant with honeysuckle, which grew in every backyard, vacant lot, and untamed wooded area of Staten Island's North Shore. The blooming rosebushes, colorful flowers, pink dogwoods, and gentle breezes represented the augurs of spring. But the ultimate rite of spring—Tennyson's poem about thoughts of love occupying young men's fancy all over the world—was absent from the skinny teacher's mind. Whether Martha had moved on or still had some feelings for her old boyfriend was a deep dark mystery to Tom.

Amon's girlfriend, Mary, no longer taught in the same school as Martha and did not appear to be the best of friends with Tom's former paramour.

A few weeks ago, Tom had bumped into Jake Gardello, Joanie's cousin. They exchanged pleasantries, but the latter was not forthcoming about Joanie's doings. The last time he saw Joanie was at St. Vincent's Hospital, where she was suffering from an undisclosed illness. He had visited Joanie with Amon, who had placed his hand on her forehead, curing her miraculously. Apparently, she returned to her husband in that faraway Midwestern state that still filled him with dread: Indiana.

With the balmy breezes inspiring him to exercise, Tom drove his old gray Pontiac to PS 21, where he took out his basketball, some Spaldings, and his worn baseball glove. Working up a sweat, the skinny science teacher practiced jump shots, sweeping hooks, driving layups, and some rim-jarring dunks from various locales on the nine-foot-high rims. Next, he proceeded to the concrete wall with the rectangular strike zone and began throwing hard, alternating fastballs with sharp breaking knuckle curves.

He was surprised that he was able to throw both sidearm and overhand without any shoulder pain. Apparently, a few years of inactivity plus exercise had healed the muscle tear in his shoulder. Now he could throw that rubber Spalding so hard that it tailed up and down, left and right. The old adage — time heals all wounds — seemed to have some validity for the skinny science teacher, who seldom missed a day of calisthenics: push-ups, sit-ups, knee bends, plus curls and presses with twenty-five–pound dumbbells,

Concentrating on throwing strikes with his fastballs and knuckle curves, Tom didn't notice the green sedan pulling up adjacent to the school yard. A pretty, curly-haired young woman with a cute toddler emerged from the hair and walked toward him. The toddler's curly hair, pouting lips, and pretty face clearly indicated that the twosome were mother and daughter. With confident familiarity, the woman said hello and asked if Tom remembered her.

Momentarily caught off balance, Tom hesitated. "Bonnie Rosolio, I haven't seen you since high school."

"It's been seven years. You look the same. Still the skinny stickball player who dashed around this playground while I read my poetry and romance novels," she exclaimed.

"I was just trying to fit in with the Elm Park kids who didn't give a damn about highbrow stuff like that. Is that your daughter?"

"Yes. Say hello to Tom, Flora."

"That's a cool name. She's very pretty … just like you."

"Why didn't you say that to me in those days. I always liked you," Bonnie said warmly.

"I was focused on my grades in high school. Besides, I was kind of backward in that area. But I was your secret admirer," Tom replied, blushing.

"I heard that you're a teacher at Curtis High School. I always knew you would do something special with your life. How's your sister doing?"

"Cara's good. She's still drawing and painting, as in her school days."

"You have a nice family, Tom."

"Well, we've had our ups and downs. You remember my dad with his drinking binges. Remember how he disrupted our poetry recital at this school?" Tom said, pointing to the small red-brick building, with the PS 21 lettering on its facade.

"I remember the recital like it was yesterday. I felt awful about it," she replied, smiling wistfully and pausing momentarily.

"I need your help. I read in the paper that you're a close friend of that Mariners Harbor man, Amon. The *Advocate* claims he has remarkable healing powers. Reporters use words like 'avatar,' 'faith healer,' and 'messiah' when referring to him."

"He is gifted in certain ways, but he's not a miracle worker," Tom replied.

Caressing her daughter, Bonnie said in soft voice, "She has seizures. They have been getting worse, and the pediatrician thinks they might be detrimental to her cognitive development."

"Isn't there medication for epileptic seizures? I had a student at Curtis who was plagued by them. His doctors prescribed medication that appeared to curtail the seizures somewhat," Tom replied.

"I'm a nurse. We've tried different meds, but nothing seems to work. It's terrible when a child suffers from seizures. She's frightened when she regains consciousness. She doesn't understand what happened to her."

Grabbing his basketball, Spaldings, and old baseball glove, Tom said, "I'll take you to him right now."

Leaving her green sedan parked on Walker Street, the pretty young mom picked up her daughter and climbed into the front seat next to her old classmate. Tom wondered about the strange turns and twists of fate that led to his transporting his elementary school heartthrob to Amon's boat in Mariners Harbor.

As luck would have it, Amon was at home in his refurbished tugboat, along with his girlfriend, Mary, who had been tidying up their maritime home. Coincidentally, Mary was acquainted with Bonnie; they had been neighbors on Winant Street, which was a few blocks away.

"I remember playing jump rope with you back in the day," Mary exclaimed after she was greeted warmly by Bonnie. "And this is your daughter? Oh, my, she's gorgeous!"

The adorable child smiled and took Mary's hand as the latter showed her some freshly picked flowers. The brightly colored, sweet-smelling wildflowers seemed to please the youngster.

Turning to Amon, Bonnie described her daughter's medical issues—the frightening seizures that had grown more frequent and more intense. Bursting into tears, the pretty curly-haired woman implored the young man, "I beg you to help us. It's awful to see her suffer such terrifying episodes."

Suddenly, Flora became agitated, as if something was disturbing her. Amon knelt down next to the child, who despite her fretfulness was drawn to the charismatic young man—cooing, babbling, and hugging him, as if he were a long-lost uncle.

Gently stroking the little girl's forehead, Amon murmured something about suffering the little children. The effect on Flora was immediate. She evinced a serenity that was uncanny.

Picking up the toddler, Bonnie asked Amon about continuing her medication.

"Sweetheart, I'm not a doctor. I'm not infallible. It's just a hit or miss with me. Only time will tell what the outcome will be," Amon replied matter-of-factly.

"How can I repay you?" she asked, hugging the adorable child, who looked at Amon with wide-eyed wonder.

"Just keep doing what you have been doing. You're a great mom."

On the drive back to retrieve her car at PS 21, Flora fell asleep on Bonnie's lap. The two former classmates talked about acquaintances from Port Richmond High School. Bonnie had starred in school plays. Unlike the Elm Park maverick, she was popular. Nonetheless, both of them shared a common distinction—they were memorialized on the high school's permanent honor roll.

"Whatever happened to that girl you were with on graduation night?"

"That was Joanie. Her family moved to Indiana. I wrote to her during college, but she met a guy and got married," Tom said, trying to sound detached.

"That's awful. When you're in high school, the world is at your fingertips. Then suddenly, you're an adult dealing with grown-up realities," she exclaimed.

"As a teacher, you carry a lot on your shoulders. Sometimes I feel I've never left high school. Except you're on the other side of the desk."

"How are your students? I bet some of the girls have a crush on you," Bonnie said with a melancholy smile.

"Most of the kids are great. No crushes that I'm aware of. At least I'm getting paid to be there. And I'm taking some courses at City College for my master's degree—free of charge."

"Well, you were always a good student. Even in the sixth grade, though you tried to hide it," she responded.

"Yeah. I was a jerk in those days."

"You weren't a jerk. You were just a boy, doing what boys do."

"Yeah. Being a pain in the ass," he replied.

As Tom's gray Pontiac pulled up next to Bonnie's green sedan, she kissed him on the cheek and left his car, holding Flora in her arms.

"You'll find someone. But don't hang out in bars, Tom," she said, standing next to his old Pontiac.

"How do you know I hang out in bars?" he asked incredulously.

"The North Shore is a small town. Word gets around that you like to drink … just like your dad," she said grimly.

"I'm not like my dad, I can assure you."

CHAPTER 59

The Mockingbird Book

Melancholy after his encounter with Bonnie Rosolio, Tom opted for some heavy drinking at Kaffman's on Morningstar Road. He frequently sought to numb his melancholia after meeting with former classmates. Bumping into Harry the Horse, he spewed out a narrative of maudlin remarks. After an hour, Harry had heard enough from the skinny science teacher. Pocketing his money from the bar, the former Pied Piper of Elm Park grabbed Tom by the collar of his shirt and escorted him out of the hazy, sour–sweet–smelling bar into the fresh air of the balmy April night.

"It's time both of us got out of there. I don't know about you, but I have work tomorrow," Harry growled, fumbling for his keys.

"Ah. Who said April is the cruelest month, breeding lilacs out of dead land, mixing memory and desire?" Tom recited, recalling Bonnie Rosolio's love of poetry.

"How the fuck would I know! I'm not a schoolteacher. You better get your ass home. Those kids are gonna give you a hard time, whether you're hungover or not."

"It was T. S. Eliot, the American expatriate, living in Paris."

"Go home, Tom. I tell you what—I'll play you in stickball Saturday. Bring your friend with you."

Pleased by the notion of challenging the formidable stickball player, Tom smiled and shook the housepainter's hand. He turned and shambled down Booker Place and was sound asleep in his sun-porch bedroom within a few minutes.

Walking into the front entrance of Curtis High School, Tom greeted the school's principal.

"Don't tell me, I'm going to be covering somebody's class today."

"Yup. By the way, you look like shit today. I hope you're not back drinking all hours of the night," the burly administrator said, eyeing Tom closely.

"Not at all. I might be coming down with something. Otherwise, I'm as fit as a fiddle. When was the last time I missed a day of teaching?"

"You got a point there. But burning both ends of the candle is going to affect your looks at some point," Mr. Stout said sardonically.

"Then I'll start living like a saint—attending church, eating healthy, getting to bed by nine o'clock, no drinking, no women, and no impure thoughts."

"Yeah, sure. The Elm Park barfly is turning over a new leaf."

"Anyway, whose class am I covering?"

"You know who—Miss Rearview Mirror. She's missing in action for the next few days. You're covering an English class," Mr. Stout said grimly.

"Would that I grab that rear appendage, an indiscretion worth dying for," Tom replied.

"Don't even think about it. Rosie Murray's husband is a New York City detective who keeps her on a short leash," Mr. Stout said, handing Tom the absent teacher's notes.

Entering Mrs. Murray's class to the usual crescendo of boos and cheers, Tom wondered how he would start a lesson on Harper Lee's novel *To Kill a Mockingbird*. He barely remembered the splendid book, which he had read in high school. Unlike his science lessons, he had no practical experiment or visual aid to motivate the lesson. How did English teachers get their ideas across without a dramatic opening like launching a match-head rocket or dropping a piece of sodium in a beaker of water? Nothing beat pyrotechnics when it came to grabbing teenagers' attention. Turning to the board, the skinny science teacher wrote the name of the book on the board as his students groaned with typical irritation and petulance.

"Come on, Mr. Haley. Do one of your practical experiments," Manny called out from the back of the room.

"Why don't you give us a free period?" someone chimed in from the same locale.

"He's just doing his job. Give the guy a break," Lora said, rattling her copper bracelets and anklets.

"Look who's brownnosing today. Yesterday you were giving Mrs. Murray a hard time," Barry replied.

"I hate that snotty bitch. Thinks she's better than everyone with her fancy clothes and her big you-know-what."

"Okay, everybody, pipe down. Let's talk about the book, which is set in a small town. When does the story take place?"

"During the 1950s," Ronnie answered.

Looking at his notes, Tom corrected her. "I believe it was during the 1930s. There's mention of Franklin Roosevelt's WPA program employing some people in the town of Maycomb, Alabama."

"It had to be a long time ago, because all the white people had black housekeepers and maids doing their work," Barry observed.

"Those Southerners were very mean to the Negroes. My dad said people from the South are still fighting the Civil War," Wendy observed.

"What about the two Finch children, Scout and Jem?" Tom asked, checking his notes.

"How can a six-year-old girl beat up her big brother? That's messed up," Barry said, shaking his head.

"Yeah, Jem must be gay like that music teacher, Mr. Schayes," Manny called out from the back of the room.

"Here's some practical advice: live and let live," Tom replied. He had heard the same advice as a CCNY student from his physics instructor in response to some derogatory remarks made by a classmate about an English professor.

"That girl Scout was the real hero of the book. Remember when she kicked that redneck in the nuts when he was getting ready to beat up Atticus?" Lora commented, shaking her copper bracelets and anklets for emphasis.

"What did you say? The proper description is to say she rattled his nuggets," Barry interjected.

Ignoring the chitchat and perusing Mrs. Murray's notes, Tom asked about the social taboos described in the book.

"We all know about that stuff. When a colored man messes with a white woman, he'll wind up dead before you can say Jackie Robinson," Barry said.

"That's only in the South," Lora replied.

"You kidding me? A white girl with jungle fever is asking for trouble … North or South in the good USA."

"What about the title, *To Kill a Mockingbird*?" Tom inquired.

"The mockingbird was a symbol of innocence. You could shoot a blue jay but not a mockingbird, which sang each morning," Wendy replied.

"Excellent, Wendy. Getting back to the book, was Atticus Finch a hero in the story, unlike most of the adults who had axes to grind?"

"He argued a good case for that black man, Tom. But the jury was prejudiced, and he was convicted of raping that white woman. I'm not a big fan of trial by jury," said Riner, a bespectacled boy who always did his homework.

"Trial by jury goes back to English common law and the Sixth Amendment of the Constitution," Tom observed.

"That white woman, Mayella, was a slut. She should have gone to jail for perjury," Manny called out from the back row of desks.

"The thing that bugs me about small towns, like Maycomb, is that everybody knows your business," Lora said, fiddling with her copper bracelets.

"Why's that? You got something to hide, girl?" Barry snapped.

"Shut the fuck up!" she screamed.

"You want to make me?" Barry yelled, getting up from his seat.

"Calm down, both of you," Tom said firmly, walking down Barry's aisle.

Moving on, Tom asked, "What about the emphasis on family and social class? Is that just a phenomenon of the South, or does it also exist in the North?"

"That's just snobbery. It exists everywhere," said Wendy, whose good looks were matched by a sharp mind.

"I agree," said Barry. "Look at Mr. Haley. He comes from a long line of whiskey drinkers, but he became a renowned Curtis High School teacher."

"Mr. Haley is cool. And he has cool friends, like that messiah man from Mariners Harbor," Lora replied.

"You ought to invite him here to talk to us," someone called out from the back of the room.

"Is he white or black?" Barry asked.

"He's mixed, like most of us," Tom replied. Actually, Tom wasn't sure of his friend's ethnic background. Lately, he surmised that Amon was a Native American.

Glancing at Mrs. Murray's notes, Tom asked what Harper Lee meant by the term "fine folks" in her book.

"That's just another name for white people," Barry replied.

"Actually, the author defined 'fine folks' as those with the good sense to do the best with what they've been given," Tom read from his notes.

"Why does everybody have to have a label? White, black, Spanish, Italian, Irish, Polish, Chinese—down deep inside we're all the same," Lora asserted.

"That's a profound sentiment," Tom concurred, folding up Mrs. Murray's notes.

"C'mon, people, now, smile on your brother. Everybody get together, try to love one another right now," Barry crooned off-key as the bell sounded, ending the class.

Amidst the good insights, irrelevant comments, laughter, and derision, and the Youngbloods' song on brotherly love, Tom's fill-in lesson for his well-endowed colleague seemed to go fairly well. Of course, how much his restless teenagers carried away from Harper Lee's memorable book about social justice in the racially divided South was questionable. From Tom's remembrances of his own high school experiences, he believed that students took away useful insights that would remain with them through the years. He recalled reading Charles Dickens's novel *A Tale of Two Cities* in high school, which began with the line "It was the best of times, it was the worst of times, it was the age of wisdom, it was the age of foolishness … it was the season of Light, it was the season of Darkness, it was the spring of hope, it was the winter of despair."

CHAPTER 60

Stickball Game

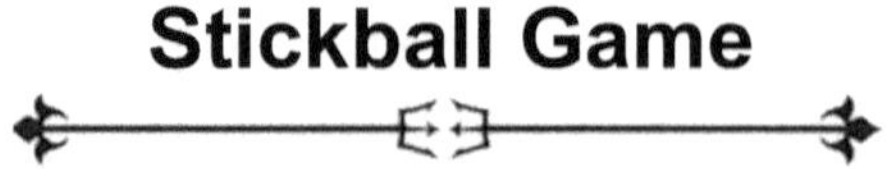

On a foggy Saturday afternoon in April, Tom pulled up at PS 21 in his old gray Pontiac, with Amon at his side. Unhappily, he noticed Harry the Horse warming up earnestly on the pavement, firing blazing fastballs and sharp knuckle curveballs. His blazing pitches hit the rectangular strike zone marked on the paved handball court wall, filling the school yard with loud rhythmic thuds as the rubber Spalding smashed against the rigid concrete wall.

"Looks like you got your good stuff today," Tom called out as he and Amon walked toward the concrete wall, which faced south toward Walker Street.

Tom carried several Spaldings, two broomstick bats, and his well-worn baseball glove. Amon had a kid's baseball glove, which was made of plastic, plus an old Brooklyn Dodger baseball cap. Fortunately, the sun began to peak through the low-lying clouds, and broad shafts of sunlight illuminated the paved school yard.

"Damned right. You better start swinging with my windup, 'cause you'll never catch up to my fastball," the Pied Piper of Elm Park replied.

After a coin toss, which Harry won, Tom and Amon batted first. Tom struck out on three pitches. Amon managed to foul off two of Harry's fastballs and was fooled on a changeup, swinging too early.

Smiling at his own ineptitude, Amon exclaimed, "You're a tricky pitcher, Harry. But I'll get to you eventually."

"It'll never happen. I'm undefeated at fast-pitch stickball."

"Ain't true, Harry. Mike Palermo and I beat you when Mike hit a ninth-inning home run off you a few years back," Tom retorted.

"Ten bucks says it's not going to happen today."

The stickball game proceeded uneventfully, with Tom baffling Harry with an assortment of overhand and sidearm fastballs, mixed with tailing curveballs and some sharp knuckle curves. Harry was unstoppable as a pitcher, with Tom managing only some foul tips and one ground ball single. Amon hit two screaming line-drive doubles and a towering pop-up, which Harry caught after a long run. The game remained a scoreless tie until Amon got hold of one of Harry's fastballs in the eighth inning and sent it over the fence, across Walker Street into the cemetery.

"Holy shit!" Harry yelled. "I've never seen anybody hit a Spalding that far. It must have traveled three hundred feet."

In the bottom of the eighth, Tom felt something give in his shoulder when he tried an overhand fastball. Changing to a sidearm delivery gave no relief to the skinny science teacher, so Amon had to relieve him. Beckoning to the Mariners Harbor resident, Tom ran to the outfield while Amon warmed up, using an unorthodox no-windup delivery. His first few warm-up tosses were off the mark, missing the rectangular strike zone by a lot. In addition, his pitches appeared to lack the velocity of Harry's and Tom's heaters.

Eagerly setting himself at the plate, Harry called out, "Just get ready to duck, Amon. Harry's gonna give that baby a ride!"

Then Amon cut loose with a fastball that whizzed by Harry at blinding speed. Harry had swung hard but did not connect. The same result occurred with Amon's next two pitches.

"Are you friggin' kidding me? Where did you learn to throw like that?" Harry exclaimed, completely overpowered by Amon's fastball.

Amon replied that he was a novice at stickball. "We didn't play stickball where I came from."

"The guy throws like Sandy Koufax and never played the game before. Shit, you should go to Shea Stadium and show the Mets your stuff. They'd sign you with a bonus—no questions asked."

"Beginner's luck. Besides, I have no control throwing baseballs. Just ask Mrs. Eggert on Pulaski Street. I broke her window."

"Good for you. I hate that woman. She was gonna call the cops on me after that guy broke her window," Harry replied, pointing at Tom.

"Amon fixed her window and did some home repairs. Now she loves him," Tom declared. "Even Granny Schmidt smiles at him."

"And you lifted that heavy beam off my chest like it was a plywood plank. No wonder they call you the Mariners Harbor Messiah," Harry said, scrutinizing Amon for the source of his physical powers.

"That came from the local papers after I rescued someone who jumped off the Staten Island ferry," Amon replied quietly.

"I think his girlfriend, Mary, was the first to use that pseudonym talking to a newspaper reporter, and it stuck," Tom chimed in.

Tom suggested they go for a few beers at K. C.'s to cool off, to which both men agreed—Harry emphatically and Amon reluctantly. Tom chose K. C.'s rather than Kaffman's because of Bonnie Rosolio's remarks about his frequenting that busy saloon on weekends.

Entering the hazy, sour-sweet–smelling bar, the three men were greeted by Pat McDean, owner of K. C.'s. "Well, the prodigal son has returned with his entourage. What are you drinking? The usual Ballantine beer brewed right here on the Island or something a little stronger?"

"Ballantine's good. There's nothing better than an ice-cold beer to celebrate a big win," Tom exclaimed.

"Don't rub it in, Teach. Without this guy, I would have beaten you easily."

"You're absolutely right. I had thrown out my arm, overhand and sidearm."

"It could have gone either way. The main thing was that it was an enjoyable experience. You can't call yourself a New Yorker unless you've played stickball," Amon said.

"I wonder if they play stickball in Chicago or Detroit," Tom replied.

"I tell you what, Tom. You go to those cities and find out for us. Next time I visit those bush-league places, I'll bring my stickball bat with me."

Amon said he had never heard of stickball before coming to the Island.

"Amon's a pretty good basketball player too. Gave me fits under the basket, and from the outside there's no stopping him," Tom commented.

"Basketball's a game I haven't played in recent years, though I like watching it on TV. I saw those big guys Chamberlain and Jabbar going at it the other day," Harry observed.

"There will never be another dominant center like Wilt Chamberlain. He once scored a hundred points against the Knicks in 1962. And that year he averaged more than fifty points per game," Tom replied.

"Jabbar is a better shooter and quicker. Wilt couldn't stop his skyhook. But my favorite player is Elgin Baylor, driving to the basket, faking the other guy out."

"Baylor is a one-man show. He's changed the game of basketball from what it used to be. Slow white guys with two-hand set shots and banked layups," Tom said, ordering another round of Ballantines for his two companions.

"What's wrong with the set shot? I had a deadly one in my day," Harry responded angrily.

"I'll have to challenge you to a game of twenty-one next time you're free."

"Shit. You with your friggin' challenges. Stick to teaching, and leave the ball games to talented athletes like me and Amon," Harry said, downing his beer and getting ready to leave K. C.'s.

"Tom's an instigator, but he's a good guy. He's helped me more than I can count and still manages to teach those Curtis kids," Amon chimed in.

"Yeah. He's harmless—like his Elm Park buddies I used to play stickball with on Pulaski Avenue," Harry replied, shaking Amon's hand and slapping Tom on the back before exiting the hazy bar.

Amon also got ready to leave K. C.'s. Tom asked him about speaking to Curtis students about volunteering. "I spoke with my principal. Many of them have heard about you from the local papers. I'm sure you'd get an enthusiastic reception from them."

"I don't know. I'm not much of a speaker," Amon replied, seemingly lost in thought. "But my time is running out. So I've got to do what I can before—"

"Of course. But what is this weird stuff about time running out?"

Dalton Trumbo

Dalton Trumbo was an American novelist and screenwriter whose career was curtailed by his association with the Communist Party in the 1940s. In 1947, Trumbo was summoned by the House Un-American Activities Committee (HUAC) to testify about his activities with the American Communist Party. Refusing to disclose his actions or the identities of Hollywood actors, directors, and writers who were members of the party, Dalton Trumbo was blacklisted—banned from working in the movie industry. Trumbo asserted that the First Amendment of the US Constitution gave him the right to refuse to answer questions about his political beliefs and his personal associations.

Born in Colorado in 1905, Dalton Trumbo began writing in his twenties while working at a bakery in Los Angeles. Anxious to move away from his menial job, Trumbo worked on short stories, novels, and screenplays. Drawing on experiences while growing up in a working-class family, Dalton Trumbo's stories appeared in magazines like *Vanity Fair* and *Vogue*. In 1934, Trumbo was hired by Warner Brothers to review plays and novels for possible movie adaptation and also to write screenplays. In 1936, Trumbo wrote his first screenplay for the movie *Road Gang*. In 1937, he wrote the screenplay for the movie *Devil's Playground*, which showed his concern for the downtrodden and disenfranchised.

In addition to Warner Brothers, Dalton Trumbo also worked for Columbia, Paramount, Twentieth Century Fox, MGM, and RKO movie studios. In 1940, he won his first Oscar for the movie *Kitty Foyle*, starring Ginger Rogers in a role about a poor girl who enters a wealthy family as a result of marriage. In addition to his movie industry success, Trumbo became involved in left-wing political causes. He joined communists and liberals in supporting the anti-fascist coalition against General Franco during the bloody Spanish Civil War.

In 1939, Dalton Trumbo wrote the antiwar novel *Johnny Got His Gun*. At that time, the Communist Party changed its anti-Hitler policy to a pro-peace orientation, as a result of the Russian–German peace treaty. The publication of *Johnny Got His Gun* coincided with the antiwar movement of the far left and far right in the United States. There was a break between President Franklin D. Roosevelt and the Communist Party, until America entered World War II as an ally of the British and the Russians.

During the Second World War, Dalton Trumbo wrote screenplays for several patriotic war movies, including *A Guy Named Joe, Mission to Moscow*, and *Thirty Seconds Over Tokyo*. In 1945, the Trumbo-written movie — *Our Vines Have Tender Grapes*, starring Margaret O'Brien and Edward G. Robinson — depicted life on a meager farm in Wisconsin. Earlier in 1943, Dalton Trumbo reportedly joined the Communist Party, which had attained the zenith of its popularity in the United States during that era.

Appearing before HUAC in 1947, along with several other Hollywood writers, Dalton Trumbo refused to answer questions or name coworkers associated with the Communist Party. This group of screenwriters, known as the Hollywood Ten, cited the First Amendment in refusing to incriminate other members of the Screen Writers Guild. Charged with contempt of Congress, Trumbo and nine other screenwriters were fined and sent to prison for ten months. In addition, they were blacklisted — prevented from working for the Hollywood studios. Unable to write under his own name, Dalton Trumbo wrote movie scripts for several Hollywood hits — including *Roman Holiday, The Brave One, and Spartacus* — using a pseudonym. Otto Preminger and Kirk Douglas broke the blacklist in 1959 by openly hiring Trumbo to write the script of *Spartacus*. He also reportedly wrote the script for *Exodus* in the late 1950s.

The Academy of Arts and Sciences (which had supported the blacklist during the 1950s) belatedly conferred an Oscar on Trumbo for his work in writing the screenplay for *The Brave One* in 1975. Despite his communist sympathies, Trumbo's writing was populist, depicting the individual fighting the establishment. Dalton Trumbo was not embittered by his ill treatment during the Cold War. He asserted that "the blacklist was a time of evil, and no one on either side who survived it came through untouched by evil … There was bad faith and good faith, honesty and dishonesty, courage and cowardice, selfishness and opportunism, wisdom and stupidity, good and bad on both sides."

CHAPTER 61

Algebra Lesson

Walking into the Curtis lobby, Tom bumped into Lou Stout, the school's burly principal, the latter dropping a sheaf of notes filled with algebraic equations. Stooping to pick them up, the skinny science teacher knew he would be guest teaching for an absent colleague.

"Goody Gootstein has a coverage for me. Isn't there anybody else capable of filling in for the AWOLs?" Tom complained wearily.

"Look at it as a compliment. You're a popular guy. Even Rosie Murray smiles at you in the hallways," Stout replied.

"I wish she'd give me more than a smile. Never mind. I'll do it. What about that assembly program on community volunteering for my friend Amon?" Tom replied, trying to arrange a quid pro quo.

"I hear you. But there's a protocol to be followed for outside speakers in the schools. Once I get the go-ahead, we'll do it."

Later that day, Tom walked into a third-floor classroom carrying a large balance scale, along with several half-pound, one-pound, and two-pound weights. In a large shopping bag, Tom removed a couple cans of soup, a jar of peanut butter, and a large box of Wheaties. The skinny science teacher also had a deflated soccer ball. As expected, students reacted with a mixture of dismay, joy, confusion, and curiosity.

"What are we doing today? Learning how to cook?" Manny called out from the back of the room.

"Nah. Mr. Haley missed his lunch period. So now he's gonna eat with us," Barry chimed in.

"Not really. We're gonna do some math. And hopefully show the connection between math and food," Tom replied.

"I know the connection between math and food. If the number of calories you eat is bigger than the number of calories you burn off, then you get chubby … like Miss Bracelet over there," Barry snapped.

"Shove it up your ass," Lora responded, rattling her copper bracelets and anklets angrily.

"Enough, both of you. Suppose I wanted to weigh this big box of Wheaties with the balance scale. How would I do it?" Tom asked the class.

Ronnie raised her hand. "Put the Wheaties on one scale, and add weights to the other scale until they balance."

Following the student's instructions, Tom kept adding small weights to the pan opposite from the Wheaties until an equilibrium was achieved.

"It looks like it weighs a little less than a pound," Ronnie observed.

"Well, the box says one pound," Tom read.

"You sure you didn't sneak some before class?" Barry asked Lora, who responded by throwing a wadded paper ball at the teenager.

"Maybe General Mills is cheating the public. Let's weigh those soup cans,"

Manny called out from the back of the room.

The cans also seemed to weigh slightly less than a pound. Tom asked for a conclusion.

"Maybe your balance scales are inaccurate," Wendy asserted. She was a pretty teenager whose intelligence was as noteworthy as her appearance.

"Well, these science apparatuses have been around as long as Curtis High School itself," Tom replied. The St. George school was built around the turn of the century, as the formidable stone gargoyles on its facade indicated.

Barry raised his hand, and Tom got ready for a non sequitur. "When it comes to cereal, Wheaties and Cheerios come in different-size boxes. So how do you compare their prices?"

"That's an excellent question. What's the answer?"

Riner, a serious student, raised his hand. "I'd buy the larger box. It's cheaper because companies save money on packaging."

"That depends on the item. Sometimes the jumbo size is not cheaper. It's a scam," Lora exclaimed.

"You should buy the no-frills brand—they're always cheaper," said Marty, who seemed to know a lot about marketing and economics.

"Only cheapos buy no-frills stuff. I buy name brands like Wheaties, Skippy, Franco-American, Chock Full o' Nuts, and Campbells," Barry replied, reading the labels of the displayed items.

Marty mumbled something about welfare spendthrifts, and Barry got up from his seat and loomed over Marty, sitting at his desk. "What did you say about welfare? My family works for a living, chump!"

Tom sprang from his spot behind the teacher's desk and inserted himself between Barry and Marty, the latter of whom remained seated but looked perplexed and intimidated. "Now sit down! Before I send you both to the dean."

"Good. I'll kick his ass on the way to the dean's office," Barry shouted.

"That's your only answer to criticism—punching somebody in the face. Grow up already!" Lora yelled, shaking her bracelets and anklets loudly.

Tom wondered why the current crop of kids were so prone to fighting at the smallest provocation. He remembered his own high school days, when fisticuffs were rare occurrences. Of course, he was in the honors "x" class, where arguments were mostly verbal and concerned the merits of rival baseball teams and occasionally entered the political realm. With the backdrop of the raging Vietnam War, Tom's generation seemed to be focused on peaceful means of settling differences. Notwithstanding teenage passions and rivalries, his classmates seemed to genuinely like one another. With the current racial, ethnic, class, and political differences wracking the country, social cohesion was notably absent in 1970s America.

Glancing at Mrs. Murray's notes, Tom asked the class about unit price.

"It's the price per pound," Wendy answered.

"That's correct," Tom said, turning to write the unit price formula on the board: Unit Price = Price/Quantity.

Next, he placed several unit price problems on the blackboard:

> Ex 1: Compute the unit price of a 12-ounce can of soda that costs 52 cents.
> Ex 2: Compute the unit price of a 16-ounce can of soup costing 77 cents.
> Ex 3: Compute the unit price of an 18-pound turkey that costs $11.69.

The class was given a few minutes to work out the solutions, and then Tom had Lora, Barry, and Wendy place the answers on the board:

> Ex 1: 4.3 cents/oz
> Ex 2: 4.8 cents/oz
> Ex 3: $0.65/lb

"So what are you gonna do with those balance scales, weigh Lora?" Manny called out from the back of the room.

"How about weighing your balls? They're probably weightless," she responded, jangling her copper bracelets.

"Why don't you come back here and see for yourself?" Manny responded with a snarl.

At that point, Tom dispatched Manny to the dean, incurring protests from the boys that he favored the girls—especially his pet, Lora. Ignoring the uproar, Tom wrote an algebraic equation on the board: 2X – 13 = 25.

"To solve this equation, we are going to use the principle of the balance scale—whatever you do to one side, you have to do the same thing to the other side."

Tom demonstrated the principle of algebraic equivalence by adding a pound to one side and then adding the same weight to the other side to restore the balance. He further demonstrated the equivalence principle by removing equal weights from each side of the balance scale.

Lora raised her hand. "Can we weigh my copper bracelets and anklets on your balance scale?"

The skinny science teacher agreed, and the cute coed removed her bracelets and anklets with great ceremony, aware that all the boys' eyes were riveted on her when she slipped them off her plump legs.

After prancing to the front of the room, she plopped them on the left balance scale while Tom carefully added weights until a balance was achieved.

"Altogether your copper bracelets and anklets come to 2.5 pounds," Tom announced.

"Wow. That's a lot of weight to carry around. You're one strong girl," Barry commented.

"Getting back to the algebraic equation: 2X - 13 = 25, how do we solve it?"

Riner raised his hand. "First, add 13 to both sides, and then divide by 2. So the answer is 19."

Tom wrote a second equation on the board: 3X + 11 = 47 and asked the class to solve it.

Wendy raised her hand. "First, subtract 11 from both sides, and then divide by 3. The answer is 12."

Tom was about to write a third equation on the board, when the bell rang, bringing the contentious lesson on unit price and algebraic equations to a close. As he gathered up his materials, he gave Barry the box of Wheaties, Ronnie the peanut butter, and Lora the two cans of soup.

"What about the soccer ball?" Barry asked.

"I was going to weigh the soccer ball with no air in it and then reweigh it fully inflated. It would weigh more with the air in it because air has weight."

"Why don't you show us now?"

Tom weighed the soccer ball empty, filled it with air, and then weighed it again. Sure enough, the air-filled ball weighed half a pound more.

"Way to go, man," Barry squealed, shaking Tom's hand.

"You're the best, Mr. Haley. But I wanted to ask you when your friend Amon is coming to speak at Curtis," the curly-haired Lora asked.

"Soon, because time is running out."

"Why is that?" Lora inquired.

"I don't know. I'm just repeating what Amon himself said to me last week."

Heartfelt Talk

Tom stood nervously next to Amon on the stage of the Curtis auditorium, looking at the congregation of students talking and fidgeting in their seats. It was a first for the skinny science teacher, who recalled the many times he had shepherded his homeroom class to assembly programs on the environment, science, current events, and the school's clubs and teams. He remembered the "x" class boys rebellion refusing to attend assembly after their homeroom teacher, Mr. Gento, had excused the girls from that obligation. A stern lecture from his guidance counselor and a letter to his mom were the punishment for that particular transgression.

The school's burly principal, Lou Stout, spoke briefly about the guest, as if he were an old acquaintance, taking credit for his contributions to the North Shore, as he had done when Tom started the holiday food basket program a few years earlier. Then, he nodded to Tom to "give the introduction for the Mariners Harbor Messiah."

"Ladies and gentlemen," Tom began haltingly, startled by the sound of his voice reverberating in the large auditorium.

"Hey, Mr. Haley, why don't you set off one of your match-head rockets?" Manny yelled from the audience.

"Not today, folks. Where were we? Ah, I first met Amon walking on Richmond Terrace more than two years ago, seeing him connecting some wires from his tugboat to a utility pole. I was stunned to see him fall from the that pole and land on the wooden pier without injuring himself. He is a skilled carpenter, housepainter, plumber, fisherman, stickball player, and faith healer. But the most impressive qualities of my friend are his kindness and compassion for the homeless, the poor, the sick, and those afflicted by alcoholism and drug addiction. Please give Amon a warm welcome."

An extended period of applause and cheering followed, which surprised Tom as Amon looked over his notes, preparing to speak. Indeed, as a result of numerous articles in the *Advocate*, Amon had become a celebrity — on par with rock stars, baseball players, and movie actors.

"Thank you, everybody, for that warm welcome. Curtis High School was one of the first places I saw on Staten Island. I really admire those sandstone gargoyles on the front of your school, plus the great view of the New York City skyline."

"Tell them about your rescue of that guy who jumped off the ferryboat," Lora called out from the front row, rattling her copper bracelets and anklets so that the jangling could be heard throughout the large auditorium.

Smiling sheepishly, Amon proceeded. "Don't believe everything you read in the newspapers. I'm no superhero, no faith healer, no clairvoyant, no avatar, and certainly no messiah. I do live in Mariners Harbor on a tugboat off Richmond Terrace. You're welcome to stop by and lend a hand. The city has given us another building in Mariners Harbor to fix up for those who have nowhere to live. Never look down on someone who is poor, for truly they are your brothers. Perhaps you can volunteer in your own neighborhoods — help shut-ins, disabled folks, and the needy. Give of yourself, and the rewards will be awesome. I am an ordinary man, faced with formidable tasks, limited resources, and little time left to accomplish these worthwhile goals.

"There is one rule which guides me in my everyday life — the golden rule stated by Jesus himself: Do unto others as you would have them do unto you. The dos and don'ts of your parents, the laws of our city and state, and our Constitution advise us to treat each other with mutual respect, regardless of our class, color, or creed. And remember, folks, errors of omission are as bad as errors of commission. Your teacher, Mr. Haley, informed me that the foundation of ethics originates with the ancient Roman stoics, like Epictetus. A Roman slave, Epictetus advocated a life of simplicity, sacrifice, austerity, and reason. He said the stoic is happy despite poverty, sickness, imprisonment, or impending death."

The student audience reacted negatively to Amon's description of Roman stoicism, causing him to pause. "Of course, this is an ideal picture of the virtuous life. Mr. Haley also mentioned the German philosopher Immanuel Kant, who stated the categorical imperative—a universal ethical principle that applies to all people, in all times, and across all societies. Such moral rules—such as do not lie, steal, or kill—are compelled by the will and by reason."

"In Jesus's own words: Blessed are the poor in spirit, the meek, the persecuted, the sick, the hungry, the workers, and the peacemakers. It's the young people like yourselves, Curtis High School students, who are the salt of the earth and the light of the world. Do not answer violence with violence. If struck on the cheek, turn the other cheek, rather than retaliating with force. Do not be consumed with material wants, to the detriment of spiritual concerns. Judge not, and you won't be judged. Ask, and it will be given to you. Seek, and you will find. Knock, and it will be opened to you. In 1960, John Kennedy said we should not ask what America can do for us. Instead, we should ask what we can do for America. Ben Franklin urged us not to waste time, for time is the stuff life is made of. I feel my own time is coming to an end, and I need you—Curtis students—to carry on my work and do good in the world."

The students burst forth in thunderous applause and cheering as Amon walked off the stage and headed down one of the aisles. Several students, including Lora and Barry, hugged the charismatic young man, whose face was overcome with emotion. There was a mixture of awe, happiness, and sadness in the crowd. And the feeling that Amon wouldn't be around much longer was palpable to everyone sitting in the Curtis auditorium.

CHAPTER 63

Life Redux

Sitting on Tom's desk were the following items: a potted geranium plant, a jar with a grasshopper amongst some weeds and crabgrass, a petri dish with bread mold, a log covered with moss, and a piece of coal. On the blackboard was a simple question: "What is life?"

As the skinny teacher's class entered the room, Barry picked up the jar, examined it closely, and started to unscrew the lid. Taking the jar from his cantankerous student, he said, "We don't want Jiminy Cricket to get loose."

"But Jiminy can't breathe, Mr. Haley. You're killing the poor bugger!"

"Look at the lid—there are several pinholes in it."

"Can the air get through those tiny holes?" Ronnie asked nervously.

"Normal atmospheric pressure is about fifteen pounds per square inch—sufficient for air to get in there," Tom responded.

Showing the class the petri dish mold, the moss-covered log, and the piece of coal, Tom asked which item represented a living organism. Someone from the back of the room said they were all life forms except for the coal, which was a mineral formed from green plants living millions of years ago.

Concurring, Tom repeated his pivotal question: "What is life?"

"Anything that moves, breathes, eats food, and eliminates waste," answered Riner, who was studious and methodical.

"You mean takes a dump," Manny called out from the back of the room.

"I hate that expression," said Lora, shaking her copper bracelets and anklets.

"Should I have said shits and pisses?" Manny snapped.

"You're very crude. We are in a classroom, sir," Barry chimed in with his falsetto voice.

Ignoring the irrelevant banter, Tom went to the board and wrote down the five conditions necessary for life. Through a series of questions, answers, and non sequiturs, they arrived at the following facts:

Conditions Necessary for Life
1. Oxygen: Except for anaerobic bacteria, all plants and animals require oxygen to oxidize food.
2. Water: All plants and animals need water. Our body cells are bathed in saltwater solution.
3. Food: Chemical energy is obtained by green plants through photosynthesis. Animals eat plants or other animals for growth and energy.
4. Moderate Temperature: Human beings can stand temperatures ranging from 30 °F to 100 °F.
5. Normal Atmospheric Pressure: Human beings require 14.7 lbs/sq in of air pressure in order to breathe.

Wendy raised her hand. "Why are our body cells bathed in salt water?"

"That fact originates with early life forms, which began in the sea. Human beings are 80 percent water by weight," Tom answered.

"Stop drinking so much water, and you'll lose most of your fat," Barry said, smiling and squinting his eyes at Lora.

Lora held up both of her arms, extending them toward her tormenter, and rattled her copper bracelets.

"Hey, she's casting an evil spell on me. I know about that stuff — it's black magic," Barry screamed in mock terror.

"I'm no gypsy. I don't do black magic," the cute curly-haired teenager replied.

"Yes, you are! Only gypsies wear those weird copper trinkets."

"Fuck off! You're the one giving off bad vibrations," Lora exclaimed.

"Good, good — good vibrations. My baby gives good vibrations," Barry chanted in his patented falsetto voice.

Moving on despite the bickering, Tom asked the class to define "food chain."

"A food chain shows how food energy is passed from one animal to the next," Wendy answered. Like most able students, she was able to ignore the many distractions occurring in the classroom and focus on the lesson itself.

"Excellent, Wendy." Turning to the blackboard, the young science teacher had his students list some examples of food chains:

Man — Pig — Corn — Nitrates
Bear — Fox — Rabbit — Carrot
Lion — Giraffe — Tree Leaves
Hawk — Frog — Grasshopper — Grass
Shark — Trout — Snail — Algae

"What is a food web?" Tom inquired.

Again, Wendy raised her hand. "A food web is interconnecting food chains."

"Wouldn't it be better to say it's a network of food chains?" Barry interjected.

"Both definitions are correct. And ecology is the study of the interactions of plants and animals in their food chains and food networks," Tom replied.

"You always favor the girls, Mr. Haley," Barry complained.

"Girls are smarter than boys—that's clear," Tom snapped as the bell rang, ending the lesson on the conditions necessary for life.

Tom recalled that he had given a similar lesson early in the school year—something that had eluded his students. He understood that repetition was a necessity in teaching and in everyday life.

Helping Tom gather his materials together, Lora asked if he really felt that girls were smarter than boys.

"Absolutely. My mom is the smartest person I know."

"Do you think we'll ever have a woman president?" she asked.

"Sure. It's only a matter of time," Tom asserted.

Smiling, Lora left the room, her copper bracelets and anklets jingling and making good vibrations all the way down the hall.

As Tom walked wearily along Curtis's dark third-floor hallway, he bumped into his old friend Tony Tumali.

"You're looking gloomy today. Are the kids getting to you?"

"Sometimes they can be a pain the ass," the skinny science teacher replied.

"I give pop quizzes when things get out of hand," Tony offered.

Just then, Dick Grimsby hobbled by. Tom was dismayed that the congenial colleague was back to wearing his steel leg brace. Were Amon's healing powers on the wane?

"Maybe you should have them recite the Common Prayer before each class: Lord, forgive me for not doing what I should have done, and for doing what I shouldn't have done," Dick replied.

"But prayer is forbidden in the public schools," Tom replied. He recalled listening to Bible readings in elementary school, but the

Supreme Court put a stop to that by the time he was in high school.

"No. That's out of the question nowadays," Tony said ruefully.

"Just go up to the one with the biggest mouth and jab him in the stomach with your finger … playfully, with a smile on your face. He'll get the message," Dick recommended.

"I couldn't do that. 'Know your limitations' is an adage I follow as a teacher. My approach is to grab their attention with a booming practical experiment."

"You can't set off a match-head rocket every day of the week," Tony replied.

"Whenever the hall is filled with sulfur fumes, the kids say it's Mr. Haley with one of his practical experiments. It's your trademark," Dick exclaimed.

"I wish I had my friend Amon's charisma. He had the kids eating out of his hands when he spoke here last week."

"He's a star, all right. But you know what happens to shining stars?" Dick asked.

"They lead us to our destiny?" Tom responded uncertainly.

"No. They burn out and fall to the earth," Dick declared grimly, pointing to his steel brace.

"Ah, don't say that," Tom said as Tony turned away and Dick smiled with a grimace that reminded Tom of his late alcoholic father, Thomas Haley. Thinking about his unhappy father, Tom felt an urge to visit Kaffman's bar for an early afternoon picker-upper.

CHAPTER 64

Jake Gardello

Driving up Morningstar Road, Tom slowed down as he approached Kaffman's on the corner of Walker Street. Then cursing at himself, he opted to turn left on Walker Street, heading for PS 21. The best way to blow off steam and forget your troubles, he realized, was with some healthy exercise.

Taking out his basketball from the gray Pontiac, Tom walked over to the nine-foot basketball court and began shooting baskets, working up a nice sweat and forgetting the ups and downs involved in teaching pesky adolescents. Before long, a pale-blue Chevy that was vaguely familiar pulled up to the school yard. It was none other than Jake Gardello, his old flame's cousin. The two greeted each other awkwardly and, as young men are wont to do, started shooting baskets together.

They played some games of horse and then a spirited game of twenty-one. Jake removed his suit jacket and loosened his tie, but his leather-soled shoes prevented him from getting the traction needed to stop, start, and change directions quickly. A stocky thirty-year-old, Jake lacked the sprightly energy of his graceful cousin. Tiring quickly, Jake finally spoke up and revealed the purpose of his visit to Elm Park.

"Joanie's marriage has broken up. It's a long story, which I don't want to go into. Let her talk about it."

"What? I'm astonished. How is she doing?" Tom replied, shooting a line drive that caromed off the front of the rim. Knowing Joanie, he figured the breakup was due to betrayal by her asshole husband.

He remembered visiting Joanie at St. Vincent's Hospital some time ago with Amon. His friend had placed his hand on her forehead, healing her almost immediately. It was one of his amazing miracles, which made him a local celebrity.

"She's good. I thought I'd find you at Kaffman's doing some elbow bending.

Then I figured you might be at the school yard playing ball."

"You know me well, Jake. Either drinking or playing ball or teaching science," Tom replied.

The skinny teacher was glad he had chosen the PS 21 school yard instead of the hazy, sour-sweet–smelling Elm Park gin mill. He recalled that wonderful softball game, so many years ago, when he had collided with a teammate in the outfield and Joanie ran over, fussing and cooing over him. Jake had played on the opposing team and probably was the reason his cousin Joanie was there as a boisterous spectator. Indeed, Tom had been so distracted by the cute teenager that he crashed into Joey Caprino while chasing a fly ball in center field.

"I'm not sure when Joanie's coming back to the Island, but it will be soon. Be nice to her! She's been through a lot," Jake declared, grabbing his jacket and heading for his sleek Chevrolet.

Later on, Tom was talking excitedly with his friend Amon about Joanie's return to the Island. Amon grabbed the skinny science teacher by the arm. "Didn't I tell you that you two were soul mates, inextricably bound together?"

They were shopping at a local supermarket, where Amon was purchasing food items and household comestibles for the residents at his Victorian boardinghouse on Union Avenue. Checking out at the cashier's register, Amon found he was a bit short on cash. Amon asked if he could put the amount he owed on his tab, as usual.

"No, sir. We can't do that anymore. Your tab keeps getting bigger, and your people come in here all the time, charging stuff—including beer and cigarettes," the clerk responded sourly.

Uncharacteristically, Amon turned red with fury. "Don't worry, you'll get your money. Friggin' money gougers. You're just as bad as the bankers, businessmen, and landlords who rip off working people trying to get by."

Reaching into his pocket, Tom paid the balance as Amon muttered epithets under his breath. Patting the Mariners Harbor resident on the back, Tom said, "You're beginning to sound like my Marxist mom."

"Well, your mom makes a lot of sense. How is she doing, by the way?"

"Good. Why don't you drop over Saturday morning? Elm Park could use a visit from the Mariners Harbor Messiah. We need someone to talk us out of our evil ways."

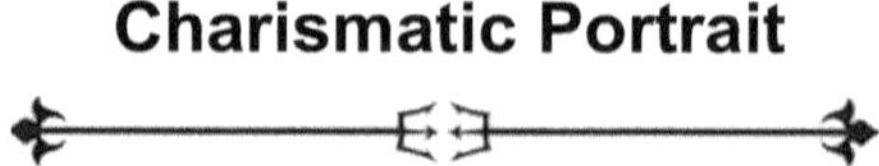

CHAPTER 65

Charismatic Portrait

As it happened, Cara was at the flat-roofed stucco house with their mom, having coffee, talking about her secretarial job in the city, and complaining about her brutish husband, Phil. The thought of his sister's unhappy marriage gave Tom pause when it came to resuming his connection with the tumultuous Martha. Answering the ring of the doorbell, Tom ushered Amon through the long narrow hall and the central TV room, to the bright sunny kitchen.

Amon gave Tom's mother and sister a hug and a kiss, exclaiming, "I'm so glad to see you again, Mrs. Haley. Tom talks about you all the time."

"I can only imagine what he says about me," Claire responded with a sardonic laugh, giving Tom an angry look.

"Oh, no! It's all good, Mrs. Haley. Tom's a good son and a loyal friend. He has done much on behalf of the homeless, in addition to his teaching duties at Curtis High School."

"Well, he damned well better be. I worked very hard—wearing the skin off my fingers, typing envelopes at night—after working as a bookkeeper all day long in the city."

"Mom, please don't get the shoebox of canceled checks from the Smiths," Cara said, shaking her head and looking up at the ceiling.

"Both of your children have inherited your work ethic—of that you can be sure, Mrs. Haley," Amon intoned diplomatically.

"I hear you're some kind of faith healer," Claire asserted, pointing to the right side of her face, which had been scarred by radium burns in her youth. "Can you do something about this?"

"I'll try," Amon responded, going over to Claire and gently touching the disfigured woman's face.

Tom sensed that Amon no longer was confident about his healing powers. The fact that Dick Grimsby was now wearing a brace and the car-crash victim, Evette, had begun complaining about an aching back gave him pause.

"You should have been around to help Tom and Cara's father. He was an incurable alcoholic."

"The rumors concerning my abilities have been hugely exaggerated by the local papers," Amon offered quietly.

"Yeah. That damned *Advocate* is a rag. They like to play up the misfortunes of working people just to sell their rotten scandal sheet. Just like those damned saloons selling booze to helpless drunks. Blood money, I called it … right to their faces."

"You're definitely a woman of strong opinions, which I admire greatly," Amon replied, sipping on coffee that Cara had given to him.

Cara also gave the charismatic Mariners Harbor resident one of her homemade cupcakes, which he seemed to enjoy immensely. Tom remembered his sister giving their neighbor Antonio, the mason, one of her special cupcakes when he was furious with Tom. Her brother had hit a pop-up, which landed in some cement Antonio was mixing to repair his sidewalk.

Surprising everyone in the small kitchen, Cara had Amon sit by the window, where she began to paint his portrait. He complied willingly, sitting motionless while the young woman sketched and painted with amazing skill. Before long, a striking resemblance of the handsome, dark-complexioned young man was completed before everyone's eyes.

"Cara, it's an extraordinary painting. It looks just like him!" Tom exclaimed.

"Cara has her father's talent. Although he painted in a room, using his imagination. He worked quickly and effortlessly, producing excellent stuff, when he was sober. Not bad," Claire said, examining the picture closely.

Putting her brushes and tubes of paint away, Cara placed the painting on the living room coffee table to dry.

"Mrs. Haley, you must be very proud of your gifted children."

"Of course I am. But don't let it go to your head—the both of you," she replied with a smile, which was more like a grimace, reminding Tom of the way his dad smiled.

Tom realized that the ability to find joy in life and to smile with your whole being was not widely disseminated in those who had gone through some tough times in life. Indeed, Claire Haley had a good sense of humor, but her laughter was usually manifested as a response to sarcasm mixed with ironic wit. Her wisdom about the world and its ways was tempered with a bitterness that sometimes surprised her son. Like many people who have had disappointments in life, she could not laugh at herself easily.

Later on, his mom and Amon had a philosophical discussion about charity. As a Marxist, Claire Haley did not believe in charity, stating that it was the role of government to eliminate poverty by moving resources from the wealthy to the poor. Amon agreed with much of what she had to say but asserted that until "the fortuitous arrival of a utopian society, we are obliged to help the poor, the downtrodden, the desperate, and the afflicted."

Surprising everyone, Cara used the term "post-office socialism" to describe her mom's political philosophy. "You want the government to own corporations and run them like the post office. Whenever I go to the post office, there are long lines and the postal employees are all sitting around in the back."

Looking askance at Cara, her mom said, "You're getting like your brother. The both of you deal with the world's problems with a snappy argument that doesn't hold water."

Getting ready to leave, Tom and Amon walked down the long narrow hallway, where the latter bumped his head on the hanging light fixture. Smiling, Tom mentioned he had learned to duck in that hallway after enduring many bumps to his noggin.

"Wait! Your picture," Cara called out as she ran into the living and retrieved her portrait of the Mariners Harbor resident. As she handed it over to Amon, the young woman did a double take.

"Look! There's a halo over your head," she called out.

"You're kidding … you're not kidding," Tom said after examining the picture.

"Com'ere, Mom. There's a halo in my picture, which I did not paint."

Ever the doubter, Claire Haley scrutinized the painting. "Yeah, sure. You must have been thinking about post offices while you were painting Amon's picture."

"Don't forget, Mom. Life must be lived on the basis of reality," Tom said, teasing his unspiritual, down-to-earth mother. As a science teacher, Tom believed that the events of life, though ostensibly random, were linked by cause and effect.

Always the realist, Claire yelled from the front porch, "I'll believe it when my face turns pretty and General Motors is owned by the government."

CHAPTER 66

Reluctant Hero

A few weeks later, Tom was treating Amon and Mary to dinner at their favorite diner beyond Union Avenue on Richmond Terrace. The dingy diner had been the scene of Amon's earliest miracle: resuscitating an elderly man who had an apparent heart attack. His wonderful feat of hands-on faith healing had prompted Mary to call her boyfriend the Mariners Harbor Messiah. This label was reinforced by the local newspapers after he rescued Perry Pantino from the swirling waters of the New York Bay.

Sitting in a booth under the neon lights, the three young people were greeted by the same gaunt, gray-haired waitress who had served them so long ago. Tom and Amon ordered hamburgers and french fries, while Mary requested her customary BLT on toast. Tom noticed that Mary had changed little in the past few years. She was still the slender sweet-faced parochial school teacher who doted on her students and adored the charismatic Mariners Harbor resident.

As the threesome chatted and ate their down-home diner food, Tom observed the fatigue in Amon's face. Gone were the radiant smile and glowing energy that were part of his friend's persona.

When the waitress came back with the bill, which Tom grabbed unceremoniously, she scrutinized Amon at length. "I remember you, young man. You saved Danny when he had a heart attack here a couple of years ago. He was a steady customer."

"Oh, yes. Whatever became of that poor man?" Mary inquired.

Pausing momentarily, the waitress replied, "Danny collapsed and died on Richmond Terrace from a massive heart attack. He was seventy-five years old, an old sailor who liked his whiskey and his rye."

"I'm so sorry to hear about that. I wish Amon had been around. He would have saved him again," Mary responded.

Shaking his head sadly, Amon disagreed. "Mary, I'm no miracle worker. So-called faith healing is akin to the placebo effect. If the afflicted person is convinced that his helper has a special gift, he feels better about his condition and therefore heals."

Tom began to wonder about Amon's special powers. Were they real? Were they receding? Dick Grimsby was wearing a steel brace on his leg again, Evette's leg—damaged in a car accident—had begun to bother her, and his mom's appearance had changed only slightly. Even that black cat, which had been struck by a car and revived by Amon, was limping badly and not eating, until Mary took it to a vet. And Amon himself seemed to be in a funk, unlike his usual optimistic self.

As the three friends ate their dinner quietly, Tom thought about the deleterious effects of time. He was no longer the raw rookie teacher often mistaken for a student in the hallways and cafeteria of Curtis High School. The good-natured Mary had a few gray hairs scattered in hair wavy dark-brown hair. Time, the ineffable stuff that life was made of, was relentlessly moving forward, carrying all of us unwillingly in its wake.

Tom's unhappy thoughts were interrupted by a commotion in the front of the diner. A husky masked man with a gun had demanded the cashier empty the cash register in his canvas bag. "Do it now, bitch, or I'll blow a hole in your head!"

Tom and Mary looked to Amon, anticipating heroics in the form of a lightning move or a fearless face-off with the gunman. Instead, Amon remained sitting, chewing on his hamburger, as if nothing amiss had occurred. Then the thief moved along the row of booths, looking for something else to snatch. He noticed Mary's silver cross, given to her by Amon himself.

The latter slowly looked up and told the perpetrator to "quit while you're ahead of the game."

"Shut up, preacher, or I'll put a hole in your chest!" he snarled at the Mariners Harbor resident. Tom couldn't quite figure out why the thug thought Amon was a man of the cloth.

As he reached over to grab the cross, Tom threw his glass of soda in the man's face, and Amon, finally coming alive, wrested the gun from the would-be assailant's face. Tom knocked the crook to the floor with a body slam, as if he was a base runner trying to knock the ball from a catcher guarding home plate. The three men tussled on the floor for a few minutes until the sound of a police siren told them the ordeal was ending.

After the gunman was taken away and the dust settled, Tom was amazed at how long it took for Amon to step in and take action. Something was amiss with the Mariners Harbor Messiah. Even Mary was puzzled by her boyfriend's slow response to the dangerous situation. She looked at him uncertainly.

Shrugging his broad shoulders, Amon responded, "I get tired of playing the hero. There are so many jerks in the world. As soon as you deal with one asshole, another comes along that you have to smack down."

Another thing that bothered Tom was that guns were so readily available to lawbreakers. Recently, one of his students claimed that it was easier to get a gun than to borrow a book at the library, in certain parts of the North Shore. Although he was raised on a South Jersey farm where hunting was common, Tom had never fired anything but a BB gun. His idea of sports was hitting a Spalding with a broomstick bat or shooting a basketball at a school yard hoop—not stalking a fleeing deer or a quacking duck with a loaded shotgun.

Harry Bridges

Harry Bridges, a native of Australia, was the leader of the longshoremen's union for more than forty years. Born in Melbourne, Australia, Bridges first went to sea at the age of sixteen as a merchant seaman. Bridges said he was inspired to go to sea by the legendary writer Jack London. In 1920, Harry Bridges arrived in the United States, where Americans nicknamed him "The Beak" because of his hooked nose. As a result of his strong Australian accent, Bridges was also called "The Limey" by his fellow dockworkers.

In 1921, Harry Bridges joined the Industrial Workers of the World, a seamen's union that participated in an unsuccessful strike. Bridges's experience with this union influenced his attitude on the importance of organizing workers to gain better working conditions and higher pay. During the early 1920s, he left the sea for longshoremen work on the West Coast. When he joined the International Longshoremen's Association (ILA), Bridges was blacklisted for several years. He was forced to join the fraudulent company union in order to get work as a rigger on a steel-handling gang.

In 1933, Franklin Roosevelt's National Industrial Recovery Act gave workers the right to organize unions. At that point in time, Harry Bridges was involved with the Communist Party, which was trying to organize sailors, longshoremen, dockworkers, and merchant seamen into the Marine Workers Industrial Union (MWIU), rather than the ILA. Although Bridges was sympathetic to the MWIU, he opted to join the new ILA. When the union held elections, Harry Bridges and his leftist cohorts were chosen to run the longshoremen's union. Bridges's group began organizing on a coast-wide basis, forming a confederation of local longshoremen and maritime unions.

In 1933, Harry Bridges's ILA union called for a strike against a company that had fired four workers for wearing ILA buttons on the job. Bridges's strike was successful, as the company backed down. In 1934, Bridges organized a West Coast longshoremen strike over working conditions and pay. The San Francisco Police participated in breaking the strike by trucking cargo to company warehouses, beating the strikers with clubs, and even shooting picketing workers and union leaders. Harry Bridges became the chief spokesman for the ILA, as well as its main negotiator. In the ensuing years, Bridges brought all the maritime unions in the West Coast together under one umbrella: the newly formed International Longshoremen's and Warehousemen's Union. This union became affiliated with the Congress of Industrial Organizations (CIO). In 1937, Harry Bridges was featured in *Time* magazine for his work in organizing West Coast longshoremen.

In 1939, due to his past association with known Communists, Harry Bridges was threatened with deportation under the Alien Act of 1918. Because he was not a member of that political party at the time, Bridges was acquitted. Then in 1949, Bridges was again subject to deportation under the Smith Act, which appeared to be targeted at the West Coast union leader. A second round of deportation hearings ensued, with the attorney general ordering that Harry Bridges be deported. He appealed in a series of court cases that led to the Supreme Court, which ruled in Bridges v. Wixon that the government had not proven Bridges was affiliated with the Communist Party. The court asserted that sympathy with Communist ideas is not tantamount to membership in that notorious political party.

In the early stages of World War II, Harry Bridges was sympathetic to the Soviet Union, opposing the alliance between Roosevelt and Churchill. Bridges's position against the New Deal was very unpopular with his membership. After Germany attacked Russia, Bridges urged companies to increase wartime productivity and supported a no-strike pledge by the longshoremen. He also supported a proposal by Roosevelt to place certain arms manufacturing under military control. After the war, Bridges opposed the Marshall Plan in Europe and the Truman Doctrine in Greece and Turkey. Consequently, Bridges's union, the ILA, was expelled from the CIO.

Despite this controversy, Harry Bridges continued to be reelected as head of the West Coast longshoremen's union year after year. As a result of challenges from black workers, he opened up more jobs to minorities during the Vietnam War, when West Coast ports were particularly busy. In 1977, at the age of seventy-six, Bridges retired from the ILA after more than forty-four years as the leader of the West Coast longshoremen. He was survived by his wife, Noriko, who was of Japanese origin. They were originally denied a marriage license in Nevada because of an 1846 statute forbidding marriage between individuals of different races. In 1958, a federal district court ordered a marriage license be issued for the couple.

The legacy of Harry Bridges is monumental in the American labor movement. The Harry Bridges Institute in San Pedro, California, does research on international economics and the effects of politics on unions. Bridges' triumphs and accomplishments have been celebrated by folk singers Woody Guthrie and Pete Seeger. The city of San Francisco named a plaza in Bridges' honor on the anniversary of his one hundredth birthday. And California Governor Gray Davis declared that day—July 28, 2001—to be "Harry Bridges Day."

Magnetic Lesson

Perched on Tom's desk were samples of several common elements—aluminum, copper, iron, carbon, iodine, chlorine, magnesium, calcium, sulfur—plus a horseshoe magnet. Hung from the blackboard was Mendeleev's periodic table of the elements. The title of the lesson was written on the board: "What are elements?"

As usual, a few students—Barry, Manny, and even Lora—milled around the front desk until Tom shooed them away. Driven by raging hormones and surging energy, most freshmen and sophomores were restless. The concept of passive, sedentary learning was flawed, although it was the most widely used approach to teaching and learning throughout the Western world.

Holding up some of the samples, the skinny science teacher reiterated the key question: "So, what are elements?"

"Pure substances that cannot be subdivided by ordinary chemical methods," Riner, a student with a good memory but little creativity, answered.

"That's correct, Riner. There are approximately one hundred elements found on the earth in solid, liquid, and gaseous forms."

"The only elements I care about are gold and silver," Barry said.

"Sorry to disappoint you, but I don't have any of those elements today," Tom responded.

"What about copper? Copper has medicinal properties," Lora exclaimed, shaking her copper bracelets and anklets.

Ignoring the cute, curly-haired youngster, Tom held up the horseshoe magnet. "Which elements are magnetic?"

"Iron and steel," Manny called out from the back of the room.

"Iron and steel are both forms of iron. There are three magnetic elements — iron, nickel, and also cobalt — which I don't have with me today." Tom demonstrated the magnetic properties of iron and nickel with the iron nail and the old nickel coin.

"Wait a minute. I have a nickel here. I didn't know it's magnetic," said Lora, getting up and handing a nickel to the skinny science teacher.

Tom placed the horseshoe magnet near her nickel, but it apparently wasn't magnetic. "Why is that?"

"Because Lora has wooden nickels, like all gypsies," Barry snapped.

"Go fuck yourself!" she yelled.

"Send her to the dean for profane language," Barry replied.

"Both of you, settle down. How about pretending we like each other and get along for a change?"

Moving on, Tom explained that most metals are shiny, malleable, and hard, and had considerable strength, with the exception of the alkali metals like sodium and potassium, which are soft and chemically active. He cut a small piece of sodium with a knife and placed it in some water. The sodium skidded around the water and began burning rapidly. The students weren't impressed, since some had seen that practical experiment before.

"Cut a bigger piece, and throw it in the water," Manny called out from the back.

Complying, Tom did exactly what was requested. This time it exploded with a loud noise, and a piece of burning sodium fell on his science notes, setting them on fire — to the joy of his students.

Tom poured some water on the notes to put out the fire, which delighted his students even more.

Laughing, Tom declared his notes needed revising anyway. "At least the sodium didn't set fire to my jacket like the last time that happened. I was forced to buy another suit jacket."

"Too bad. John's Bargain Store sure needs the business," Barry snapped.

"No. J. C. Penney needs the business," Tom replied, thinking of that pretty salesgirl who had sold him his first teaching wardrobe—some sports jackets and a business suit—some years ago.

Relentlessly pushing forward, Tom mentioned one of the most common elements found on the earth: carbon. "Carbon is found in the atmosphere in the form of carbon dioxide, in green plants, and in fossil fuels like coal, oil, and natural gas."

He showed the class the charcoal and the pencil—both composed of carbon.

"I heard that pencils contained lead, since they're called lead pencils," Wendy observed.

"Don't believe everything you hear, girl," Barry chided.

Unlike the feisty Lora, Wendy ignored her classmate's barbs, focusing on the matter at hand.

"That's a misnomer—lead pencil. Pencils contain a certain form of carbon called graphite. Diamonds also contain carbon, plus other elements, subject to heat and pressure for millions of years, eventually forming one of the hardest substances known to man—diamond."

"What about charcoal, the stuff you barbecue hamburgers with?" someone asked from the back of the classroom.

"That's still another form of carbon. Virtually all the fuels we burn for energy contain carbon. What happens when we burn carbon fuels?"

"It produces carbon dioxide in the atmosphere. And the carbon dioxide tends to trap the earth's heat, causing global warming," Wendy answered.

"That's a good thing. I hate snow, ice, and winter. Skiing and ice-skating are dumb sports meant for crackers in white-landia—not for us ghetto folks," Barry replied half-seriously.

"Ah, give me a friggin' break," Lora said, rattling her bracelets.

"Besides, if the earth's average temperature rises by a few degrees, the ocean levels will rise, flooding the coastal areas of Staten Island, Brooklyn, and Manhattan," Tom mentioned, thinking of the Mariners Harbor area where the Kill Van Kull fronted Richmond Terrace.

"We'll build dikes like those Dutchmen did in Holland," Manny called out.

"That's why they all wear wooden shoes, so they can float in the Zuider Sea," Barry said, unperturbed by the prospect of coastal flooding.

"It's called the Zuiderzee—not the Zuider Sea," Riner corrected his outspoken classmate.

"Only a weird dude like you would know about the Zuiderzee."

"Now that's enough, Barry. We all have something to contribute to class discussions," Tom said, aware that Barry dominated classroom proceedings.

At that juncture, the bell rang, bringing the class to an end before Tom could introduce the Mendeleev's periodic table. Lora came up to Tom and apologized for her profane language. Tom suggested that she spin her copper bracelets and anklets whenever she felt like cursing someone out.

"You mean spinning them brings on good vibrations that could neutralize the bad vibrations of jerks like Barry?"

"Not exactly, but it could help you cope with negative energy of others," Tom asserted, trying to convince himself, as well as his naive student.

"I'll give it a shot. Anything to snuff out his annoying motormouth," she replied, following the stream of students prancing out of the room, her copper bracelets and anklets jingling all the way down the long, dark hallway.

CHAPTER 68

The Elements Redux

Following up on his previous lessons on the elements, Tom had on display the elements of the previous day: aluminum, copper, iron, carbon, iodine, chlorine, magnesium, calcium, sulfur, and mercury. As with the day before, Mendeleev's periodic table of the elements was hung on the front blackboard. In addition, Tom had a big jar of marbles on his desk, which drew some interest from Barry and Manny. Through a series of questions and answers, definitions for the three basic kinds of substances were placed on the board.

Element: a pure substance that cannot be subdivided by chemical means.
Ex: aluminum, carbon, iron, gold, silver, sulfur, oxygen, hydrogen.
Compound: two or more elements chemically united in definite proportions.
Ex: water, salt, sugar, alcohol, rust, limestone, plastic.
Mixture: two or more substances mixed together, but not chemically united.
Ex: air, salt water, sugar water, oil and vinegar.

Tom showed the class some matches, which he said were mostly made from sulfur. Then he took a strip of magnesium and ignited it with a match. The magnesium burned with an intense white light. "What would be an application of magnesium?"

"Magnesium bracelets for medicinal purposes, like copper bracelets," Lora replied, nodding her curly head.

"Girl, only gypsies believe in that bullshit," Barry snapped.

Growing angry, she shouted, "Why you …" Then spinning her copper bracelets and anklets, Lora regained her tranquility and smiled sweetly at her long-term foe.

Seizing the rare moment of tranquility, Tom asked about the periodic table of elements, which was hung on the blackboard.

"It shows the elements arranged in order of increasing weight. It was invented by that Russian guy Dmitri Mendeleev," Riner, a serious student, replied.

"What is the most important feature of Mendeleev's periodic table?"

"The vertical columns represent families of elements. These elements have similar properties, which is why they're called families," Wendy responded. She was another serious student, but unlike the short, bespectacled Riner, Wendy combined brains, beauty, and a pleasant manner. In addition, she had learned to ignore the snide remarks of her rowdy classmates.

"That's correct, Wendy. Metals are to the left, and nonmetals to the right of the table, with the transition elements in the middle of the periodic table. You'll find the most active metals on the left — the alkali metals like sodium and potassium, and the alkaline earth metals like magnesium and calcium. The most active nonmetals are the halogens, like fluorine and chlorine, and the less active nonmetals, like oxygen and sulfur, are on the right side of the periodic table."

"What about that group of elements on the extreme right side of the periodic table?" Ronnie asked.

"Those are the noble gases — helium, neon, argon, and krypton," Riner said.

"Correct. The noble gases are chemically inert, meaning they don't react with other elements," Tom replied.

"Krypton is the superman element, which made him a weakling," Manny called out from the back of the room.

"Well, copper makes me strong and impervious to evildoers," Lora declared resolutely.

"Oh, yeah? Catch this!" Barry exclaimed, throwing a rubber ball at his classmate, who blocked it smartly with her bracelets, causing the ball to rebound off his head — to the delight of the entire class.

"Shit! Them damn bracelets have black magic," the pesky teenager complained.

Ignoring the troublesome twosome, Tom asked the class what Jacob Berzelius was known for. Nobody knew, and few cared, but the skinny teacher pushed forward. "Berzelius developed the system of symbols we use today to represent the elements and compounds used in chemical formulas."

"How come scientists have such dumb names like Berzelius, Newton, Galileo, Volta, Ohm, Planck, and that guy Gay-Lussac, who sounds gay to me?" Barry remarked.

"By the way, Mr. Gay-Lussac discovered the chemical formula of water: H_2O. If you make a discovery in chemistry or physics, they'll name a unit after you.

How about the Barry — as a possible unit of random disorder or chaos?"

"Very funny. By the way, is Halley's Comet named after someone in your family?" Barry asked.

"No. Different family and a different spelling."

"The Haley family is better known for drinking booze. One Haley equals two gallons of beer — the usual consumption of our teacher on a good drinking night," Manny called out from the back of the room.

"Flattery will get you nowhere," Tom quipped, turning to the board.

Instructing his students to get out their science notebooks, Tom began writing the major elements with their symbols on the blackboard. He explained that most chemical symbols come from the first letter or first two letters of the element's name. A few of the symbols come from the Latin names of elements, such as gold, silver, iron, copper, lead, mercury, sodium, and potassium.

Symbols of Key Elements

Carbon: C	Hydrogen: H	Oxygen: O
Nitrogen: N	Phosphorus: P	Sulfur: S
Iodine: I	Fluorine: F	Helium: He
Nickel: Ni	Silicon: Si	Aluminum: Al
Calcium: Ca	Lithium: Li	Magnesium: Mg
Chlorine: Cl	Zinc: Zn	Platinum: Pt
Copper: Cu	Iron: Fe	Uranium: U
Gold: Au	Silver: Ag	Radium: Ra
Sodium: Na	Potassium: K	Lead: Pb
Mercury: Hg	Chromium: Cr	Tungsten: W

Raising his hand and scratching his head, Barry said, "Wait a minute, didn't we cover the symbols of the elements before?"

Skimming through his lesson plans, Tom smiled sheepishly. "You're right, but the elements are such an important topic that they bear repeating. Repetition is the key to learning."

"And drinking is the cause of amnesia," the rude teenager replied.

"What did you say your name was?" the skinny science teacher retorted.

Tom mentioned that certain elements like radium and uranium were radioactive, emitting dangerous radiation. "Years ago, people working in clock factories would paint radium on the clock faces, so the numbers would glow in the dark. Many of them came down with tongue cancer as a result."

He recalled his mother's terrible experiences with radium as a youngster. Doctors had tried to use radium to remove a purplish spot from her face. It caused severe burns on her face, requiring years of surgery and disfiguring of that side of her face. Suffering comas, she had spent most of her adolescence in hospitals and hardly attended high school at all. Her parents did send her to business school to learn typing and other secretarial schools so she could find work. Forty years later, Claire Haley was still doing office work, which, along with reading, was the supreme joy of her life.

Stirring the skinny teacher from his reverie, someone from the back asked Tom what he was going to do with the mercury.

First, he showed that an iron nail could not float in water, because iron is denser than water. Then, he placed the iron nail in the beaker of mercury, where it actually floated on the surface of the liquid metal. "What does this demonstrate about the metal iron?"

Wendy raised her hand. "That iron is more dense than water but less dense than mercury."

"Right on, Wendy," Manny yelled from the back of the room.

"Incidentally, scientists have found high levels of mercury in tuna fish due to contamination of the oceans with methyl mercury, a by-product of coal-burning power plants," Tom lectured.

He thought about Amon fishing in the polluted Kill Van Kull, which likely had high levels of methyl mercury. Perhaps his friend's weakened physical and mental condition could be attributed to the fish he had consumed over the years from that murky body of water. Tom made a mental note to warn Amon about fishing in that contaminated North Shore bay.

"Does density have to do with how close the atoms are packed together?" Ronnie inquired.

"Yes. Density is obtained from the following formula," Tom replied, turning to the blackboard.

Density = Mass / Volume

Next, he listed the densities of several common substances on the board.

Densities:

Water = 1.00
Alcohol = 0.78
Iron = 7.86
Copper = 8.92
Silver = 10.60
Gold = 19.31
Wood = 0.71
Aluminum = 2.70
Lead = 11.34

"Then why do ships made out of steel float on rivers and oceans?"

Again, Wendy responded. "Because ships are hollow with lots of space for air. So their overall density is less than water. But if they spring a leak so ocean water rushes into the hull, they will sink. Like the *Titanic* did when an iceberg tore a hole in its hull."

"Excellent, Wendy!"

"How come you always say 'excellent' when Wendy answers a question? But when I answer a question, you just say 'correct,'" Barry said half-seriously.

"You're right. I've been remiss. The entire class was excellent today. It was like everyone was wearing those magical copper bracelets that Lora has." This remark caused Lora to rattle her copper bracelets and anklets joyfully.

"And to show my appreciation, I'm handing out these magical glass marbles, which will give you all positive energy and good vibrations."

Tom walked down the aisles, handing out marbles to his students — most of whom accepted them happily — proving that people will accept freebies, regardless of their minimal value.

Barry grabbed more than his fair share, asserting he would sell them to the little kids on his block, proving that the entrepreneurial spirit was alive and well in America's teenagers.

The Berrigan Brothers

The Berrigan brothers, Daniel and Philip, were deeply involved in the antiwar movement during the Vietnam War. Daniel Berrigan was a Jesuit priest who taught theology at Le Moyne College in Syracuse, New York. Philip Berrigan served in the army during World War II as an artillery officer, fighting in the Battle of the Bulge.

Both Berrigan brothers participated in the Vietnam-era antiwar movement, organizing protests and writing letters to newspapers urging an end to the war. Philip Berrigan was arrested for nonviolent protests and was sentenced to six years in prison. Daniel Berrigan traveled to Hanoi during the Tet Offensive in 1968 to take custody of three American airmen who had been released by the North Vietnamese government.

In 1968, Daniel Berrigan signed a pledge refusing to make tax payments in protest of the Vietnam War. He changed his tactics from nonviolent to violent in the form of using homemade napalm to destroy the draft files of the Catonsville, Maryland, draft board that same year. Berrigan was arrested and sentenced to three years in prison for his actions against that draft board. However, Daniel Berrigan went into hiding before being apprehended by the FBI.

Philip Berrigan also became embroiled in the antiwar movement during the late 1960s. In 1967, Berrigan and three others poured blood on the Baltimore draft board's records. When arrested, Philip Berrigan calmly handed out Bibles and lectured draft board employees on the "terrible waste of American and Vietnamese blood in Indochina." In 1968, Berrigan asserted that the Catholic Church, the Protestant churches, and the synagogues of America were complicit in the American war effort because of "their silence and cowardice in the face of the country's silence." Philip Berrigan went on to accuse the American religious bureaucracy of overt racism and indifference to the poor.

After the Vietnam War, Daniel and Philip Berrigan and others formed the Plowshares Movement, which operated against munitions manufacturers. At one point, they trespassed onto the General Electric nuclear missile plant in Pennsylvania. At this facility, they damaged nuclear warhead nose cones and poured blood onto documents and files. Both Berrigan brothers were arrested and charged with felonies and misdemeanors, eventually spending two years in jail after ten years of appeals.

The Berrigan brothers also inspired other antiwar efforts by the "Catholic Left." A group organized by Jerry Elmer took action against corporations fulfilling military contracts during the 1970s. This group was willing to do jail time as a consequence of its actions against the military-industrial complex. There were actions against Dow Chemical, which produced napalm for use in Vietnam, and against General Electric, which had contracts to produce incendiary weapons employed in Vietnam.

Near the end of his life, Philip Berrigan spoke against the scourge of nuclear weapons — mining uranium, manufacturing the bombs, and using them in future wars. He said these weapons are "a curse against God, the human family, and the earth itself." Daniel Berrigan continued to be involved in the Plowshares Movement. Both brothers were opposed to American intervention in Central America, the Middle East, and Afghanistan. In recent years, Daniel Berrigan spoke out against abortion, against capital punishment, and in support of the Occupy Movement to address economic inequality. Daniel Berrigan was not an admirer of American material success. He thought of it as a death trap. Berrigan felt that "each person must struggle to stay alive and be of use as long as he can." Philip did not believe the ballot box lead to reform:

"If voting made any difference, it would be illegal."

The Undesirables

Returning to the flat-roofed white stucco house on Pulaski Avenue, Tom's plans of checking his students' science homework were interrupted by a panicky phone call from Mary, Amon's girlfriend.

"Amon's been arrested for beating up a man in the Simonson Avenue house. He's being detained at the St. George precinct," she said in a feverish voice.

"Beat up a guy? That doesn't sound like Amon. What happened?"

"He's a new resident at the Simonson Avenue house. Moved in a few weeks ago with a woman friend. They had a big fight, and he smacked her around. So Amon intervened and punched him out. When the police arrived, Amon started arguing with them, and he was taken into custody."

"You don't argue with the cops. He should know better," Tom replied.

"Amon hasn't been himself lately. Either he's too laid-back and doesn't want to intervene, or he jumps into situations with both feet," Mary related sadly.

"I'll call Stan, the Elm Park lawyer. He helped us when those developers were trying to seize his tugboat for that dumb condo project."

"By the way, those people have begun bulldozing the Terrace waterfront a few blocks from us. He's very upset about that also. Sid Davidoff came around again and spoke to Amon, but there's little he could do to deter the big shots from their ambitious projects," she explained.

"Friggin' developers. Urban renewal, they call it. But it's really poor people removal. Don't worry. We'll get him out. They can't pull that shit with the Mariners Harbor Messiah."

"The police were taunting him about that epithet. There's a lot of ill will directed toward Amon. The local people resent the so-called undesirables he's bringIng into the neighborhood," she said.

"Yeah. Staten Islanders are not crazy about undesirables. I don't know how they put up with themselves."

Within an hour, the congenial attorney Stan Mislicki had sprung Amon from jail, posting a modest $2,500 bond. A few weeks later, Amon and Stan stood before the black-robed Judge Taylor. The judge, a wise gray-haired magistrate, who was aware of Amon's good standing in the community, admonished him to "restrain your passions in helping the sick and the poor. Remember, young man, Jesus said the meek, not the mighty, shall inherit the earth."

Embarrassed by his angry display of violence, so uncharacteristic of his past behavior, Amon replied, "I am very sorry for my actions. I promise you, sir, it won't happen again. I shall turn my cheek to all attacks—verbal and physical—upon myself. Blessed are the peacemakers. They are the sons of God."

On the way back to Mariners Harbor, the three men stopped for a drink at K. C.'s bar, where Pat McDean greeted him. "Aha, the prodigal son has returned to the fold. What are you guys having?"

Tom ordered a Ballantine beer for himself, and his two companions indicated that the same beverage would suffice for them. Tom noticed that the place was jumping that night—attributing it to a full moon.

"Have you noticed that crime rates go up during a full moon?" he asked his companions.

"As Shakespeare once said, the fault, dear Brutus, is not in our stars, but in ourselves," the young lawyer declared.

"That crime pattern follows the moon's phases sounds like an old wives' tale," Amon observed.

"How is your teaching going?" Stan asked the skinny science teacher.

Tom replied that his teaching job was coming along, now that he had more control over his restless charges. Teaching is about "stuffing as much information into their craniums as possible, keeping them busy so that there's no time for troublemaking."

"St. Paul said it best: Idle hands are the devil's workshop," Amon commented.

"Well, Tom. You were always busy as a kid. Delivering the *Herald Tribune*, going to school, and playing stickball in the street," Stan replied.

"I remember you working in the bakery on Morningstar Road. The only time I ever saw you uncovered in white flour was when you were carrying that old briefcase, going back and forth to law school."

"The road to law school was strewn with doughnuts, sweet rolls, and cheesecakes. It's still hard to believe I became a lawyer," Stan said in his usual self-effacing manner.

"And a damned good one, to boot," Amon asserted.

"The best lawyer in Elm Park," Tom concurred.

"Actually, the only practicing attorney in the neighborhood, since Bob Whitman retired a few years ago," Stan replied with smile.

"Mr. Whitman was my mom's lawyer when she bought her house on Pulaski Avenue. It seems like you need a lawyer nowadays to get permission to spit, piss, or fart. People run to court at the drop of a hat," Tom said.

"Indeed. We are becoming a litigious society," Stan replied.

"There are so many rules, regulations, ordinances, and laws that a person is afraid to step outside his house," Amon said mournfully.

"What's the alternative? Living in the sticks like a hermit?" Tom asked.

"Sounds good to me. Maybe I should go to the desert and live by myself," Amon declared more to himself than to his companions.

Coming and Going

It was Friday night, and for the lack of alternative plans, Tom decided to stop into Kaffman's, where Rudy greeted him with a smile and an overflowing glass of Ballantine beer. The place was packed, as befitting a full moon.

Looking around the noisy, sour-sweet–smelling saloon, Tom observed his former girlfriend Martha sitting at the end of the bar. He sat on a stool next to the tall, attractive brunette and said hello. Propitiously, the young woman smiled tepidly and asked him about his teaching.

"Not bad. I've become Curtis's super-sub, covering classes for those missing in action during my prep period," he replied, looking at his old flame wistfully.

"I heard it through the grapevine that your buddy Amon was arrested for punching someone out," she said grimly.

"He intervened in a domestic dispute. Amon doesn't tolerate bullies."

"Yeah. The Mariners Harbor Messiah playing the hero, at the drop of a hat," Martha grumbled as she sipped some white wine. "He's a good guy in a world filled with money-grubbing SOBs."

"So how's your love life?" she inquired bluntly.

"I love playing stickball. I love teaching, especially the summer break. And I love drinking Ballantine beer," he said with a wry smile. "How about you?"

"I'm seeing somebody. A guy from a good family, who knows what he wants in life," she replied with a half grin.

"Good for you," he replied magnanimously.

At that moment, Tom sensed the presence of someone in the bar, which caused him to turn abruptly toward the entrance. It was his old flame Joanie, who smiled sweetly at the skinny science teacher. As he got up from his stool, Tom was punched squarely in the jaw by the androgynous Martha, knocking him to the floor. As the blood spurted from his nose, Tom was dimly aware of two actions: Martha storming out of the crowded saloon and Joanie hovering over him with a hankie, daubing his throbbing nose. The fracas caused a momentary stir of Kaffman's patrons, before everybody resumed their merrymaking.

"We have to stop meeting like this," he mumbled happily. Years ago he had first met Joanie, lying dazed on the ground after colliding with a teammate while chasing a fly ball in the outfield.

"Oh, shut up, you big jerk. Why don't you learn to duck when people swing at you?" she said with a giggle.

"What can I tell you? It's a full moon, and I'm an easy target," he replied, getting up slowly and asking Rudy Kaffman to get Joanie a ginger ale. A confirmed teetotaler, Joanie distained alcoholic beverages of any type—a trait that Tom, despite himself, hoped to emulate.

"How's your friend Amon? I'll never forget how he helped me when I was sick at St. Vincent's. They thought it was a brain tumor. As soon as he touched my forehead, the pain subsided."

"Amon's fine. That special gift of healing seems to have diminished a bit. He fixed up an old Victorian house for the homeless in Mariners Harbor. But some local people are opposing it and making trouble for him."

"Why would anybody oppose a person doing good things in the world?"

"It's that old saying—not in my neighborhood. People are worried about their property values," Tom explained.

"Why does everything have to have a dollar sign attached to it?" she asked.

"Money makes the world go round."

"No. Love makes the world go round." The jukebox began playing a popular song by the Carpenters. "Come on, Tom. Dance with me," Joanie said softly, taking his hand and leading him to a small dance area at the rear of the bar.

It was a new experience for Tom. When he dated Joanie that summer after graduating from high school, they had never danced. Dizzy from the beers he had consumed and from Martha's shot to his head, the skinny teacher managed to slow-dance with the graceful young woman, who held him closely. No longer the cute, lissome teenager, Joanie was in the full bloom of womanhood.

Feeling light-headed, Tom took a deep breath and closed his eyes. Was this a dream? Slowly they whirled round and round, keeping time with the Carpenters' haunting melody—their faces touching, inhaling each other's breath, and kissing long and slow. The twists and turns of fate in that social whirlwind called life had led the two of them to this unlikely convergence.

Karen carpenter's soulful voice filled the smoky bar:

"Long ago and so far away , I fell in love with you before the second show. Don't you remember you told me you loved me, baby? You said you'd be coming back this way again, baby."

They went back to the bar and sat and talked awhile about general things. Tom wondered about Joanie's personal life. Was she attached to someone back in Indiana? Had the relationship been severed? He didn't really care, as long as she was with him in the here and now. With true love, all that mattered was the existential present. The past was irrelevant, and the future was uncertain. His mom's often-repeated axiom that life must be lived on a basis of reality was preposterous.

As customary in crowded bars, the music grew louder and louder as the hour grew later. Joanie and Tom just sat on their stools, looking into each other's eyes and holding hands. They had attained that level where conversation was not needed. As Joanie stroked Tom's face, she began to cry. Tom asked her why she was crying.

"I'm so sorry for leaving you. You were devastated when you found out. I never really liked Indiana. They made fun of my New York accent."

"Well, you do talk funny."

"You've become such a wiseass, Tom. Quick with the put-downs."

"When you teach high school kids, a sharp tongue is a necessity."

"It was just as hard for me as for you. My parents really liked you. They said you were the all-American boy, delivering newspapers every morning before school on your rickety red bicycle."

Tom started to say something, when suddenly Jake Gardello appeared next to them. Tom was stunned and didn't know what to say to Joanie's cousin. Apparently, he was there to take Joanie home. Kissing Tom good-bye, she said that she would be in touch with him soon.

"Is your phone number the same?" she asked.

"Yes. Same phone number, same address. Nothing has changed."

"That's what I love about you, Tom. You live in the same place, wear the same clothes, and you're just as nice as ever."

"I wouldn't go that far," he replied, causing Joanie to smile radiantly.

Tom felt that he could travel the one hundred or more countries scattered across the seven continents of the world and never meet another woman like Joanie. Her beautiful brown eyes, full red lips, wavy black hair, flawless tawny complexion, voluptuous figure, graceful movement, and sweet demeanor had always captivated the skinny teacher. Alcohol, music, loneliness, and sentimentality added to his feelings for his high school sweetheart.

Such is the halo effect of the beloved upon the lover. Adjectives for such a state of mind range from dumbstruck to moonstruck, from spellbound to love smitten, from captivated to enchanted. Love is an all-or-nothing state of mind; one cannot be partially in love. Tom stumbled out of Kaffman's, greeting the mild night air with a loud "Whoopee" and a big leap, touching the ten-foot-high neon sign for the first time in his life.

CHAPTER 71

Messiah Attacked

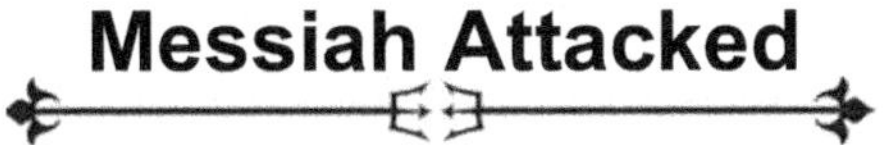

At the end of a busy teaching day at Curtis, Tom got a notice from the main office to call Mary, Amon's girlfriend in Mariners Harbor. She had just arrived home from her teaching job at St. Mary's to find him lying on a couch in his Victorian boardinghouse. He was badly bruised and battered, with some missing teeth, as a result of a beating administered by several thugs.

Rushing over to the refurbished Victorian house in his old gray Pontiac, Tom wondered about Amon's recent propensity to get into fisticuffs. Instead of turning the other cheek, the charismatic young man was prone to behave recklessly, rather than prudently, to achieve worthwhile goals. The goodwill built up in recent years from positive press reports was being squandered by his rash behavior. In addition, his faith healing, keen sensitivity, prophetic ability, and prodigious energy were waning. Indeed, Amon appeared to have aged noticeably in the past several months.

Entering the small, dingy bedroom, Tom saw Mary tending to Amon, who was shifting restlessly on a narrow cot under some torn, faded blankets.

"How are you doing?" Tom inquired, taking in the run-down state of the Victorian boardinghouse.

"I've been better. I'm afraid I bit off more than I could chew today," the young man replied in a slurred manner.

"You look like they worked you over pretty good."

"Well, you should see what my attackers look like. It ain't pretty." Gone were the rudiments of his western accent. Amon now spoke in the fast, clipped New York vernacular.

"Amon gave as much as he got. But he was outnumbered three to one," Mary asserted grimly.

She went on to explain that Amon had rescued a young girl from prostitution in Port Richmond. As expected, her pimp took offense and paid him a "friendly visit" with two allies, for the purpose of teaching Amon a lesson.

"Amon, why didn't you call the police about that situation? It's their job to handle things like prostitution and drug dealing," Tom replied.

"That's exactly what I told him myself. This isn't the Wild West, where you can be a lone-wolf vigilante, rescuing the damsel in distress," Mary said in an exasperated tone.

"There's so much bullshit going on in the world. Sometimes you just have to take a stand and let the chips fall where they may."

"There are injustices in the world you just have to accept. We can't right the wrongs of the world in one day. Progress is incremental," Tom asserted.

"That doesn't sound like you, the son of a Marxist," Amon retorted.

"My mom is an armchair Marxist. Her greatest joys are working as bookkeeper for the Royal Canadian Bank, reading the *Staten Island Advocate*, going to Great Books, and attending off-Broadway shows in the city."

"The point is I'm running out of time, and I must do what I can before my time is over," Amon declared.

"He keeps talking that way about dying, which upsets me so much," Mary whispered to Tom.

"What are you talking about? You're a young man with your whole life ahead of you," Tom said, in spite of his fears that his friend was in danger. It seemed that America had a way of knocking off its mavericks — social and political.

As they left Amon's room, Mary indicated that the city was getting ready to seize Amon's tugboat as part of their renewal project on the Kill Van Kull waterfront. "They've already cleared the old ships and rusty hulks from the harbor. Notices to vacate have been placed on the tugboat, and the utility wires, which Amon himself put up, have been torn down."

On the following Saturday, Tom helped Mary cart their furniture, clothes, books, old newspapers, and other possessions to the Victorian boardinghouse on Simonson Avenue. He recalled his first meeting with Amon when he was connecting the electricity wires from the tugboat to the utility pole — a dangerous job in which Amon had received an electric shock, throwing him to the soft, rotted wharf below without injury.

Tom was in awe of the strapping young man, whose concern for the poor and the downtrodden was Christlike. With the city's help, Amon eventually converted the ramshackle twelve-room Victorian house into a much-needed shelter for down-and-out alcoholics, ex–drug addicts, the homeless, and other lost souls of Staten Island's North Shore. His gifts of faith healing, surreal sensitivity to events of the past, heroic efforts in saving others in danger, plus his exceptional kindness and generosity earned him the pseudonym of Mariners Harbor Messiah — given by the local newspapers. But recently, the tide of public opinion had turned against Amon, with even the *Staten Island Advocate* publishing an article critical of the "so-called Messiah with his half-cocked vigilante actions and his run-down boardinghouse filled with ne'er-do-wells, misfits, drunks, drug addicts, and jailbirds."

CHAPTER 72

Age of Aquarius

Claire Haley had pointed out the article to Tom one Saturday morning as mother and son chitchatted over second cups of coffee. "What's happening to your friend? The paper's chastising him for taking on the local pimps and drug pushers. Of course, if the police did their jobs instead of hanging out in diners, getting their free coffee and doughnuts, the Island would be a lot safer."

"Mom, you're so cynical. The cops enforce the law, but they can't be everywhere at the same time. Einstein said that for event A to cause event B, they have to be separate points in the space–time continuum."

"You know what, McGee? You should have been a lawyer, because you could convince a jury that the moon is made out of chopped liver," she retorted.

"By the way, remember Larry Adamo?"

"Of course, I remember that skunk. He was messing around with your sister back in high school," she replied angrily.

"Mom, he was very nice to her. Much nicer than the guy she's married to right now — Phil, the sanitation engineer. Anyway, I heard Larry's become a cop."

"Well, anybody can become a cop. And anyone can become president, like that crook Richard Nixon," she snapped with disgust.

"Actually, Mr. Nixon is in Red China, talking to Mao Tse Tung. You know Chairman Mao — the guy who said that war can only be abolished through war. And in order to get rid of guns, you have to take up a gun."

"The Red Chinese are crazier than those redneck Southerners, barring the schools from little Negro girls in pigtails," she snorted.

"Gee, Mom. You're putting down the Red Chinese. You must be getting smarter in your old age."

"I've been smart enough to work and put food on the table all these years. With you going through a big pullman loaf every week, just about eating me out of house and home."

"Did you hear that California Governor Reagan said he was cutting welfare by sending the welfare queens back to work?"

"That no-talent movie actor never did an honest day's work in his life. Though he does look good in a business suit," Claire replied, rustling her newspaper.

"Anyway, I'm worried about Amon. He doesn't seem like the same sensible guy. Now he's become a vigilante, hell-bent on saving the world from itself."

"I'm sure he's made some enemies in high places. But don't believe everything you read in the papers, especially the *Staten Island Advocate*. By the way, I see that Al Shanker has gotten a raise for the teachers. Maybe I should increase your monthly board."

"Mom, as you just said, don't trust that scandal sheet. Anyway, I gotta get to that front hedge," Tom replied, gulping his coffee and getting ready to leave the kitchen.

Years ago, the *Advocate* ran a front-page story about Thomas Haley's nephew robbing a liquor store and leaving the bag of money at their white stucco house, complete with names and the address. It resulted in many months of ribbing from the neighborhood kids before the incident was forgotten. "Jailbird" is an epithet that's not funny when you're on the receiving end.

"Incidentally, I met Joanie last night at Kaffman's. It was great to see her after a year and a half. She had been very ill at St. Vincent's Hospital, whom Amon helped by just touching her forehead."

"I thought she had married someone in Indiana," his mom said, putting her newspaper down and staring at her son in amazement.

"It's the Age of Aquarius. Things like that don't matter anymore," he replied, getting up before she could query him about his old girlfriend. "I have to trim the hedge from hell before it reaches the roof."

Shrugging her shoulders, Claire Haley went back to her newspaper. "I never liked that Catholic school teacher—Martha, holier-than-thou hypocrite," she said out loud, looking out the kitchen window.

As usual, Mr. Caprino was puttering around in his flower garden. "Now that's a good man—straight-shooting, hardworking, and sober. Not like Thomas Haley, the Elm Park boozer. Yet I miss the son of a bitch," Claire intoned sadly.

Albert Shanker

Albert Shanker was president of the New York City public school teachers' union, called the United Federation of Teachers (UFT) from 1964 to 1985. Shanker then moved on to head the national teachers' union, known as the American Federation of Teachers (AFT) from 1974 to 1987. While growing up, he remembered listening to Franklin Roosevelt and Winston Churchill, hoping to emulate them with regard to their roles in shaping history. As it turned out, Albert Shanker played a big role in the development of teachers' unions—fighting for salary increases, better working conditions, and a greater role in shaping the teaching profession.

Albert Shanker was born in Manhattan's Lower East Side to Russian Jewish parents, who immigrated from Eastern Europe during the 1920s. Later on, his family moved to Long Island City, in the borough of Queens. Shanker's father delivered newspapers, and his mother worked long hours in a sewing factory. The poor working conditions, seventy-hour workweek, and meager wages motivated the young Albert Shanker to think about labor unions as a force to improve the lives of workers in all fields of endeavor. As a boy, Shanker was an avid reader of newspapers and history. He admired such American icons as Franklin Roosevelt, Senator Robert Wagner, lawyer Clarence Darrow, and civil rights leader Bayard Rustin.

Albert Shanker graduated from Stuyvesant High School in Manhattan, where he headed the debate team. Moving on to the University of Chicago, Shanker was a member of the Young People's Socialist League and the Congress of Racial Equality (CORE). He was active in campus politics, including picketing segregated restaurants and movie theaters in Illinois. In 1949, Albert Shanker graduated from college and enrolled in Columbia University to work on his master's degree. After obtaining his master's degree from Columbia, Shanker began teaching mathematics full-time in an East Harlem public high school in 1952, remaining there until 1960.

In the late 1950s, Albert Shanker began working as a union organizer, helping to form the Teacher's Guild, which was originally founded by American pragmatist philosopher John Dewey in 1917. In time, the Teacher's Guild merged with a high school teachers' association to form the United Federation of Teachers (UFT) in 1960. During the 1960s, Shanker got national attention plus considerable criticism for his aggressive union tactics and tough bargaining stance. But his strong bargaining paid off in sizable salary increases for underpaid New York City teachers. Like the transit union's Mike Quill, Albert Shanker went toe-to-toe with New York Mayor John Lindsay in lengthy teachers' strikes during the late 1960s. As with the legendary Mr. Quill, Shanker served a jail sentence for leading his teachers in a strike that lasted several weeks. By the late 1960s, Albert Shanker had left his teaching post to become a full-time union organizer.

With respect to union philosophy, Albert Shanker believed that teachers must share common goals, as well as common tactics. As with all unions — industrial and professional — unity of purpose was essential for survival. In addition to fighting for better teacher pay, Shanker opposed the decentralization of New York City schools into community districts, where local politicians would run things. Consequently, the UFT went out on strike, effectively closing the schools for five weeks. In 1975, Albert Shanker held a five-day strike, which was settled by a pay freeze and the investment of $150 million from the Teachers' Retirement System in municipal bonds. In return, the city canceled the fines assessed on the UFT for the strike.

During the Vietnam War, Albert Shanker and other labor union leaders affiliated with the AFL-CIO refused to speak out against the unpopular war. There was extensive criticism of Shanker's position from peace advocates of that era. With regard to charter schools, Shanker opposed them because they were largely run by for-profit businesses and were advancing the concept of school privatization. He believed that charter schools would eventually siphon off scarce resources destined for public schools. In the early

1980s, Shanker spoke out against President Ronald Reagan's desertification of the air traffic controllers' union as a result of their strike. President Reagan's actions had a profound chilling effect on the labor movement throughout the nation in subsequent years.

A lifelong supporter of public schools, Albert Shanker felt that the schools hold our nation together, bringing children of different races, languages, religions, and cultures together. Our schools "give children a common language and a common purpose." He likened spending public money on private schools to spending public money on private pools. There was a quote attributed to Shanker: "When school children start paying union dues that's when I'll start representing them." However, union researchers have never found evidence of that quote's authenticity. Indeed, Shanker felt the duty of a union to preserve public education is as essential as its duty to negotiate a good teachers' contract. After his death, Albert Shanker was posthumously awarded the Presidential Medal of Freedom by President Bill Clinton.

CHAPTER 73

Playing for Fun

"Oh, not again! I'm totally off my game," Joanie exclaimed after throwing her second gutter ball in a row. Though the ball ran afoul, she threw with the same effortless grace that Tom remembered from years ago.

"It's all right. You're just a little bit rusty," Tom said, suppressing a smile.

They were bowling at Gooley's run-down alley, where Richmond Avenue intersected the Terrace a few hundred feet from the murky Kill Van Kull. He wasn't doing particularly well himself. Unlike his former girlfriend Martha, Joanie was not competitive, immersing herself in the sheer joy of whatever activity in which she engaged. This noncompetitiveness was a trait shared by Tom, himself, whose approach to sports was to have fun. The obsession with winning at all costs—inherent in organized sports—did not appeal to him.

Tom recalled a ping-pong game he had played with Martha when they were dating. It was a close hard-fought game when Martha smashed a shot that Tom somehow returned with equal velocity. The ball landed squarely on her left boob, causing the skinny teacher to giggle. This infuriated the tall husky woman, who threw her paddle at him. Unlike his barroom fights when he was an easy target for tough guys like Wayne O' Toole, Tom managed to duck, avoiding the hurtling paddle.

After a couple games, Tom went up to the dimly lit bar and started to order a Ballantine beer. Then he changed his mind, ordering a

Coke for himself and a ginger ale for Joanie. Whether Joanie noticed the change in his drinking preferences, she made no comment about his unusual choice. The serene brown-eyed beauty had the ability to take the good and the bad that life presented without losing her equanimity. She wasn't one to analyze and dissect a person's behavior to the detriment of enjoying life in all its manifestations. Whatever misfortunes had beset Joanie prior to her reacquaintance with Tom, she was not anxious to talk about them. Her authenticity was manifest in that Joanie was fundamentally the same person no matter what circumstances or company she was thrown into.

Sitting at a booth, they drank their beverages and nibbled some pretzels. Smiling at the skinny teacher, she said, "I remember the first time I saw you, riding that old red bicycle, with the canvas bag of newspapers on your back, delivering the paper early in the morning."

"That was my *Herald Tribune* paper route—seven days a week, in rain or snow, I delivered that damn paper."

"It probably made you the special person you are today. Hardworking and dedicated to your students," she said with admiration.

"There were days, especially during winter, when I wanted to quit. But my mom said no way."

"She felt it was a good experience for you. Your mom has smarts."

"That she does. But I'll tell you one thing: during the four and a half years I had that paper route, I never caught the flu, had a cough, or a cold. And it gave me the strength and endurance to compete in sports at a fairly high level."

"Why didn't you deliver the *Advocate*, like most of the boys?" Joanie asked.

"You had to know somebody to get a paper route delivering Staten Island's favorite newspaper, which was an afternoon paper."

"I wanted my dad to order the *Tribune*, but he said it had stale news," she said with a smirk.

"Stale news or stale buns?" he chided her.

"Now you're being fresh. If only your students could hear you now."

"The *Herald Tribune* was a good newspaper, comparable to the *New York Times* in terms of news coverage. And they had great writers: Red Smith, Walter Kerr, Walter Lippmann, Tom Wolfe, and Jimmy Breslin."

"My dad liked reading the community news, the sports section, and the obituary column in the *Avocate*."

"Too bad your dad didn't read the *Trib*. I would have gotten to know you sooner. Imagine seeing you snatch the paper from your front porch in your pink nighties."

"How did you know I wore pink PJs?" she asked, scrutinizing him at length.

"I didn't. Just a guess. You're kind of a pink cotton pajamas girl. I can't quite see you in a diaphanous negligee," he replied, smirking.

"Wow! So fresh—no longer the sweet honors student."

Changing the subject, Tom brought up the *Herald Tribune* again. "It was a really good paper, founded by Horace Greeley. You know, the guy who said, 'Go west, young man, go west, and grow up with the country.'"

"Only you would know a ridiculous fact like that, Tom. Just like the time you told me about the old Dutchman Peter Stuyvesant buying Manhattan from the Lenape Indians for twenty-four dollars."

"How did you remember that, Joanie? That was … what, seven years ago?"

"I remember like it was yesterday. We were sitting on a wooden bench in that little cemetery across from your old elementary school."

"PS 21 on Walker Street, in the heart of Elm Park," Tom related, picturing the two of them on their last date before he got the terrible news of her moving to that faraway Midwestern state, Indiana.

"Yeah. You were an Elm Park boy, and I was a Graniteville girl — star-crossed lovers torn apart by evil fate."

"It kind of sounds melodramatic, but it was one of the worst things ever to happen to me, along with having to leave my foster parents in South Jersey for the Island, which is my favorite place in the entire world. Thomas Wolfe said it best: 'You can't go home again.'"

Joanie's eyes filled with tears as she reached over and held his hands. "I'll never leave you again … ever. I promise."

"Just looking at you sitting across from me seems like a dream. I'm afraid to pinch myself, because I might wake up and you'll be gone."

"Maybe everything that happens in life is a dream. And we don't wake up from this dream until we die," she said dreamily.

"Amon once said that we were destined to be together. But for reasons of my own, I couldn't buy into it. I had to get on with my life — going to school, learning how to teach, and doing the nitty-gritty things to survive in this world."

"Talking about Amon, how is he doing?" she asked.

"Amon's had some rough times lately. But he's a strong person, and he'll overcome anything they try to throw at him."

Joanie shuddered momentarily, as if she had seen a ghost.

"What's the matter?"

"Nothing … I hope. I just had a premonition about Amon."

Tom looked at her closely and then sighed loudly. "It's weird when I look at all the things I've done in my life—farm boy, newspaper boy, security guard, and now a science teacher at Curtis High School. But I'm best known for being Amon's sidekick."

"You've done well for yourself. The Elm Park boy who became a schoolteacher. Betcha that none of those other kids that played stickball with you have accomplished what you have, Tom."

"Joey Caprino is a stockbroker on Wall Street. Albert Cloots was on his way to becoming a famous mathematician until he was killed in Vietnam. Your cousin Jake is an insurance agent. Stan Mislicki is a lawyer with an office right on Morning Star Road. And there are plenty of others from Elm Park who made good. Not to mention my sister, Cara, who will make a name for herself as an artist."

"Think of it this way. The years we were apart and all the things that happened led to this special moment and all the moments we will spend together for the rest of our lives. And we'll never take each other for granted," Joanie said fervently in a low voice.

"So what color nighties do you wear?"

"You'll just have to wait and see," she replied with a sly grin.

CHAPTER 74

Teachers vs. Students

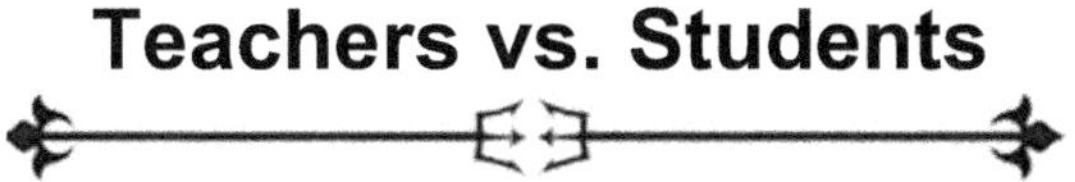

Tom had an idea that he brought to Curtis's principal, Lou Stout. The Curtis High School faculty would play a basketball game against the nonvarsity seniors, with the proceeds going toward Amon's boardinghouse on Simonson Avenue.

Aside from Mary's low-paying teaching job at St. Mary's, there was no income coming into Amon's household. *Maybe Amon should find gainful employment, but how do you tell a prophet to get a job?* Despite the bad publicity concerning the Mariners Harbor Messiah in the local papers, there was still a lot of approbation from his wondrous deeds and his good work helping the sick, the afflicted, the homeless, and the downtrodden of the Island's North Shore.

"I don't know. Your boy has lost some of his luster, messing around with pimps and pushers like some crazy cowboy, with nothing to back him up but his balls," the administrator said, keeping his eyes on the students milling about the hallways.

"How about splitting the proceeds into other worthwhile charities, in addition to Amon's Mariners Harbor boardinghouse?" Tom suggested.

"Let me think about it. I'll get back to you in a couple of days. Meanwhile, you better get in shape. Work on your game, and give up the booze."

"I have been playing basketball and stickball right along. And I haven't had a beer or anything stronger in a month and a half," Tom asserted.

"What happened? Did you join AA?"

"No, a new girlfriend. Actually, an old girlfriend from years ago who has just returned to the Island."

"Well, there's hope for everyone." At that moment, Rosie Murray walked by in a tight skirt, nodding at the two men.

"Maybe you can get Mrs. Murray to lead the faculty cheerleaders," Tom said.

"Now you're talking. I wouldn't mind seeing her in one of those skimpy cheerleaders' outfits," Stout replied as he eyed her ambling down the hall.

The Curtis High School gym was packed with students cheering and jeering as the teachers gasped for air and tried to keep up with the swift seniors as they raced up and down the court. The faculty was led by six-foot-five-inch Arthur Jansen, who had played college basketball at Wagner College. Other faculty stalwarts included Tony Tumali, Alan Katz, and Dick Grimsby hobbling back and forth, in addition to Amon, whose athletic skills had mysteriously declined since Tom had played with him at the nine-foot rims of the PS 21 school yard. Tom himself played fairly well after tossing a couple airballs during the first half. He hit two long jump shots from the top of the key and grabbed several rebounds before running out of gas, trying to keep up with the energetic seniors.

The teachers were backed by their own cheerleaders, led by Rosie Murray displaying her chubby legs and substantial butt to players and spectators alike. Some of the dropped passes and missed baskets on the part of the faculty could be attributed to sidelong glances at the well-endowed math teacher. At one point, Lou Stout ran into Rosie, grabbing her around the waist to keep from diving into the stands. Tom scarcely gave her a look, since he focused on

Joanie sitting demurely and waving at him shyly from her perch at the top of the stands.

It was noteworthy during the game that whenever Amon scored a basket or grabbed a rebound, the students roared their approval. The Mariners Harbor resident was embarrassed by all the attention he received, not quite knowing what to do. Though somewhat tarnished in reputation and diminished in stature, the charismatic young man was the cynosure of all eyes, particularly for the students.

"Just tip your hat like baseball stars do when the fans cheer their exploits," Tom advised his friend.

"I'm not wearing a hat, or can't you see well?" Amon said, vexed by his celebrity status.

"Then, acknowledge their cheers with a polite wave like British royalty are wont to do when their subjects pay homage to them."

Everyone, students as well as faculty, had a wonderful time in a contest where winning or losing was secondary to having fun. Consequently, the basketball game was an artistic and financial success, with the senior eking out a narrow victory. A total of $978 was collected for charity, half of which went to Amon's boardinghouse on Simonson Avenue.

When the game was over. Lora ran over to Amon and gave him a copper bracelet, engraved with crosses and stars, made by her mother. "My mom wants you to have this bracelet for good luck."

Amon, who was out of breath, thanked the curly-headed coed warmly, wiping the tears from his eyes and promising that he would "wear this bracelet forever, in this life and beyond."

Later on, when the faculty team was changing back into their civilian clothes, Tom joined Amon, who was standing in front of a mirror. As the skinny science teacher combed his hair, he was astonished to see Amon's image fade in a swirling cloud. Grabbing his friend's arm, the Mariners Harbor Messiah signaled that this phenomenon should be kept confidential.

"Death is nature's remedy for all things. Please don't mention this to Mary."

Tom was too shaken to say anything. A cold hollow feeling took hold of him, and he shivered uncontrollably.

John Lindsay

John Lindsay was elected to Congress in 1958, representing Manhattan's Upper East Side for four terms. Lindsay was a native New Yorker, born on West End Avenue to an upper-middle-class family of English and Dutch ancestry. Lindsay attended prep school at St. Paul's and Yale University in New Haven, Connecticut. Upon completing his college studies in 1943, Lindsay joined the navy as a gunnery officer during World War II. Obtaining the rank of lieutenant, John Lindsay earned five battle stars through action in Sicily and several landings in the Pacific. After the war, he worked as a bank clerk before entering Yale Law School and receiving his law degree in 1948, ahead of schedule.

After marrying Mary Anne Harrison, a distant relative of US presidents, in 1949, John Lindsay was admitted to the bar. In 1952, he became president of the New York Young Republican Club and was active in New York City politics. In 1958, with the backing of prominent Republicans, Lindsay was nominated and then elected to Congress, representing the "Silk Stocking District" of upper Manhattan. In Congress, John Lindsay established a liberal voting record that put him at odds with the Republican Party. He was a staunch supporter of federal aid to education, Medicare, and the federal department of Urban Affairs. Lindsay earned a reputation as a maverick, opposing federal interception of communist literature and obscene material. He justified his votes by asserting that communism and pornography were the two major industries of the "Silk Stocking District." A strong supporter of civil rights, John Lindsay was the leader of a group of liberal Republicans in Congress who voted for LBJ's Civil Rights Act of 1964.

In 1965, John Lindsay was elected mayor of New York City on the Republican ticket, defeating Democrat Abraham Beame, the city comptroller. One newspaper columnist described Lindsay as "fresh, where everyone else is tired." Lindsay inherited a city with serious fiscal woes, in the face of declining manufacturing jobs and a dwindling middle class. In addition, municipal workers—

including teachers, firemen, police, sanitation, subway conductors, and bus drivers—demanded higher pay and increased benefits. During the twelve-day transit workers strike, Mayor Lindsay jailed TWU leader Mike Quill, who referred to the youthful mayor as "Mr. Lindsley." Mr. Quill said, "The judge can drop dead in his black robes because I would sooner rot in jail than call off the subway and bus strike." Soon, Mayor Lindsay was besieged with a series of municipal strikes—including transit, sanitation, and teacher strikes—forcing the mayor to walk four miles from his apartment to city hall each day. Trying to make light of things, John Lindsay remarked, "I still think it's fun city," from which the sarcastic term "Fun City" was derived.

In 1968, the United Federation of Teachers, under Albert Shanker, initiated a strike that lasted until the middle of October, opposing the decentralization of the New York City school system into thirty-three separate school boards. That same year, there was also a nine-day sanitation strike and a three-day Broadway strike. The quality of city life reached a low point as mounds of garbage caught fire, strong winds blew refuse through the streets, and the rat population of Manhattan exploded. With the schools shut down, the police involved in a slowdown, the firefighters threatening job actions, the city accumulating uncollected garbage, and racial tensions beginning to explode, the city teetered on the brink of anarchy. Somehow the unlucky mayor weathered the urban storm, settling the strikes with sizable increases in labor contracts for New York's municipal workers.

After the assassination of civil rights leader Martin Luther King, John Lindsay was one of the few white politicians (besides Robert Kennedy) who could walk into black neighborhoods and talk to the disenfranchised and gain their trust. As a result of his early opposition to the Vietnam War, John Lindsay was called the "red mayor" and "a traitor." After criticism for alleged neglect of the outer boroughs, the Lindsay administration became more pragmatic and efficient in delivering vital services to the entire city. In addition, the Lindsay administration brought 225,000 more jobs to the city, put 6,000 more cops on the street, and hired hundreds of new teachers and paraprofessionals for the classroom. And unlike cities like Detroit, Los Angeles, and Newark, New York City did not experience devastating urban riots and widespread looting. Mayor Lindsay was also credited with rejuvenating the city's parks, as well as the arts and culture, particularly Broadway, transforming New York into an international tourist attraction. Under John Lindsay, New York City became more prosperous, more just, and more diverse. Indeed, despite the social unrest of that era, New York really was Fun City!

CHAPTER 75

Return to the Cemetery

Out of a sentimentality that tries to recapture an irretrievable past, Tom and Joanie returned to the old wooden bench in the abandoned cemetery at the top of Walker Street. Streetlights cast ghostly shadows on the PS 21 school yard, the scene of so many fast-pitch stickball games in Tom's youth. Years ago, they had sat on the bench together—rather, Joanie had sat on Tom's lap. Kissing, hugging, and groping, they had progressed to that enchanting precipice where their romance would be consummated. Slightly older and more mature, Tom stopped his advances, settling for the sight, touch, and taste of Joanie's swelling breasts. Delaying gratification for the goal of a college education had been hammered into the depths of his brain by his no-nonsense mom.

Nearly a decade later, the two star-crossed lovers were perched on the same wooden bench in the same little cemetery amidst the worn tombstones, desiccated crabgrass, and overgrown shrubs. This time the lovemaking was more purposeful, as if making up for lost time. Despite setbacks and sidetracks, the bond between them was unshakable. They were true soul mates, their love surviving the obstacles of time, separation, other people, and the very stuff of life itself.

Enchanting and graceful as ever, Joanie had magically shed her undergarments without removing her light cotton dress. She appeared to be a devotee of William Occam, who said it's foolish to do with more what can be done with less.

Awkward and clumsy as ever, Tom managed to take off his shirt and lower his pants without too much fumbling.

At this point, Mother Nature took over, and time itself seemed to slow down, as if the gears of the universe were grinding to a halt. And the two lovers rhythmically merged as men and women have done since the dawning of time. There isn't much unique about the act of intercourse itself. However, each person's life cannot be replicated—it's the emotional trappings that are unique. Aside from chirping crickets, buzzing mosquitoes, and the rumbling of a few passing cars, the only sounds echoing from the old cemetery were the pants and sighs of two lovers joined as one, after so many impediments and years of separation.

CHAPTER 76

The Last Supper

Amon decided to have a special dinner for Tom and Joanie to thank him for his efforts in getting Lou Stout and the Curtis staff to participate in the faculty–senior basketball game for charity. Several teachers from Curtis were invited, including Dick Grimsby, Tony Tumali, union rep Alan Katz, as well as Amon's biggest fan, the curly-haired Lora, clattering her copper bracelets and anklets — to the distraction of everyone around her.

Mary and Amon had worked hard cleaning and decorating a large dining room, in which a long table was set with dishes and utensils that were mix-and-match pieces. There was a clean linen tablecloth and a big crystal vase filled with wildflowers picked from the North Shore's woods. Amon, dressed in a white dress shirt and white cotton trousers, sat at the head of the table below Cara's portrait of him with the miraculous halo. Mary, wearing a simple white summer dress, sat calmly next to her soul mate. The stress of the past few months with regard to the city's clearing the harbor of its abandoned ships, corroded hulks, and rotting docks, as well as its seizing of his tugboat, was written on her pretty careworn face. Loyal, steadfast, hardworking, and totally devoted to Amon, she was the very personification of saintliness.

Tom thought about his first acquaintance with Martha and Mary from his days of hanging out at Kaffman's bar on Morningstar Road. Both young women were novice teachers, like himself, struggling to adapt to that demanding profession.

In the ensuing years, Martha had remained the same strong-willed, petulant woman, while Mary had grown in character, transforming her beliefs and values into concrete actions of caregiving to those in need. An objective observer might associate Martha with stagnation and Mary with enhancement.

Turning to Dick Grimsby, Tony Tumali said, "Well, Dick, are we going to witness any miracles today from Amon?"

"Maybe not. His healing powers aren't quite what they were a few years ago."

"How's your leg? I noticed you've been wearing that brace again."

"The leg's all right. It's still better than it was before Amon intervened," the congenial biology teacher replied.

"Amon helps everyone who crosses his path. He is a very kind person who brings out the best in people," Lora said reverently, rattling her copper bracelets gently.

"Of course. I wonder if that old black-and-white TV set I found on that abandoned ship is still working," Tony replied.

"Actually, it still works. They have it in the boardinghouse on Simonson Avenue. You have a talent for retrieving old junk and giving it a second life," Tom interjected.

"Well, I found you, Tom, drinking in some bar on the Island. And I rehabilitated you," Tony snapped.

Joanie giggled, to Tom's dismay. "Well, your friend is very funny."

"The stories about my drinking are grossly exaggerated."

"They're gross, but they're not exaggerated. Tom is a recovering barhopper," Tony declared.

"And Tony is a recovering tightwad," Tom replied.

"No, Tony is a recovering penny-pincher," Dick chimed in. "Considering the average paycheck of schoolteachers in this city, we all have to be frugal in our spending," Alan Katz, the teachers' union rep, commented.

"Maybe it's time for another strike," Tom said.

"This guy's a friggin' troublemaker. You better keep him on a tight leash," Tony said, motioning to Joanie.

"I'll try, but Tom has a mind of his own. He tends to go off half-cocked without rhyme or reason," she replied mischievously.

"Half-cocked, you say? Anyway, striking is the weapon of last resort," Tony said.

"Sure. I recall a certain member of the science department who crossed the picket line a few years back," Alan snapped, nodding at Tony.

"Union contracts set the standard for wages and working conditions across the country," Tom asserted.

"Absolutely. We had sweatshops and kids working in factories before unions existed in this country. The very idea of the weekend — time off from the workweek for workers — was created by unions," Alan continued.

"Trade unions created the weekend. That's an amazing fact," Tom replied.

"They had weekend drinkers like you in mind," Tony jibed.

Becoming more annoyed at Tony's barbs, Tom was about to curse out his friend but was halted by Amon's pre-speech preparations.

At that moment, Amon stood up, fumbling with a piece of paper that had a few paragraphs of a speech hastily scribbled on it in pencil. The young man who had come to be known as the Mariners Harbor Messiah seemed to be nervous.

"Thank you for coming here tonight. A great deal of hard work, blood, sweat, and tears have been given in rehabilitating this residence for the poor, the homeless, and the downtrodden of Mariners Harbor. My friend Tom was the first Islander that I became acquainted with, welcoming and helping me in more ways than I can recount. In this secular society of ours, it was gratifying to experience the kindness and generosity of the good people of the North Shore," he recited, pausing to glance at Tom.

"Truly, their spirit has brought this wonderful old Victorian building back to life again. It's nothing less than a miracle and a renaissance: creating a caring environment for the people who enter it from a world where indifference, neglect, and despair often abide. As in the pop song "Everyday People," it makes no difference what group we're in. We are all everyday people."

Pausing to look at his paper again, Amon mentioned a passage from the Bible, Paul's letter to the Corinthians: "'Love is not arrogant or rude. Love does not insist on its own way; it does not rejoice in the right. Love bears all things, believes all things, hopes all things, and endures all things.'

"There is a famous poem by John Donne that echoes the highest sentiments of people in all walks of life, reaching out to help one another: 'No man is an island entire of itself. Therefore, send not to know for whom the bell tolls, it tolls for thee.'"

Everyone in the audience was moved by Amon's heartfelt words, particularly Mary, his devoted, long-suffering partner in all his endeavors. The tears flowed down her pretty, careworn face as she hugged her man passionately, unwilling to relinquish him in her grasp. Joanie looked at Tom fearfully, as if she foresaw an impending tragedy. A general sense of foreboding pervaded the large dining room, imposing an awkward silence on the celebrants. One by one, the Curtis teachers and Lora slowly left the Victorian house, gripped by sorrow and regret. As Lora left, her copper bracelets and anklets seemed to reverberate mournfully. The gentle ringing of the Curtis coed's jewelry reminded Tom of a funeral dirge, commemorating the death of a Good Samaritan.

CHAPTER 77

The Apocalypse

On a sunny Saturday in early May, Tom and Joanie went for a leisurely stroll down Morningstar Road, as they had done years ago as love-struck teenagers. Alternately musing, joking, and chatting about mundane things, the two young people still had not come to terms with the twisting of fate that had reunited them. Human nature can be resilient with regard to unexpected setbacks but is uncomfortable with regard to unanticipated rewards. Perhaps the trite adage that nothing in life should be taken for granted tempered the happiness of their morning jaunt.

The circumstances behind the breakup of Joanie's marriage remained unclear to Tom, who was hesitant to query her about these painful events. She clearly didn't want to discuss her marriage. As a person who had gone through some rough times as a youngster, Tom understood the idea of allowing past events to remain in the past. *All we have in life is the existential present, the uncertain future, and good intentions. Everything would be easier if people just tried to act constructively, as exemplified by the Mariners Harbor resident.*

Appearing to read his thoughts, Joanie mentioned Amon's speech, quoting St. Paul: "Love is patient and kind. It's never mean or jealous. Love endures all things and hopes all things. It's one of my favorite passages in the Bible."

"Me too. Amon spoke from the heart. He really is the Messiah of Mariners Harbor—with all the good work he has done for the

North Shore. Yet, he has made some enemies in the Harbor," Tom replied.

"Amon healed me when I was at the hospital. As soon as he touched my forehead, the awful pain that wracked my head immediately stopped," Joanie exclaimed.

"I saw him bring an elderly man back to life who had just suffered a fatal heart attack at a diner on Richmond Terrace. It's definitely a gift that defies rational explanation," Tom concurred.

"So why do those people hate him?" she asked.

"To put in words — greed and pettiness, the root of much of the trouble in this country. Instead of stressing what we have in common, people get hung up on our differences — ethnic, religious, class — whatever divides us in the name of the good old American dollar."

"Well, I think there's more good than evil in the world. And in the end, things turn out for the best," Joanie replied.

"I don't know. I'm not that optimistic. Good intentions don't always lead to good ends. There's too much bullshit in this crazy world," Tom retorted.

As they reached the end of Morningstar Road and turned west on Richmond Terrace, they heard shots ring out from the harbor area where Amon had fixed up the derelict tugboat a few years ago. Running along the Terrace, Tom noticed an old battered sedan speed off and a woman bent over the prone body of a stricken man.

The two young people crossed the Terrace to where Mary was tending to Amon, who was bleeding profusely, having been struck in the chest by a bullet. Desperately she tried to staunch the bleeding with her head scarf. Tom took out a handkerchief from his back pocket to aid in this effort.

"They shot him as we walked along the waterfront this morning. It was an old beat-up Chevy, and the driver was wearing a black mask covering his eyes."

Joanie ran across the street to a nearby house, banging on the door to get the residents to call an ambulance.

Gasping for breath, Amon tried to speak to Mary, who stroked his cheeks and urged him to rest quietly and wait for an ambulance. Already the head scarf and handkerchief were soaked through with his blood.

Determined to speak his final words, Amon said, "Forgive them. They know not what they're doing. Mary, promise me you'll continue helping the good people living with us."

Mary assured him she would do so, and turning toward Tom, she signaled the skinny teacher to talk to her common-law husband. Crossing the street, Joanie joined the two young people, whispering that help was on the way.

"Amon, you're gonna pull through this. A dumb bullet can't stop the Mariners Harbor Messiah." Tom recalled the first time he saw Amon attaching wires from his tugboat to a nearby utility pole. He had gotten a shock and was thrown to the ground, landing on a soft rotted wharf, apparently unscathed.

"You were my first and best friend on the Island," he uttered weakly.

"Please. Speak no more," Mary urged frantically.

"Remember, use the time given to you — the days, the hours, and the minutes — to help the poor, who will always be with us," Amon continued in a halting manner.

"My love, don't fret. Please don't leave us," Mary begged, sensing that Amon's strength was flagging.

Somewhere off in the distance, the groaning siren of an ambulance could be heard. Was it too late? Like the police and firemen, often too late to render the help desperately needed by the victims, the sufferers of the world. At the same time, the mournful sound of church bells tolling could be heard. Tom recalled hearing church bells from deep in the Harbor when he first met Amon long ago.

Suddenly, Amon's face beamed with a radiant smile as he looked at his beloved wife, but his breathing was labored. Borne by a strong gust of wind, a huge gray cloud abruptly covered the sun and darkened the bright blue sky.

"No! No! I cannot bear it. Don't forsake me!" Mary wailed, stroking his face.

"Amon is strong. He'll make it through this," Tom asserted, trying to convince himself and Mary.

The sudden darkening of the sky was a bad sign. Tom wondered what would happen to Amon's boardinghouse and his other endeavors. He understood that Amon's legacy would endure only if his friends continued his good work.

Joanie rushed over to them, bent over the prone Mariners Harbor Messiah – desperately trying to staunch the surging blood from his chest, which had ceased panting. She whispered that help was on the way. Like the head scarf and Tom's handkerchief, her white hankie was crimson with blood.

The young man smiled weakly, and then his face went blank and still. Immediately, the gray cloud dispersed and the sun emerged, pouring golden rays of light and warmth upon them. This sign of nature's rebirth stunned the three young people, mitigating their despair and giving them hope for the future.

THE END

About The Author

The author has taught science and mathematics for many years on the high school and college levels. His approach to teaching is to make abstract principles concrete by connecting them to real life experiences. The students ought to come away with facts and ideas, the ability to solve problems, and most importantly – make ethical decisions. This book is about a compassionate young man with remarkable gifts, who is brought down by the tide of public opinion. It represents the third book of the Tom Haley trilogy: 1950s-1960s Fable, 1960s-1970s Fable, and The Mariners Harbor Messiah.